ARGENTIA STATION

GEORGE WALLACE

DON KEITH

Severn River Publishing
www.SevernRiverBooks.com

ISBN: 978-1-64875-662-7 (Paperback)

ALSO BY THE AUTHORS

The Hunter Killer Series

Final Bearing

Dangerous Grounds

Cuban Deep

Fast Attack

Arabian Storm

Warshot

Silent Running

Snapshot

Southern Cross

The Gibraltar Affair

The Tides of War Series

Argentia Station

Darkest Before Dawn

Also by George Wallace

Operation Golden Dawn

Cold is the Deep

Also by Don Keith

A Call to War Series

Never miss a new release! Sign up to receive exclusive updates from authors Wallace and Keith.

severnriverbooks.com

PROLOGUE

Stan Ward settled back in his seat and stared out the bus window at the familiar countryside. The sun was setting on the flat Kansas plain that unrolled to the horizon, an endless vista of wheat fields, interrupted only by the occasional cattle ranch and brief stops in towns with only a few structures and fewer folks. The big blue Greyhound Super-Coach was the only thing moving across the open prairie, for as far as the eye could see in all directions.

The unchanging-but-always-changing brown-green view was conducive to deep reflection. Some people, especially those who grew up in big cities, sometimes experienced a physical reaction to the openness and the flat ground. It could cause people from other geographies to experience dizziness and disorientation when first visiting the sprawling plains. Even the magnificent sunrises and sunsets out here were abrupt, as if chopped off by a hatchet at the edge of the planet.

One phase of Ward's young life had just as decisively been completed. Now he was off on the next journey, one that promised to carry him far from his birthplace and home, the dusty dryland farm outside of Lamar, Colorado, in the eastern part of the state, nestled up close to the Kansas border.

The journey had actually started five years before, the beginning of his high school senior year. Stan knew that he had to leave Lamar, Colorado, if he did not want to end up a dirt-poor farmer like his father, barely eking out a meager living. The Depression had left nothing there for a young man, but he could not see any way out. College was not even a remote possibility. The situation appeared hopeless; his options nonexistent.

That all changed one day in American history class. They were deep into the Civil War when Mrs. Robinson, the teacher, mentioned that Ulysses S. Grant was born a poor farm boy, but a college degree became possible when he received an appointment to West Point. Stan latched onto that bit of trivia, and he got to work researching the US Military Academy and how to get an appointment. From there he became even more tenacious. The application letter to his Senator was on its way within a week.

Stan was amazed when he received an appointment, but it was not to West Point. It was to the Naval Academy at Annapolis. It was only later that he found out that the Colorado Senator who so generously provided the appointment had somehow thought he was a member of the politically powerful Ward family in Denver, not the dirt-poor Wards of Lamar. By then, the Denver Stan Ward had told his dad in no uncertain terms he was going to college in Southern California and not off to some military school. Since the Senator was politically weak in the eastern part of the state, he simply allowed the appointment to proceed and added another line to his campaign literature.

Meanwhile, Stan Ward from little Lamar, Colorado, went on to spend four hard years trying to prove that a farm kid could compete in the academically and culturally challenging world of Annapolis. He was not sure about the cultural part, but he was satisfied when he finished in the top half —barely—of the class of '39, not embarrassing himself or his folks by "failing out."

He thought back on what had already been a long, eventful day. Up before dawn to do the chores one last time. Then washing off the dust and changing into his brand-new dress blue uniform with a single gold ring on each sleeve. His leave after graduating from the Naval Academy was over. It was time to get on the Greyhound and travel to his first duty station as an Ensign, USN. A bona fide commissioned officer in the US Navy. He had time to tuck into Mom's hearty farm breakfast before a tearful goodbye.

Stan knew Sarah Ward would not cry at the bus station in Lamar because it was out in public, and nobody had died or was getting married. The tears, however, flowed abundantly before they left, back there in her big, aromatic kitchen.

Jonathon Ward, Stan's father, had been quiet about the Academy thing from the very beginning. He trusted his son's judgment in the matter. Now, with the morning chores done, breakfast completed, and his oldest boy all gussied up in about the fanciest uniform Jonathon had ever seen, he loaded his boy's bag into the back of the dilapidated Model T pickup. All three of them—his two younger brothers and sister were in school, and Jonathon maintained they would be better off there—squeezed into the truck's tiny cab for the bumpy, dusty, ten-mile ride into town. The bus was early, just pulling to the curb at Lamar's redbrick station when the Wards pulled up. The town was so small and remote that the one building served as not only the bus station and train depot but also the home of the Rexall drugstore.

While other passengers disembarked or boarded the bus and his mother yet again repacked the big bag, Jonathon Ward pulled his son aside so that Sarah could not hear the conversation. Jonathon rarely talked of serious things with his children, other than religion and crop rotations, but Stan always knew this chat would come.

"Son, I don't know much about all this Navy stuff. I was on a ship twice, once to France and once back to New York with a bunch of other grateful doughboys but I mostly just throwed up all the way there and back." His dad's tone was dead serious. "But I do know somethin' about the military. There's a war a-comin. I can feel it. You're gonna be an officer, so you prepare yourself to do what you have to do to keep yourself and your men safe if the shootin' does start. Remember, if somebody's trying to kill you, you don't hesitate. You take his life if you have to. Understand? I don't wanna be havin' to tell your mother that her son ain't comin' home. I had to do that with too many buddies from the last war."

His time in the trenches in the Great War was something the elder Ward had never talked about. Stan only knew that his father had made it home when many other Colorado men, some from Lamar, were not so lucky. He talked far more about the ridge-and-furrow network on their 320 acres than he ever did about being in Europe, getting shot at, the War to End All Wars.

Jonathon Ward fished around in his overall bib pocket and retrieved his pocket watch. The shiny, gold Hamilton 992 Railroad watch was his prized possession. Stan never knew how his dad came to own such an expensive timepiece. He only knew that it came out solely on special occasions. Weddings and funerals.

Jonathon Ward checked the time, then handed the Hamilton to Stan. "Here, son, she's yours now. Grandpop Ward gave it to me when I went off to the war. It was my good luck piece over there and I reckon it must've done its job. I came back. Now, it's your good luck piece. Keep it—and you—safe." He shook his son's hand and then enveloped him in an uncharacteristic giant bear hug. There was a final embrace from Mom, too, and then a not-so-subtle signal from the bus driver that it was time to jump on board the Greyhound.

Somewhere in his reverie, not long after the sun dropped below the horizon, and with the soothing hiss of the bus tires on the pavement and the peaceful dark night sky, Ensign Stan Ward fell fast asleep.

It was sometime later when he was brutally awakened. Thrown from his seat, his ears ringing from the rending, tearing scream of tortured metal on metal. He tried to grab the seatback in front of him, the overhead luggage rack, anything to keep him from flying around the darkened cabin. Utter blackness and a cacophony of noise and screams filled the void. The heaving, tossing movement finally stopped, but something was not right.

Up was not where up was supposed to be.

He could feel the crunch of glass and upholstery beneath his shoes. Even in the darkness, there was enough light from somewhere that he could tell he was standing on the bus windows and right-side panel.

The Greyhound was on its side. Would it stay there or roll some more?

Then he smelled smoke. Fire? That was what supplied the limited light. Ward worked to calm his racing heart. This was not the time to panic. What should he do? He had noted that there were probably a dozen other passengers on the bus. A family with a small baby and a toddler. Two middle-aged couples. Several men traveling alone. One appeared to be a traveling salesman, the others probably workers searching for jobs in the next town. Now, they were all together in this smoke-filled wreckage.

They had to get out of the bus before the fire spread. But how? There was only one exit door toward the front of the vehicle, but the bus had rolled over and was resting on it. There was no other exit. They were trapped and the bus was starting to burn. Stan knew he would have to break out a window on the other side of the bus, which was now above him, and try to climb out through it.

Ward wrapped his uniform jacket around his fist and punched at the window above him. Nothing. His fist only bounced off unyielding glass. He struck it again and again, until his fist hurt too much to try anymore.

The smoke got thicker. He could smell diesel fumes. There was a fuel leak. It was only a matter of time before the bus would be engulfed in flames. The baby was crying and the toddler screaming for her mother, but Stan could not see the woman.

Someone yelled, "My wife! She's pinned under the seats! Dear God, help us!"

"I need something to break the glass," Ward shouted. "Anybody have something?"

"Here, try this." One of the workers handed Ward a heavy Ford wrench from the contents of his toolbox, now spilled everywhere. Even banging away at the glass with the metal wrench, it took him several whacks to finally break through. But the glass broke in long, sharp splinters. He quickly used the wrench to clear the frame of the dangerous glass daggers before he helped one of the men up and through the opening.

Ward took command. He ordered the guy to stay there, to reach back down and to lift people up as Stan and others raised them to reach the opening.

Once the passengers, those who were able, were climbing up through the shattered window without needing help from him, Ward turned his attention to the trapped woman. She was firmly wedged between the seat and the crumpled side panel and was in a panic.

"Please don't leave me!" she screamed. "Dear God, I don't want to die here! Not like this!"

Pulling with all his strength, Ward could not make the seat budge. The smoke was so thick, he could hardly see. And he could now feel the heat from the flames. Time was running out. He kicked at the seat in frustration. And felt it give, but just a little. He braced himself against the next seat in front and lashed out with both feet. The woman screamed in pain, but the seatback broke away. It only took a quick tug to pull her free and, with all the strength he could muster, shove her up through the broken window to helping hands.

Ward stopped, looked around. How sure was he that everyone was out? The driver slumped over the steering wheel, not moving. Ward grabbed the inert form, dragged him back, and with the last of his strength, shoved him up through the window. Then he started to climb out. It was way past time to be out. As he stuck his head through the window, he was glad to see the men had ushered everyone, including the injured woman and unconscious driver, on down the roadway, away from the bus.

He was halfway out the window when the bus exploded. There was an otherworldly sensation of flying as he felt himself being launched through the chilly night. And past a million stars.

Then there was only darkness.

1

The sun was just clearing the hills out to the east, back toward Mystic and Newport. Its first rays illuminated the misty haze that hung over the Thames River. A fishing boat made its way downriver, engulfed in a swirling cloud of hungry seagulls, looking for any morsel for breakfast. Their squawking upended the morning quietness. Adding to the noise, the Block Island Ferry sounded three deep-throated blasts on its horn before it backed away from the New London ferry terminal to begin its morning run out to the island. It promised to be another crisp "early autumn in New England" morning. The cloudless sky presented the rare, bright cerulean-blue colors that the locals cherished and the Chambers of Commerce up and down the Connecticut coast loved to boast about.

Alistair MacLean III was not at all interested in the scenery or the sunrise, though. He was in a hell of a hurry. And his head felt as if Fred Astaire had stepped off the screen from *Follow the Fleet* to tap dance on his skull. He mashed down hard on the throttle of his brand-new Packard Eight convertible. The powerful straight-eight engine sent the car rocketing ahead, but he had to jump on the brakes with equal vigor when traffic signals, milkmen, and slow-moving drivers bound for the day shift at the Electric Boat submarine shipyard kept getting in his way.

The shiny Chinese-red-colored machine had been a graduation gift from his father, Alistair MacLean Jr. And now, he needed every bit of the vehicle's horsepower, or he would for sure find himself in deep water on day one. After four years at the US Naval Academy at Annapolis, Ensign MacLean had spent most of his summer making up for lost time, becoming a regular fixture on the very active and enticing party scene on the Connecticut shore. His dress white uniform, contrasting sharply with the yachting jackets that most of his civilian male friends wore, perfectly created the desired effect with the ladies. The previous night's bash at the tony Old Saybrook Point Yacht Club had been a memorable topper to the mostly carefree summer. At least as much of it as he could remember. The bash or the summer.

Hopping off the Thames River drawbridge, he shot north on the old Military Highway. He glanced at his wrist at another graduation gift. His mother had given him the brand-new Rolex Oyster. It had just ticked past 0600. He was cutting it close. Not good form at all if one's goal is someday marrying well and landing some swell command in a place with a beach and warm breezes. He had already decided Pearl Harbor in Hawaii might be a nice place to enjoy a long career. Very pleasant and certainly out of the way. And with minimal chance of ever getting shot at.

Too much to drink and then spending the night on Daphanie Maria's yacht probably had not been a good plan for the night before he was to report aboard his first duty station. The pounding behind his temples and the gritty taste in his mouth already promised a painful day ahead. He pondered stopping at one of the bars that lined the road for a bit of the hair of the dog that bit him but immediately thought better of it. He pushed on.

Count Basie Orchestra was belting out "Jumpin' at the Woodside" on the Packard's radio—though it was not helping MacLean's headache—when he rolled to a stop at Submarine Base New London's main gate. The Marine corporal manning the gate glanced curiously at the car radio—he had not seen many of them before, nor many newcomers driving red Packards, for that matter—and took his sweet time perusing MacLean's orders. He had likely caught a whiff of the stale liquor smell, and, shaking his head, waved the young Ensign through the gate. But not before adding, "Sir, I suggest you shower and change into a fresh uniform. Commander

Flynn will have your ass if you show up at Sub School looking and smelling like that."

MacLean had to work around a lot of construction. It seemed that every inch of the submarine base was getting some kind of new building. Construction material, stacks of steel I-beams, and massive piles of red brick were piled up everywhere. He had to carefully work his way through the obstacle course.

The Packard's wide whitewalls spun gravel as he slewed into the BOQ parking space. He checked the Rolex one more time. Maybe he did have just enough time to dash to his room, take a quick shower, and then jump into his service dress blues. The bugle was sounding the call to morning colors when he finally dashed through the main entranceway at the Navy's Submarine School.

He paused for just a second to read the brass plaque hanging above the door.

"Their want of practice will make them unskillful and their want of skill, timid. Maritime skill, like skills of other kinds, is not cultivated by the way or at chance times. Thucydides, 300BC."

So that was the Sub School motto. MacLean was surprised that he would find a bunch of sailors quoting a fourth century BC historian.

MacLean found himself at the tail end of a line of young officers, all waiting patiently to check in and present their orders. The Ensign standing directly in front of him turned and grinned at him.

"I was wondering if you would be able to tear yourself away from the party scene and show up this morning, Trip." It was Fred Wurster, friend, Academy classmate, and a fellow who had pulled Alistair out of more than a few tight spots the many times they had gone over the wall at Annapolis, doing their own version of "navigation practice."

"Freddy, you sure you're in the right place?" MacLean responded with a mock-serious look on his handsome face. "I heard you had to be smart to be here. No place for a dumb jock, for sure."

Wurster had been the starting fullback for Navy until he got carried off the field just before halftime during an ugly six-point loss to Army. Graduating in the lower half of the class of 1939, he would be the first to admit that his prowess on the gridiron did not extend to mastery of subject matter in the classroom.

"The selection board was brutal," Wurster said with a laugh. He did not take to heart the goading of his buddies. He preferred viewing it as a sign of affection. "As a contingency for waiving the requirement for brains to get into Sub School, I had to promise to keep you and your roommate on the straight and narrow. So, they smiled and added my name at the bottom of the list for Sub School Class 3902. But I gotta tell you, you guys are already putting my billet in jeopardy."

MacLean shook his head. "I'm here, aren't I? I'm not one to bilge a classmate. But speaking of roommates, where the hell are Brad and Stan?"

Wurster waved his hand toward the long, unmoving line. "Ensign Ward hasn't reported in yet. Probably still chasing some cowgirl around Colorado. He's going to be in a world of trouble when he finally decides to show up. Ensign Johnson pulled his pappy's rank and marched right on up to the head of the line. It's amazing what having an Admiral in the family will get you in this man's Navy. He's probably already sipping a cup of coffee and telling sea stories with Commander Flynn."

"You two guys, all that jawing's holding up the line," the Chief Petty Officer sitting behind the desk growled impatiently. "Give me your orders and get moving." When the CPO reached out to take their papers, the embroidered dolphin insignia on his right sleeve became plainly—and symbolically significantly—visible.

The two new Ensigns realized then that they had just entered a new realm. Rank, background, family wealth, political connection, Academy grades, none of that mattered for much now. They were nothing more than NQPs, "Non-qualified Personnel."

They were now within the domain of qualified submariners. And until they earned the right to wear those dolphins, they would remain decidedly inferior to those who already had.

∞

Stan Ward's eyes blinked open. Then he shut them again just as quickly. He was not sure where he was, but the brilliant white light blinded him. He groaned. His head throbbed. His back hurt. His upper leg ached mightily. In truth, he felt pain pretty much all over. He tried to move, but something restrained him. And trying to move made everything hurt even more.

"Looks like our patient is back with us." The unfamiliar voice came from somewhere outside his limited field of vision. Then a smiling female face moved into Stan's sight. He could just make out a white nurse's cap resting on a disorderly pile of gray hair.

"You're a very lucky young man," the nurse told him. "And quite a hero, too."

"Wha...at? Where am I?" Ward stammered. It was difficult to talk.

"You're in Asbury Hospital, in Salina, Kansas," she answered. "You were in a bus wreck just outside of town. Biggest thing to happen around here in quite the while. To hear the others tell it, you single-handedly saved everyone on that burning bus. Except the driver. He didn't make it. But you sure tried, young man. Sure tried." She paused for a moment as she checked a tangle of tubes from somewhere above him. "When the sheriff brought you in, he said you pulled everyone out of the bus just before it blew up. You've got some second- and third-degree burns on your legs, a broken leg, and probably a concussion. We're going to see a lot of bruising showing up over the next couple of days."

She reached out to take his arm and carefully wrapped it with a blood-pressure cuff. "You're also a bit of a mystery," she said as she pumped up the sphygmomanometer. "All your identification was lost in the explosion and fire. Folks on the bus said that you were dressed as some kind of military officer. Navy, somebody thought."

He started to respond, but she shushed him while she listened for his pulse. "140 over 80. Pulse of 75. Little high for a young buck like you," the nurse said, "but expected, considering all you've been through."

Stan Ward took this information aboard. So, nobody knew where he was. Not his parents. Not the Navy, who were expecting him to show up in Groton, Connecticut. When? He realized that he had no idea what day it was.

"My name is Stan Ward, ma'am," he said. "I guess that should be Ensign Stanley Ward, from Lamar, Colorado. I need to let my folks know that I'm okay and let the Navy know that I'm going to be late reporting."

"Enough with the 'ma'am' stuff." The nurse laughed. "I'm Florence Dibble. You can call me Flo. We'll call your folks and let the Navy know you ain't AWOL. You'll not be going anywhere for a while. You broke your left femur in that explosion and the third-degree burns on both of your lower legs are going to take a while to heal up."

"Well, Flo," Ward answered, "we don't have a phone on the farm. Best call the sheriff in Lamar. He can drive out and tell my folks."

He paused as he considered the second half of the quandary. A broken leg and third-degree burns. What did that mean for his orders to Submarine School? Would they still take him? Or was his accidental Navy career over before it even started? Maybe they would just let him pick up with the next class. Maybe.

"My Navy orders were in my suitcase," Ward offered. "You should be able to find someone to call from them." Then he remembered. Flo had said they were burned up in the fire. Somebody else would have to figure all that out. His head hurt too much.

Their discussion was interrupted by the door swinging open. A middle-aged man wearing a white lab coat and with a stethoscope dangling from his neck strode in uninvited. He grabbed the clipboard hanging at the foot of Stan's bed and took a quick read. Then he glanced up and noticed that Ward was awake.

"How's our mystery patient?" he brusquely asked the nurse.

"Dr. Brown, this is Stan Ward," Nurse Dibble answered. "He just regained consciousness a few minutes ago."

The doc nodded and scratched some notes on the chart before he said anything to Stan. Then he looked up with a serious frown. "Mr. Ward, now that you are back with us, we need to talk. It's your left leg that we're most worried about. You have a compound fracture of the femur. That's your thighbone. You're real lucky that you didn't rupture your femoral artery. If you had, you would have bled out before the sheriff even got you here."

"Well, that's a good..." Ward started but quickly ran out of breath.

The doctor glanced down at the clipboard before continuing. "We're going to have to amputate your leg. With the compound fracture wound combined with the burns, there is just too much chance of infection.

Gangrene or sepsis sets in and you're a dead man. Sign these papers and we'll schedule the operation for the morning."

Ward was in wide-eyed disbelief. Dr. Brown's brutal diagnosis had just turned his world upside down. "You're not taking my leg!" he shouted, tears rolling down his face, now finding all the breath he needed to protest. "That ain't happening! There's gotta be something else you can do!" Facing the world as a cripple was not an option. The day before, he was starting an exciting new life as a submariner. Now he would be lucky to have any kind of life. At least one worth living.

Dr. Brown looked hard at his patient and dryly answered, "There is a procedure called the closed-cast method. I saw it used in the Great War, but it's very risky, takes months to heal up, and you'll probably still end up losing your leg if it doesn't kill you first. I've never done one, but I've seen it performed. I suggest you think about this real hard. I'll be back in the morning for your decision and we'll go from there."

With that pronouncement and nothing more, Brown turned and exited the room.

"Boy, he sure has a heartwarming bedside manner," Stan commented with ill-disguised sarcasm.

"He can take a little getting used to, I admit," Flo Dibble answered. "But he's the best doctor in all of Kansas. You need to listen to what he's saying. I'm not trying to persuade you one way or t'other, but if he says it's risky, it really is. Either way, you're going to be here for a while. It's a lot for a young man to think about. I'll talk to Dr. Brown about at least waiting until your folks can get here and y'all can talk it over. In the meantime, I'll see if I can find somebody in the Navy to speak to."

"Thank you, Nurse Dibble," he told her.

She looked back over her shoulder as she walked out. "Bless your heart, darlin'. Bless your heart."

2

"Did you see the today's *New York Times*?" Trip MacLean asked as he, Brad Johnson, and Freddie Wurster made the walk from the Submarine School back to the BOQ. "Front page headline. Germany invaded Poland. The paper's talking about something called a *blitzkrieg*, some new type of warfare the Germans have invented."

"Why should we care?" Wurster asked. "The Nazis are going to be stuck between the Poles on one side and France and England on the other. From everything I've read, they'll make short work of this Hitler guy and his henchmen. Besides, it's none of our affair anyway. Berlin's what? More than four thousand miles away? That'd be one hell of a...what'd you call it, Trip? A *blitz*-what?"

"Maybe so," MacLean said. "And besides, President Roosevelt says no way we get involved in another war in Europe."

"Enough of this war talk. Let's go grab a beer," Brad Johnson interrupted, changing the subject. "I'm thirsty and we need to unwind."

The trio had just endured a brutal week in the classroom. Submarine facts and figures, the "whys" and "hows" of going to sea on a submarine, had been coming at them fast and furious. Flank speed. The instructors worked hard to embed the information into their heads, always stressing the reality that both their lives and the lives of their shipmates depended on them assimilating and retaining everything they were being fed. By now, the Ensigns were starting to understand the stress that went along with being a submariner. Especially a submarine officer.

"Where we going, then?" Trip MacLean asked. "I'm not up to testing fate and hitting the dive bars over on Water Street. Navigating the Thames River Bridge with a snoot full of beer just don't sound like that much fun."

"Party pooper," Johnson shot back, laughing. "Just because you have the only car."

"Got an idea," Freddy Wurster offered up. "The quartermaster that was teaching navigation mentioned a place called Solomon's Tavern. It's just outside the main gate, walking distance, and it's supposed to be a real hoppin' place on a Friday night."

"Okay by me," MacLean replied. "Rather walk a few blocks than explain to Dad why the Packard's back in the body shop again."

"Well, let's do it," Johnson answered. He grabbed his coat and headed for the door all in one motion.

Solomon's Tavern was indeed right across Crystal Lake Road from the base's main gate. Although the place looked seedy and run down, the parking lot was full of cars, and sailors crowded to get in the door. About the only thing that looked new and modern inside was the Seeburg Symphonola jukebox. It blasted loud enough, and enough sailors and their dates were on the dance floor so that it seemed the whole building was vibrating.

The three worked their way through the crowd and wormed themselves up to the bar. The female bartender looked up from wiping the bar top. "So, what'll it be, boys?" she asked with a grin. "Red Tops are a nickel a bottle tonight."

Brad Johnson decided she was kind of cute and broke into his best broad smile. "My kinda place. Walking distance, cheap beer, and a gorgeous bartender. We'll take three Red Tops right now and have three more at the ready."

"Wow! Big spenders!" she responded with a wink. "I'm Debbie. Need anything, just whistle." She proceeded to demonstrate with an ear-piercing wolf whistle.

The three grabbed their beers and moved over to a table that serendipitously came open just then. It wasn't quiet, but far enough away from the music and dancing that they could hear each other over the noise. They were well into the evening, with a growing mound of empties crowding the table, when the cute bartender sauntered over with another tray containing three more cold bottles.

"Hi, guys." She started up a conversation as she cleared away the empties and set down the cold ones. "Don't think I've seen you around before. Must be in the new class at Sub School."

"Yep, that's us. Class 3902's finest gift to the fleet," Brad Johnson answered, turning his infectious smile up a notch. "I'm Brad." Pointing at Wurster, he said, "This ugly mug is Freddie and the chump on my right is Trip."

"Well, welcome to—"

"Hey, Debbie," someone from across the bar hollered. "We need some more brews over here if you got a second."

Debbie glanced over, sighed, and shook her head. "Excuse me, handsome. Gotta go make the customers happy. Don't be a stranger around here, okay?" Then she aimed another wink at Johnson before walking away toward the bar with a noticeable and seductive wiggle to her hips.

All three submarine officers watched with interest, then turned up their beers in unison and drained them. Two of them stood to go but Brad lingered a long moment, watching the cute barmaid at work.

∞

He was swimming, looking for the surface. Swimming upward through a thick fog. Even when he broke through into bright light everything was blurry. He was having a terrible time trying to focus.

Where was he? What the hell was going on?

"Welcome back."

The voice came from somewhere above him. Two words, but it was still the sweetest melody he had ever heard. Angelic. Stan Ward blinked hard several times until his eyes finally began working again. He had been right about the voice.

He could now see it was, indeed, an angel.

"Mr. Ward, your operation's over." And that beautiful angel was smiling, speaking to him. Was he dead, in heaven? No, she seemed real, all right. And the reality led him to ask her a crucial question.

"My...my leg?" he stammered. "Do I still have my...?"

"You did great. Dr. Brown had to remove a good bit of damaged tissue, but it's all dressed and in a plaster cast now. You have a couple of pins through your thigh for the traction device. As soon as the plaster dries, we'll wheel you back to your room and hook you up to it." God, she was beautiful. She gently wiped his brow with a cool sponge. "I'll give you some ice chips to suck on. They'll help with the dry throat."

Just then Dr. Brown walked into the room and looked down at Stan. "Mr. Ward, you are one stubborn SOB. You're really going to need that trait, I assure you. I think we cleaned out anything that could cause an infection, but only time will tell for sure. We're going to remove that cast and replace it with a new one in a couple of days just to make sure that nothing's growing that we can't see. If all goes well—and that's a hell of a big *if*—we'll start your physical therapy first thing next week. Nurse Kamp here... Karen...will be supervising your therapy. I warn you, it will not be easy, and it will be painful."

Though Ward was still groggy, this all sounded good. "Thanks, Doc. Now, how long before I can get back to the Navy?"

Brown frowned and snorted. "That's between you and the Navy. You're going to need some long-term rehabilitation and likely have some significant impairment. The Navy will put you on the Temporary Disability Retired List. Don't let the name fool you. I was an Army doc. I know there's nothing temporary about this particular status. You will be retired."

Ward looked over at his angel. Nurse Karen Kamp. "Well, let's get this rehab thing going, then," he said with a weak grin. "Doc Brown's diagnosis is correct. I am a stubborn SOB. And, by God, I'm still going to be a submariner."

∞

Sublieutenant Geoffrey Chandler walked into the Junior Officer Mess, hungry and eagerly anticipating the evening meal. His Majesty's Ship

Courageous, when the air group was aboard, had a crew of over twelve hundred sailors and more than two hundred officers. That meant the ship was large enough for the junior officers and the senior officers to each have their own mess.

The steward handed the young officer a glass of claret to sip while he waited for the second sitting. That was one of the problems with having all these pilot officers aboard. They seemed to always be first in line for meals. Regular ship's officers, who had duties to perform running the large aircraft carrier, were usually relegated to eating at the second sitting.

"Hey, Geoff! Over here!" Randall Macallister called out from across the mess. Chandler saw the ruddy Scotsman waving him toward an empty seat at his table. The two had been shipmates and drinking chums since they reported aboard the old carrier three years before.

"What's happening up in the wireless shack?" Macallister asked as Chandler plopped down. Chandler was the ship's communications officer. He spent most of his day in the radio room, or wireless shack, encrypting outgoing messages and decrypting incoming ones.

"Just the usual," Chandler responded as he nodded to the steward to serve him his soup. "Random sightings being reported of Herr Hitler's submarines. Nothing anywhere near us. Looks like the Admiralty assigned us to a very quiet part of the Western Approaches. All the action is happening over in the North Sea."

Macallister tasted his soup. "Bean soup again. Mess treasurer must have landed a deal on navy beans. Well, let us hope it stays quiet out here. Mrs. Macallister gave her favorite son strict orders to eventually come home but not come home a war hero."

A sudden vicious, jarring jolt sent the bowls of soup flying off the table just as the cacophony of a horrendous explosion roared forth. The lights flickered once and then blinked out, leaving the mess totally dark. A second explosion, even sharper and more violent than the first one, brutally shook the mighty ship. Chandler could feel the vessel already listing to port.

"Randy, let's get out of here," he shouted, grabbing his friend's shoulder and leading him toward where the door to the passageway should be. The passageway was just as dark as the mess, but it was already crowded with panicked sailors running about in all directions, some seeking duty stations, most looking for a safe spot. No one seemed to know what had happened or what to do about it. Mostly from memory, Chandler found the ladder that headed up to the next deck. The hatch above him opened onto the lower hangar deck.

The ship's list was becoming much worse by the minute. Chandler guessed it must be better than twenty degrees by now. He could hear heavy gear screeching and screaming as it succumbed to gravity and slid across the hangar deck.

Someone shouted, "Abandon ship! They have ordered 'Abandon Ship'!"

Macallister and Chandler scurried up the ladder to the upper hangar deck.

"The flying-off deck," Macallister panted. "We can better abandon ship from there!"

The pair ran out on the short lower flight deck, an obsolete remnant left over from the days of Sopwith Camel airplanes. The ship's listing was so bad by now that it was difficult to walk out onto the flight deck without sliding right off the edge. The night was fittingly dark, with a waxing crescent moon playing peekaboo with the clouds.

Chandler could just make out the silhouettes of a couple of destroyers racing toward the stricken carrier. He heard a deep, ominous groaning sound emanating from somewhere within the guts of the ship. All he could think was it was the moan of a dying vessel. He did not really relish a dip in the cold Atlantic waters off Ireland, but it was clear the time to get off the stricken vessel had arrived.

"Randy, it's time to jump," he shouted to Macallister.

"You go ahead," his friend answered. "I'm staying here, Geoff." Then, after a short pause, he mournfully added, "I can't swim."

"Well, by God, you can't stay here," Chandler pleaded. "The ship's sinking, mate. We're under orders to abandon ship. Come on. We'll just have to find something to float on until we get picked up."

"I'll look for a lifeboat," Macallister answered. "Don't worry about me."

The ship gave a sudden lurch and heaved over dramatically. Chandler lost his footing and promptly slid off the deck. The last sight he had of Randy Macallister was of the Scot holding on to the lifelines with both hands. Then Chandler hit cold water.

After a seemingly long time, and after swimming as hard as he could, he surfaced, spitting out saltwater. Partly by training but mostly by common sense, he knew he needed to swim as far away from the *Courageous* as he could manage. That he needed to get distant enough from the ship so it could not roll over on him or suck him down when it inevitably got swallowed up by the sea.

He heard shouts and cries all around him but was unable to see anything at all besides the hulk of the heavily listing carrier, still looming above him. He hollered for Macallister but did not hear any reply. But he did hear a deep, low, sighing moan, ramping up to a point a thousand times louder than any human could make, emanating from the carrier.

Then he looked back and saw an impossible sight. The *Courageous* was slipping beneath the waves. His ship was gone.

Chandler forced himself to swim around in the frigid water until he found some wreckage to climb onto. He was not at all sure what it was. It looked like a crate of some fashion, but it was just enough to keep him afloat and mostly out of the water. Where were those destroyers? It seemed like he had been in the sea for hours when he spotted a motor whaleboat. He shouted out, waved, begged for help. He was exhausted, half-conscious when he felt strong hands pulling him from the water and wrapping him in a thick blanket. Someone poured a cup of steaming coffee from a thermos and handed it to him.

As he drank, he looked around. There were twenty other survivors crowded into the motor whaleboat.

Randall Macallister was not one of them.

∞

"I just don't understand this crap!" Fred Wurster threw his notebook down hard onto the table in front of him and pounded it with a fist. "What the heck is 'TVG' and why is it so damned important?"

Wurster, Alistair MacLean, and Brad Johnson were arranged around a table in the BOQ lounge. They were not lounging, though. They were grabbing any opportunity to study together. Only three weeks into the six-month basic submarine officer school, the three young Ensigns were admittedly struggling. Facts and figures came flying at them furiously. Four years at the Academy—immersed in all kinds of technical subjects—had not been nearly so challenging. Nor, apparently, had it prepared them for the tsunami of technical information they would need to assimilate. And absolutely not for the rate at which it was being thrown at them. Even the few minutes before the evening meal—a time typically reserved for playful banter and a bit of relaxation—was being used to cram for a key upcoming exam the following Monday.

This week's topic was the submarine battery. The batteries that provided the juice to run the boat's electric motors to turn their screws and push them through the water.

MacLean looked up from his own notes. "Fred, this one's pretty simple. TVG is 'Total Volts Gassing.' When you're charging the battery, you charge at a constant current and let the voltage rise until you get to TVG. That's about 2.3 volts per cell or about 140 volts for a 60-cell battery. It depends on the temperature, though. Then all you need to do is maintain a constant voltage and let the current drop until you get to the float current."

"Sounds simple when you say it," Wurster grunted. "Chief Crawford doesn't say it that way up there at the chalkboard. But why is it something we need to know?"

MacLean laughed. "If I try to map out all the anions and cations for the lead-acid reactions at the positive and negative plates in a battery, it'll just fry what few brain cells you still have, Freddy. The easiest thing to remember is that if you raise the voltage above TVG, you'll start generating excessive hydrogen. Hydrogen is explosive and that is bad inside a submarine."

"I get it!" Wurster's eyes brightened. "Going beyond TVG causes hydrogen. Hydrogen causes BOOM!" He threw his arms up into the air and loudly exclaimed, "Boom bad!"

Brad Johnson playfully punched Wurster's shoulder. "Hey, jock, you ain't half as dumb as you look."

The other would-be submarine officers in the lounge cheered whatever it was Wurster was yelling about. The steward opened the door to the dining hall just then and rang the dinner bell. The three friends charged through the door toward the waiting food as if it might disappear if they did not hurry. Chow times had become the favorite part of their day. They grabbed a table and immediately commenced to eat without further conversation.

"Hey, I got a letter from Stan today," Brad Johnson finally offered up during a brief lull in his chewing. He and Stan Ward had been roommates since their plebe year at Annapolis. "He says he should get out of traction this week."

"Man's got to be going stir-crazy," MacLean observed. "Same four walls for over a month. At least we get outdoors between classes and hustling from here and back."

"Maybe not," Johnson replied. "They got more than cows and pigs out there on the prairie. It seems one of the young nurses is falling for the charms of our naval hero. This is the third letter now that he has mentioned someone named Karen."

Fred Wurster shoveled another generous helping of roast beef, gravy, and mashed potatoes onto his plate. "Has he heard any word on what the Navy's gonna do with him? He damn well needs to skedaddle out of Kansas before Karen's daddy finds out he's a sailor."

"It's not looking promising," Johnson answered. "Stan says he has at least another couple of months in a wheelchair before he can even try to walk without crutches again. BUMED's planning to hold a review board sometime after the first of the year. They'll decide if he gets to stay in the Navy or is 'medicaled out.' Precedent is not on his side. I doubt the Navy has much use for an Ensign who has to limp around a boat. These sewer pipes are hard enough to get around in with two good legs."

Fred Wurster was chewing hard on a piece of roast beef. He massaged his jaw. "I've got shoes that ain't this tough," he complained, "and probably taste better. What happened to submariners gettin' the best chow in the Navy?"

"Gotta be at sea for that benefit," Trip MacLean explained. "But then we simultaneously give up a whole bunch of other wonderful stuff we enjoy. Things like girls, elbow room, girls, sunshine, girls, fresh air, girls, towels that don't smell like piss and diesel fuel..."

Wurster chewed a bit more and then swallowed before saying, "Brad, can't your old man do something for Stan? I mean, he is an Admiral, after all. Couldn't he pull some weight with that medical board."

Johnson took a swig from his Coke, then answered, "I'll see what I can do. Dad always liked Stan. He said he was a stabilizing influence on me." He laughed. "But then, Dad didn't know about all the times the two of us snuck out over the seawall to get a beer downtown. Good thing, too."

"Hey, guys," MacLean chimed in. "Speaking of which, I talked to Daphanie Maria a little bit ago. They're having a dance at the Stonington Country Club on Friday night. They'll have a band, plenty of free booze, and easy women. She promises a couple of friends if you two are looking for a good time. Believe me, the girls at the club get all misty-eyed over a man in a Navy uniform."

Wurster chewed for a while, then shook his head. "Naw, got to study. If I don't figure out how that TVG battery thing works and pass that test, by Christmas I'll be out ridin' an old four-stacker tin can on a cold, rough sea, seasick as a dog."

Bradley Johnson had a frown on his face, too. "Yeah, count me out. Dad's already told me he's not bailing me out if I flunk Sub School. Something about me having to grow up on my own someday."

"Truth be told..." Alistair MacLean started, then shook his head no. "You guys done shamed me into cuddling up with my notes all weekend."

Johnson reached for his slice of apple pie. "But I'll see what Dad can do for Stanley. Hate to see the old boy have to go back to the pigs and cows for companionship."

3

Admiral Devin Johnson sat high in the gallery. His perch offered him a commanding view of the gaming floor that stretched out below him. Members of the Naval War College, Newport, Rhode Island, class of 1940, were scattered across the big floor, moving set pieces that represented the naval fleets of the United States and the Japanese Empire, both arrayed across the broad stretches of the Pacific Ocean. And their manipulation by the class members simulated real-world naval warfare between the two nations as the game judges called out each move and countermove.

As Admiral Johnson looked on, the latest iteration of "War Plan Orange" was being gamed out on the floor. It was not going well for the US Navy. Far too many of the little blue models were being set aside in the "sunk" box and not nearly enough of the orange pieces. Something in the game assumptions was causing the US to badly lose this major simulated battle. And it was Johnson's task to figure out what the problem was and do something about it. The US was not at war with Japan or anybody else, and President Roosevelt had promised not to involve the country in another foreign war. But tensions at various hot spots around the globe were building. The general consensus held that war could be just over the horizon. The Navy had to find a solution to this War Plan Orange problem and be ready to use the plan if it should ever become necessary in real life.

Johnson grabbed a pen and a pad of paper and did some quick calculations. Then he signaled his flag aide that he had a task for him.

"Phil, get me Secretary Edison on the telephone," the Admiral ordered. "He needs to know what we saw here, and quick."

"Yes, sir," Lieutenant Phillip Sherman responded, jumped up, and trotted off in search of a telephone so he could call the Secretary of the Navy on behalf of his boss. Luckily, he found a telephone in the first office down the long hallway. It took ten minutes before the operator could connect him to Secretary Edison's office. Admiral Johnson strolled into the room just as all the hookups were made, a set of concise notes in hand.

"Secretary Edison, good afternoon, sir," Admiral Johnson started out.

"I hope you're bringing me some good news from all that play-acting you all have been doing," Edison said in his usual direct manner.

"I'm afraid that the war game results are even worse than we suspected. When we tried out the latest iteration of War Plan Orange, the fleet was destroyed. It took a little longer this time, but the results were the same. Then I had the gamers add fifty submarines from the proposed *Gato*-class. The very long range of those boats made all the difference. The *S*-boats are okay for guarding ports and harbors, but we need true fleet boats, fast enough and with the range to move with the fleet. And ones that can be aggressive, offensive. The *Gato*s will do the job, Charles. Sorry...Mr. Secretary. I highly recommend that we start lobbying for adding more of those boats into the budget. We're going to need them if push comes to shove."

Secretary of the Navy Charles Edison was President Franklin Roosevelt's point man to rebuild the US Navy, first as Assistant Secretary of the Navy and now as Secretary. He had taken it as his personal responsibility to see that the United States had a fleet second to none. After the Navy drawdowns during the doldrums and treaty negotiations of the 1920s and the crushing Great Depression, he had a lot of work to do. Now, he was well underway with his efforts. There was still too much to do. And politics threw up barriers every way he turned.

Admiral Devin Johnson, one of his trusted advisors and a longtime friend, was informing him that they needed even more ships. Especially new and technologically advanced—and very expensive—submarines.

"Devin, you know a lot of the Navy thinks battleships and carriers will do what we need to get done," Edison responded. "Those dreadnoughts and floatable airfields cost a lot of money. Submarines are beyond the imagination of most Senators and Congressmen. And especially if they have shipyards in their states that build carriers and battleships. Besides, those big-gun ships are named after states, not fish. And I don't need to remind you, fish don't vote."

"They aren't looking at our blue-and-orange models here. Nor do they understand what that new class of subs will be able to do. Maybe tell them more about the capabilities of the German U-boats. They should be well aware of what those bastards are doing out there already."

"You know it. I know it. But they'll all be a tough bunch to sell," Secretary Edison responded. "We will add your recommendation into our planning and budgeting. Right now, I have a different task that requires your personal attention. Our friends across the pond have requested that we meet. As we Navy types like to ask, is your seabag packed? The *Houston* is standing by there in Newport. She weighs anchor in the morning to transport you to Portsmouth, England. You meet with the First Sea Lord next week. I believe you know Sir Roger Whittaker."

Johnson chuckled. "Yes, Sir Roger and I have shared a pint or two over the years. But I gather this meeting isn't a social call."

"I'm afraid not," Secretary Edison said. "The Brits have requested some advanced planning discussions for possible future coordination. Herr Hitler is causing them significant angst with this 'Phony War' of his. They're concerned about what might happen when the other shoe drops. I want you to see what's on their mind and report straight back to me."

"Will do, Mr. Secretary."

"And Devin? Your boy, Bradley? He went to Submarine School out of Annapolis, right? That why you're so sold on more subs for the fleet? Really expensive subs?"

"Yes. For my son. But also for everybody's sons. The next war we fight will be different from anything we've been in before. A strong Navy might just deter somebody from trying to claim the whole damn planet. Japan will be the US Navy's problem. Hitler's 'Phony War' is a land battle right now despite what they're doing to Atlantic shipping bound for Britain. Even if it breaks out into real fighting again, it's going to primarily stay a land battle in Europe. Britain and France together should be able to contain Hitler. But if we have to fight Japan, they will present a whole different conundrum, and our games here prove it. Distance and acreage will present enough of a challenge, let alone the hardware they got in the pipeline over there. Hirohito is building a major fleet, and the Pacific is a very big portion of Planet Earth. We will have a real naval fight on our hands."

"Let's hope we're both wrong, Devin, but you know I totally agree. We damn well better have a strong Navy. And by the way, that's the mission the President gave me."

Johnson hung up the phone and turned to his aide. "Phil, get our seabags packed and down to the pier. We sail for 'jolly olde England' with the morning tide. I'll be at the Officer's Club for a final wrap-up from the game and dinner with the War College President and his staff. Please have my car pick me up at 2100. I'll see you bright and early, 0700, at the pier."

With that, Admiral Johnson grabbed his cover and marched off in the direction of the Officer's Club.

∞

Stan Ward angrily threw his crutches across the room.

"This is impossible!" he vented. Equal measures of pain and frustration left deep furrows across his perspiration-soaked brow. "At this rate, I'm never gonna walk again!"

The shooting pain in his back and the ache radiating up and down his leg only added to his mood. After two weeks of therapy, he still was not able to put any weight on his bum leg, nor even manage a faltering step. Maybe Doc Brown was right. He was not supposed to ever walk on that leg again. Maybe he would have to give up on his Navy dream.

"C'mon, now. Give it one more try," Karen Kamp cajoled after retrieving his crutches. "Then we'll break for lunch. Promise." The nurse knelt to adjust the straps on his brace. "You're the one always talking about the old Navy try."

Ward could not help but smile. Karen seemed to take his recovery as a personal challenge and saw Stan as more than just another patient. She was becoming his own angel, sometimes gently encouraging, other times more than willing to kick his butt when he needed it. And her intuition about which tactic was required always seemed to be spot on.

Ensign Ward was also beginning to harbor some hope that her interest in him was more than simply professional. As she adjusted the straps, he reached into his robe pocket and fondled his dad's Hamilton pocket watch. Maybe there was still some good luck left in it after all.

He forced a smile as she stood up, hands on hips, a dare-to-defy-me look on her pretty face.

"Okay, let's give it another shot," he agreed. "Then we can make our bet on what flavor Jell-O they'll bless us with today."

"You're on, sailor boy," she told him. "You're on."

∞

It was just a little before midnight when the *U-47* broke the surface. The crescent moon was low on the horizon, but the brilliant, brightly colored aurora borealis made the night almost as bright as daylight. The Orkney Mainland was clearly visible to starboard. Gunther Prien, Captain of the German submarine, worried that his boat might be spotted and the alarm raised before he could even enter Scapa Flow, Britain's mighty naval base in the north of Scotland.

The Royal Navy Home Fleet typically rested in Scapa Flow's quiet anchorage, protected by the encircling Orkney Islands. Only the heavily guarded Pentland Firth, opening to the south, allowed access. But Admiral Karl Dönitz, Supreme Commander of the German Navy's U-boats, had been informed that there was a narrow, shallow back channel, a back door, into Scapa Flow, that a skillfully driven U-boat might use. Prien had been ordered to test that back door.

The channel between Orkney Mainland and the tiny island of Lamb Holm was reported to only be about four hundred meters wide and two fathoms deep. Prien threaded the *U-47* between two sunken block ships, but snagged his submarine on a cable strung from one of them. Ringing up maximum power, he pulled free from the entangling cable and then found himself inside the anchorage.

But he could see only one target worth shooting. The Home Fleet was not home. Only the old battleship *Royal Oak*, too slow to run with the battle fleet, swung at anchor in the expansive harbor.

Prien decided to accept what he was offered. He carefully took aim and launched a four-torpedo salvo from his bow tubes. One torpedo hung up in the tube. Two torpedoes missed. One struck the target but there was no indication of explosion or damage.

Unperturbed, he swung *U-47* around to line up his stern tube, but that shot missed, too. Prien calmly reloaded the three operable bow tubes and swung back around to reattack the *Royal Oak*.

This time, all three torpedoes hit the battleship and exploded. A few seconds later, a massive secondary explosion erupted from the hapless ship, illuminating the night sky far more brilliantly than had the northern lights.

The *Royal Oak* quickly capsized and sank even as the *U-47* was threading its way back through Kirk Sound and toward the North Sea beyond.

Eight hundred thirty-five British seamen died in the attack.

∞

The bitter-cold wind, blowing across Long Island Sound and up the Thames River, churned the river water into a nasty gray soup and quickly chapped the skin of anyone in its way. Alistair MacLean, Fred Wurster, and Brad Johnson stood in ranks with the rest of their Submarine School class on the head of Pier 6, waiting, trying to ignore the bite of the breeze. Today was Sub School Class 3902's first time to go to sea on a real, live submarine. Though it was just for training and only for the day, there was still a sense of excitement mixed with a little anxiety at the prospect.

Every one of the twenty-four Ensigns hugged their reefer jackets around them in a vain effort to stay warm. They could see the diesel smoke being exhaled from the four submarines tied up alongside the pier, straining at their moorings, as if just as eager as the newcomers to get underway. Diesel exhaust burbled from the subs down near the waterline and then was whisked away by the wind. The smoke looked warm, but none of that welcome heat made it up to the shivering men while the officer in charge, Lieutenant Blythe, took his sweet time sorting out who was going out to ride which boat for the day's run.

Finally, happy with his list, Blythe started calling out names and boats, among them:

"Wurster – *R-1*."

"MacLean – *R-4*."

"Johnson – *R-10*."

Each of the gray boats was easily identifiable. It had its number painted on the side of the sail in big white figures inside a black square. As each officer's name was called, he marched over and stood by the brow of the submarine, the walkway from the pier to the deck of the boat he had been assigned to ride. Soon there were six officers standing, still shivering, in front of each of the four boats.

These *R*-class boats had been built at the end of the Great War but were delivered too late to see service in that conflict. Prior to that, the US Navy mostly considered submarines to be a novelty with limited usefulness. The Germans, with their U-boats, and especially against commercial shipping, showed otherwise. After the war, these particular subs had spent most of their useful lives patrolling the seas while the Navy figured out what it was that they needed submarines to do. Now they were assigned only as training subs, and these four appeared to have seen years of hard service. Streaks of rust trailed down the sides. The casings were pocked with numerous dents, the result of inexperienced officers banging them into piers and pilings while making practice landings.

Ensign Fred Wurster stepped across the brow onto the deck of the submarine *R-1*, his emotions very similar to the first day he ran out onto the football practice field in a Midshipman jersey. He saluted the national Ensign that blew briskly from the jackstaff and happily dropped down the hatch into the torpedo room, out of the chill wind. He immediately realized that he was in a completely different world, surrounded by pipes, valves, and machinery. But the thing that struck him first was the smell, the aromatic mixture of hot oil, diesel fuel, cooking smells, and the unwashed bodies of sailors. Well, these things were called "pig boats" and "sewer pipes" for a reason.

One of the crew, dressed in a ratty, sweat- and oil-stained pair of dungarees, pointed toward the hatch to the next compartment and said, "Sir, you're supposed to report to the control room. It's just through the forward battery."

Wurster nodded and ducked through the watertight door, then worked his way past the tiny officer staterooms and equally small wardroom that claimed most of the forward battery compartment.

"Hey, get your butt up to the bridge!" The speaker, dressed in a dirty sweater of some indeterminate color and a well-crushed officer's cover, stood in the middle of the cramped control room, arms akimbo. "We're casting off lines in five minutes and you're driving."

Wurster had just entered the control room, his eyes not yet adjusted to the dim light. He looked around to see to whom the man's order had been directed.

"Damn it, Ensign, I said get to the bridge!" He pointed to a ladder that disappeared upward into a compartment directly above them. "Skipper's up there and he's been waiting on your ass."

Wurster swallowed hard but did as he was told. He climbed up the ladder into the conning tower and then continued up another one that went on up to the bridge. He emerged onto a small platform about eight feet above the main deck. The bridge was surrounded by a waist-high steel enclosure that afforded only meager protection from the wind.

"Glad you could join us, Ensign!"

Wurster looked around and saw an officer wearing a heavy reefer coat with the two gold stripes of a Lieutenant on his shoulder boards.

"I'm Jim Moore, Skipper of the good ship *R-1*, and you got the honor of taking a voyage with us today." He stuck out his hand. "You got a name?"

"Wurster. Uh, Fred Wurster," the hapless Ensign stammered.

"You ever get a boat underway before, Fred?" Moore asked.

"No, sir. Just the yard craft at the Academy a few times."

LT. Moore chuckled. "What you're gonna want to do is not a whole lot different than that. The *R-1* is just bigger and a little slower to respond." He clapped his hands and looked out toward the river. "Let's get this show on the road and you'll see what I mean. You're in luck today. We're on the downstream side of the pier. All you need to do is cast off the lines and let the current push us away from the pier while you back into the channel. Once we're clear of the pier, twist her around to fair up to the channel and away we go. You'll have to really work hard to screw it up. Got it?"

"Yes, sir," Wurster responded.

Moore pointed down at the line handlers miserably standing by on the deck, ready to get below and out of the cold. "Just yell down and tell them to cast off all lines." Pointing toward the voice tube, he added, "Then you yell down that pipe there and tell the XO that we are underway and order a back two-thirds on both shafts."

Sure enough, the submarine backed smoothly out into the current. Once it had cleared the pier, the natural flow of the Thames River started to really push them downstream. Wurster ordered the starboard motor to answer "ahead one-third" while the port motor stayed at "back two-thirds." That combination, along with the power of the Thames, smartly twisted the boat around until it was aimed downriver.

"Well done, Mr. Wurster," Moore told him, obviously impressed. Wurster grinned proudly. Somehow, it all seemed natural to him. Maybe he actually would be at home on the bridge and in the conning tower of a submarine. "Now, the important stuff. Call down to the conn and get some coffee sent up. Then we can enjoy the trip downriver. We've got right at two hours to the dive point. We might as well take in the sights."

Fred Wurster looked back over his shoulder. He could see the other three boats lining up behind him as they all headed toward the Long Island Sound. He wondered if either of his buddies had gotten to be on the bridge for the underway.

Eastern Point was abreast to port when Fred first felt the motion of the long rollers from the North Atlantic. The *R-1* started to pitch as the swells built. The winter wind was blowing in off the ocean. That promised a rough ride, at least until they dove. By the time they passed Race Rock, the swells were breaking over the main deck and sending frigid spray up to the bridge.

"Okay, Mr. Wurster," LT. Moore shouted above the wind, "I don't need another saltwater shower. Let's get this boat underwater. Sound the diving alarm and then get yourself through that hatch and below."

Wurster smiled broadly as he hit the diving alarm twice. "*Aoogha!*

Aoogha!" Then he ordered, "Dive! Dive!" and headed for the hatch. The two lookouts coming down from their perch above the bridge beat him there. He had to wait for a moment.

Then Moore shouted, "About to get real wet here, so best you hurry!" And the Captain was already tromping on Wurster's fingers as the Ensign dropped down the ladder as quickly as he dared.

The Skipper pulled the heavy hatch shut over his head and deftly spun the handwheel just as cold seawater spilled over the bridge. He called out, "Last man down, hatch secured!" as he landed with both feet on the conning tower deck. He stepped over to the periscope and started to swing it around, taking a look at what was happening outside.

Wurster had already noticed how surprisingly quiet it was. The diesel engines were secured, and the boat was operating on its batteries. Silence. The "Silent Service."

From the control room, one deck below, Wurster heard the Chief of the Watch call out, "All Kingston valves open, all vents open, flooding negative." The *R-1* angled noticeably downward.

Moore called out, "Scope's under. Lowering the scope. Dive, make your depth seven zero feet and get a good one-third trim."

Wurster looked around wide-eyed. He was amazed. He was actually on a submerged submarine, and everything seemed normal. It was hard to believe that outside those thin metal walls was the cold, gray Atlantic Ocean. Well, Block Island Sound to be precise.

Moore looked at the navigation chart and ordered, "Helm, steer course one-two-zero." Turning to the six Ensigns that pretty much filled the conning tower, he said, "Gentlemen, we're going to spend the day familiarizing you with submarine life. The XO, LT. Johansson, has a schedule laid out for each of you."

The CO pointed toward a man Wurster recognized as the officer in the greasy sweater who had yelled at him when he first came aboard.

Johansson nodded and said, "We're going to do a series of evolutions for you to watch. You've seen each in the books and on the chalkboard but now each of you are going to spend time with the major underway watches." He paused to stare hard at the young officers. "One simple reminder. A submerged submarine is a dangerous place to be. And you guys are non-quals. Don't touch anything unless you're told to. If we have a problem, I want you to stand back, out of the way. You will be told what to do, if necessary. Everybody understand?"

Six heads nodded and, in unison, answered, "Yes, sir."

The six dispersed to their first assigned stations. Fred Wurster ended up in the maneuvering room, watching and listening as the on-watch electrician explained how the submarine's batteries supplied power to the main motors when they were submerged and how the two NELSECO 6-EB14 diesels both charged the two 60-cell batteries and supplied the main motors when the sub was running on the surface. By the end of two hours, all the switches, controllers, and gauges were starting to make sense to Wurster.

He next made his way up to the torpedo room for his second watch. The submarine's JP sonar system was operated from there. The *R-1* JP system had a sonar head that lowered below the hull and another one that raised from the deck above. The lower one, or the "supersonic head," was useful for detecting very high frequency noise such as a destroyer using its own active sonar to search for a submarine. The upper head resembled a long bar and was trainable to get a bearing on any detected sonic noise.

Wurster listened to the outside ocean through the headset. The clicks and pops of various sea life were fascinating. He had no idea of the noises that things as small as shrimp or as large as whales made. The sonar operator was in his element, enjoying pointing out the various sounds as he spun the wheel that rotated the upper sound head.

"Hear that? That's the Montauk Ferry," he said as they listened to the churning of the ferry's screws. The noise had a *chug, chug, chug* sound.

"The ferry hit the pier a couple of months ago and bent a blade on one of its screws," the sonar operator explained. "That's why it makes that particular sound. Next time you're out, they'll have fixed it maybe and it'll sound different. Now, let's see where those whales got to."

He spun the wheel around so that the sound head was looking out toward the open Atlantic. Suddenly, they heard not the sound of a pod of whales but a loud, rushing, whooshing noise. Wurster was not sure if he was listening to a waterfall or a rainstorm. Then he noticed the expression on the face of the sonar operator. The man looked alarmed.

He grabbed the microphone and yelled, "Conn, Sonar. I'm hearing a submarine diving and it's close! Dead ahead!"

Wurster felt the submarine suddenly angle up and, at the same time, saw that they were dramatically changing course. His first thought was that this was all part of the training, but if it was, the sonarman was one talented actor.

"Jesus. Looks like the Skipper is going up to take a look," he said as he slowly turned the handwheel to keep the sonar head aimed at the intruding submarine. "Whoever it is, that guy is sure taking his sweet time diving."

Up in the conning tower, Jim Moore raised the periscope. Then, just as it broke through the surface, he was staring at a sight he never imagined he would see. There was a German Type 1A submarine and it was only a couple of hundred yards away, steaming straight at them on a collision course. He could see the mist blowing up from the German boat's ballast tank vents as it settled lower into the water, in the process of slowly diving. There was a swastika painted on the front of the boat's conning tower.

"Dive! Make your depth one hundred feet! Ahead flank!"

The best move appeared to be to dive beneath the other sub. Trying to duck or dodge might just result in a far worse T-bone crash.

The Chief of the Watch sounded the collision alarm and announced, "Rig ship for collision!" The crew—who had never had to do this operation except in drills—scurried to shut watertight doors and ventilation flappers as they hustled to make the sub as watertight as possible.

They only had seconds to get out of the way. Moore stared through the periscope at the German submarine as it loomed larger, completely filling his view. It was only a few seconds, but it seemed to be an eternity until the periscope dropped below the surface. Moore lowered it.

The Diving Officer shouted out the sub's depth as they dropped down toward safety, and hopefully quicker than the apparently unaware German boat was diving.

"Depth fifty feet, coming to one hundred! Depth sixty feet coming to one hundred! Depth seventy feet—"

The *R-1* suddenly heeled over sharply to port. Simultaneously there was a grating, screeching, grinding sound that filled the narrow confines of the conning tower. The submarine leaned over even farther and was shoved downward hard as the grinding noise grew even louder. Then, just as suddenly, the noise stopped, and the boat snapped upright again, as if released from some giant hand that had pushed it downward.

"Flooding! Flooding in the engine room!" The announcement sent a shiver of fear through the crew. And the six trainees. "Flooding through the main induction line!"

There was no telling yet how much damage the collision had caused, but water was flooding into the people tank. That meant it was time to get to the surface in one hell of a hurry.

"Dive, blow all main ballast! Surface the ship!" Moore ordered. He then turned and tried to raise the periscope. It would not go up. He turned to try the number two periscope. It was also jammed in place. There was no way to tell if they were surfacing directly into a fishing boat, a ferry, or that damned damaged German submarine.

The *R-1* bobbed blindly to the surface. Jim Moore jumped up the ladder and spun the handwheel to open the bridge hatch. Thankfully, the mechanism still worked, and he was able to lift and open it. Then he climbed out onto the bridge and took a look. The German sub was on the surface, maybe a hundred yards away. It appeared its bow was caved in badly, but as the Skipper watched, the vessel swung around and headed out to sea. It certainly was not waiting around to see if Moore's submarine and crew needed any assistance.

Kirk Johansson yelled up the ladder, "Skipper, flooding has stopped. Maybe 'cause we're on the surface. We're pumping the engine room bilge. I've ordered the diesels started. Recommend we head back home before we spring a leak somewhere else."

Moore looked aft for the first time. Toward the stern of his aged submarine. Most of the afterpart of the conning tower superstructure was gone. It simply was no longer there. Just some jagged, bent, and torn metal.

"XO, I agree. Come to course three-one-zero, ahead two-thirds. I don't think the body shop is going to be able to just rub these dents out."

Johansson yelled, "Skipper, looks like the radio antennas are gone. We can't raise SUB Base."

"Guess we'll surprise them when we show up at the pier," Moore answered. Then he thought for a moment before he continued. "There's going to be a whole lot of interest when we come in dented and dinged. I expect things are going to be coming fast and furious. Before we get in, have everyone write down what they saw. Especially Sonar. I think I'm the only one who actually saw that Nazi bastard. People are not going to believe us unless we have some backup information."

"Skipper, we're in luck," the XO replied. "We had one of those Ensigns listening to sonar. He was up to the bridge behind you and got a glimpse of the Nazi boat, too. That kid Wurster. He's already writing down everything that happened and what he saw and heard."

"Good. Damn good."

4

The pub at the Officer's Club was crowded and everyone was in a happy mood. Thursdays were ten-cent "cheeseburger and a beer" night. The place was decorated in dark mahogany and shiny brass. The smoky, dimly lit pub would have been right at home in London or Midtown Manhattan, except for the fact that every male patron wore a US Navy uniform. The smattering of females in the club mostly sat in booths along the back wall, quietly nursing a gin and tonic or other cocktails with their husbands or boyfriends. The bar itself was jammed with young submarine officers drinking their dinners while they loudly discussed how the Midshipmen's defense could possibly handle the Cadets' brutal running attack in the upcoming Army-Navy football game. The bartenders were kept busy trying to keep the zinc bar top clear and clean and all their customers' plates and mugs filled.

Most of Submarine Class 3902 were seated around two large tables in the center of the room. The tables were strewn with the remnants of devoured cheeseburgers and mostly empty beer glasses. A couple of pitchers showed up just in time to remedy the latter situation. Their just-completed first underway was the main topic of discussion among these men. For most, the run out into Long Island Sound had been exciting, informative, and uneventful. But by now, the entire class had walked past the heavily damaged *R-1* and seen firsthand what the German U-boat had done to the submarine.

Even as they listened to Fred Wurster and his five shipmates describe yet again their close call, a hotly contested game of liar's dice competed for the young officers' attention. The dice cup made its way clockwise around the two tables. At a dollar a chip, the game was both a source of entertainment and a way to raise money for the class's planned graduation party. They calculated that they were almost halfway to their thousand-dollar goal. That would be enough to pay to rent the club's party room for an evening of dinner and dancing and maybe even a live band to play.

Brad Johnson gave the leather dice cup a hearty shake before slamming it down on the table. Then he carefully lifted one side of the cup to peek underneath.

He smiled, shook his head up and down, and announced, "Four sixes and a deuce," before passing the cup to Trip MacLean.

MacLean did not even consider the cup. Instead, he looked Johnson dead in the eye. He had gambled with his friend many times and had discovered early on that Brad always blinked when he was bluffing. Such a tell had won MacLean considerable money. Now Johnson merely looked at MacLean and smiled. No sign of a blink.

Only then did MacLean take the cup and peek under it. A pair of twos, a three, a four, and a six. He smiled at Johnson, pulled out the single six, put the rest of the dice in the cup, and said, "You lying lowlife!" He shook the cup vigorously before slamming it down. Without even bothering to look at what he had rolled, he announced, "Five sixes," and passed the cup to his left, to Fred Wurster.

Wurster laughed. "Bull! You're lying, Trip." He lifted the cup with a flourish to reveal four sixes sitting there to go with the fifth on the table, just as promised.

Flipping a chip into the growing pile in the middle of the table, he complained, "Trip, you are unconscious lucky. If that Nazi sub had hit your boat, it would probably have flooded the conning tower with cold German beer."

But nobody laughed. The room had suddenly gotten eerily quiet.

"Nobody saw any German submarine." The voice was stern, gruff. The speaker, dressed in a black trench coat and with a dark gray fedora pulled low over his eyes, hiding most of his face, stood beside Wurster's table. He was flanked by two similarly dressed men. He reached into an inside coat pocket and pulled out a little wallet. When he flipped it open, there was a brass badge pinned to it.

"Special Agent Ralph Flannigan," he said as he held the badge up for all to see. "FBI."

The room remained completely silent as Flannigan returned the badge to his pocket before anyone could inspect it more closely.

"Let me repeat myself," he said. "No one saw any Nazi sub because there wasn't any. Do I make myself clear?"

Several of the Ensigns at the table shook their heads. Fred Wurster stood and started to protest, "Mister, I know what I saw, and it was for damn sure—"

Special Agent Flannigan stopped him short with an upheld hand. "Ensign Wurster, you are mistaken. The *R-1* struck a submerged log. Telling any other story is a violation of national security. Do you want to go to jail, young man?"

Wurster shook his head and meekly sat back down. Whatever game Special Agent Flannigan—if that really was his name—was playing, he clearly held all the cards. He not only knew about the collision, but he also knew Fred Wurster's name. He probably had a list of everyone in the club this night.

Flannigan continued, his voice a low and very effective growl. "I'll be perfectly clear. Any further discussion, on base or off, of this so-called collision with a Nazi sub will be considered a violation of the Espionage Act. If one word of this story leaks out, we will find out who did it. We will put you in prison and throw away the key. There was no German sub. Just a very unfortunate sunken log."

Flannigan turned and walked to the door. He stopped and over his shoulder said, "We'll be listening and watching." Then he touched the brim of his hat and added, "And have a nice evening."

∞

Eloise Morton—Ellie to family and friends—brushed the hair back from her eyes. Saturday was typically a slow day at Morton's Pharmacy. This cold December Saturday had been especially slow, though. A bitter wind blew a wet mixture of sleet and snow down Main Street. That certainly discouraged customers from venturing out unless they really needed headache powder or a bottle of her dad's special cough syrup. She sighed as she stared out the window. Another boring day in a boring town.

Ellie could not wait until she had earned enough money to pay for nursing school. The pert nineteen-year-old had already been accepted to the Massachusetts General Hospital Training School for Nurses. That would take her to the exciting city of Boston. All she needed was the money to pay for it.

The store had seen only one "customer" since opening. As usual, Agnes Fortright had come in to peruse the magazine rack, leafing through the latest edition of *Harper's Bazaar*. But Eloise knew from experience Mrs. Fortright would read for a bit while she got warm. Then, after consuming much of the magazine and without spending a nickel in the pharmacy, she would venture down the street to the Mystic Grocers to stay warm and read the latest edition of *Collier's Weekly*. Indeed, that was precisely what she did this dreary morning.

Ellie grabbed a towel and began wiping down the soda fountain countertop one more time. Her father, the owner of Morton's Pharmacy, expected her to keep the fountain area immaculate. It typically made more money for the store than all those pills and potions did.

She was busy wiping the counter when she heard the tinkling of the doorbell. Finally, a real customer. She looked up to smile and greet the newcomer, a handsome young man in a Navy uniform. Her smile brightened considerably. Involuntarily.

"Good morning, ma'am." The rich baritone voice grabbed even more of Ellie's attention. "I was wondering if I could get a cup of coffee?" he asked. "Take the chill off."

She flashed an even warmer smile and answered, "Sure! One coffee coming up. Just finished brewing a fresh pot."

Just finished brewing it two hours before, when she first opened the drugstore. But that made it, she figured, reasonably fresh. She filled a cup from the steaming pot and passed it to the sailor as he eased down on one of the bar stools. He slid a nickel across the bar to her, took a sip, and smiled at the tall, attractive blonde.

"Oooh, that sure hits the spot on a cold day like this." He glanced at his watch. "I got half an hour 'til my bus. You mind if I wait here out of the wind and buy a few more cups of that special coffee of yours?"

Mystic, Connecticut, was a few miles removed from the Navy's submarine base, so it was not really a Navy town, but it was still close enough that sailors were not a rarity. Ellie knew from what her mother and many of her friends had told her that she should be wary of them. That especially applied to submarine sailors. Besides drinking, sailors usually had only one other thing on their minds, and it wasn't coffee or cough syrup.

But this one seemed different. Interesting. Nice. And with no ulterior motives at all.

"I have an apple pie back here if you have time," she offered. "Just baked it. Still warm."

"Sure," he answered. "If it doesn't cost too much. And if you'll stay here and keep me company while I wait."

"Oh, no charge! And as you can see, we're not exactly awash with customers this morning."

The pair discussed the weather, small-town life, and a host of topics as he nibbled the pie. They were both surprised that a half hour had passed when the orange Groton and Stonington bus pulled to a stop in front of the pharmacy.

He stood, started for the door, but stopped, turned back, and took her hand. "I'm Fred. Fred Wurster. I'd like to come back and see you sometime, if that's okay."

She blushed. "My name's Ellie. Ellie Morton. I'd like that."

Wurster grinned and rushed out to get onto the bus. But he stopped again, turned, and waved before climbing the steps.

Ellie Morton smiled and waved back. It had turned out to be not such a dull Saturday after all.

∞

Admiral Devin Johnson stepped out of the blue Morris Super Six taxi and looked up at the white granite pile of London's distinctive Admiralty Arch. The massive, curved building, constructed at the behest of King Edward VII in memory of his mother, Queen Victoria, connected Trafalgar Square to the Mall. It served as both home and office for the First Sea Lord of the British Navy.

Tonight's dinner meeting would bring to a conclusion the series of discussions that Johnson had already conducted that week with the First Sea Lord. All the talks were very private, held in Sir Roger Whittaker's inner office. Even Phil Sherman, Johnson's flag aide, had been required to sit outside the closed doors and wait. The two men had covered a lot of ground but had not reached any specific accord. The only thing they fully agreed on was that US involvement in the war between Great Britain and Germany and its allies was inevitable. And that it would be prudent for both the US and Great Britain to rapidly shore up their respective navies. However, they had not reached agreement on how much growth or even what types of ships they needed to build to prepare for the inevitable. Certainly nothing had been decided about how the two navies might work together against a common enemy. Or how to do so when so many within their two governments were adamant about not getting dragged into another major conflict in continental Europe. In Great Britain's case, even though hostilities had already commenced.

Sir Roger's invitation to dinner had stipulated that it was to be a small, informal affair at his official flat. A quiet evening for two old seafarers to rehash the week of intense discussion over brandy and cigars before Admiral Johnson headed back to the States.

Sir Roger's flag aide met Johnson at the north entrance and escorted him up to the First Sea Lord's flat on the third deck. After a discreet knock on the door, the aide disappeared back down the long hallway.

Sir Roger opened the door, smiling, whiskey glass in hand. "Devin, so glad you could make it this evening," he welcomed as he showed Johnson into the flat. "I must apologize. We are playing bachelors tonight. 'She Who Must Be Obeyed' is off to an evening at the theatre. Some Eugene O'Neill play that she has been prattling on about. She asked that I give you her best and insist you bring your beautiful wife along next time."

"I'll certainly tell her, Roger. She fusses because she gets to accompany me on so few of my business trips."

Nodding toward the butler, who waited nearby, Whittaker went on. "James will take your coat. Let's get you a drink. You must be positively parched, all the jawing we've been doing. Our other guest is running a few minutes late." Sir Roger laughed. "Once he arrives, the bar will become quite crowded, and the whiskey supply will be in serious jeopardy."

"How is your son?" Johnson asked. "We heard the dreadful news from Scapa Flow."

Sir Roger's face lost its joviality. "William was navigator on the *Royal Oak*. By God's good graces, he survived the ordeal, for which we are eternally thankful. Too many of our boys did not. But he was seriously wounded. I'm afraid he lost his arm."

"I'm very sorry to hear that," Johnson said.

"But, on the brighter side," Sir Roger continued, "we have taken to calling him Horatio, since he now takes after Admiral Nelson."

Reaching for a cut glass decanter, Roger poured a generous dram into a tumbler and nodded toward a small pitcher of water on the bar. Offering Johnson the drink, he said with proud enthusiasm, "I believe this to be the finest fruit of Scotland. From a tiny distillery up in the Highlands. I have it privately bottled just for my personal use. And for special guests, of course."

Johnson took the tumbler and lifted it to his lips.

Sir Roger held up a hand to stop him. "Wait. You really must add just a splash of water. It opens the aroma and taste."

"Yes, you must!" a deep voice boomed from behind the pair. Both turned to look at the newcomer. "A chemist once explained to me that the water severs the guaiacol molecules from the ethanol ones and they rise to the surface, carrying the aroma and flavor with them. All very scientific, you see. Roger, so long as you are pouring, a healthy dram for me, if you please."

"Winston," Sir Roger said. "Glad you could join us. Busy day at Westminster, I presume?"

"Yes," Churchill said with a laugh. "The PM was still trying mightily to explain why his policies left us so woefully unprepared for this current war when I dozed off. And the windbag was still preaching his drivel when I awoke later, far better rested but still unconvinced." Shifting to his more stentorian parliamentary voice, he went on. "As I have said before, an appeaser is one who feeds the crocodile, hoping the creature will eat him last."

Everyone laughed. The trio made small talk as they gazed out the large plate glass windows and down at the traffic busily coursing through Trafalgar Square.

James, the butler, entered the room and announced, "Sir Roger, gentlemen, dinner is served."

The dinner conversation was light as they discussed with good humor the foibles of the various members of Parliament. Churchill seemed to have a funny anecdote about each, regardless of the member's party or politics. As James cleared away the last course, Whittaker rose and offered, "Gentlemen, cigars and cognac in the library. Winston, I have stocked in your favorite La Aroma de Cuba and the wine merchant just delivered a case of Hine Bonneuil 1895."

Once they were comfortably ensconced in a trio of deep leather club chairs, each cradling a snifter of cognac and enshrouded in a haze of cigar smoke, Churchill intoned, "Devin, I asked Roger to host his little dinner so that we could get a chance to talk. We are in agreement that this current war is going to deeply entangle Great Britain but also the United States eventually. Mr. Hitler will ensure that prophecy is fulfilled. The time to prepare for us to fight cooperatively is now but too many people in leadership positions in both of our countries refuse to see the obvious."

The other two men nodded agreement.

Churchill took a sip of brandy and then a long, appreciative draw on his cigar before he continued. "Despite my vast experience in the military and government, no one wants to hear what I have to say. As you know, I have only recently resumed the role as First Lord of the Admiralty. We warriors are being called upon once again. I mean to do everything possible to answer that call. But to be effective and to begin laying the groundwork, I need a back-channel means of communication with your Secretary of the Navy. Secretary Edison says you are the man for the job."

Churchill's request came from way out in left field. Johnson needed a few seconds to think. He took a slow sip of brandy and then, his mind made up, he smiled. "Winston, if Secretary Edison is on board with this, I'm your man."

Churchill leaned forward in his chair, his head shrouded in cigar smoke. "Devin, let me caution you. You must be very discreet about this. For both political and diplomatic reasons, we cannot afford for anyone to discern that we are looking at a level of collusion between our two navies at a time when your country is ostensibly neutral. If the wrong people—here as well as over there in the colonies—should find this out, it could not only stymie our preparations but could become quite dangerous for all of us."

"Understood, Mr. Churchill. Understood."

The two men shook hands as Sir Roger looked on, now smiling broadly.

The quiet moment was disturbed by someone out in the hallway. Whittaker looked up and said, "It sounds as if the ruler of the household has returned to her domain."

Churchill pulled his pocket watch from his vest and glanced at the time. "I really must be going. Off to the Carleton. Eden wants to discuss working together to quash this 'appeaser' drivel."

Taking his signature bowler and coat from James, he said, "I'll go out by the Spring Street exit, if you don't mind. Devin, kindly give me a few minutes and then use the Mall exit. Can't afford to be seen leaving here together so late in the evening." He chuckled as he chewed on the stub of his cigar. "The town would be positively awash with rumors if we old warriors were spotted out together this time of night. Those of us who advocate common sense will always fall under suspicion from those who possess a zero sum of that precious commodity."

After Churchill left, Admiral Devin Johnson thanked Sir Roger Whittaker for his hospitality, wished his wife a good evening, and promised to convey her best wishes to Faye, his wife. By the time the social courtesies were completed, enough time had elapsed for Churchill to have completed his departure. Johnson headed back out the way he had come in. A cab waited for him at the north Mall entrance.

Lost in thoughts of the night's heavy conversation, Johnson failed to notice the lone figure lurking back in the black shadows of the Admiralty Arch. Someone watching with great interest as the American Admiral climbed into the cab and it pulled away.

Only then did the man emerge from the darkness, pulling his hat down low over his face, and saunter off toward Waterloo Place.

5

Stan Ward stared out the hospital window just as he did for so many long hours, all day, every day. Having consumed all the magazines and the few books in the hospital library and being strapped to the Thomas splint looming above his bed, gazing out the window was about the only other thing he could do to pass the hours. Even so, there was little to observe out there. Only the wind howling across the empty winter prairie, driving the snow into massive drifts against every building, tree, and fence that got in its way. And then watching the sun slowly set on another dreary day, leaving only black, depressing darkness outside his sole window on the world.

The all-knowing US Navy, working in its own usual mysterious way, had abruptly decided to transport him from the Asbury Hospital in Salina, Kansas, to the Army hospital at Fort Riley, Kansas. Here he had the distinction of being the only Navy officer on an Army post in the middle of the country, surrounded by thousands of soldiers. The move left him alone and lonely, even farther away from family and friends back in Colorado. The distance and weather made it difficult for them to come visit him. While spending the first couple of months after the bus accident in Salina, impatiently waiting for his broken leg to mend, he had made many friends among the doctors and therapists and fellow patients. Even Nurse Dibble, who had become something of a mother figure.

But the person he missed the most was another nurse, Karen Kamp. He truly missed her laugh, her always-smiling face, and the obvious fact that she seemed to care more for Ward than the typical caregiver did for a patient.

As he watched the latest winter storm blowing in, Ward was feeling especially abandoned when he heard a faint knock at the door. The wind, blowing stuff around outside? Not another nurse to subject him to physical therapy torture. That was yesterday. No, most likely it was the orderly bringing him his medications, though his knock was never timid. Neither was the guy's attitude toward a patient who still refused to take any pain meds. But the salves the burly orderly brought him for bedsores were a godsend, so Stan tried to put up with him, even if he had the bedside manner of an Army mule.

"Come on the hell in!" Ward grumbled irritably.

"Is that any way to greet an old friend?" It definitely was not the orderly bearing bedsore salve. It was a female voice. And one with a wonderful laughing lilt attached to it.

"Karen, what are you...?"

"I thought you might be lonely," she replied. She carried something. A tin of what could only be her walnut cookies. The best medicine ever dispensed in any hospital. "I decided to just pop over and plump your pillow up for you."

It was a good sixty miles from Salina to Fort Riley over wintry Kansas back roads and with a minor blizzard blowing in. Karen Kamp had certainly not just "popped over."

Stan Ward's smile stretched from ear to ear as the young nurse gave him a quick kiss on the forehead and took his hand.

"You won't believe this, but I was just thinking about you," he blurted out. "I really miss you."

"I miss you, too, Stan," she responded sweetly, with a shy smile and a deep blush.

They were still smiling at each other, maximizing the moment, when someone burst through the door without knocking or asking. The hospital administrator, an especially irritating Major, offered no apology and did not acknowledge Stan's visitor.

"Ensign Ward, sign this form," he brusquely directed, pointing to a line at the bottom of the last page of a thick sheaf of papers. He offered a pen while impatiently tapping with his knuckles on Stan's bedside table.

"What is it that you're ordering me to sign?" Ward asked.

"It's your request to resign your commission for medical reasons and forego your obligations to your country," the administrator answered, looking at Stan over the tops of his spectacles. "The paperwork came through from Washington in today's mail and I need to get it off my desk to make room for some more. Now, sign it and make the Navy happy. Then we can start the wheels turning. It'll still be a month or so, but then you'll officially be a civilian again and free to go back home."

"But as I have told everybody who will listen, including you, Major, I have no intention of resigning," Ward shot back, an angry edge to his voice. Karen still held his hand. She squeezed it reassuringly. "Tell me. What would I do if I went back to Lamar? I have a degree in naval engineering from the US Naval Academy. That won't do me much good coaxing wheat out of the dirt a thousand miles from saltwater."

"Not on my list of problems to solve today, Ensign. Your only option is to request a waiver, which generates still more paperwork for me," the administrator grumped. "Look, the Navy's not going to have a lot of use for an Ensign who walks with a bad limp. But I can't keep you from trying if you intend to."

Ward looked up at Karen with a grin. "Reckon you could get me a pen and some paper? Looks like I've got some letters to write."

She squeezed his hand again and smiled back.

"Happy to help."

∞

Ensign Brad Johnson sat in the back row of the classroom, struggling mightily to stay awake. Every time Lieutenant Blythe, the instructor for this class, turned to write on the blackboard, Johnson's head fell forward, chin on chest. And each time, it took a well-timed jab in the ribs from Trip

MacLean, sitting at the desk next to him, to jerk him awake before his friend let out a snore or Blythe turned back around and caught him.

"Damn it, Brad!" MacLean hissed, he assumed low enough that he would not be heard in the front of the classroom. "If you're going to scream with the eagles every night, you've got to scratch with the chickens in the morning."

"You have something to share with the class, Mr. MacLean?" Blythe asked pointedly as he spun from the blackboard to face the students, chalk poised midair.

"No sir!" Trip MacLean quickly answered. "We were just trying to figure out the difference between 'normal course' and 'normal approach course.' They sound like the same thing to me."

Blythe lifted an incredulous eyebrow, then turned back to the blackboard. He quickly drew a diagram showing a target ship on a straight course across the top and a submarine, labelled "own ship" down at the bottom. "Okay, for Mr. MacLean's benefit and for the sixth time for the rest of the class, for a normal course, you simply turn 'own ship' so you are approaching the target ship at ninety degrees to its course. For example, if the target is on course zero-nine-zero, normal course would be course north. For a normal approach course, you turn 'own ship' so that the target always has a ninety-degree relative bearing. By any chance do you see the difference now, Mr. MacLean?"

The young Ensign smiled and answered, "Yes, sir. I think I understand now. Thank you, sir." But when the instructor turned back to the blackboard, MacLean gave Johnson an unmistakable "you owe me big-time" look.

Blythe eventually reached a stopping point and looked at the clock resting on his desk. It read 1650. He pulled a stack of mimeographed pages and a bunch of circular slide rules from a nearby bookshelf and placed them alongside the clock on the desk. "Because we were required to repeat some of the material multiple times, we won't have opportunity to cover all I had intended today, particularly using the 'Is/Was' to calculate optimum approach courses." He pointed at the two stacks. "Everybody grab an 'Is/Was' and the instructions. You can figure it out from there. If you need help, I'll be in my office until 2000." He sat down. "Don't forget that we have a test in the morning covering approach geometry. I recommend you be well prepared. Dismissed!"

As Class 3902 shuffled out of the classroom, Trip MacLean caught up with Brad Johnson and Fred Wurster.

"You want to thank me for providing a little entertainment during class, guys?" MacLean asked with a grin.

"You and Bradley? You did break up the lecture nicely," Wurster said. "But look, I'm lost, guys. This ain't making sense. Why don't we get together after dinner and go over this stuff?"

"I'm in," MacLean answered without hesitation. "We can put it in football terms for you, Freddy, then you can translate it back to us."

But Johnson was shaking his head. "I've enjoyed about as much of this approach geometry stuff as I can stand. Look, there's a Red Top Ale with my name on it waiting for me down at the Solomon Tavern. Debbie promised to keep it especially cold for me. You guys are welcome to come watch me get tipsy."

"Brad, be serious," MacLean retorted. "You don't pass that exam in the morning, you could be out, no matter what kind of strings your old man might pull for you. How you gonna explain to him that a few beers were more important than passing this test?"

Johnson laughed. "You men study hard and give me the gouge over breakfast."

Then he trotted off in the direction of the main gate and some cold Red Top Ales.

∞

Lieutenant Blythe walked into the classroom and began distributing the completed examinations. He paused in front of Brad Johnson's desk, handed him the papers, and gave him time to notice the failing mark on the top sheet.

"Mr. Johnson, Commander Flynn wants to see you in his office." He glared down at the Ensign. "And right now, mister!"

Johnson slowly walked down the passageway to the SUBSCOL CO's office, planning exactly how he would remind the Sub School's commanding officer that his dad was Admiral Devin Johnson. And, if that failed to impress, he would tell the CO he had come down with a nasty stomach bug the night before the exam. He knocked, opened the door, and stepped inside.

Snapping to attention, he announced, "Ensign Johnson, reporting as ordered, sir!"

Commander Roderick Flynn looked up from the letter he had been reading. The look on his face was anything but reassuring.

"Mr. Johnson, I can only conclude that you think Sub School is some kind of personal vacation for you," he growled. "Am I correct in that assumption?"

Bradley Johnson, still at attention, crisply answered, "No, sir! My dad always made sure I understood the importance—"

"Let's leave your dad out of this for the moment. How do you explain the fact that you were seen leaving Solomon's Tavern after midnight the evening before an important examination? Approach geometry, if I am correct. And if that report is accurate, you were more than a little wobbly and certainly not in proper shape to drive back to base, yet you did just that. And had a few choice things to say to the gate guard." Flynn's voice had gone lower as he went along. It was downright menacing toward the end. He took a deep breath and went on. "The following morning, you were observed being tutored over breakfast by two classmates, though you were reportedly in no shape to accept such aid. While your friends were studying together that evening, you were out drinking. They worked hard for their grades. You, on the other hand, skated. Does that seem fair to you?"

"No, sir," Johnson responded.

"Now, about your dad. Your father and I served together back on the old *North Dakota*. He was the XO when I reported aboard as an Ensign in 1918. He made sure that this young submarine officer got started out straight. That means I owe it to him to do the same for you. But the main reason for this chat this morning is to explain how your lax attitude could have deadly effects on those you might one day serve with. If you somehow make it through Sub School—and at the moment I have serious doubts—you will likely become an officer aboard a submarine at some point. Then, as with every other man on that boat, sailor or officer, the lives of every crewmember and the integrity and effectiveness of your submarine will depend on you doing the right thing, not just some of the time but every time. You will not have the benefit of having an Admiral as a father. He won't be able to help you when you have an emergency situation at two hundred feet. Nor be able to rely on shipmates to cover for you if you are fighting a fire or loss of control on a dive. Do you understand?"

"Yes, sir," Johnson answered. And he did.

Flynn tapped the desk with his fingertips for a long, long moment before going on. "You are hereby restricted to the base. Against my better judgment, I am giving you one more chance to pass that approach geometry test. Not just pass it. Get a perfect score. And if I hear that you are even thinking about another beer down at Solomon's before an exam, you will find yourself on the open bridge of an old four-stacker tin can on North Atlantic patrol before you can even pack your foul-weather gear. Do I make myself clear, Mr. Johnson?"

Brad once again crisply replied, "Yes sir!"

"Dismissed!"

"Aye, aye, sir!" He turned to leave and then looked back at the CO. "Thank you, sir. I do appreciate the second chance."

"Don't make me regret it."

6

Stan Ward threw down the letter in disgust. "Damn! The Navy's ordering me on the Temporary Disability Retired List just like Doc Brown said they would. I don't think anybody even bothered to read my letter."

Karen Kamp leaned closer and took his hand. "We just have to take the next step. Who do we appeal to next?"

She had been sitting with Ward in the Army hospital's waiting room when an orderly handed him the letter. While she had not exactly moved to Fort Riley, she had been spending most of her days off from her nursing duties at the hospital in Salina driving back and forth between the two small Kansas towns. Her visits were the high points of Ward's otherwise miserable existence, and it was not just the food and reading materials she brought him.

"The only one who can overrule the medical board is the Secretary of the Navy. Ain't much chance of him listening to me," Ward lamented. "I'm just a nobody from East Nowhere."

"Stan Ward!" Karen harrumphed with a mock frown. A stunningly beautiful mock frown. "Listen to you! That's just about enough feeling sorry for yourself. We need a pen and paper. We've got some more writing to do. Didn't you say that your roommate at the Academy was related to an Admiral or something?"

"Yeah, Brad Johnson's dad is Admiral Devin Johnson. Nice guy, and way up the command chain at the Main Navy Building in DC. He and Bradley's mom had me over for dinner several times when we were in the Academy," Ward reminisced. "But your chocolate cake is much better than Mrs. Johnson's."

"Thank you," she told him.

The two sat close together on one end of a ratty couch, taking advantage of the warm sunlight filtering through the waiting room window. Outside, spring had come to the Kansas prairie, at last. The pawpaws and the redbuds were just starting to show their blooms. Goldfinches and meadowlarks played happily in the thick prairie grass.

She glanced at the elderly female attendant sitting at a desk at the entrance to the room. "Dear, you have a pen and some paper we could borrow? Let's get to corresponding, Ensign."

"Look, I don't want to bother him. The Admiral's got far more important things on his mind than some crippled kid out here in Kansas."

Karen stepped quickly to the desk and retrieved the offered paper and pen. "I betcha he'll happily take two minutes to read your letter since he already knows what a fine submarine officer you'll be. Besides, dummy, what could be more important than our future? I mean your future." She swatted Ward with the writing paper. "You get busy writing to the Admiral. Then we'll write to the Secretary of the Navy. And then, who knows? President Roosevelt?"

Stan Ward rolled his eyes but took the pen from her, slid one of the magazines she had brought him beneath it, and started putting words together.

He had not missed Karen's slipup, her reference to "our future." That left him with a warm glow and a nervous flutter in his chest.

The two of them had clearly reached a real turning point in their relationship.

∞

"Congratulations!" Commander Roderick Flynn stood in front of the assembled Class 3902 with a proud, fatherly smile on his face. Then he spread his hands and offered a broad wink. "Against my better judgment, I have been instructed to send you on to the US Navy submarine force."

The class of young would-be submariners stood at attention, listening to their boss, then laughed politely at his witticism. It was the last day of Submarine School for the class. Excitement ran high. Tomorrow, they would head off to all points of the globe to join their newly assigned boats.

"Since you have successfully completed Submarine School—some of you just barely—we will now depend on our experienced submarine sailors to teach you what you really need to know before you pin on your dolphins signifying you are 'qualified in submarines.' Let me give you one last bit of wisdom. You should always strive to keep the number of surfaces equal to the number of dives." Again, polite laughter, though everyone suspected Flynn used the same bit of humor with each class. "On a personal note, this is the last class I will have the honor of graduating, as the Navy has reassigned me for new duty, commanding a yet-to-be-determined squadron, so some of you may not be finished with me yet. It has been my honor. Now, Lieutenant Blythe will pass out your orders. Good luck and smooth sailing. Dismissed!"

The Ensigns crowded around Lieutenant Blythe's desk as he called names and handed out envelopes. Then the grads wandered off to read their orders and find out where in the world the Navy was sending them.

"Where you going?" Trip MacLean asked Freddy Wurster when he caught up with him.

"About a quarter mile. I got the *S-52* right here in Groton," Wurster answered excitedly. "What about you?"

"I'll be riding the *S-53*, likely berthed right next to you," MacLean said, but his tone was glum. "No offense, Freddy, but I was really looking forward to Pearl Harbor. You know, swaying palm trees, tropical nights, fancy, fruity cocktails, and hot wahines."

"What's a wahine?" Wurster asked, puzzled. "Some new kind'a car? Never heard of one."

MacLean shoved Wurster playfully and laughed. "No, you dumb jock. They're native Hawaiian girls, and I hear they know how to really keep their men happy. And not just by doing the hula for them."

"Yeah," Brad Johnson joined in. "I understand from reputable sources that they don't wear anything under those grass skirts. But I guess none of us are going to find out. And by the way, looks like I'm going down to the *S-54*, close enough to you guys I can spit on both your boats. At least we'll all be in the same division starting out." Johnson poked out his tongue and tapped it with a fingertip. "Guys, I'm thirsty as hell. What say we all head over to Solomon's? I haven't been allowed over there in a couple of months now."

"You thirsty?" Wurster questioned. "Or you just hungry to see that Debbie gal you always talking about?"

"Since when do I gotta choose?" Johnson asked. "Can't a man be thirsty and hungry at the same time?" He put his hat back on his head and took a step toward the door.

Trip MacLean spoke up. "Brad, before we journey off to satisfy your lusts, you mentioned you'd heard something about the fourth member of our little group?"

"Yep, Dad got a letter from Stan asking for help appealing the Med Board's decision to medical him out." Johnson's tone was serious for a change. "He's going to see what he can do. Probably speak with the Secretary, but Dad's not hopeful. Secretary Edison's not an easy man to persuade."

"Let's keep our fingers crossed," Fred Wurster said hopefully.

"It's all we can do," Brad said, once again heading for the door. "Except go get the coldest, wettest beer in all of Groton, Connecticut."

∞

It was a bright spring morning. A light breeze blowing up the Thames River brought just a hint of salt water. Ensign Fred Wurster was excited. Today would be his first day to actually be part of a submarine crew. He checked his dress blue uniform multiple times in the mirror until he finally felt everything was perfect before he left his BOQ room and headed down to the waterfront and Pier 3. His mother had always told him the importance of first impressions. And that was doubly true today.

He spotted his boat, *S-52*, tied up to the north side of the pier. *S-54* was directly across the pier, on the south side, but he saw no sign of Brad

Johnson in the midst of all the activity around the boats. He could also see *S-53*, Trip MacLean's new home, tied up on the south side of Pier 4.

Wurster pulled himself up tall and strutted down the pier and across the brow. There seemed to be a lot of activity all around his submarine, including topside on the boat itself. Lines of men were moving boxes across the brow and down the submarine's after hatch. That seemed unusual for so early on a Monday morning.

Midway across the brow, Wurster came to attention and smartly saluted the national ensign flying in the fragrant breeze at the submarine's stern. Turning to the sailor on duty as the quarterdeck watch, he saluted again and loudly proclaimed, "Ensign Fred Wurster reporting for duty. Request permission to come aboard."

The quarterdeck watch, a young seaman, briskly returned Wurster's salute and said, "Permission granted." Pointing toward the hatch, he continued, "The XO's in the wardroom. He's been expecting you. Expecting you for a while." Then the sailor looked sideways at Ensign Wurster. "Where's your seabag? We get underway in an hour."

"An hour?" Wurster gasped. "Nobody told me. How do I get my stuff? What do I do?"

The seaman shrugged. "Best ask the XO," he said and pointed toward the hatch.

Wurster dropped down the hatch into the cramped boat. There were people everywhere, everybody busy, jostling each other just to get around. It reminded Wurster of a fumble drill scrum on the football field. He did his best to make his way forward without getting into a pushing match with anyone, then ducked through the hatch leading to the battery compartment. When he stuck his head into the tiny wardroom, he saw a man, a cigarette in his mouth, smoke encircling his head, sitting at the table behind a tall stack of papers and a half-empty cup of what might have been motor oil but was more likely coffee. An ashtray overflowing with cigarette butts sat off to the side. The guy was dressed in what was once probably a white sweater but now was grease- and sweat-stained to a mottled tan/brown.

The man looked up. "You Wurster?" he queried, then frowned. "Where the hell's your seabag?" Seeing Wurster's perplexed expression, he answered his own question. "Damn Ensigns! They make 'em dumber every year. Get your worthless butt back to the BOQ and get enough stuff to cover up your ass for two weeks at sea." The Executive Officer glanced up at the ship's clock on the wardroom bulkhead. "You've got one hour before we cast off lines and we won't be waiting for you. You best haul ass or you're going to miss movement."

In a panic, Fred Wurster hurried back down the passageway, up the ladder, and then ran full speed all the way back to his BOQ room. He tossed stuff willy-nilly into his seabag. There was no time to plan out what he might need or to neatly fold everything. Again, as his mom had taught him to do. As he ran back down the pier, he could see the crowd around the boat and on the deck had disappeared except for a few line handlers. Diesel smoke poured from *S-52*'s exhaust. The mooring lines were already singled up.

He dashed across the brow. It was pulled away from beneath him as soon as his foot hit the submarine's deck. Then, as he dropped down the hatch, lines were being cast off. He had made it back by only a few seconds. Leaving without him had been no idle threat.

The XO met him at the bottom of the ladder. "Glad you could join us, Mr. Wurster," he said sarcastically. "Dump your stuff in the bottom rack in stateroom one, change into working khakis, and meet me in the conning tower. You've got two minutes."

Wurster dashed forward, tore a khaki uniform out of his seabag—sighed in relief that he had actually packed one—and changed out of his dress blues. But he could not find his gold ensign collar devices, his "butter bars." He must have left them in his BOQ room.

This day was not turning out at all the way he had imagined it.

Wurster climbed the ladder from the control room up into the tiny conning tower, where he found the XO gazing through the eyepiece of the periscope. The exec pulled away from the scope long enough to nod toward the new officer and say, "It's time for you to learn how to be a submariner. You probably didn't get the word either that we're heading out for a couple of weeks for an ASW sweep around Bermuda, looking for U-boats. By the time we get back, you'll be qualified as surface Officer-of-the-Deck and well on your way as Diving Officer. Do I make myself clear?"

"Yes, sir!" Wurster responded, nodding vigorously.

"Good." The XO inclined his head toward a young sailor hunched over the chart table next to him. "Obrien here will show you how to navigate down the Thames. Get busy." He clamped his eye back to the scope and called out, "Railroad Bridge Center, bearing, mark."

Wurster watched intently as Petty Officer Clancy Obrien plotted out the bearings on a paper chart using a three-armed protractor. After looking on for a few minutes, Fred smiled. Plotting the ship's position was something he already knew how to do. He was nowhere near as fast as this experienced sailor was, but this was something he could do already.

"Wow, did I piss him off!" Wurster mumbled to Obrien as they worked to plot a fix.

"Who, Mr. McNeely?" Obrien replied. "Don't read too much into it. That bark is just part of his charm. He don't bite. Much anyway." Obrien winked.

By the time the XO called out confirmation that Race Rock Light was abeam to port, Petty Officer Obrien was sitting back, enjoying a cigarette, and watching as Fred Wurster proudly plotted the fixes all by himself.

"Look at him go, Clancy," Lieutenant Simon McNeely said with a wry smile.

"I know, sir. Now, if he can just find Bermuda out there in the middle of the ocean, we might have to let him be a submariner."

∞

It was near midnight when the train pulled into Washington, DC's Union Station, puffing smoke and its brakes squealing. Work on tracks somewhere in rural Ohio delayed the arrival by more than twelve hours.

Once the train came to a stop, Ensign Stan Ward stood and stretched. It was still a strange sensation after being on his back for so long and unable to stand. He reached out to help the person seated next to him to rise to her feet.

"We've arrived in our nation's capital, Mrs. Ward," he said with a broad smile. Saying that last part was another strange—but very pleasant—sensation to which he was not yet accustomed.

"I still love the sound of that, Skipper," Karen Kamp Ward cooed. "Say it again."

"Okay, Mrs. Ward," he said with a laugh. "But you best quit calling me 'Skipper' out in public. I'm a long way from command, even if by the grace of God I get to stay in the Navy." They slowly made their way down the aisle with all the other tired, frustrated passengers. "Hey, we better hurry and get the porter to help with our bags and find us a cab. We got an early appointment in the morning."

It was well after one a.m. when the newlyweds finally arrived at Mrs. Williams's Boarding House, though it was not far from the station. They had to hammer on the door to awaken Mrs. Williams, the landlord, but she was most solicitous toward the limping Ensign and his young bride. She even offered a snack, but they thanked her, explained they had a big day starting in only a few hours, and hurried on to their room.

Ensign Stan Ward's appeal before the Medical Review Board was scheduled at Main Navy on Constitution Avenue at 0800. He was dog tired, his back hurt, and his leg ached, but he intended to be there, on time, and not showing any of the wear and tear. Even if he continued to contemplate the hundred or so reasons why the board would ultimately deny his petition.

He and Karen rose at 0400, just to be sure. And indeed, the Review Board procedure commenced promptly at the appointed hour in a nondescript conference room on the third deck of the Main Navy and Munitions Building, popularly called just "Main Navy." As directed by staff, Stan sat across a broad oak table from a Navy Captain, two Navy doctors, and a civilian lawyer, while Karen waited outside. His thick medical file rested unopened before the members as each of them nodded politely, their faces all frustratingly noncommittal.

A couple of thin folders, a tan one and a blue one, lay directly in front of the Captain as he called the Review Appeal to order with a curt, "Good morning," and no other indication to Stan of how the panel might be leaning.

"We are meeting today to review and decide on an appeal of the decision to place Ensign Stanley Ward on the Temporary Disability Retired List by reason of his severely disabling injury sustained in a vehicle accident. By the way, Mr. Ward, this panel salutes you for the exemplary bravery you demonstrated in that tragic situation."

That was a positive sign, Stan thought. *Maybe.*

But the Captain went on, saying, "We have reviewed all the pertinent medical information and the recommendations of the military doctors who treated this injury. Based on that information, the decision for a Temporary Disability Retirement is a very compelling one. It is and always has been the policy of the US Navy to honor the decision of our fine doctors. They know best, both for the affected person's own best interests and for the fighting readiness of the Navy."

Stan Ward's heart fell. Everything had swung the other way now, as if this appeal process was perfunctory. Clearly, the decision had already been made.

There was a long pause as the Captain appeared to be searching for the best way to tell this brave young Ensign that his career was over before it ever began. "However, additional information has just been presented for our consideration," he finally said as he reached for the two thin folders. He opened the tan one and pulled out a letter. "The attending physician, Dr. Daniel Brown, who performed the surgery and prescribed the rehabilitation regime for Mr. Ward, a civilian physician from Salina, Kansas, has corresponded with this Board. His prognosis is that Ensign Ward will make a near full recovery with better than ninety percent of his ability to walk, though he will still have a pronounced limp and limited mobility, especially in cramped or cluttered spaces."

The civilian board member seemed impressed, but the Captain and the two Navy doctors simply shook their heads. Though heartened by the introduction of Doc Brown's letter, Stan sensed that it might not be enough to change the minds of the majority of the board's members. Even so, it had at least been mentioned, so things were looking decidedly better than they had two minutes before.

The Captain reached for the other folder, the blue one. "And we have two additional letters to consider. Admiral Devin Johnson writes of his personal interactions with Ensign Ward while the young man was matriculating at the Naval Academy. Admiral Johnson, by the way, is Personal Advisor to the Secretary of the Navy. He writes to advise this Board that based on his estimate of Ensign Ward's potential valuable contributions to the Navy and the nation as a naval officer, that he be retained on active duty as an intelligence officer, assigned to Commander Submarine Patrol Force Staff and to other classified duties yet to be determined."

Stan Ward sat up straight and smiled. Brad Johnson's dad had come through in a big way. And he wanted Stan to serve on the Submarine Patrol Force Staff. Ward knew that group controlled all the submarines in the Atlantic Fleet from their headquarters in New London. Best of all, that specific position left open the possibility that he might be able to sneak his way back into submarine duty after he recuperated and went through a bit more therapy.

Looking good, he thought. *But not a done deal.*

The Captain pulled a second letter out of the blue folder and passed it to the other board members. "This correspondence is from Secretary Edison himself. He approves Ensign Ward's appeal and is directing that he be ordered to Submarine Patrol Force Staff immediately."

It was all Stan could do to keep from jumping up and letting out a very inappropriate whoop. That should seal it! But he remained outwardly calm, quiet, waiting for the board to make it official.

"Mr. Ward, this appeal is therefore accepted. All the best to you in your career and in your service to your country. This board is adjourned."

Stan Ward still had to fight to stay in control of his emotions. Smiling from ear to ear, but with traces of tears in his eyes, he stood, reached across the table, and shook each member's hand. Then he thought of a question he needed to ask.

"Could any of you recommend a nice place where I could take my new bride for celebration dinner tonight on an Ensign's pay?"

7

"Mr. Johnson."

Brad Johnson looked up when he heard his name called. He was hunched over, down on his knees and in an awkward position, tracing out the fuel system for the port—or number two—diesel engine. He would very soon have to describe from memory every inch of it to one of the Chiefs to have it checked off his qual list.

"Yeah, what?" Johnson responded irritably as he glanced up to see the duty messenger standing at the engine room hatch.

"There's a civilian topside asking to talk with you. Duty Chief sent me to find you and let you know."

Johnson stood, grabbed a rag, and wiped as much of the dirt and grease from his hands as he could. After only a couple of days on board the *S-54*, his working uniform was already splotched and streaked with oil and he was certain he would never be able to get the grit and grease from beneath his fingernails. It would not be long before he was just as grubby as every other sailor on this "pig boat." And stink like the boat, too.

More curious than aggravated, Johnson sighed and climbed up the engine room ladder to emerge out into surprisingly warm afternoon sunshine. Spring had arrived at the Connecticut shore, but the young officer was spending so much time in the bowels of the submarine that he had not even noticed.

When he got topside, the only civilian he saw was someone in a gray suit and black fedora with his back to Johnson. The visitor stood on the sub's deck by the brow, talking with *S-54*'s Skipper, Lieutenant Stephen Brewster. Johnson walked over and saluted Brewster.

"Excuse me, sir. The messenger said there was a civilian here who wanted to speak with me."

The man turned to face him. Johnson recognized him at once as the FBI agent who had made the ominous visit to the Officer's Club. Special Agent Ralph Flannigan, or something like that. But why would the FBI want to talk with him?

The agent flashed his badge for a quick moment, just long enough for Johnson to see the gold shield, and then said, "Good afternoon, Ensign. Remember me?"

"You're Agent Flannigan, from the O Club a few weeks ago," Johnson answered.

"That's right. We need to talk." Turning to Brewster, he said, "Excuse us, Lieutenant, but this needs to be a private chat."

Brad could not believe that this guy had the audacity to so rudely dismiss the Skipper on his own submarine. He clearly had an enhanced sense of his own importance. But LT. Brewster only paused for a beat, nodded, and walked away, dropping down the hatch, back into the guts of his submarine. Agent Flannigan guided Johnson over behind the conning tower, where they would be out of earshot of anyone topside and out of view from anyone on the pier. There was only the squawking of seagulls seeking supper out in the river, beyond the end of the pier.

"Ensign Johnson, I will make this quick and to the point," Flannigan said in a voice so low that Brad had to strain to hear him. "You have been frequenting an establishment called Solomon's Tavern of late."

"Me and half the men from Sub Base New London. Why does the FBI care if I like a beer occasionally?" Johnson shot back. He had no idea where this guy was going but Agent Flannigan's presence and this whole conversation were giving him a very bad feeling. And this guy was...what? *Oily*. That was the best word. Or maybe *slimy*.

"Only if it becomes a matter of national security," Flannigan replied pompously. "You, Mr. Johnson, have a security clearance and that gives you access to classified information. Information that enemy agents would generously pay for."

"Are you accusing me of being a spy?" Johnson shot back angrily. Then he said the next thing that popped into his mind. "Do you know who my father is?"

Flannigan held up his hands, palms out, in a placating gesture. "Hold your horses, Ensign. Nobody's accusing you of anything. But we understand you have been seen spending a great deal of time lately with someone named Debrorah Schultz, who works there as a waitress."

"Barkeep," Johnson corrected Flannigan. "Debbie's a barkeep."

"Yes, well, whatever," the agent responded, his train of thought seemingly interrupted. He quickly got back on track. "But her father is a man named Heinrich Schultz, an immigrant from Germany. He works as a ship fitter with the Electric Boat Company, building submarines. Let's just say that Mr. Schultz's loyalties have come under suspicion. The Germans have taken considerable interest in what's going on at Electric Boat, and especially with the new class of subs they're building down there. We—the FBI —want you to get close to Miss Schultz—something we think you are doing quite successfully on your own already—and report any suspicious activity to us."

Brad Johnson saw red. "You lowlife son of a bitch! You want me to spy on my girlfriend?" He squared off, both fists raised. "I ought to..."

"Just hold on," Flannigan growled back, raising his hands to fend off any possible blows. "Stop and think how it would look if the world should learn that Admiral Devin Johnson's son—a naval officer in his own right—was found to be cavorting with a known agent of Nazi Germany. And at a time when our relations with Mr. Hitler are so volatile." The sun had suddenly become very hot there on the deck of the *S-54*. Brad could smell his own sweat, even over the odor of diesel fuel. Flannigan, despite the dark suit and hat, was not perspiring at all. "Look, you do as we ask or that could well be the headline in *The New York Times* one morning soon. Don't even think for a second that we can't or won't make that happen."

Brad Johnson dropped his fists and his head in defeat. Surrender tasted terrible. But he had no choice. He would have to swallow whatever the G-man was serving up.

∞

"Wurster, get in here!" the XO on *S-52* called out. Simon McNeely was not known for his patience. Or diplomacy.

Fred Wurster was sitting in his cramped little "stateroom," trying to draw on a blank sheet of paper the old submarine's ventilation system from memory. Before he could be "signed off" on the system, he would have to be able to correctly locate and describe the function of every component, as well as precisely shift it to every possible configuration. But when he heard the exec's gruff summons, he jumped up and stepped across the passageway to the wardroom.

"Yes, sir," Wurster responded. "You need something?"

McNeely, wreathed in the ever-present cloud of cigarette smoke, shoved a couple of thick notebooks across the table toward the young Ensign.

"Congratulations. I'm making you the supply officer," he announced. "I'm sure you don't know a damn thing about the supply system, but you'll learn. Your job is to make sure that this fine submarine of ours is always stocked with the best food, and that we always have every part and tool that we need. You will keep a record of all that in these notebooks. Understand?"

Wurster knew nothing about the Navy supply system other than it was notoriously complicated and that a supply officer could get in really big trouble if he screwed up. He gulped. "Yes, sir. But are you sure, sir?"

McNeely gave a wicked laugh. "A good supply officer is always only one step ahead of the brig. That's why we use Ensigns for ours. They're expendable and easily replaced if they get caught. But keep good records and stay out of the brig and it might help you make Admiral someday." He laughed again but it quickly morphed into a deep cough.

The *S-52* was five hundred nautical miles southeast of New London, a bit more than halfway outbound on their two-week journey around Bermuda and back. They had been heading toward the mid-Atlantic island at a leisurely pace, watching out for German U-boats as they progressed. So far, the journey was uneventful. The old boat's pair of MAN diesel engines vibrated reassuringly as they pushed the submarine along. They were making six knots good, beating against the Gulf Stream's four-knot current. The weather was warm and calm. A light breeze barely disturbed the brilliant blue waters. Bermuda's inviting beaches and welcoming bars were only three days away and there had been hints about liberty before they headed back to homeport.

Wurster picked up the two notebooks and was about to get back to the ventilation system drawings when a loud bang reverberated up and down the length of the vessel. He wasn't sure, but it sounded like the noise came from aft, back in the general direction of the engine room. Sure enough, the reassuring rumbling vibration of the diesel engines immediately came to a stop. Almost at once, he could feel the boat start to bob in the waves as it slowed, and the wind and waves began pushing them around.

LT(jg) Brent Halloran, the sub's Engineer Officer, passed by and told McNeely and Wurster, "Number one diesel just bit it. Chief Wankel says it's a crankcase explosion." The officer shrugged then headed aft.

"Anybody hurt?" the XO asked.

"Not as far as we know," Halloran called back over his shoulder. "But the engine is wounded pretty bad."

McNeely groaned and shook his head as he pulled himself to his feet. "Come on, Wurster. Let's go see what this old bitch has in store for us today." He, too, went aft, toward the control room. The *S-52*, built in the early 1920s, the first class of submarine designed for blue-water service, was an old boat, not noted for reliability. Every underway had strong potential to be an adventure.

Lieutenant Don Gorman, *S-52*'s Skipper, tall and lean and blessed with plenty of patience, stood calmly in the middle of the control room talking to a short and burly Chief Fritz Wankel, the senior engineman. Gorman glanced over at McNeely, shook his head, and said, "XO, Chief Wankel is pretty sure that number one diesel is OOC with a crankcase explosion. He and the other machinists need to be off the watchbill while they fix it."

"Yes, sir," McNeely responded. "That's going to put a bunch of people on port-and-starboard watches, but we can handle it. Guess we have to. Any idea how long?"

"At least a couple of days," the engineman answered. "Maybe three, depending on what we find when we crack that crankcase open. I think we have the parts we need. Guys are breaking them out now, so we'll know soon enough if that last supply officer knew what he was doing."

Gorman nodded. "About when we're due in Bermuda." He did some quick arithmetic in his head and added, "We can still make six or seven knots with one diesel. We should still make port on schedule."

But then, as if on cue, the conversation was interrupted by another loud banging noise, again emanating from aft. The men looked at each other in disbelief, then, seconds later, one of Chief Wankel's machinists stuck his head in the control room.

"Chief, number two just died. Same as number one."

Chief Wankel threw his hat on the steel deck and stomped on it. "Damn the luck!" he growled. "All right, men, let's get number one fixed, then we'll worry about number two." The machinists disappeared through the after hatch, heading toward the engine room.

Gorman wryly acknowledged their situation. "The old girl is up to her tricks again. XO, call back to Sub Div 21 and tell them we're going to need a tow into port." He paused for a second and then added, "Again."

Fred Wurster had an idea, though. "XO, I know this is going to sound really dumb, but why don't we sail to Bermuda. I read a story once that the old *R-14* rigged sails one time when they ran out of fuel. They sailed her all the way back to Hilo that way."

McNeely was about to yell at Wurster for being an idiot when Don Gorman held up his hand to stop him. "Listen, that just might work. XO, get the COB to muster everyone not working on the diesels. Mr. Wurster, it's your idea, so you are appointed the sailing master. Make it happen. Seems like a nice day to go sailing."

Fred Wurster spit and sputtered for a minute. The only sailing experience he had was a few times out on the Academy's seventeen-footers. That was a couple of sunny afternoons on the Severn River, not at all like turning a submarine into a sailboat in the middle of the Atlantic. It was a challenge, and the Skipper had given the order. He would do his best.

"Don't sweat this, Mr. Wurster," QM-1 Clancy Obrien said quietly, so that only Wurster could hear. "Couple of us have been sailing since we could climb over the gunnel. And the torpedomen can jury-rig anything out of nothing. Just you stand back and watch."

It took the rest of the afternoon, but the crew managed to jury-rig a couple of masts using the radio antennas, some torpedo loading equipment, and most of the blankets they had on board. The *S-52* would never be mistaken for an America's Cup racing yacht, but the makeshift sails filled with the wind and the boat gradually started to move. By carefully adjusting and trimming the sails, the submarine/sailboat picked up speed. Nightfall found them making three knots in the direction of Bermuda. At that pace, and if the wind kept blowing, the subtropical island was four days over the horizon.

Chief Fritz Wankel's team worked around the clock to repair the recalcitrant MAN diesels. After three days of nonstop labor, they were buttoning up number one engine when the bridge watch called down to the control room, "Control, to the Captain. Officer-of-the-Deck sends his respects. New contact, bearing one-four-zero. Looks like a destroyer and he's heading toward us."

LT. Gorman was standing in the conning tower, taking advantage of the height above the sea of number one periscope to get a good look at the approaching ship. He grabbed the microphone and answered, "Thank you, Mr. Halloran. Good eyes. He's barely over the horizon. We see him. Looks like a Brit tin can and he is definitely heading our way. Let's get ready to haul in our laundry so he can tow us into port."

Chief Wankel tugged on Gorman's shirt sleeve. "Excuse me, Skipper. Repairs on number one diesel are complete. Request permission to light it off and test it."

Starting air was cut into the now repaired engine. It rolled, coughed and sputtered, then it fired, roaring to life.

Don Gorman ordered the diesel placed online for propulsion. Then he called up to the bridge, "Officer-of-the-Deck, signal the Brit and request that he stand by to accompany us back to port. I think the old girl might just make it on her own power, this time."

∞

The drive up from Washington, DC, to Connecticut in their beat-up, second-hand Chevy roadster had been something of an adventure for Ensign and Mrs. Stan Ward. The normally two-day drive had stretched to four after they got lost somewhere in New Jersey. Then, after passing through some place named Goshen, New York—and even before they realized they were lost again—the old car overheated outside of Cornwall-on-Hudson. They had to wait for two days while the gas station mechanic located and installed a new water pump. Making the most of their forced stay, Karen and Stan found a charming little rooming house with an upstairs window that looked right out on the picturesque Hudson River. From there, they could watch river traffic from the comfort of their bed.

The rest of the journey was less adventurous—and far less romantic—and soon the couple finally drove down Military Highway and right up to Submarine Base New London's main gate just in time for Stan to report for his first day at his new command. The Marine sentry saluted smartly and directed them to the Commander Submarine Patrol Force headquarters building.

Once there, Stan climbed out of the roadster and grabbed his cane from behind the seat. The long drive had not been easy on his bad leg but walking around, getting the blood flowing again, helped. So did giving Karen a long, parting embrace. They had been together almost constantly since the wedding. Now, he was surprised how bad he felt parting with her for a few hours.

Kissing her on the cheek, he said, "Well, Mrs. Ward, it's time I went to work and started earning a living to support us."

Karen laughed and replied, "You had better work hard, Ensign Ward. You know I expect to be kept in exquisite comfort, complete with all the finer things in life."

"Just don't forget to pick me up right here at 1600," Stan Ward told her, grinning broadly. "And you had better have a fine dinner waiting when we get back home."

"You know as well as I do that dinner will be whatever Mrs. Miller has on the boarding house table," Karen shot back. They had spent all of one night in their new accommodation so far, checking in too late the previous night for dinner. Breakfast was pretty good, though.

She eased into the driver's seat, cranked up, let out the clutch, and slowly progressed out of the parking area and down the street. Stan waved, then watched her until she was out of sight, missing her already. Only then did he slowly limp up the stairs and into the large brick building.

A young sailor sat behind a wooden desk just inside the door. He jumped to attention when Ward entered. The sailor directed him to the admin office where his check-in would start. He had barely begun the process when a tall, slightly overweight Commander walked into the room. A thick ring of aromatic pipe smoke followed him around.

"Morning, Ensign," the Commander said, offering his hand. "I'm Ollie Oglethorpe. I run the intel office here. You'll be working with us." Glancing at Ward's cane, he added, "Your fame has preceded you. It's not everybody who can wrangle a waiver for a bum leg like that. Look, you can finish checking in later. Come on down to the basement with me. I want to show you around."

The pair headed down a back stair into the building's basement, Oglethorpe politely matching his pace with Ward's. Once there, a heavy steel door blocked their way, held firmly shut by a large, impressive lock.

"We like our privacy," Oglethorpe told him as he unlocked the door with a key retrieved from his pocket. They stepped into a large, brightly lit room. The walls were mostly covered with large, detailed charts of various parts of the Atlantic Ocean, plastered with symbols signifying the ships and convoys steaming back and forth across the vast expanse of water. A half dozen sailors were busily updating the charts, using information from clipboards holding pages of message traffic.

"We like to think of this as the brains of the Submarine Patrol Force," Oglethorpe explained. "From here, we track and correlate every ship in the North Atlantic."

Stan Ward was impressed. He noted that several of the symbols sported swastikas, and some were shaped like U-boats. Clearly there was a whole lot going on here.

"Where does it all come from?" he asked. "The information for the charts I mean."

"Lots of places," Oglethorpe answered. "Some of it comes from reports filed by ships or planes. Some of it's from agents in various ports of call. But

I admit a lot of the information is conjecture based on putting together bits and pieces. That, in a nutshell, is our job." Oglethorpe pointed at himself and then Ward. "That's why an intel officer gets paid, for cobbling together all those bits and pieces and trying to make sense of it."

"One big old puzzle..." Ward said, mostly to himself. But he had to admit he was intrigued.

"Here's your office, Stanley," Oglethorpe said, pointing to a battered steel desk set off in a corner of the big room. It was obviously no office.

"And Stan's fine, Commander. Maybe you can tell me—"

But just then, a young Lieutenant poked his head through another heavy steel door. He spotted Oglethorpe talking with Ward. "Boss, we need you back here."

Ollie Oglethorpe nodded toward the Lieutenant and held up a finger, indicating he would be there in a minute.

"What's back there?" Ward asked.

"You're not cleared for any of that yet," Oglethorpe answered. "For now, just assume it holds the 'Tree of Knowledge.'"

∞

His Majesty's Royal Naval Dockyard Bermuda was literally humming with activity. A dozen or more destroyers and a pair of cruisers were tied up at Kings Wharf, some waiting for Liverpool-bound Convoy BHX 13 to form up in the Great Sound, some standing by for battle repairs in the dockyard. *S-52* was the only warship in the harbor that was not flying the White Ensign that showed them to be British Royal Navy vessels. The damaged US submarine had tied up inside the Camber, at the jetty across the water from the floating drydock.

While Chief Wankel and his boys struggled to properly repair the diesels, most of the crew decided to take advantage of the sunny beaches or old English pubs that proliferated on the island. With the ready availability of both British gin and Caribbean rum, some of the crew thought they must have arrived in submariner's heaven. Consuming too many rum swizzles had just become an occupational hazard.

As the noon meal was wrapping up in the wardroom, LT. Don Gorman folded his napkin and pushed back from the table. Glancing over toward the XO, he asked, "What's on tap for this afternoon?"

"The Brits have laid on a tour of old St. George for the crew," McNeely answered. "At least the ones who aren't off getting soused. Sounds like it might be interesting, though."

Fred Wurster chimed in, "Yeah, thought I might catch that one. They're touring all the old fortresses. Real history."

"Hold your horses, there, Fred," the XO interjected. "Last time I looked, you were behind on your quals. You're supposed to be surface OOD by now and you're not there. Dinks are restricted to the boat, so looks like you're not going anywhere."

"But...but..." Wurster sputtered. "I spent all that time working the sails we rigged to keep moving. That time doesn't count for something?"

McNeely shook his head. "Nope. You didn't learn anything on that chore that you can use runnin' a boat."

Don Gorman shook his head and added, "The sad fact is, Fred, while you did a good job in getting those sails rigged and moving us toward Bermuda when the diesels were OOC, the XO is right. Your quals suffered and you are dink. If we make an exception for you, what do we tell the other non-quals?"

Wurster nodded glumly. They had him. "Yes, sir. I understand." He stood. "If I may be excused, I'll head aft. I guess it's as good a time as any to finish my diesel checkout."

He grabbed his notebook and headed back to the engine room, where he found the engineman chief up to his elbows in the bowels of the number two diesel. Parts, tools, and oil-soaked rags filled every available horizontal surface around the engines. Wurster found a spot back in a corner where he could quietly observe while staying out of their way. But he was soon passing tools down to the sailors, becoming more and more involved in repair work. Before long, he was just as grease covered as any of the mechanics, and his knuckles were scraped and bleeding.

"Mr. Wurster," Fritz Wankel called out from his position deep under the diesel crankcase. "Pass me a crescent wrench if you ain't too busy."

"What size you need, Chief?" Wurster asked as he looked at five different wrenches laid out on the diamond tread deck.

"It don't matter," Wankel called up. "I'm just gonna use it for a hammer anyway."

As Ensign Wurster watched and helped reassemble the engine, he gradually became intimately familiar with the inner workings of the four-cycle, air-injection equipped, 600-horsepower, 8-cylinder MAN diesel engine. As they worked, the machinists took time to explain to him how fuel oil made its way into the cylinders, how the heat of compression caused it to burn, and how the explosions in each cylinder made the crank-shaft rotate. And since he was a good listener, seemed to really want to learn, and was willing to get dirty, they accepted the young Ensign as part of their little team.

Wurster lost all track of time. Dinner was a quick sandwich and cup of coffee, eaten with the team. He had no idea what time it was when they finally tightened the last nut on the cover plate. He only knew that the stars were glistening overhead when he went topside to go find the duty officer to ask permission to start and test the diesel. He was dead tired when the test run was finished. He finally was able to strip off the greasy uniform and fall back into his bunk.

Wurster's final thought before he fell into a deep slumber was that he was happy that the XO had restricted him to the boat. He had learned far more than he ever could have from pictures and diagrams. Plus, Chief Wankel and his guys saw him as an officer who was not afraid of getting his hands dirty or doing his part with a nasty job.

Both of those, Wurster figured, could be valuable someday.

∞

Sublieutenant Geoff Chandler had so far been unable to stop the trembling of his hands. He gripped the railing hard as he stood alone on the bridge of his ship looking out over the darkened Great Sound of Bermuda and at the dozens of ships riding at anchor there. Chandler was having a very difficult time convincing himself that he had the courage to go back out once again into the war-torn sea. Being hesitant could prove fatal, he knew. He could not shake the image of his friend Randall Macallister, drowned because he was too frightened to abandon the sinking carrier

Courageous after a German submarine attack. Or the screams of those still on board as the mighty ship slipped beneath the waves.

After he was fortuitously plucked from the cold water off Ireland, Geoff Chandler was sent home to Devonshire for thirty days' survivors leave to recuperate from the trauma, physical and mental. His father, a retired merchant marine sailor who had survived his own ship being sunk in the Great War, advised Geoff to get back to sea as soon as possible, to get back in the saddle, to conquer the fear. Chandler had reluctantly followed his father's advice.

The Royal Navy, needing every warm body it could muster to crew its old fleet, immediately posted him to the naval trawler *Blackthorn* as the communicator and third officer. These little ships were intended primarily for coastal minesweeping and harbor defense duties, but the demand for convoy escort vessels had now grown intense. The scarcity of destroyers and corvettes left the Admiralty with little choice but to press every ship that could carry a few depth charges into escort duty. The *Blackthorn*, at a little over five hundred tons and with no Asdic sonar system or radar, could only act the role of a blind sheepdog, trying hopelessly to protect its flock from wolves it could not see or hear until they attacked.

Convoy BHX 13 was scheduled to depart Bermuda that night, bound for Liverpool. His new ship (at least to Chandler), a *Tree*-class trawler, was to be one of the anti-submarine escorts herding the twenty-seven slow-moving freighters past German U-boats that likely lay out there eagerly awaiting such a nice, easy array of targets. The *Blackthorn* was very different from Chandler's last ship, the ill-fated *Courageous*, but the U-boat threat was precisely the same.

This evening, Chandler stood on the trawler's bridge, enjoying the warm breeze off the Gulf Stream, waiting for the signal from the escort commander to strike out to the northeast with the convoy. This assemblage of vessels had been designated a slow convoy. Several of the old, coal-fired freighters struggled to make anything over six knots. While it was frustrating to the escort commander on one of His Majesty's fast destroyers, the slow convoy was a good thing for the *Blackthorn*, which could barely break twelve knots.

The flashing-light signal from the escort commander told Chandler that it was time to depart the safety of the Great Sound. Normally, the trawler's master would be on the bridge for an underway like this, but both he and the first officer had spent most of the last day in port at the Sea Winds Pub, drinking their problems—and U-boat trepidations—away. They were in no condition to conn a ship. Instead, they were passed out, down below in their staterooms. Chandler had discovered on his first day reporting to the *Blackthorn* that both LT. Rodney Jeffries, the master, and First Officer LT. Ian MacDonald were patrons of the bottle and neither wanted to go to sea on the trawler. So, by no choice of his own, Chandler had the bridge and all the responsibility for getting underway to himself.

At Chandler's command, the *Blackthorn* swung away from the wharf and headed out to take station escorting the merchant ships of Convoy BHX 13. As Chandler maneuvered the trawler to guard the convoy's after port quarter, he recalled that several of the trawler's crew had expressed concern about the numbering of this assemblage of ships. Thirteen was bad luck. And sailors were a notoriously superstitious lot. But there was nothing he could do about it, other than not speaking the number out loud unless absolutely necessary.

A total of four trawlers were assigned as close-in escorts while the destroyer and two corvettes—often termed "greyhounds of the sea"—raced around further out, pinging away with their Asdic sonar units to attempt to detect any German submarines before they could fire their torpedoes at elements of the convoy. Or, better still, maybe they could scare the U-boats away.

It was just past midnight when Chandler sent the messenger down to the galley to fetch him a cup of coffee. It was proving to be a long night. Neither Skipper Jeffries nor First Officer MacDonald had yet roused themselves to relieve him on the bridge. Chandler nursed his coffee and settled in, praying for a peaceful, quiet night.

Dawn found Convoy BHX 13 fifty nautical miles north-northeast of Bermuda. The twenty-seven merchant ships, each flying the Red Ensign of a British ship, were huddled in five columns. They were struggling to keep formation, which was supposed to be five hundred yards between ships and the same distance between columns. But none of the ship masters had experience steaming in formation. The picture that was now spread out in front of Geoff Chandler more closely resembled a gaggle of geese than it did any prescribed geometric formation. The four trawlers were still stationed on each corner of that gaggle with the destroyer and corvettes fanned out in front.

By the first light of dawn, keeping his eyes open was a challenge for Chandler. Coffee, strong and bitter as it was, was not working anymore. He was just too tired.

But then the sound of a sudden brutal blast jarred him fully awake. For just a brief moment, he was back on the sinking *Courageous*. Then he saw flames and clouds of black smoke erupt from the tanker nearest to him, the third ship in the outboard line.

Torpedo! And to strike where it had, the weapon had passed mere feet in front of *Blackthorn*. They were under attack from a U-boat! Chandler grabbed his binoculars and searched the dark seawater for a telltale periscope even as he ordered the *Blackthorn* to battle stations. It was a nearly futile effort, he knew, trying to spot a skinny pole sticking out of the vast expanse of blue-gray water in such dim light. But just then he thought he spotted a ripple that could have been caused by a sub's periscope. He estimated it was a thousand yards to the north. But if it was a U-boat, now was his chance to get some retribution for his previous experience and the loss of his friend and fellow officer. The forward gun on *Blackthorn*, a 12-pounder, was manned and ready. It was a simple matter to estimate the range and bearing of that slightest of disturbances in the water, then point and fire the gun in that direction.

A bleary-eyed Rodney Jeffries emerged onto the bridge just as Chandler ordered the 12-pounder gun to open fire. The first gun blast almost knocked the hungover master down.

"What the blazes ya doin', man?" Jeffries angrily demanded.

"Convoy's under attack. I saw a periscope," Chandler reported and pointed in the direction of the ripple. "I took it under fire. Recommend we signal the escort commander."

"Very well," Jeffries growled. "Damn, my head hurts. Get me a cup of coffee," the master told the messenger. Then he slumped into his bridge chair, rubbing his temples. The 12-pounder's blasts were only making his hangover more intolerable.

The escort commander's reply was prompt. He directed the *Blackthorn* to search for survivors at the spot where the tanker had sunk while the corvettes looked for and attacked the U-boat. Meanwhile, the convoy would continue on course toward Liverpool without slowing down.

Chandler could see the corvette, HMS *Arabis*, plowing a huge bow wave as it ran hard toward the suspected U-boat. Her four-inch gun was already blasting away at Chandler's ripple. He continued to watch as *Blackthorn* swung around and as depth charges rolled off the corvette's stern and into the water. The water astern of the corvette erupted in huge, boiling masses of white water. *Arabis* wheeled around smartly and made another pass over the same spot, again dropping a string of depth charges. If there was a submarine down there, Chandler could only imagine the pounding it was taking.

He carefully steered the trawler over to where the tanker had sunk, aware there were likely—hopefully—survivors in the water. He found the sea covered with a thick slime of foul smelling, dark crude oil. Chunks of flotsam and debris bobbed in the mess. Here and there, they could make out survivors clinging to wreckage, some waving frantically for help, some merely holding on and hoping. By noon, they had fished a dozen seamen out of the foul brew, some hurt, some just cold and wet, all covered with thick oil.

That was all that was left of the torpedoed tanker, its cargo, and its crew of forty men.

Then they put on all the speed they could manage to catch back up with the convoy. The sun was dropping below the western horizon when *Blackthorn* resumed her station alongside the group. The escort commander signaled a Bravo Zulu—job well done—to *Blackthorn* and informed them the *Arabis* was claiming one sunken U-boat.

Meanwhile, Convoy BHX 13 steamed on, still 2900 nautical miles from Liverpool and safety. Still twenty dangerous days to port.

8

Ensign Fred Wurster climbed up the ladder from the conning tower to the *S-52*'s open bridge. The crystalline blue waters of Bermuda's Great Sound sparkled in the early morning sunshine. Wurster could feel the old submarine vibrate, almost as if the boat was eager to be underway once more. The sub's mood matched the excitement that Wurster felt as he grabbed the binoculars hanging from the binnacle. His job today was to get the boat underway as the Officer-of-the-Deck and this would be the first time doing it by himself. When the day was done, he would be qualified to operate the *S-52* even when the captain was asleep or otherwise predisposed.

That Skipper, LT. Dan Gorman, stood to one side and smiled at the young Ensign. "Well, Mr. Wurster, you ready for your big day?" he asked and looked out over the harbor. "Some rules for today before we get started. I expect you to conduct yourself like I am not up here. The only time I will speak to you is if you are doing something unsafe and I need to interfere. In that case, you will have failed your qual watch. Any reports that you would normally make to me or any permissions that you need from me, call down to the XO. Understand?"

Fred Wurster's heart was in his throat, but he nodded that he understood. He grabbed the microphone and said, "Conn, Bridge, XO, to the

Captain, ship is ready to get underway. Request permission to cast off all lines and get underway."

The reply was prompt. "Bridge, from the Captain. Get the ship underway. Proceed according to the OPORD to the rendezvous point."

Wurster leaned over the bridge fairing and called down to the Chief of the Boat, standing on the main deck, "COB, cast off all lines."

When he saw all the lines—"ropes" to the uninitiated—fall into the water, then quickly pulled to the pier by the line handlers stationed there, Wurster ordered, "Port engine ahead one-third, starboard engine back one-third."

He glanced aft to confirm that water churned around both screws. As the boat twisted and the bow swung out into the channel, he commanded, "All stop." Waiting a few seconds, he then ordered, "All ahead one-third. Helm, steer course two-one-six."

The sub slowly moved away from the wharf and headed down toward the mole. Wurster looked over to LT. Gorman, just to see if there was any reaction. The Skipper's face showed no sign of how Fred might be doing.

Out of the corner of his eye, Wurster caught a glimpse of a light flashing from the bridge of a cruiser tied up at the dockyard across the Camber from the King's Wharf. It was HMS *Ajax*, a light cruiser and the senior ship in the harbor at the time.

Wurster was trying to figure out what the proper response was when he remembered something that Chief Wankel had told him while they were putting the diesels back together. "Mr. Wurster, you ain't got enough hands to do it all yerself. Youse gotta pay attention to the important stuff an' get someone else to do the rest."

Wurster smiled. Right now, he figured getting the boat safely out of the harbor was the "important stuff." He grabbed the mike and said, "XO, we're being signaled by the *Ajax*. Have the quartermaster copy, report to the Captain, and draft and send a response." Then, without missing a beat, he ordered in a voice that was becoming more and more confident, "Helm, come right. Steer course two-two-seven."

Then he saw the Skipper allow the slightest of a smile and nod. So far, so good.

"Bridge, XO," the speaker blasted. "Responded to *Ajax*'s challenge. She wished us good hunting. Recommend coming left to zero-nine-zero to conform to track."

Wurster looked around in all directions. They were well clear of the mole, the harbor's manmade breakwater. It was time to steam out into the Great Sound for a few thousand yards before turning north.

The Great Sound was almost entirely open to the Atlantic Ocean from the north. Wurster could already feel the *S-52* starting to surge and pitch with the waves in open water. When they came around to a course of north, the sub seemed to lope along happily as it rose and fell in the swells.

"Officer-of-the-Deck!"

Wurster heard the cry from above him. He glanced up toward the periscope shears at one of the three young sailors serving as lookouts, standing there on tiny platforms. "New contact fine on the port bow, low down on the horizon. Looks like she might be our escort."

Wurster lifted his binoculars to take a look. He could barely make out a plume of smoke and a single tiny mast where the lookout had indicated. Being ten feet higher up in the shears, he had a better view and could see more of the ship's superstructure. Fifteen minutes later, the old coal-fired ocean-minesweeper *Abingdon* came into better view. Laid down at the end of the Great War, she was from the same era as the *S-52*. They were both long in the tooth and, it appeared, on the verge of serving in their second world conflict.

The minesweeper fell in company with the sub, five hundred yards to starboard, as the two headed out to the north. The *Abingdon* would stay with them primarily to protect them from accidental attacks from patrolling British aircraft searching for German submarines. The minesweeper was really useless for any ASW protection.

Wurster hollered up to his lookouts, "Guys, on your toes. There was a U-boat attack just north of here last night." He could see the lookouts clamp their binoculars even tighter to their eyes and lean in harder to their supports. He turned back around to see if Gorman still looked upon Wurster's work as OOD approvingly. But he was just in time to see the Skipper drop down the hatch into the conn. Standing alone on the bridge —except for the three sailors above him—he could only conclude that his evaluation was done. And that he must have passed since he had not been relieved and was still standing there on the bridge of a US Navy submarine.

He was jarred from his thoughts when a Short Sunderland flying boat roared overhead, no more than a hundred feet above them. The four-engine patrol bomber would be on its way out to sweep the waters, diligently looking for U-boats. The big, ungainly aircraft waggled his wings as he blasted past and then gently banked to the northeast.

Unexpectedly, the *Abingdon* signaled then that she was returning to port, low on coal. She was scheduled to escort the *S-52* until dark, still several hours away, but would not be able to stick around that long. The vessel turned around and slowly chugged past *S-52*, back toward Bermuda, just over the horizon to the south.

The submarine was alone in the ocean with just the wind and the waves. Then, more unexpected company. A pair of bottle-nosed dolphins appeared, playing tag off the submarine's bow. Wurster knew the old maritime superstition was that dolphins brought good luck. He also caught glimpses of silvery flashes as flying fish, disturbed by the sub's passing, leaped from the water and glided for a few yards before splashing back down again. Wurster noticed what a truly beautiful afternoon it was. For the first time in several hours, he leaned back, relaxed, and called below for delivery of a cup of coffee to the bridge.

I could get used to this, he thought.

"Mr. Wurster, I think I have a contact broad off the port bow," the port lookout called down, interrupting the pleasant reverie.

"What you got?"

"I can't make it out, but something bobs up every once in a while."

Wurster grabbed his binoculars and searched out on the port side. He could not see anything out there except blue water and more flying fish. "I don't see anything," he called up. "You sure you saw something?"

"I thought maybe I saw something," the lookout stammered. "But I ain't sure."

The fact was they were in hostile waters. Attacks by U-boats in this area were common nowadays. Better safe than sorry. He called down to the conn, "Take a periscope sweep broad off the port bow. Possible contact on the horizon."

Less than half a minute later, Don Gorman's voice came back over the bridge speaker. "Mr. Wurster, dive the ship! Looks like you might have found yourself one of Mr. Hitler's U-boats!"

A jolt of electricity shot through him as Wurster yelled, "Clear the bridge!" He counted out loud as the three lookouts dove down the hatch next to him. Then he announced, "Dive! Dive!" and hit the diving alarm.

As he jumped through the hatch, he grabbed the lanyard and swung the hatch shut. Spinning the closure ring, he yelled, "Last man down, hatch secure!"

The conning tower was cramped but surprisingly quiet. The Skipper was peering intently through the attack periscope while Simon McNeely, the XO, was setting up the plots and the TDC, the mechanical torpedo data computer, a relatively new innovation that did the job of older torpedo-targeting devices such as the circular slide-rule-like "banjo."

"Mark this bearing," LT. Gorman called out.

"Bearing three-three-six," McNeely answered.

"Helm, steer course three-three-six," Gorman ordered. "Ahead two-thirds. Down scope."

He slapped up the training handles on the scope as the silver tube dropped down into its well.

"I can't make it out plain yet, but I think we have a U-boat on the surface," Gorman said as he wiped sweat from his forehead. The conning tower had quickly gotten very warm and humid without the cool air coming down the hatch from the bridge. And with too many sweaty bodies jammed into too small a space.

After ten minutes, it was time to take another look. "Ahead one-third," Gorman ordered. "Make your depth five-zero feet. Raising number one scope."

The scope slid up smoothly. Gorman squatted on the deck and caught the training handles as they emerged. He rode the scope up with his eye already fixed to the eyepiece.

"Bearing, mark."

"Bearing three-three-four."

"Range, mark. Set range five thousand yards. Down scope." Gorman stepped back as the scope slid out of the way. "Pretty sure he's a U-boat.

But I still can't see all of him. He's on the surface but riding low in the water."

The speaker came to life with a raspy voice. "Conn, Sonar, I'm hearing something on the bearing to the U-boat. Not anything I've ever heard before." It was the sonar operator down in the forward torpedo room.

Gorman looked up. "Mr. Wurster, you're probably the only one aboard who has heard a U-boat before. Get your butt down there and see if you recognize what Sonar's hearing."

Wurster dropped down the ladder into the control room and stepped aft to the tiny sound room. He clamped the headsets to his ears and listened intently.

Sure enough, that was the same noise he had heard just six months before in Long Island Sound. The noise of a German diesel submarine. But there was something strange about this one. He could not hear the rhythmic sound of the vessel's screw turning. But there was some kind of rhythmic knocking noise, almost like someone hammering on something made of metal.

"Conn, Sonar," he reported, "confirmed this sounds like a U-boat. But I'm not hearing his screw, and it sounds like someone's beating on something."

Gorman nodded. "That might explain why he's on the surface in the daylight in shipping lanes only seventy miles from Bermuda. He's trying to repair something damaged. Could be he's the U-boat from that attack last night."

"That's good to know," McNeely responded. "Even if the Brits did claim they sank that one. But what do we do about it? Last time I looked, we weren't at war with Germany. Not yet anyway."

"We tell our Brit friends," Gorman replied. "Let them see if they can take care of the problem this time."

"And if he fixes his damage and dives before they can get here?"

"Then we find some excuse to shoot the bastard, even if he doesn't give us a good reason first," Gorman answered. "They're sinking cargo vessels and killing innocent people just about every day out here in international waters. Look, let's open out over the horizon to where he can't see us and call back to Bermuda. XO, get a message drafted up to Flag Officer Bermuda."

Nighttime was making its appearance by the time they had messaged the Brits on Bermuda and were back watching the U-boat bobbing on the surface from a safe distance. They had a front-row seat as the German crew struggled to repair what was obviously considerable damage to their boat. The moon had not yet shown up when Fred Wurster heard a change in the sound he continued to monitor on sonar.

The U-boat's screws had begun turning.

"Conn, Sonar, sounds like he's underway," he reported.

Lieutenant Gorman could now see that the Nazi submarine had started to move. Then it suddenly swung around so that it was pointed directly at the *S-52*.

"He's pointing us!" Gorman growled. "He's seen us, and the bastard's going to shoot!" That was the only provocation *S-52* needed to launch a defensive attack. But they needed to be quick. Once the U-boat dove, he would be nearly impossible to hit.

"Shoot tubes one and two!" the Skipper ordered. He waited a moment, then ordered, "Shoot tubes three and four!"

Down in the forward torpedo room, high-pressure air was ported into the four torpedo tubes, ramming the Mark X torpedoes out into the Atlantic. The alcohol-fueled, steam-driven weapons turned on their preset gyro course toward the German submarine and ramped up to their thirty-six-knot top speed. With an estimated range of three thousand yards, the torpedoes had a ninety-second journey to their intended target.

Gorman could easily see four arrow-straight white bubbly wakes leaving his boat, swimming directly at the oncoming German. He knew that if he could see the wakes of his weapons, so could the Germans. The best hope for getting a hit on the narrow profile the U-boat presented was for the spread of torpedoes to be wide enough that the Germans could not dodge all of them.

Suddenly Fred Wurster heard a new sound, a very high-pitched whining noise.

"Conn, Sonar, I hear incoming torpedoes! The German has shot at us!"

Don Gorman's response was instantaneous, though he had never had to make such a call in anything other than drill situations. "Dive, make your depth two hundred feet, left full rudder, all ahead flank!" They had to do some of their own dodging and ducking if they were to get out of the way of the onrushing torpedoes. If the Germans had ninety seconds to live, the Americans had even less.

"Flood negative! Full dive on the bow planes! Full dive on the stern planes!" *S-52*'s diving officer yelled. The old submarine popped and groaned as it arrowed down into the increasing water pressure of the depths.

"Seventy-five feet coming to two hundred!"

"One hundred coming to two hundred!"

No one needed a sonar to hear the high-pitched whine from the German torpedo screws as they raced by just overhead. Really close overhead. The sound reverberated through every nerve of every sailor on the *S-52*. Several men unconsciously ducked, as if that made them smaller, harder to hit.

The German torpedoes had barely passed them by when they were rocked by a tremendous explosion. Dust sifted down everywhere. Bulbs blew out. Anything not tied down fell to the deck. So did many of the crew of *S-52*. They all braced for inrushing seawater.

But after a few moments, they realized that the explosion was not from the German torpedoes striking their own submarine, ripping it apart. It had come from farther away, from the direction of the U-boat.

By the time they got back up to the surface to continue checking for damage, there was nothing visible of the *unterseeboot* but a spreading oil slick sprinkled with bits of flotsam.

This particular U-boat had sunk its last merchantman.

9

The name Ieusterfiord appeared only on a few very select, very highly classified German maps. To the rest of the world, the narrow stretch of ice and water, bound on either side by near-vertical granite cliffs that reached five hundred meters into the sky, was just another narrow, uninviting, and unnamed fiord. Greenland had hundreds of these stretching up and down the entire length of its Atlantic coast, its eastern side. Most were unexplored and devoid of human life. There was little reason for men to risk life and limb forcing their way up these fingers of frigid water into the bleak, ice-covered interior.

Ieusterfiord was the exception. Located some two-hundred-odd miles north of Cape Farewell, Greenland's southern tip, this fiord offered nearly everything the Germans required. Its access from the sea was well hidden in a maze of channels and small islands. That made it easy for a U-boat to remain hidden while it offloaded men and supplies, and then to sneak back out and submerge into the Atlantic. There were plenty of nooks and crannies, sheltered from the wind, in which to hide a base camp, concealed from anything but maybe a low-flying aircraft passing directly overhead. That would be a most unlikely prospect. The climb up to the ice plateau was reasonably easy for the hardened German troops, even if it was not so much the case for the meteorologists tasked with the job for which the base was intended, making weather observations and predictions. The region provided another benefit. The Germans would have to make the weather reports back to Berlin by radio. They rigged a single long wire across the valley. The wire formed a horizontally polarized high-frequency antenna. Its height above the ground and horizontal polarization enhanced the skywave propagation required to reach the Fatherland. However, the surrounding mountains effectively formed a geographic shadow zone that made intercepting the transmission very difficult from any position other than straight down the fiord, which conveniently pointed directly toward Germany.

But the conclusive reason for choosing Ieusterfiord was that the weather that crossed that part of Greenland today—assuming no other mitigating factors—would be over London and key RAF airfields in two more days.

The Germans arrived in Ieusterfiord in the early summer of 1940. A U-boat dumped off a dozen *Marinetosstrups*—literally naval shock troops, the *Kreigsmarine*'s answer to the US Marines—along with three meteorologists and a radio team. It took an entire day to ferry all the men and equipment, along with the food and fuel they would need for a month alone in the icy wilderness, to the narrow, stony beach. The *Marinetosstrups* schlepped all the gear and supplies up to their predetermined campsite while the radio team set up their communications equipment and got the generator running. They set up camp and immediately began burrowing in. With more than twenty hours of daylight each day during the summer, the industrious Germans had plenty of light to explore the surrounding areas and to construct a comfortable bivouac. And to compile a shopping list for next month's resupply U-boat to bring to them.

By the end of the first week, the little group was busy sending daily reports back to Berlin. There, the information was fed directly into the planning for bombing raids bound for Great Britain. The Nazi Luftwaffe pilots knew exactly what weather to expect over London before they ever left their airfields in the Netherlands and northern France. Or to not make the run at all if the conditions were too bad.

The effectiveness of the raids increased significantly.

∞

Trip MacLean was frustrated enough to take a bite out of the bridge rail on his submarine. Nothing was going his way. He was supposed to be enjoying a leisurely Navy life on the golf course at Pearl Harbor or basking on the beach at some palm-tree-studded tropical naval base. That had been his plan, but the Navy had other ideas. Instead, he was working his tail off in the shipyard at Electric Boat, doing all he could to get a beat-up old submarine ready for a war that many said would never happen but others claimed was a certainty. Either way, there were no leisurely mornings nursing a mimosa on a golden beach, no moonlight filtering through swaying palms, no wahines showing their special kind of appreciation to him for his service to his country. No, his every waking minute revolved around this smelly, rusty, steel sewer pipe they called a "*Sugar*" boat, named for the phonetic for the letter *S*.

And, just to top it all off, Daphanie Maria was making loud noises about marriage.

"Mista MacLean!" the XO's voice roared. "Get youse ass in heah!" Alphonse Dinnacetti was a proud product of Brooklyn. His accent became especially rich when he was angry. Right now, it was well marbled with generous amounts of Bedford-Stuyvesant.

MacLean had been nursing a cup of coffee in the wardroom, killing time before he was scheduled to supervise loading new battery cells into the battery well. Each cell was nearly five feet tall and weighed almost a ton. He figured that loading 120 of those monsters would kill the entire afternoon, even if he would not actually need to exert any effort beyond lifting his coffee cup as he watched some shipyard cranes do the heavy work.

But now the XO wanted something, and he did not sound happy about it. MacLean jumped up and hurried into the control room. With the boat torn up by shipyard work, the navigation table was the only flat work surface available onboard. Dinnacetti had appropriated it for his "office."

MacLean found him standing there, clutching a sheet of paper in a way that indicated it may have offended him in some manner. His face was brick red and a vein on his neck throbbed rhythmically.

"What is the meaning of this crap?" Dinnacetti growled, waving the paper at him. His tone was low and nasty. "I should have your worthless ass keelhauled for this."

MacLean shook his head and held up his hands innocently. "XO, I don't have a clue what you're upset about," he responded. "Can I see what you got there? Maybe I can explain it if I know what it is."

"It's a friggin' letter from the Bureau of Navigation." Dinnacetti's face took on an even darker hue of crimson. He threw the offending document at MacLean.

"Seems some United States Senator is unhappy about the duty assignment his precious little kid got. The poor little boy ain't being treated fairly by the nasty officers on his boat." The XO's growl was menacing. "You don't happen to know any Ensign whose papa is a US Senator, now do you?"

Trip MacLean gulped as he glanced at the letter. Dad had gone and swung his weight around to get his boy off this tub. It would have been nice if Dad had given him a heads-up. Now he had an irate XO that he needed to calm down before the guy blew a gasket or had a heart attack right there in the messy control room.

"This is a complete surprise to me," MacLean said, a placating tone in his voice. "I'm betting someone in Dad's office just overreacted. Let me check."

"Don't try that horseshit with me, kid," Dinnacetti roared. "Signature on that thing is Alistair MacLean Junior. That's your pappy, ain't it? Now, here's what's going to happen. You are going to draft up a response to the Bureau. If I had my way, that response would say that you were unsuitable for submarines and available for assignment for any seagoing garbage scow that needed an officer. But I don't have a choice here."

He pointed to a typewriter taking up the corner of the plotting table. "Get busy writing. You got yerself an appointment with the Division Chief of Staff in two hours." He glanced at his watch. "One hour and forty-eight minutes."

Commander Lawrence Yancey, the Division Chief of Staff, was no happier than the XO with having to deal with this particular problem. He had enough on his hands trying to get a squadron of Great War–era submarines repaired, manned, and ready to fight a war that he had to assume was coming. Handling some demand about an unhappy Senator's son just should not be a priority. But Yancey knew only too well that the junior Senator from New York had abundant political clout. More than ever, the Navy needed as many friends in Congress as they could get. Especially ones who served on key military appropriations committees. Word had filtered down to him that he should handle this situation with the utmost care.

When Trip MacLean arrived, he was immediately ushered into the Chief of Staff's office. There he stood at attention across the metal desk from Yancey as the COS read the draft response, trying to gauge the expression on the Commander's face.

Finally, Yancey looked up at the Ensign and said, "Mr. MacLean, you have effectively poisoned any chance that you might have had on the *S-53* and in this division. Here's what's going to happen. First, get your seabag packed. Your train departs New London at 1803. You have three days to be in Long Beach, California, to meet your new boat. So, there is no opportunity for missed connections or sightseeing. The *S-55* is deploying to Cavite Naval Base in the Philippines. You will...you WILL...be on board when she leaves Long Beach. Understood?"

Ensign MacLean nodded and offered the only response he could muster.

"Yes, sir."

∞

"Hey! Shut up! I want to hear this." Brad Johnson's command was greeted by a few hoots but then silence from most of the other bar patrons. A rare quiet fell over Solomon's Tavern. Only the big Hallicrafters shortwave receiver on the shelf behind the bar could be heard.

"This...is London," Edward R. Murrow's deep bass voice rang out from bursts of static, the beginning of another live report from bomb-ravaged England. The journalist was delivering one of his nightly broadcasts from the British capital, graphically describing the blitz and Londoners' response to the terror and damage from Hitler's air force.

"Not very friendly to the locals, telling them to shut up," someone noted as he slid onto the barstool next to Brad. It was Fred Wurster. "When did you get to be so interested in the news?"

Johnson's head shot up. "Freddy! When did you get in?" Johnson signaled Debbie, the bartender, to shove a glass of Rheingold in front of the new arrival.

"This afternoon," Wurster answered. "Oh, and look what I got while we were gone." He tapped the shiny gold dolphins on his left breast.

"Congratulations!" Johnson exclaimed sincerely. Then, before Fred could stop him, Brad shouted out, "Hey, everyone! Freddie just got his dolphins! Next round is on him!"

While Debbie helped deal with the resulting mad stampede, Johnson put an arm around Wurster's shoulder and pulled him closer. "Otherwise, how was the trip?"

Wurster shook his head and snorted. "A lot of blue water and a few seconds of absolute terror. I can tell you all about the blue water, but I'm afraid that's it, Brad. Our favorite FBI agent was there to meet the boat when we tied up. 'Very' Special Agent Ralph Flannigan made it clear to the whole crew from the Skipper on down that what we did out there didn't really happen. So, I can tell you all you want to know about blue water, fixing diesel engines, and pumping out bilges. But I can't discuss those few seconds of terror I didn't just mention. The ones that never happened."

Johnson's face took on a decided scowl as he said, "Yeah. I've come to really dislike that SOB."

Wurster looked at Johnson, surprised at the venom in his voice. Normally, Brad was about as mild mannered and easygoing as anyone he knew. He let it slide and grabbed his beer.

Their reunion was interrupted by another newcomer before Wurster could take a swallow of Rheingold.

"Got a stool for a cripple?"

Wurster and Johnson turned to see Stan Ward standing there, supported by a walking cane. They noticed again how much gaunter and more drawn he looked since their days at the Academy. Clearly, he had not fully recovered from the bus accident.

"Stan!" they shouted in unison.

"Might've known I'd find you guys at the closest bar to base gettin' soused and talking about girls you'll never get in a million years."

"The ball and chain give you liberty tonight?" Jonhson asked. "I thought you newlyweds didn't surface after the workday for at least the first year of marriage. Some kind of Kansas custom."

"Karen's up at the new base hospital tonight," Stan Ward answered as he eased down on a stool and leaned his cane against the bar. "She's talking to them about volunteering as a Navy nurse."

"That's great," Fred said. "I got a feeling we're going to need a lot of nurses."

"Not sure how I feel about that," Stan glumly responded. "Tough enough reading all the reports coming out of Europe..."

He paused and nodded toward the shortwave radio, where Murrow was just beginning a graphic description of a midnight Luftwaffe bombing raid on the heart of London. One still in progress as he reported.

"...and realizing what we are probably going to be up against without worrying about my wife going off to war, too." He took a sip of the newly arrived beer and tried to shake off the gloom. "Speaking of nurses, you still seeing that little thing over in Mystic? The one you wrote me about?"

It was Wurster's turn on the hot seat. He smiled shyly. "Matter of fact, I had a letter from Ellie waiting for me when we tied up. She's up in Boston now at the nursing school. Started class a couple of weeks ago. I'm heading up that way this weekend if they don't cancel leave and make me scrape barnacles off the hull or something."

"Sounds good," Brad said. "But old Stan here can confirm you gotta watch these nurses. Liable to slip something in your drink, and next thing you know, you wake up married."

Then Stan held up a hand, pointed to the radio, again asking everyone to quiet down. "Did you hear that?"

Brad shook his head. "Something about a 'bombers' moon.'"

"Exactly," Ward responded. "Nazis are over London in full force tonight.

Sky's clear and the moon's out, so they can actually see their targets. They never showed up last night because there was a hundred percent overcast."

"So?" Johnson asked.

"How do they know until they get there what the weather's like over their targets? That weather blows in off the Atlantic, from the west. The bomber runs are coming in from the east. But they know far enough ahead of time so they don't even make the run if London's socked in." Stan Ward suddenly stood and grabbed his cane. "Guys, I gotta head back to the basement! I got an idea."

"Wait, Stan! You're abandoning a full cold bottle of beer?" Fred asked.

"Gotta go!" But he stopped and turned. "Congrats on being the first of our bunch to qualify in submarines, Freddy. Maybe you're good for something besides being a tackling dummy after all."

As Ward hobbled out of Solomon's, Edward R. Murrow intoned on the radio his signature signoff: "Good night, and good luck!"

∞

Stan Ward was down in his basement office, staring hard at the big map on the wall, when Ollie Oglethorpe walked through the door to the room, long since dubbed "The Tree of Knowledge." He was passing by and noticed the lights on. The Commander was surprised to see his new protégé sitting there, deep in thought, transfixed by the small-scale map of the North Atlantic.

Not wanting to derail the younger man's train of thought, he took a couple of puffs on his ever-present pipe before he spoke. "What are you doing here so late, Stan? Shouldn't you be home with that new wife of yours?"

Startled, Ward looked up. "Sorry, boss. Didn't see you come in. I was just doing some thinking."

"Yeah, I could see that," Oglethorpe said with a laugh. "I could hear the wheels spinning. The question is, what were you thinking?"

Ward rubbed his chin for a moment and then stood, bracing himself against his desk. "Well, you know how you told me that our job is to take all the bits and pieces, find the pattern that makes sense, and then put them together like a jigsaw puzzle to convert it all into a pretty picture?"

"Yeah, that kinda sounds like something I might say," the senior officer answered. "But that still doesn't tell me what you're doing here in the middle of the night, Stan."

"Well, I was down at Solomon's this evening, having a beer with some friends," Ward related. Oglethorpe had a confused frown on his face. "Edward R. Murrow came on the radio. He was talking about tonight's air raid on London and the bombers' moon. I got to thinking. How do the Nazis know what the weather will be over England before they send a bunch of bombers that way? They have to have some reliable weather information that gives them enough lead time to plan and execute a raid. That means about a day in advance. I guess they could get data from spies on the ground in the area, but that would be real localized and still wouldn't tell what it would be like in twenty-four hours." He pointed at the map. "Ain't no place for a weather station to the west of Britain until you get to Greenland. I'm thinking there's a good chance the Nazis have some sort of secret weather station hidden over there and that's how they're getting such accurate information."

It was Oglethorpe's turn to study the map. "Makes sense," he mused. "Getting a good weather report would be worth the effort, too. Not many people around to see what's going on. Plenty of places to hide up in those fiords. Question now is, how do we find this weather station if it really is there?"

"Well, I figure somebody's got to be supplying them and they could lead us right to the spot," Stan Ward answered. "Why don't we just send out a patrol along the coast and see what turns up?"

Oglethorpe laughed. "Stan, take a closer look at the map. You have any idea how much coastline Greenland has? Even if we limit it just to the southeast side, the most likely area, we're talking about several thousand miles. And the Germans are going to go out of their way not to be found." Oglethorpe paused for a bit, deep in thought. Then he said, "I have an idea that should work. The Brits have set up a top secret network of receivers to DF U-boats when they come up to the surface to report in. They call them 'huff-duff stations.' Maybe they can DF this theoretical weather station.

That would tell us if your hunch is correct and would also give us some idea of where to look for it."

Oglethorpe sat down at his own desk and started to write. "Let's talk to the Admiral in the morning. This would have to go way up the food chain. What resources we have out there are old and scarce and we've got most of it tied up helping the Brits without anybody noticing. We need to get our ideas down on paper so we give the appearance of having a well-thought-out plan. You want to call Mrs. Ensign Ward? Looks like you're going to be late getting home tonight."

10

Brad Johnson reached down and grabbed the handle for the ship's whistle. It was his first time as OOD for an underway. Sounding the whistle started the adventure. With one prolonged and three short blasts from the whistle, he signaled to everyone within earshot that the *S-54* was backing out from Golf Pier into the Thames River.

It was a grand morning to be heading out to sea. A light north wind had blown the morning haze out toward Long Island Sound, revealing a bright sunlit sky overhead. Even so, Johnson was feeling troubled. Not even sounding the whistle had eased his mind.

On one hand, Brad was feeling comfortable and happy with his duty as a submarine officer. Whether it had been inherited from his Admiral dad or was an acquired feeling, he felt perfectly at home standing on the submarine's open bridge, guiding it down the river and out into the open ocean.

But another part of him was uneasy, unsettled. His relationship with Debbie Schultz, the barkeep, had grown much deeper than he ever anticipated. Or intended. He could feel it was getting serious. But it seemed FBI Special Agent Flannigan was always lurking in the shadows, poisoning everything he felt and said when it came to not only Debbie but his own naval career. And even the legacy of his father. He knew that if he and

Debbie were to have a chance, he needed to come clean and tell her about Flannigan, the FBI, and the agent's blackmail threat. But if he did that, he could wreck their relationship while ruining both his and his father's careers. Maybe even landing Brad in the brig. The young Ensign was at a loss.

A honking car horn broke through his thoughts. Johnson glanced over toward the riverbank. And there she was. Debbie was parked at the end of Crystal Lake Road, standing on her car's running board, hitting the horn and waving wildly at him. And she was wearing his favorite pink dress. Even from several hundred feet away, he could see she was smiling broadly. Somehow, seeing her did not make him feel any better.

LT. Stephen Brewster, CO of the *S-54*, nudged Brad, startling him, and said, "Got yourself an admirer, Brad? That's your girl, right? You know it's not a violation of Navy regs to smile and wave back."

Thankfully, the current shoved them downstream, allowing Brad only time for a quick return wave. The honking horn and waving girl were quickly lost astern. Soon, they passed under the railroad bridge, then floated past the massive Electric Boat shipyard facility. The company had been involved with building submarines since the first practical one, the USS *Holland*, back in 1899, and in this location on the Thames for almost thirty years now. Brewster held his binoculars to his eyes so that he could get a good look at the activity over there. The shipyard had four new subs on the building ways.

"Man, do you see those *Gato* boats over there?" Brewster enthused. "Sure wish we had one of those to play with. Can you imagine four brand-new Fairbanks-Morse diesels and ten torpedo tubes? And they'll shoot that new Mark 14 torpedo. The Germans and the Japs better not mess with us once we got those babies commissioned!"

Brad Johnson smiled and nodded. All he could think about was that over there in one of those buildings, Henrich Schultz, Debbie's dad, was hard at work, not suspecting the FBI was watching his every move.

"You're not very talkative today," Brewster said as he glanced over at Johnson.

"Sorry, Skipper," Johnson replied glumly. "I just got a lot on my mind right now."

"Well, get your mind back in the game," Brewster directed. "This is going to be a busy run. I'll give everybody the skinny after we dive. But I'll need everyone, including you, in top form." He looked down at the activity on the main deck, then back to see several sailors enjoying a smoke on the cigarette deck. "We'll dive as soon as we are past Race Rock. Get everyone below decks except you and your lookouts. I'm going below. I'll be in the conning tower talking with the XO."

"Yes, sir," Johnson answered, but realized he was only responding to himself. Brewster had already dropped through the hatch. By the time they had made the short run across Long Island Sound, the *S-54* was ready to dive. Race Rock had just passed astern to port when Brad Johnson called down to the conning tower. "To the Captain, Race Rock is astern. Request permission to dive the boat."

"Mr. Johnson, dive the boat."

Johnson looked up at his lookouts and yelled, "Clear the bridge!"

As the last sailor dropped through the hatch, he announced, "Dive! Dive!" and sounded the diving alarm. The boat was already taking a down angle as he dropped through the hatch, pulled it shut above himself, and spun the handwheel to seal out the seawater.

"Last man down, hatch secured," he called as he dropped to the conning tower deck, then continued on down the ladder to the control room, where he would take his station as diving officer. It only took a few minutes of pumping and flooding to get a satisfactory trim on the ship. Then they were heading out of Block Island Sound into the open Atlantic.

Johnson was just settling in as the diving officer when the Chief of the Boat, Delbert Lafour, a grizzled old Chief Machinist with almost twenty years on submarines, stepped into the control room. "Mr. Johnson, Skipper wants all the officers in the wardroom," he reported. "I relieve you as dive."

Johnson rushed forward and crowded into the cramped wardroom, anxious to hear what might be different with this run. Something not as routine and boring as what they had been doing. And that would keep him busy enough so he would not have time to stew about the FBI situation. There was no open seat, so he leaned back against the forward bulkhead.

When Stephen Brewster saw that all the officers were present, he started the briefing. "Guys, I figure you all want to know what's up. We are not heading out this week to play rabbit for the destroyers trying to find a submarine. Our orders are to head up to Greenland and look for U-boats. Seems that somebody got the wild idea that the Nazis may have put up a secret weather station up there to help the Luftwaffe keep pounding London like they're doing. It's most likely being supplied by U-boats. Our job is to find them and let them lead us to the weather station."

"What do we do when we find them?" The XO, LT. Clark Manson, asked the question they all had, as he stubbed out a cigarette in the wardroom "ashtray." It was really a cutoff section of a four-inch shell casing from the boat's deck gun.

"Right now, our orders are to tell the Brits what we learn and then slink out of town before anybody ever notices we were there," Brewster answered. "We've got a five-day transit to get everything ready for this job. I want each of you to look at your divisions and see what needs fixed for this boat to be ready for war, just in case things get dicey. And, just to make things interesting, we will be passing right through a major convoy route coming and going. You guys know what that means. If the Brits detect a sub, they'll shoot first and not bother checking to see if we might be friendly. That means we keep on our toes. We avoid every ship that we see. We ain't got no friends out there. Everyone understand? Any questions?"

There were a bunch of worried faces, but no more questions.

At least none that were asked out loud.

∞

"Anything helpful from those huff-duff stations?" Ollie Oglethorpe asked as he poured himself another cup of coffee. The pot had been stewing long enough that the liquid looked more like a thick, black syrup.

Stan Ward shook his head. "Nothing we can really work with yet. The stations at Keflavik over in Iceland and the Sligo Station in Ireland are reporting detections of very brief and apparently low-power signals. Looks like our German weathermen...if they actually exist...are using some kind of burst transmitter and shortened codes. Probably that new *kurzsignale* system that we heard about. Each time, they're on the air for only a few seconds. If we didn't have huff-duff, we'd probably never hear them at all.

The bearings are jumping around so much that the best the Brits can say is that the transmitter is someplace in southern Greenland."

Oglethorpe frowned. "That's really helpful. But our meteorologists tell me that would give them a pretty good place to be if they wanted to predict the weather in a couple of days over Piccadilly Circus. So, where are our submarines now?"

Ward pointed up to the map where little icons showed four US *S*-boats traipsing northeastward across the North Atlantic, each pointed to Greenland's Cape Farewell.

"*S-54*'s leading the way. She reports that she's still a day south of Greenland. *S-51* and *S-52* are each about a day behind the *54* boat. *S-53* just finished repairing her number one main motor. Look out the window. She should be heading downriver as we speak."

Both men knew there were no windows in the basement intelligence facility. It was a running joke.

"So, the forces are gathering," the senior intel officer mused as he rubbed his chin, chewed on another sip of coffee, and stared at the chart. "Suggest you don't ever let those sub sailor friends of yours know it was your idea to send them way up there. You may get your ass keelhauled." Oglethorpe studied the tags representing the submarines for a full minute, then said, "That begs the question we have something like one whole day to answer: What do we do with the subs if we can't get a good DF from the Brits? Not much in the way of a liberty port in that part of the world."

Ward slowly stood, got his balance, and made his way over to the chart. "I've been giving that some thought. The only thing I can suggest is we give them each a box to search, say one fifty miles long. That would cover the lower two hundred miles of coastline. Then we move further north if necessary. We move the *54* boat the furthest north and then fill in behind her as the others show up."

Oglethorpe sucked on his pipe and nodded. "Sounds good. Even if they don't know for sure what they're looking for. But I guess up there, anything is something. Call over to Ops and see if we can make it happen."

"Commander, we can make it happen," Ward said as he studied the long, jagged shoreline of Greenland. "At least you can. But you gotta know what we call this back on the high plains of Colorado."

Without hesitation, Oglethorpe answered, "Needle in a damn haystack."

∞

Fred Wurster had just finished shooting the morning round of stars to try to determine their precise position in the Atlantic. He now sat in the back of the control room, performing the calculations that reduced his sextant altitude readings into lines of position for each of the six specific stars in the night sky he had chosen to observe. The intersection of all those "LOPs" resulted in the famous "cocked hat," a vaguely triangular shape on the chart. The position of *S-52* should be located inside that cocked hat. But something was not right, and it had Wurster perplexed. The cocked hat was a whole lot larger than it should be. Instead of knowing their position within a mile or so, the position error was more like ten miles. Out in the open Atlantic, that was not really a problem, but they were headed toward an unfamiliar rocky and jagged coastline. Just to add anxiety to uncertainty, the weather this far north, at this time of year, was frequently unsettled. Storms, rain, fog—pick the poison—any one of them could suddenly reduce decent visibility to a few feet. And in wartime, even if there were the normal navigation aids, like lighthouses, available in this desolate territory, they would be turned off.

LT. Simon McNeely stumbled into the control room, accompanied by a rough, hacking cough. He pulled a pack of Lucky Strikes from his pocket, fished out a smoke, and lit it before even offering a "good morning."

"XO, what you doing out of your rack?" Wurster asked him as he observed McNeely's bloodshot eyes, sunken into his pallid, grayish face, and fever-flushed cheeks. "Didn't Doc tell you to stay down and get some rest?"

"It's just a damn cold," McNeely growled. He drew deeply on the cigarette, blew out a cloud of smoke and tapped the butt on the ashtray hanging alongside the chart table to discard an impossibly long strand of ashes. "Damn sawbones. He'd order an autopsy on a hangnail. Anyway, thanks for taking the morning fix. We should be seeing Cape Farewell sometime this evening."

Fred Wurster nodded. "Yep, the DR track has us making landfall about midnight." He pointed to the path, the "dead reckoning" track, that the submarine was following between navigational fixes. Then he pointed to the fix that he had just plotted from his celestial observations. It showed them to be well to the southeast of the DR position.

"Something isn't right here, though," he admitted. "I checked my calculations a dozen times. I know the magnetic pole gets the compass all scrambled up the farther north we go, but the stars ought to be where they're supposed to be."

McNeely coughed some more, caught his breath, then said, "If your calcs are right, the problem is either the sextant or the operator." He reached out. "We all know an Academy grad and brand spankin' new submariner would never make a mistake. So, let me see the sextant."

Wurster reached under the plot table and retrieved the device's wooden storage box. The photo-engraved label read, "Naval Sextant, Mark II." Some sailor with a typical submariner's deviant sense of humor had long before scratched out the "tant" part of the label. Fred opened it, pulled the complicated device from its nesting place, and handed it to the XO.

McNeely grabbed the sextant and began to carefully look it over. He nodded and looked up. "Here's your problem. The indexing mirror has been knocked loose. It's way out of whack. You'll have us making port in Timbuktu with this cockeyed thing." Grabbing a screwdriver, the XO tightened down on the lock screw, then he worked with the horizon glass to correct the index error and adjusted the mirror perpendicularity. He handed the sextant back to Wurster. "All ready to go."

Fred started to return the instrument to its box. McNeely stopped him. "What you think you're doing?"

"Sun's up," Wurster answered. "No stars."

McNeely shook his head. "Man! JOs! They make 'em dumber every year. You got a waning crescent moon. It's still up and visible. You go and shoot the moon and a couple of sun lines. Then at least we'll know what ocean we're in the middle of, maybe." He was interrupted by the onset of another hacking cough. He closed his eyes and leaned on the chart table for a moment. "Look, I'm gonna grab a couple of aspirins and lay down for a minute. Call me when you have the observation plotted."

The XO disappeared forward, headed for his stateroom. Fred Wurster draped the sextant lanyard around his neck and climbed up toward the bridge, frigid air, and icy sea spray.

∞

Stephen Brewster tried to read over the radioman's shoulder as he typed each letter of the message he was copying. It seemed to be taking forever. The Skipper of the *S-54* finally gave up, paced around the control room for a bit, but then stepped back to the little nook that housed the submarine's radio.

The radioman had copied two more words since the captain left on his short hike. At this rate, it would take the message an hour to *dit* and *dah* its way to the end.

Clark Manson was the *S-54*'s Executive Officer, second-in-command. He leaned back against the conning tower ladder and commented, "Skipper, you bugging 'Sparks' every couple of seconds ain't going to make that traffic get here any faster."

"Yeah, XO, I know," the anxious Skipper grumbled in response, "but we're stuck here, not knowing what to do, while some long-winded desk jockey in Groton is telling us why and how to suck an egg. Why can't he just say where he wants us to go, and be done with it?"

"'Cause he's probably never been stuck on the other end," Manson dryly responded, "with his butt hanging out all exposed while he's trying to listen to Mr. Morse's finest code."

"Dive! Dive!" the 1MC suddenly blasted. That was followed immediately by the "*Aoogha! Aoogha!*" of the diving alarm.

Manson and Brewster collided as they both rushed for the ladder from the control room up to the conning tower. Brad Johnson was dropping down from the bridge as Brewster pulled himself up to the cramped compartment.

"Last man down! Hatch secured," the breathless junior officer said. He turned to see Brewster staring at him, an inquisitive expression on his face. Why had he suddenly given the order to dive the boat? Johnson, still panting, explained, "Plane! Came out of the clouds! Maybe a couple of miles out, way too close for comfort. Not sure that he saw us, but he was coming right at us."

Brewster yelled down to the control room. "Right full rudder! Ahead flank! Steady course zero-nine-zero!" Turning to Manson and Johnson, he explained, "If he saw us, I want to be somewhere else by the time he gets here."

A massive explosion rocked the *S-54*, as if punctuating the Skipper's words. The boat pitched and heaved. Crewmen were knocked off their feet. Light bulbs shattered and dial faces spider-webbed, scattering glass fragments all over the deck. Cork and dusty debris sifted down, clouding the air with a thick haze.

As Manson picked himself up off the deck, he felt something dripping down from his forehead. When he brushed it aside, his hand came away red with blood, his blood.

"You okay, XO?" Brewster asked as he handed Manson the cleanest dirty rag he could find.

"Yeah," he replied, "Must'a bounced my head off the TDC. Better check to make sure my hard head didn't break anything on that machine."

Brewster looked around as men slowly pulled themselves up. Everything appeared nearly normal, or at least as close to normal as he could expect after someone tried to bomb them. No reports of fire or flooding. That was a good sign. But they still needed to get further away before that plane came around for a second shot.

"Dive, make your depth two hundred feet." He ordered, so they could get some water over their heads.

Delbert Lafour, the COB, stuck his head up from the control room. "Skipper, boat's okay, far as we can tell. Got some scrapes and bruises, but nobody hurt bad. We was lucky." He caught a glimpse of Manson's bloody face. "And I'll get Doc up here to look at the XO."

There were a couple more explosions, each much farther away than the first. They had apparently gotten out from beneath their attacker.

Stephen Brewster smacked his hand down angrily on the plot table. "Damn! This is what happens when you get stuck on the surface during the day!" he growled. "Those idiots at COMSUBPATFOR need to send message traffic at night, not during the day when it's convenient for them. And they need to be a hell of a lot shorter or sent a hell of a lot faster. Sparks can copy what? Twenty-five or thirty words a minute? XO, make sure all that gets into the patrol report."

Manson nodded, pressing the rag against his head wound. "Yes, sir. I'm just glad I don't have to write it in blood. I may be coming up short here in a minute."

Brewster half chuckled, then he turned to Johnson. "Brad, good job in not screwing around and in getting the boat down quick like that. What can you tell me about the plane?"

"It all happened so quick," Johnson admitted. "He just dropped out of the clouds and already saw us for sure. It looked like one of those flying boats. You know, like those Pan American Clippers. Definitely four engines and real big."

Brewster nodded, then pounded the plot table in anger once again. "Probably a Short Sunderland. Boys, our Brit friends are trying to kill us. Like I said before, we ain't got no friends out here!"

11

"Damn! Bean soup again!" Brent Halloran complained as he stirred a spoon through the gray broth. "This is the third day in a row with bean soup for lunch."

Simon McNeely looked down the wardroom table at his Engineering Officer. "You got a problem there, Brent?"

"Yeah, XO," Halloran shot back. "Subs are supposed to have the best food in the Navy. I haven't seen anything but bean soup this whole run. Where's all that great grub?"

McNeely looked over at Fred Wurster. As the boot Ensign on board, Wurster was the boat's supply officer. Among other things, he was responsible for the food that was stocked on board. "Freddy, want to defend yourself?"

Wurster had been trying to keep out of the conversation, feigning intense interest in the noontime repast. But he should have known the displeasure would be deflected his way. It came with the job. He reluctantly looked up from the bowl. "We left New London in such a big hurry I requisitioned whatever I could get that was edible. There were a lot of beans in the warehouse. Not many steaks. We've been out here long enough that the dry stores are getting pretty bare." He smiled and glanced over at Halloran.

"Brent, another week out here and we'll be stewing your shoes and serving them up with a little steak sauce and you'll be glad to have them."

Halloran grimaced at the thought, then he added, "Another week out here, too, and we'll need to get towed back home. We won't have the fuel to make it to the next wavetop."

Dan Gorman looked up from his seat at the head of the table. "Well, we already know the way to handle it when the diesels ain't pushing us anymore, don't we, Freddy?"

Wurster smiled and nodded. "Yep, Skipper, COB hung onto those sails. He's got 'em stowed in the torpedo room, just in case."

Turning serious, Gorman looked over at McNeely. "XO, draft up a message to COMSUBPATFOR. Tell them that we'll stick here for two more days, then we're heading to Reykjavik for fuel."

"Yes, sir," McNeely answered. "Just as soon as I have myself some dessert, which means another bowl of this delicious bean soup."

"Captain to control!" the 1MC blasted, interrupting any further discussion of beans or dessert.

Gorman threw down his napkin, jumped up, and rushed out of the wardroom. He sprinted into the control room and then up the ladder to the conning tower, where he found Jim Shelton, the on-watch OOD, peering through the periscope.

"What you got, Weps?" Gorman asked.

LT(jg) Shelton, the boat's Weapons Officer, stepped back from the scope and said, "Nothing visible, Skipper. Sonar says they're hearing a diesel on the JK sound head. But it ain't one of our NELSECO engines. Sonar's not positive, but he's sayin' what they're hearing sounds a lot like that U-boat off Bermuda. Best bearing is three-five-two. I'm not seeing anything on that bearing."

Gorman put his eye to the periscope and stared out to the north. Nothing out there but sky and sea. "Come around to course three-five-two," he ordered. "Let's see what's swimming up that way."

Simon McNeely called up from the navigation plot down in the control room. "Skipper, our boundary with *S-54*'s patrol area is only a mile in that direction."

Gorman replied, "Yeah, thanks, XO. Let's find out what we got."

Lowering the periscope and turning to Shelton, he ordered, "Weps, sound battle stations. Let's be ready just in case this guy's in a bad mood."

The *S-52* slowly moved to the north, in pursuit of the sonar signal.

"Captain, Sonar reports the signal's getting weaker." Shelton still held the phone handset to his ear as he reported to Gorman. "No sign that he has changed anything, just opening out."

"Let's see if we can speed up and still hold him," Simon McNeely suggested.

"We'll give it a try," Gorman agreed. "Come to ahead two-thirds."

The old submarine slowly accelerated. They were up to six knots when Sonar reported, "We lost the signal. It faded. Last bearing, north."

Gorman smacked the periscope barrel. "Damn! Not our lucky day." Turning to McNeely, he said, "XO, get a message ready to COMSUBPATFOR and *S-54*. Tell them that the U-boat is heading their way. And tell COMSUBPATFOR we will stay here another two days, then head to Iceland to resupply. I'm tired of bean soup."

∞

To Brad Johnson, all this was a great adventure. Standing on the bridge of a submarine—even if it was old and creaky—patrolling just a couple of miles off a mountainous, icy coast, searching for an elusive Nazi submarine that may or may not be anywhere around. It seemed to him to be a scene pulled directly off a Navy recruiting poster. This was exhilarating, just him and three lookouts, the blue sky, deep blue sea, and granite-colored mountains lining the western horizon.

"Control, Bridge. Captain to the bridge."

The announcement came simultaneously with Stephen Brewster's head appearing at the hatch. The Skipper stood, took a deep breath of the cold, fresh air, and then scanned the horizon before speaking. Then, turning to Johnson, he said, "Brad, keep a sharp eye out. We just copied a message from the 52 boat. They picked up a possible U-boat and confirmed it is headed our way. The information was several hours old, but if it's good dope, and the guy is coming our direction, we should see him about sunset or a little after."

Johnson nodded and mumbled, "Yes, sir." He was not sure exactly what he should be doing, other than keeping his eyes to the south. And he was not at all comfortable with a U-boat heading toward them. The Nazi submarine could be sneaking up on them right now, and he knew they would not hesitate to shoot if they thought the Americans were close to some top secret base ashore. The first time he would know about it would be when one of the lookouts spotted the frothy white wakes of torpedoes inbound. Spotted them if they were lucky. Their "hello" could be a torpedo strike that cut the *S-54* in half.

"Brad, the XO and I studied the charts. There is a whole gaggle of fiords over there that look like they could lead back into protected water, making it real convenient for a U-boat dropping supplies." Brewster waved toward the mountains over on the Western horizon. "I want you to make sure the battery is completely topped off. Then submerge and head over toward the coast. We'll get a couple of miles off the rocks. Then we'll patrol parallel to them. If we're lucky, this guy won't be comfortable going up any of those fiords submerged and will run on the surface. That'll make our job a lot easier."

"What do we do, though?" Johnson asked.

"Why, we follow him in and find out what he's doing and with whom," Brewster answered calmly.

"Submerged?" Johnson gulped.

"Of course," Brewster answered. "He ain't gonna like us hanging around, tailing him, waving to him, now is he?"

"Roger that, Skipper," Johnson sheepishly agreed. "We just completed a normal battery charge. We're ready to dive."

"Very well, dive the ship," Brewster ordered, then dropped back down the hatch.

Half an hour later, the *S-54* was submerged and at periscope depth, cruising parallel to the rocky coast of Greenland, searching for, of all things, a German U-boat.

The sun had just dropped behind the mountains when sonar reported, "Hearing a noise source to the south. Squeaking, sounds like a possible shaft rub."

"What's the bearing?" Brewster demanded. "Give me a bearing a tad better than 'south.'"

"Best bearing is two-zero-zero, but it is rough," the sonar operator responded. "The noise is really weak, going in and out."

Brewster spun the periscope around so that he was looking directly down the estimated bearing. Nothing in that direction except darkening sky and steel-blue water. Then he saw a ripple emerge. The ripple turned into a periscope. Then the gray shape of a submarine sail. A U-boat filling his scope! Up on the surface and obviously heading toward one of the fiords.

"Mr. Johnson, get in behind him," Brewster ordered. "I want to follow this guy until we find out what he's up to. Come around to course three-two-seven."

The *S-54* slowly maneuvered until it was a thousand yards directly astern of the Germans. Brewster could easily see the sailors emerging as they clambered out to the submarine's deck and manned the deck guns. Clearly, they were not taking any chances of being caught unprepared, unlikely as such a thing might be way up here.

"He's slowing," Brewster announced. "Ahead one-third."

The *S-54* kept pace as the U-boat snaked its way through the very narrow passage. Brewster swung the scope to port and starboard. All he could see was steep, rocky cliffs stretching to the sky. It appeared he was driving his submarine into a cave. Ahead, the channel seemed to neck down to nothing. What was the German up to? And how much longer would the two subs fit through this maze?

"Sounding thirty fathoms under the keel," the fathometer watch called out, confirming the channel might be skinny but at least it was deep.

The U-boat suddenly turned sharply to starboard. Webster could not see far enough ahead yet, but the channel must have veered sharply that way. He blindly steered the *S-54* around the steep headland and found they were in another channel. This one snaked around to the north-northwest. They followed the other guy until the channel finally ended in a glacier-fed lagoon.

The German stopped and anchored a few hundred feet from a narrow rocky beach. The captain could see a party of men waiting on the beach, then watched as they shoved off in a pair of inflatable boats and paddled out toward the U-boat. The submarine crew was already busy, manhandling box after box of what were probably supplies, pulling them topside and then offloading them down into the inflatables when they got there.

Stephen Brewster faced a quandary. This was proof that the weather station really did exist. Now, what to do about it? If they had been at war, there was a perfect solution to this problem. Just sink the U-boat right here in the icy lagoon and then shell the shore party. An aerial bombing attack could take care of the weather station, which had to be nearby. But that option was not open to him. The only thing he could do was to sneak back out of the fiord without scraping the fenders and report. Maybe the Brits—who were at war with Germany—could get here in time to do what needed to be done. If nothing else, maybe that damned unfriendly Short Sunderland flying boat was still around and could be useful instead of trying to sink Brewster's boat.

He turned the *S-54* around and backtracked, making his way out the winding channel. He glanced over to see Johnson was drawing a detailed map of each turn. Once they were well out of sight of the Germans and in a spot where he thought a radio signal might propagate, he surfaced the *S-54* and began broadcasting his report. They had just cleared the fiord when the XO stuck his head out of the bridge hatch.

"Skipper, we just established comms with British Convoy Command Iceland. They report they have a pair of destroyers being diverted our way. But at best, they're four hours out. And our favorite seaplane is on patrol an hour away. They request we stay on station and on the surface at the mouth of the fiord to guide the Sunderland in."

"Acknowledge their request. Tell them we'll comply if they promise not to try to sink us this time."

∞

British Convoy Command Iceland, the command responsible for routing and protection for all convoys traveling between the southern tip of Greenland and the Western Approaches, west of Ireland, took up two floors in an old stone warehouse on Grandabakki in the heart of Reykjavik Port.

The Royal Navy had appropriated the building, much to the ire of its Icelandic owners, a couple of days after the Royal Marines landed and seized control in late May. The invasion was meant to forestall any Nazi occupation of the island when the king of Denmark capitulated. The Icelanders weren't quite sure if they were an occupied nation or a British ally. The Royal Navy was not sure either, but they still held the strategically vital bit of real estate. The result was the harbor teemed with warships refueling and re-arming before heading back out for patrols and convoy duty. And a tense truce had descended over the waterfront pubs lining the harbor.

A stiff predawn wind blew across the harbor, rattling the warehouse windows, the chill finding its way through into the drafty old interior. The Operations Center Floor drew meager heat from a couple of coal-fired stoves. The WRENs—members of the Women's Royal Naval Service—who plotted out all of the North Atlantic activity on a giant map painted on the floorboards, huddled around the stoves, warming their hands whenever possible.

The message that came clacking across the radio telegraph came as a surprise. And very little surprised Chief WREN Sallie McGinnis. She had been around for too long and seen too much to be surprised by a simple message from a submarine. But nobody on the Ops Center Floor knew anything about an American submarine operating in their waters. The very early morning hour meant that it took several minutes to roust the watch officer from his bunk and then awaken the Center Commander at his lodgings over on the Old West Side.

By the time the two Royal Navy officers had wakened enough to comprehend what was happening, Sallie McGinnis had analyzed the situation, found what resources were available, and had a message reply sent back to the *S-54* Yank sub. The only assistance anywhere close were a Royal Navy trawler, the *Blackthorn*, and an old coal-burning sloop left over from the Great War who had just departed Reykjavik and were headed down south to help escort an eastbound slow convoy. That and a Short Sunderland flying boat finishing up an ASW patrol off of Cape Farewell.

Messages to all three were drafted and sent before the Commander's car pulled up to the warehouse. He was sipping his first cup of tea when the replies rolled in. The ships reported heading to the rendezvous at best speed but were at least four hours out. The Short Sunderland aircraft reported that it was returning to base with a failed number two engine.

∞

A rogue wave heaved green water up over the vessel's forecastle, submerging the number one gun mount before it washed back along the main deck, crashed into the deckhouse, then sluiced back into the sea. Royal Navy Sublieutenant Geoff Chandler, the *Blackthorn*'s Third Officer, spit and sputtered as the spray drenched him where he stood on the trawler's mostly unprotected open bridge. The waters off Greenland were always cold and rough. With the early onset of another Arctic winter, they were now downright unfriendly, particularly to those manning a tiny Royal Navy trawler like the *Blackthorn*.

Chandler stole a quick glance over at the nearby HMS *Flying Fox*. Although twice the size of the *Blackthorn*, the sloop was also struggling in the North Atlantic seas. The *Flying Fox* had been built at the end of the Great War and spent most of its service in the Volunteer Reserve fleet. The battered, rusty ship, streaked with black from its coal-fueled boilers, looked like it had seen hard use. But at least, Chandler thought, the deck officer on that ship had a little more protection from the weather and the cold, driving seas than did his own vessel.

"Mr. Chandler," LT. Ian MacDonald, the First Officer, yelled across the bridge. "Orders been changed. We be a'needin' ta come 'round ta west-sou-west. Best ya be steerin' west by south three-quarters west." MacDonald's heavy Scottish brogue and his stubborn adherence to the old compass points of steering made his order both hard to hear and to comprehend.

Chandler turned to the helmsman and yelled, "Come right, steer two-five-zero true." Then he yelled over to MacDonald, "First Officer, should we signal *Flying Fox*?" But the Scot had already disappeared back into the shelter of the deckhouse.

The Captain of the *Flying Fox* was senior to the master of the *Blackthorn* and that put him in charge of this little flotilla. He should be the one ordering these course changes. Or at least be told about them.

Chandler aimed the Aldis lamp toward the sloop. Flipping the handle on the lantern, he slowly spelled out the course change. A flashing light on *Flying Fox* confirmed the change. It also directed them to get to a point off southwest Greenland as fast as possible. Chandler informed the sloop that his trawler was straining to make twelve knots. The *Flying Fox* should race ahead. The question of why the sudden change in plans and urgency was left both unasked and unanswered.

Heavy, black smoke poured from the sloop's single tall stack as the old ship literally poured on the coal. It surged ahead, diving into the head seas, shuddering before leaping free and then plunging into the next wave. Chandler watched as the ancient warhorse raced toward the horizon while the *Blackthorn* plodded along behind.

Then, an hour later, the *Blackthorn*, still doing all she could to maintain twelve knots, steamed right on past the *Flying Fish*. The old vessel was dead in the water. In a flashing light exchange, the sloop signaled that they had a boiler casualty that would take several hours to repair. The trawler pushed on ahead.

It was almost dawn when Rodney Jeffries, the *Blackthorn*'s CO, appeared on the bridge. The man was wearing a heavy oilskin sou'wester and wool watch cap to protect him from the weather. Chandler, chilled to the bone and soaked from his long exposure to the elements, stared enviously at the master's warm, dry clothing and the steaming cup of coffee that he was nursing.

Jeffries scanned the approaching Greenland coast with his binoculars, carefully studying every headland and inlet. Finally, he turned to Chandler and asked, "Third Officer, where is *Flying Fish*?"

"Captain, she's broken down two hours behind. I sent the messenger to inform you when it happened," Chandler answered. It was not unusual for the ship's master to forget a report delivered to him during the night.

"Of course, of course," Jeffries answered, waving away the reply. "Must have forgotten. Asleep and all. Let's get on with the show. Should be a Yank submarine around here somewhere and a Nazi one hidden in one of these coves." He waved toward the coastline, only a couple of thousand yards away. "Get the guns manned and clear the decks for action."

"Mr. Chandler, sir," the port lookout called out. "There's someone coming down that fiord ahead. I can see his smoke. Just coming around that bend up the channel."

Geoff Chandler grabbed his binoculars and searched in the direction the lookout pointed. He could just make out what looked like a U-boat on the surface, heading out to sea. He wiped off the lenses of his binoculars and looked again, even harder, to make sure it was a German craft, not the American sub. Then he saw a bright flash and puff of smoke from the sub. A sound like a fast freight train whistled past the trawler. Then there was a tall column of water a couple of hundred yards away.

"I do believe he is firing at us," Rodney Jeffries said calmly. "I suggest you return fire before he gets lucky."

The *Blackthorn*'s quick-firing 12-pounder opened up, sending its first shell high up onto the rocky bluff to the starboard of the emerging submarine, much to the dismay of a bunch of nesting cormorants. Two of the 20mm Oerlikon machine cannons came alive, spraying the oncoming submarine with four-ounce shells in short bursts that were at a rate of over two hundred rounds a minute.

Chandler pointed the trawler toward the oncoming submarine, moving the rudder back and forth, snaking the wake to at least give the Germans a moving target. A splash from another near miss sprayed frigid water up onto the open bridge. The 12-pounder barked, and barked again, as they charged forward. Chandler could see a row of flashes and sparks stitch across the submarine as one of the 20mm cannons found the range to the German, punching a neat, straight row of holes into the sail. That might prevent the submarine from diving, but it would not be enough to sink her.

Chandler felt the trawler shudder even before he heard an explosion aft. He turned to see the after deckhouse blasted away and ablaze. He could not tell much more because of the smoke and flames. One thing he knew for sure, though. If the fire got to the depth charges sitting in their racks on the stern—just feet away—the *Blackthorn* would promptly and loudly disappear in a greasy black cloud. He was in the process of ordering them jettisoned when he saw them roll off the ship and into the sea. Someone back there had the same idea. The depth charges sank to their preset depth of two hundred feet before detonating, leaving a trail of boiling water behind the trawler.

Chandler had just turned back to see the gun battle when one of the 12-pounder rounds found the U-boat. It looked like the round penetrated the hull just forward of the sail and then detonated with a huge blast. A thick column of smoke poured up out of the sail. The submarine lurched drunkenly across the narrow channel, driving itself high up onto the stony beach.

The 12-pounder and the two 20mm Oerlikons continued their deadly fire at the now immobile hulk. Even so, German survivors were climbing out of the submarine and rushing up the hillock, trying to get away from their stricken boat, now a sitting duck.

Chandler looked around to find the Captain. Normally, in battle, he would expect him to be on the bridge directing all the action, but he was nowhere in sight. And no sign of the First Officer either. That left Chandler in charge.

"Cease fire!" he ordered. The Germans were no longer a threat, but the heavy, black smoke from aft told him that *Blackthorn* still had a fire to worry about. He looked aft, but he still could not see much except smoke and someone occasionally running by, fighting the fire. The ship was feeling sluggish, and it was now obvious that she was riding lower in the water.

"Steer toward the beach," he ordered the helmsman. "Ahead one-third." If the *Blackthorn* was sinking, maybe he could drive it up onto the beach to save it or at least give the crew a chance. No one would last long in this cold seawater.

But where was LT. Jeffries? The master should be the one making these crucial decisions, not the Third Officer.

He felt the ship come to a lurching, grinding halt, striking bottom, just as a smoke- and dirt-covered Ian MacDonald emerged from aft to say that the fires were out. However, there was four feet of water in the engine room and the ocean was pouring in through a gaping hole they could not repair.

The *Blackthorn* would not be going anywhere soon without a lot of effort.

12

Stephen Brewster watched the gun battle between the little trawler and the U-boat with fascination, all through the periscope of the *S-54* submarine. With both ships ultimately driven up on the beach and afire, one on either side of the narrow fiord, it was obvious his sub was the only ship around that could conduct any type of rescue.

"Mr. Johnson, battle-surface the boat," Brewster directed. "COB, as soon as we sort out whether anybody is going to shoot at us, get a rescue party ready topside to render assistance to that trawler. Looks like we may end up fighting a fire on her. XO, get in comms with those Brit Command Center folks and see what help they can send."

The *S-54* silently emerged from periscope depth and immediately steered toward the mouth of the fiord and the two distressed vessels on the beach. Once surfaced, the diesels coughed to life as the gun crew raced to man the four-inch deck gun. Men passed the heavy shells up through the gun access trunk. One of the brass shells was slammed into the cannon's breech and made ready for firing. The gunner spun the weapon around to point in the general direction of the U-boat. A pair of sailors lugged a .50 caliber machine gun up and stuck it on a pintle on the cigarette deck. The COB climbed up onto the bridge where he handed each lookout a Tommy gun. Turning to Ensign Brad Johnson, he held out a .45 pistol and holster.

"Here, Mr. Johnson," he said. "Just keep this in its holster. It's loaded. Please don't pull it out unless necessary. I don't want no one hurt."

Johnson was not quite sure if the grizzled old chief was serious or having some fun with him. The look on Chief Lafour's face did not confirm either way.

They were still manning the guns when the trawler challenged the submarine with its flashing light. The radiomen were below, talking with Iceland. The quartermasters were busy plotting their positions and not available. Johnson realized he was the only person on the bridge who could read or transmit Morse code. The problem was, he had not done that since his Boy Scout days. He was very rusty, but as he watched the flashes from the smoking ship, it came back to him. He slowly worked the Aldis light handle to send a return message of acknowledgment, telling them that they were an American submarine and asking what the trawler needed.

Johnson grabbed a pencil and slowly wrote out the reply as the operator over there kindly matched Brad's slow sending rate. "Fire out. 4 feet water in engine room. Aground. 10 injured. Burns, wounds. 5 dead. Need assistance with wounded."

The young Ensign read and then reread the cryptic return message. This suddenly made the war very real to him. It was no longer simply a gallant adventure. People were hurt and dying right over there.

He blinkered back, "Sending boat. Be ready to transport wounded. Convoy Command notified."

Brewster and Johnson carefully maneuvered the *S-54* to get as close to the stranded trawler as they safely could without running themselves aground. They managed to drop the anchor with less than a fathom of water under the bow and were only a hundred yards from the stranded Brit trawler.

It took a few more minutes to get the inflatable boat on deck, pump it full of air, and be ready to ferry men back and forth to the trawler. The first load of wounded sailors was just being hauled aboard when Clark Manson stuck his head through the bridge hatch.

"Skipper, Brit Convoy Command Iceland says that they scrambled a Short Sunderland. They're saying three hours for it to get here." Manson then nodded over to the other vessel on the shoreline. "Skipper, did you take a look over at the U-boat?"

Brewster shook his head. "No, I've been busy with the Brits. Why?"

"They're forming up on the beach," Manson said. "I think they're figurin' on surrendering."

Brewster stood up, took his binoculars, and scanned the far beach. It was less than a thousand yards across the choppy waters to where the German U-boat lay, still smoking. It appeared that a couple of dozen sailors stood in ranks further up the beach.

"I don't suppose you speak German, Brad?" he asked.

Johnson quipped, "*Nein, Herr Kapitaine.*"

Brewster shook his head at the Ensign's brashness. "Well, signal them in English to lay down any weapons," he ordered. "Tell them they're prisoners of war and will be picked up shortly."

Brewster turned back to Manson. "XO, see if we can get *S-52*." He had to speak louder because of the clacking of the Aldis lamp as Johnson sent the message. "They can probably get here as soon as that flying boat can. If we need to ferry all these Brits and the Germans back to Iceland, it's going to get real crowded."

It took almost an hour to bring all the injured members of the British crew over to the *S-54* and to get them stabilized below decks. The last group had just been lowered down when Clark Manson again popped his head through the bridge hatch. "Skipper, the Captain of the *Blackthorn* was in that last load," the XO reported. "He's in your stateroom. Passed out. The man is drunker than a South Alabama skunk."

Brewster shook his head in disbelief. Then he glanced over at the Germans, hunkered down on the beach, just above the highwater line. With the inflatable raft now available, it was time to do something about them.

"Mr. Johnson, take the COB and a couple of men over to take charge of the Germans. If any of them speak English, explain to them that they are now prisoners of war and that a ship is on the way to haul them all to Iceland. Make them understand somehow. And make sure that none of them is armed. Don't allow any of them back aboard that U-boat. There might be valuable intel on it. And just like us, they would have orders to burn what they could."

Brad Johnson nodded, then he asked, "Skipper, can we even make them POWs? We aren't at war with Germany. At least not yet."

"Brad, I'll let the smart lawyers figure that one out," Brewster said with a wry chuckle. "Right now, I just want them under guard and not shooting at us. Think you can handle that?"

Johnson promptly answered, "Yes, sir!" He climbed down off the bridge onto the main deck where the COB waited with a couple of heavily armed sailors. It only took a few minutes to paddle over to where the Germans casually lounged on the shore. They obviously recognized their situation.

The U-boat commander identified his boat as the *U-102*. He said that they were surrendering and demanded to be treated as prisoners of war as provided by the Geneva Convention. Johnson answered that as long as the submariners were peaceful, they would be well treated. The *U-102* crew was docile and cooperative, content to sit and wait for rescue, even if that meant spending a while—including the rest of any possible war—in a POW camp.

It was late afternoon before the steel-gray Royal Air Force flying boat kissed down in the open waters at the fiord's mouth. It was still taxiing toward the anchored US submarine when the *S-52* steamed over the horizon to the south. The *Flying Fish*, her boilers at least temporarily repaired, arrived shortly afterward. The sun was falling behind the bulk of the mountainous coast of Greenland to the west when the last of the crew members were loaded aboard the various transports. The flyboat ferried the more seriously injured back to Iceland while the rest of the two crews—trawler and U-boat—were carried by the odd little flotilla of three Great War relics: two American *S*-boats and a British coal-fueled steam sloop.

∞

Commander Ollie Oglethorpe, his head wreathed in the inevitable cloud of pipe smoke, stuck his head through the door to the "Tree of Knowledge" and yelled to Stan Ward.

"Stan, my boy, come in here. We have cause to celebrate. Your guess was right. Our boys ended up capturing the U-boat that was supplying the weather station you predicted. They rescued the crew of a Brit ship at the same time. The cast of characters are heading to Iceland as we speak. Looks like the Royal Marines are going in to deal with the Nazi weather guessers and make sure they go dark. The Royal Navy is sending a Bravo Zulu all around."

Ward was in the process of drafting an intel message. That was all good news, but was his boss actually inviting him back into the forbidden room, the place where the secrets were really held? Stan's clearance still did not allow him such access.

"Come on, boy," Oglethorpe cajoled. "It's time you see what we really do here and for you to earn your keep and help out." He impatiently waved the Ensign through the door. "And by the way, you are out of uniform."

Ward stared at Oglethorpe. He was wearing an old knit sweater over a plaid shirt, corduroy slacks, and slippers. Stan had to stifle a laugh at the incongruity of the Commander's statement.

But now Oglethorpe fished in his sweater pocket and pulled out a small box. He flipped it to Ward and said, "Here, put these on. Your promotion and clearance both came through this morning. Congratulations, Lieutenant Ward."

The box contained the silver bars of a Lieutenant junior grade. He wanted to immediately call Karen and let her know the good news, but the Commander was waving him on into the adjacent room.

Now legal, Ward stepped through the forbidden door to find himself in a room that was maybe half the size of the intelligence center he had just left. The far wall was a mass of radio receivers, dials glowing yellow. A half dozen operators sat in front of the equipment, wearing headphones, busily scribbling on pads of paper. Another dozen people sat at desks strewn around the room. They were pecking away at really odd-looking typewriters. He glanced at Commander Oglethorpe for an explanation.

"Stan, what we have here is our window into Nazi Admiral Dönitz's operation." He pointed over at the far wall. "We are intercepting the radio messages he sends out to his U-boats. The guy is really talkative, so we have a lot of traffic to intercept." He waved at the cluster of desks. "These men are trying to decipher the messages. The Germans use something we call the Enigma code. A couple of Polish mathematicians figured out the basics back in the early '30s but the Germans have gotten a lot more sophisticated since then. Those devices you see there are our crude version of an Enigma machine."

"So, we're reading their mail?" Ward asked enthusiastically.

Oglethorpe pondered his answer for a bit. "Not nearly what we can do with the Japs and their code. From the Krauts, well, maybe ten percent of it, but usually only after we've played with it for a couple of weeks, and by then, it's old news. The Brits are doing better than us, but they're not sharing. They don't want to let slip what little they can do, or the Nazis would change the code in a New York minute.

"Lots of high-level math involved, way above what you or I would understand. What we really need is an operational machine, and to be sure the Germans don't know we have it. Then we'd be eavesdropping on the U-boat party line pretty near real time." He shook his head sadly. "We were hoping that we would get one from that U-boat, but reports are that it was pretty much gutted by the explosions and fire. And the crew took a sledgehammer to it just to finish it off."

Stan Ward looked around the busy room. He instinctively knew that this work was very important. Intelligence analysis coming out of this basement could shorten the war for the Brits. It might even keep America out of the war. He was thrilled to be a part of it.

"What can I do to help the cause?" he blurted out.

Oglethorpe smiled. It was exactly the reaction he expected from the eager Ensign-now-Lieutenant. "I need help taking the bits and pieces to put together the puzzle. You've already shown a bit of talent for that. We're going to really put it to work. But I need to warn you. It is highly likely no one will ever know what you do here, no matter how spectacular and history-changing it might be. If you're looking for glory, or to climb the career ladder, this basement is not the place. You won't even be able to tell that young wife of yours what you do. Ever."

∞

The twinkling band of lights popped above the dark horizon like a long string of white pearls. Reykjavik was up ahead, promising a calm, quiet berthing and, even better, fresh food. But first, they had to get themselves into port. The route was straightforward enough, but both the American submarines were down to the last few drops of their fuel supplies. It was going to be touch and go to get alongside before the tanks ran completely dry. Otherwise, they would have to suffer the ignominy of being towed into port.

Brad Johnson carefully steered the *S-54* in the wake of the *Flying Fish* as the Royal Navy sloop skirted around the north side of Akurey Island. The small, uninhabited bit of land was just a dark mass off to starboard, guarding the western approach to Reykjavik harbor. The lighthouse at the north end of Engey Island marked the little convoy's turn down that piece of land's west side. Lights blinked at them from the windows of a small cluster of houses huddled just back from the island's shore, a greeting to the seafarers as they headed south toward the harbor.

The submarine slowed as it passed between the moles protecting the inner harbor. Johnson watched as the *Flying Fish* peeled off to tie up at the very end of the Nordurgardur Wharf. He knew her crew was even more pleased to have made the voyage from Greenland, pumping water the whole way, and hoping repairs to the vessel's engines held up. Brad steered the *S-54* to berth outboard of an old American four-stack destroyer, the USS *Craven*, moored to the Grandabryggja. The *Craven* was one of fifty obsolete US destroyers that were in the process of being turned over to the Royal Navy, much to the dismay of some in the US government who wanted to maintain strict neutrality and stay out of a "European war." Johnson could see several other old four-stackers in Reykjavik's inner harbor undergoing the transfer. Several brand-new 1500-ton US destroyers —nicknamed "gold-plated" by old destroyer men because of their "overly lavish facilities"—were mixed in with British warships. They were there to refuel and resupply before heading back out for clandestine convoy escort duty. Five of them, all of the new *Sims*-class, were nested alongside at the Midbakki Wharf. For an out-of-the-way island in the middle of the North Atlantic, the harbor was certainly crowded and busy.

The *S-52* followed Johnson's sub into port and moored outboard. Johnson was amazed that a fuel barge immediately pulled up alongside and began offloading diesel fuel to both submarines, even though it was well past midnight. Johnson breathed a sigh of relief as the precious diesel fuel flowed into the near-empty tanks. But he wondered what the hurry was.

Clark Manson climbed up through the bridge hatch. He surveyed the crowded harbor, watching various small craft as they scuttled back and forth across the oily water.

"Rush hour in Reykjavik," he noted, then turned to Johnson. "Brad, as soon as you have full fuel load, cast off the fuel barge. There should be a barge with stores showing up at 0400. Work with the COB for a stores loading party to hurry and get the groceries on board and stowed. Skipper and I are headed over to Convoy Command Iceland to debrief our little adventure. I expect we are going to get our orders, too. Make sure the boat is ready to get underway by noon."

"No shore liberty?" Johnson asked, surprised by the very quick turnaround.

Manson shook his head. "Not this time. Except for official business, all hands are restricted to the ship. Orders from the top. Guess someone is worried about anything leaking from our little adventure before they have a chance to sweep it all under the carpet. Never happened, right?"

Johnson grimaced. This "what just happened never happened" stuff was getting old. And he was really looking forward to a cold beer. And something hot and fresh to chew on. That was not going to happen.

Manson and Brewster disappeared up the brow, off the submarine and onto the *Craven*, and then out of sight, down the other side of the old ship. Johnson got a quick glimpse of the pair, along with the CO and XO from the *S-52*, as they strolled down the pier in the direction of an old brick warehouse.

It was well past noon when the two senior officers stepped back onto the deck of the *S-54*. Brewster immediately called all the officers into the wardroom.

"Gentlemen, it's time to head west." The Skipper's words were met with cheers. Going home was much better than a day of liberty in Iceland. "We're getting an escort back as far as Argentia, Newfoundland. Those *Sims*-class tin cans are heading on back to help escort the next eastbound convoy. They are going to give us a head start and meet us down by Cape

Farewell. From there, they'll give us safe passage across the shipping lanes. Or as best they can. There's plenty of German subs cruising around out there."

Brewster paused for a second and then looked down the table, directly at Ensign Brad Johnson. "Brad," he said, "You are staying here for a bit. The Brits are sending a squad of Royal Marines into that fiord on one of their trawlers. They asked for someone who was familiar with the water, right up to the lagoon. That would be either me or you. Guess which one of us drew the short straw." Brewster smiled. "They are getting underway tomorrow, so you get a night's liberty in scenic downtown Reykjavik, then a pleasure cruise to Greenland and back. The Brits promise they'll get you home on the next westbound destroyer."

"That's what I get for asking the XO about liberty," Johnson groused.

Clark Manson threw up his arms, laughed, and exclaimed, "Another satisfied customer!"

An hour later the *S-54* followed the *S-52* out of the harbor and through the breakwater. From there, the two submarines circled up around Engey and Akurey Islands before turning to the southwest and toward the southern tip of Greenland.

Brad Johnson stood on the pier and watched them go until they were out of sight.

13

First Sea Lord Roger Whittaker was experiencing difficulties with the telephone connection. The static on the transatlantic line made conversation difficult. Nuanced conversation was almost impossible. He found himself shouting out every phrase and then repeating it several times. Admiral Devin Johnson, on the other end of the call in the USA, was required to do the same thing. Whittaker was almost to the point of just writing everything in a letter and then dispatching a courier across the Atlantic to hand-deliver the crucial message. Only the urgency and delicacy of what really needed to be a real-time conversation prevented him from doing just that. And the fact that a letter would leave a record of the conversation.

"Devin, the Prime Minister has asked that you carry this message directly to Secretary Edison," Whittaker shouted. "He can pass this on to President Roosevelt or take action himself, as he deems appropriate. It is a matter that must be kept most secret and absolutely off the record."

There was another burst of scratchy static and then Johnson shouted back, "I understand. What is the message?"

Whittaker was again questioning the wisdom of his decision to call. Maybe he should have climbed aboard an aircraft and made the trip. But with things changing so rapidly on the home front, it would have been inadvisable to be away for a week. Still, it was so devilishly difficult to convey the proper nuances when one had to shout to be heard. "As you know, we are currently engaged in two major battles. Quite frankly, the outcome of both is seriously in question. Herr Goering's Luftwaffe blitz attacks have proven devastating to our people. They are driving our economy into the ground and general morale is buried deeply in the peat bogs already, I fear. There is a real possibility of this aerial assault forcing the government to explore a negotiated peace, even over Winston's very strong objections."

Sir Roger paused to let that news sink in. Or at least be acknowledged. A negotiated peace was a diplomatic subterfuge for what would really be a surrender. Without the threat of Britain, the Third Reich would be virtually unchallenged from the West and would soon control most of the European continent. It was not common knowledge, but Lord Halifax, from his seat as British Foreign Minister, had already sent feelers out through diplomatic channels to explore a peace agreement with Hitler.

"That is indeed distressing news," Devin Johnson finally shouted back. But then, midway through his sentence, the line suddenly cleared so that his reply blasted through Whittaker's handset. In a more moderate tone, the Admiral continued. "With the upcoming Presidential election over here and the strong isolationist sentiment in parts of this country—even our national hero Lindbergh is leading rallies opposing involvement in another European war—the President is going to be very constrained in what action he can take. At least publicly. So, what are you asking of us, Roger?"

The First Sea Lord answered, "Winston quite understands the realities of your election cycle and political pressure. As to the blitz, there is not much that America can do but keep us supplied with bullets and fuel. But that brings us to the real quandary and the second major battle I have mentioned. Herr Dönitz's U-boats are bleeding us dry. We need assistance there. Even those destroyers that you so kindly 'lent' us are not nearly enough against the submarines."

Whittaker paused for a long moment. The line thankfully remained clear. "But you are seeking specifics. Winston is asking that your Navy takes over escort duty west of forty-five degrees west longitude. Maybe you could do this under the guise of protecting neutral rights or some such."

Again, Sir Roger paused for a stretch, letting his words sink in. Johnson finally said, "Go on."

"Devin, we must take the fight to the U-boats. Simply making shooting galleries of our convoys is tantamount to admitting defeat. We cannot go on much longer taking the losses we are taking with no resistance shown to the Reich. We need to fight back, to sink U-boats. We *must* sink U-boats. The RAF's Coastal Command simply doesn't have the long-range aircraft necessary to keep up a viable search of the North Atlantic and the Royal Navy lacks other assets. We need a threat to really keep the U-boat commanders worried. To demonstrate we are now fighting back."

"What did you have in mind?" Devin replied.

"Submarines," Sir Roger shot back at once. "A whole lot of submarines patrolling a corridor between twenty-five west and forty-five west, from Greenland as far south as Newfoundland. Sort of a manned minefield that the U-boats have to negotiate. You could station them out of Argentia, Newfoundland. It's both convenient and out of the way. Someplace where no one would ask any questions, and I doubt even the Nazis have bothered to place spies."

Devin Johnson did some quick mental calculations, and gasped. "But, Sir Roger, that's six hundred thousand square miles. Do you have any concept of how many submarines that would require?"

Roger Whittaker had obviously considered this problem. He had an answer ready. "Devin, getting into the Germans' minds and making them consider the problem is a win of sorts. The convoys have drawn them into a much smaller area like fish to bait. Just a few submarines showing up and doing damage would cause great heartburn to the *Kriegsmarine*, who have operated thus far mostly unchallenged. Maybe a squadron or two would accomplish our goal. It would be like planting a couple of mines and then claiming the whole area is mined. Everyone will treat the area as mined until they expend much time and effort to prove otherwise. And that could provide us with the distraction we need to improve our success rate. Frankly, we have no other answer unless you there in the colonies agree to provide much more robust surface and aircraft escort for our convoys. And you and I both know that is not likely in the current political climate over there."

The telephone line remained static-free with only a slight hum as Johnson pondered the British Sea Lord's plea. When he finally responded, his words were crystal clear.

"Let me pass this up to the Secretary and see what I can do," Admiral Johnson said.

"That's all I can ask." Whittaker replied.

∞

Ensign Brad Johnson sat on a bollard and watched his submarine, the *S-54*, follow the *S-52* through the breakwater and out toward the North Atlantic. For some reason, he felt pangs of loneliness as he watched the hull and sail of his boat disappear into the sunset. He stood and watched until she was gone, did his best to shake off the melancholic feeling, then ambled down the wharf to the old stone warehouse. That was where his Skipper had told him to go, along with the time to arrive there, but nothing else.

Stepping through the big oaken door, Johnson found himself immediately confronted by a middle-aged, slightly dowdy woman in a WREN uniform. "Good day to ya, sir. You must be the American Ensign," the WREN said.

Johnson nodded. "I must be."

"I'm Chief McGinnis," she continued without a pause. "Welcome to the Operation Center for Convoy Command Iceland. I understand that you are here for Operation North Wind."

"Huh?" was all Johnson could say. He was confused. He had never heard of anything called Operation North Wind, let alone that he was to be a part of it.

"Just follow me," the officious Chief ordered and promptly marched off down a long hallway. "They are all in the briefing room, waiting for you. Get a leg on now, sir. We need to get this brief down so the boys can get a pint this evening. Underway is at dawn, you know."

Johnson knew nothing of a sun-up underway, but he remained quiet as the Chief herded him into a small conference room filled with British officers, all smoking, all drinking tea, all talking. He noticed at once that he was the only person in the room wearing an American uniform.

A dapper officer at the far end rapped the table with a pointer for attention. The room quieted at once and those still standing grabbed seats. Brad found one. At the head of the long conference table.

"I say," the officer started. "I see our Yank has honored us with his presence. What say we begin. I'm Captain Reginald Hiscouth of His Majesty's Marines. I will be in charge of this little caper."

Caper? Johnson tried to maintain a noncommittal expression.

Pointing to the Royal Navy Officer sitting beside him, Hiscouth went on. "This is Lieutenant Jamison Cochrane, who will be commanding the trawler *Chestnut*. The bloke next to him is Sublieutenant Geoff Chandler, late of the *Blackthorn*. Mr. Chandler was on the bridge of the *Blackthorn*, directing the first phase of this battle. He will be helping us with the second phase, to take out the Hun weather station."

Swinging his pointer toward Johnson, he added, "And the Yank is Ensign Bradley Johnson of the American submarine *S-54*. He took his submarine into and out of that fiord, so he knows the waters far better than we. Now, let's get down to briefing. I, for one, have a powerful thirst and the bar will not be open until the briefing is done."

Johnson was sitting next to Geoff Chandler. The last time the two had spoken was during the rescue effort from the grounded and burning trawler. Except for a scratch on his forehead, he looked none the worse for that experience. The two shook hands and then listened as Captain Hiscouth addressed a chart of the fiord on the wall of the room. But the map did not look at all like Johnson remembered those waters. Or how he had depicted them on his hand-drawn map. He listened for a few minutes before raising a hand to interrupt. It took a few minutes for him to redraw the twisting, turning channel as it snaked between the near-vertical walls of the fiord, until it looked more like he remembered. Then he explained how it ended in a large lagoon with a small, stony beach that sloped up to a hilltop on the western horizon with a clear pathway leading upward.

When Johnson completed his input, the trawler Skipper smiled and nodded toward Johnson. "I guess we can see now why you were invited along. Welcome aboard. Now, let's go find a pint."

"Capital idea, old boy!" Hiscouth said. "We will brief on a specific plan while en route. At the moment, such folderol would only interfere with adequate libation, am I right?"

The morning sky was still dark when Brad Johnson stepped onboard the Royal Navy Trawler *Chestnut*. He found the deck crowded with a couple of dozen Royal Marines in full combat gear, along with stacks of their equipment. Geoff Chandler intercepted him and guided Johnson to the trawler's small wardroom. They each grabbed a cup of coffee and clambered up to the little ship's open bridge to await the planned underway. The sun was just rising in the east as the *Chestnut* eased out into open water.

At eight knots, it was an uneventful three-day cruise to the west/southwest, down to the fiord's mouth. The wreckage of the blackened, charred *Blackthorn* and *U-102* still marked the entrance to the fiord. The crew stood silently at attention as the little trawler cruised by the wreckage. Chandler snapped off a salute to his old ship and the shipmates who had died there.

As they passed, everyone looked for signs that anyone else had been there since the shootout. There were none. Had the Germans missed the *U-102*? Were they anticipating a raid on the weather station? Was an ambush awaiting them once they entered the tight waterway?

The *Chestnut* slowly made its way up the narrow twisting channel. To Brad, the granite cliffs somehow did not seem nearly as high or foreboding from the deck of the warship as they had while gazing up through *S-54*'s periscope. It was near midday when the trawler made its final turn into the lagoon. They anchored just off the rocky beach that Johnson remembered. Skid marks in the dirt and rocks from where the Germans had dragged their boats were still visible.

The Marines were rigging out their boats and stowing their gear when Reginald Hiscouth stepped up to the bridge. Seeing Chandler and Johnson avidly watching his men at work, Hiscouth asked, "Say, would you two like to accompany us? See this through to the end, as it were?" When the two jumped at the chance, he produced a pair of Webley Service Revolvers and holsters. "Here, these may prove useful. Go down and have the Colour Sergeant issue you some combat togs. Just try to keep your head down and out of the way. We have no idea if or what kind of reception they might have for visitors."

The boats made the short paddle across the water from the *Chestnut* to the stony beach. They quickly found where the Germans were stowing their inflatable boats and could see the well-worn path up the steep hill behind the beach. Johnson and Chandler followed the Marines up the hill but at some distance behind.

Cresting the hill, they could then see the campsite, nestled in the shadow of a high, rocky escarpment that pretty much protected it from view from all directions except directly overhead. With the wave of a hand, Hiscouth deployed his Marines out to encircle the camp. The encompassment was almost complete when someone in the camp spotted the Marines and yelled the alarm.

A shot rang out. Then a lot of guttural shouting as a dozen or more Germans piled out of the tents, grabbed their rifles, and began firing blindly up toward the ridgeline.

The Marines returned fire with their .303 Lee–Enfields. The stutter from Hiscouth's and the Colour Sergeant's Sten guns echoed off the slopes, adding to the deafening cacophony. Then their gunner opened up with his Bren light machine gun. The gas-operated weapon ripped apart anything in the campsite that its bullets hit. In a matter of minutes, the Germans stopped shooting. A white flag materialized. It was only a towel tied to a short pole of some type, but it effectively signaled that the fight was over.

The Marines and sailors spent the rest of that day and most of the next tending to the few wounded meteorologists, herding the prisoners aboard the *Chestnut*, and searching for anything of intelligence value.

The *Chestnut* arrived back in Reykjavik just as an American destroyer was getting underway for a trip west to the States. Brad Johnson had just enough time to say goodbye to Geoff Chandler before jumping onboard the tin can for a ride to a spot much closer to home.

14

A polar jet stream shoved a river of frigid Arctic air down from the top of the world, through the Davis Strait, and out over the Labrador Sea. There, it pushed the freezing-cold Labrador Current into the wintertime North Atlantic. Once over the deep waters east of Newfoundland, the icy Arctic air slammed head-on into the warm atmosphere hovering above the Gulf Stream. The resulting maelstrom churned the wind to hurricane strength. Hundred-mile-an-hour winds pushed waves to sixty and seventy feet high before ripping off their peaks into wind-driven blasts of stinging spume. Nature's massive heat engine gained intensity while it spread over the ocean all the way from the shores of Canada to the mid-Atlantic ridge.

Convoy OB-23, outbound from Liverpool and destined for Halifax, consisting of thirty-seven freighters and tankers in ballast, was caught directly in the path of the raging winter storm. With waves crashing high over the cargo ships, threatening to swamp them, and winds howling with such force that it was hazardous for anyone to go on deck, the convoy commander faced a difficult choice. Either they could drive ahead into the teeth of the storm's fury, or he could direct them south to try to skirt its slightly less volatile edge. But that would send the convoy directly into the path of a U-boat wolfpack known to be prowling in the mid-Atlantic, waiting to pounce on any ship that might be trying to escape the storm.

Faced with this quandary, the commander rolled the dice and chose to stay on course, plowing through the foul weather, hoping the storm might abate or they would make it through.

A hundred miles to the north of Convoy OB-23, five brand-new American *Sims*-class destroyers and two elderly *S*-class submarines were doing their best to ride out the same dangerous weather.

Fred Wurster, strapped down on the bridge of *S-52*, gritted his teeth and braced himself for another bitter, cold baptism. A towering wave raced up the submarine's bow, first lifting the vessel up and then driving it underwater, with the boat completely swallowed up by the mountainous wave's front wall. Wurster prayed that his canvas harness would keep him tied to the submarine as the wave crashed over the bridge fairwater with unbelievable force. He took a deep breath just before going under, grabbed a stanchion, and held on with all the strength he could muster. There seemed no end to the dunking. He was just beginning to wonder if he would ever see daylight or sky again—or draw an uninterrupted breath—when the boat abruptly popped up high and out of the wave.

Wurster looked up to the periscope shears to check on his pair of lookouts. The sailor on the port side was dangling from his safety harness, sputtering, coughing, and yelling for help. The starboard lookout was doing his best to pull his shipmate back aboard and get re-strapped in before another wave finished the job on him.

Wurster scanned the horizon. Or at least the tiny sliver of it that was not blocked by the heavy seas piled up in all directions. There was no sign of the *S-54* or any of the destroyers. It appeared *S-52* had this dangerous, storm-tossed patch of ocean all to herself.

Wurster was reaching for the phone to tell the XO that it was not safe up on the bridge, but that was when the next wave swept over them. A wave even larger than the last. The world suddenly got very dark and very cold. Wurster had no chance to suck in a deep breath of air before he was again under water. His ears were ringing, his heart pounding wildly. Would they ever pop back up to the surface?

Lungs searing, he was at the point of giving up and breathing in seawater when the bridge finally emerged into meager daylight. The Ensign gasped for breath as he looked up to again check on the lookouts.

No one was there. The periscope shears were a mass of tangled wreckage but no sign of the two young sailors.

"Man overboard!" Wurster yelled into the 1MC, fighting off panic. "Both lookouts overboard! All stop!"

The boat slid to a halt as Wurster stood high and searched the heaving sea for any sign of the two men. Nothing out there but gray-clouded skies and roiling, darker-gray seas.

"Right full rudder, ahead full," Wurster ordered, hoping that was the right command to give. The only thing he could think to do was a Williamson turn to reverse course back down the track they had just come. Maybe they could still find the two sailors before the cold seawater claimed them.

"Passing two-nine-zero, no ordered course," the helmsman called out. "Passing three-zero-zero."

The Williamson turn was a maneuver that turned the ship around 180 degrees and placed it right back down its former track but in the opposite direction. The theory was the boat could just steam back down the track until they found the missing men. First the ship was turned sixty degrees in one direction with a full rudder. Then the helm shifted the rudder to a full rudder on the other side. When the boat had swung around to where it was twenty degrees from the reciprocal of the old course, the rudder was put amidships. Then they would slide right down the old track. That was the theory, anyway. The storm was determined to not make it an easy operation.

Fred Wurster had just shifted the rudder to left full when the CO, Don Gorman, climbed up to the bridge and hastily tied his safety harness. As he worked, he asked Wurster, "Any sign of them?"

"No sir," Fred called out over the wind. "One minute we had just come out of a wave. They were both up there. Then we got driven under again. When we came up, they were gone."

Wurster looked at the compass card. It was coming up on one-one-zero, twenty degrees off the zero-nine-zero course that he wanted. "Rudder amidships."

Gorman had his binoculars to his eyes, intently scanning the ferocious seas dead ahead. Nothing. Nothing out there.

"Bridge," the XO's voice blasted over the speaker. "We see something on the search scope. One point off the starboard bow. Maybe five hundred yards."

The search scope offered more elevation and the benefit of magnification.

"I see him!" Gorman yelled and pointed. "Come to all stop!"

The *S-52* slid forward, then came to a shaky stop only ten yards from one of the sailors. The man was just floating on his back in his kapok, his face out of the water. But he showed no signs of life.

"Port ahead one-third, starboard back one-third," Gorman ordered, skillfully twisting the sub to put the sailor on the lee and to slide over closer.

"Can you grab him, Fred?" Gorman asked. "No time to get people topside and we'd probably end up with more people in the water."

"I'll try," Wurster replied with a gulp. He would have to untie his harness. Climb down onto the deck. Tie back in. Then he would have to reach over while maintaining his balance and try to grab the sailor, all before they got inundated by another wave.

On his first try, Wurster failed to reach the inert sailor. His arms were simply not long enough. No grappling hook or other tool nearby, either. His only option to reach the lookout would be to climb down over the side, all the while braced for a body slam of water.

Finally, he was able to grab a handful of hair. And not let go. It took every ounce of strength that he could summon to lug the man up against the hull and then grab him under the arms and pull him up and onto the deck.

Gorman helped lift the man up to the bridge and then down through the hatch just as another angry wave crashed over them. It slapped the almost motionless sub around so that it was now broadside to the waves, a position that threatened to capsize them with the next wave.

"Ahead two-thirds," Gorman ordered as he struggled down the ladder into the conning tower, icy seawater cascading down on top of them. "Steady course zero-nine-zero."

With both Gorman and Wurster back up and strapped in on the bridge, they spent another hour fruitlessly searching for the remaining lookout.

Finally, reluctantly, they had to admit that all hope was lost. No one could have survived more than a few minutes in such cold water, let alone more than an hour. With the decision made, they headed back west and submerged to at least get under the worst of the effects of the storm.

They had just gone under when Doc Jones stepped into the control room. Gorman looked up from the chart table where he had been working, already writing a narrative of the man-overboard casualty.

"How is he, Doc?"

The corpsman stubbed out his cigarette and grimly reported, "Seaman Grudson's alive, sir. Breathing. Still unconscious. I'm doing all I can to get him warmed back up. Blankets, hot water bottles. Everything I can think of to bring his body temperature up. Another couple of minutes in that water, and he'd be gone for sure."

Jones lit another cigarette and gave Fred Wurster an appreciative nod. "I expect when he comes around, we're going to find out he has more injuries. Probably some broken ribs and maybe a busted arm. But for right now, we can only pray that he survives the hypothermia."

Gorman nodded. "Just keep him alive, Doc. We've still got four days until we can pull into port."

Jones answered, "I'll do my best, sir. I hope it's enough. See, I've never lost a man before."

"Me neither, Doc," the Skipper admitted. "Now, maybe two of 'em the same day? Almost feels like we're at war or something."

∞

Dawn was breaking on a dreary day when Convoy OB-23 finally emerged from the winter storm and steamed into welcome, calming seas. Bits of seaweed floated on the waters amid all the other debris strewn on the surface, flotsam left from previous U-boat battles, reminders of ships lost and sailors drowned in their efforts to feed the British war effort.

For OB-23, the journey was almost completed. The safety of Halifax was only two days away to the west. It promised a brief, calm respite before the ships were quickly reloaded and pointed back across the ocean toward the British Isles.

But Convoy OB-23 was not alone. A lookout on the German Type VII-C U-boat *U-23* spotted the nautical parade as it steamed over the horizon. The U-boat Commander, *Oberleutnant* Helmut Schmiel, promptly dived his submarine and maneuvered until he was in a position just ahead of the approaching convoy and a kilometer off his best guess of its track. He watched intently through his periscope and carefully counted the ships. He could see twenty vessels, a mixture of freighters and tankers, in four columns, plus half a dozen escorts circling like so many sheepdogs protecting the flock from stalking wolves. Schmiel knew that there could easily be more ships still over the horizon yet. But he did not have time to devote to counting them all. There were plenty enough targets visible to deserve his attention.

His primary job was to get safely off the convoy's track and radio back to U-Boat Command in Germany with details of what he had found steaming out of the storm. Headquarters would vector the nearest wolfpack to intercept this convoy before it reached its intended port, likely Halifax. Schmiel and *U-23* would continue to track the convoy from well off to the side, promptly informing U-Boat Command of any changes in course or speed. And then to be close enough to pick off stragglers once the wolfpack attack had done its damage.

Ahead and to the south, gray steel hunters soon emerged from the deep and raced ahead toward their flock of targets. Six wolves ran to intercept the convoy just after sunset. A nighttime surface attack was usually their best tactic. Once the sun was eclipsed by the horizon, darkness hid the killers from the escorts, making the attacks easier and less risky. The U-boats formed a rough line across the convoy's estimated track to wait. When OB-23 steamed into view, they were in place and ready.

The boats surfaced out ahead of the clustered convoy and then made individual slashing surface attacks, launching their torpedoes as they sped between and among the helpless merchant ships. Soon, the night was illuminated by exploding, burning ships. Gunfire from the freighters and escorts zipped off aimlessly. Flares and star-shells arced up into the black sky to illuminate the dark night and hopefully to allow them to see their attackers. But even if they did, there was no way to fix their aim on the darting, ducking U-boats.

In all, the attack took less than an hour. By then, ten ships were burning and sinking. The carefully ordered convoy had broken down into a hopeless, disorganized gaggle of ships steaming about crazily in every direction. In their panicked attempts to avoid torpedoes, two of the cargo vessels collided, a tanker T-boning a freighter and nearly cutting it in half. The escorts raced around, randomly dropping depth charges in a desperate attempt to scare off the German sea wolves.

Helmut Schmiel calmly watched the battle from the bridge of the *U-23*, a couple of kilometers to the northeast, as if enjoying a film at the cinema back in his hometown of Hamburg. Judging from the fires and explosions he observed, it was easy to see that the attack was a success. Several of the *Kommandants* would be claiming considerable tonnage on this action, upping their scores, impressing U-boat Supreme Commander Karl Dönitz. There might even be an Iron Cross or two available for the top claimants. Schmiel had already decided he needed to get *U-23* involved or all he would receive for his trouble would be a "thank you" from the successful warriors for spotting the convoy in the first place.

He watched as one of the merchants obligingly steamed in his direction. The cargo ship belched black smoke and kicked up a broad, foamy, churning wake in its panicked drive for safety. That meant getting as far away from its sinking sisters as it could. Schmiel calmly watched and waited until the freighter was only nine hundred meters away and was presenting nearly a broadside aspect. A fat, unsuspecting sheep. When fired, the German sub's two G7a compressed air torpedoes left arrow-straight white wakes pointing directly back at his vessel. But it did not matter. In the chaos, no one on the freighter was looking anyway.

The first torpedo hit just under the forward king post. The second erupted directly beneath the ship's bridge. Schmiel watched as the burning ship slowed until it was dead in the water. The frantic crew tried to lower lifeboats to escape the doomed vessel. The German Skipper watched as one of the lifeboats jammed in its davits. The boat crashed bow-first into the water before bobbing back up, capsized. Sailors struggled to climb up onto the inverted boat.

Schmiel could only shake his head. There was nothing he could do except grumble about the incompetence he was witnessing.

He was just ordering his gun crew on deck to put the freighter out of its misery when the ship suddenly made its final, roaring plunge into the deep, sucking down a couple of nearby loaded lifeboats with it.

Helmut Schmiel shrugged, then turned the *U-23* back toward the remnants of the convoy to see if he could find another straggler to add to his list of claimed tonnage.

∞

In the darkness, sea smoke drifted above the glass-smooth, freezing-cold waters of Placentia Bay. A waning gibbous moon hung low on the western horizon as the little group of American warships rounded Point Lance, officially leaving the Atlantic and entering the bay.

The five new *Sims*-class destroyers happily raced out ahead, vying for the best anchorages in the harbor at Argentia. It was Christmas morning. Liberty lured the cold, weary sailors. That was the case even if shore leave was only to be in a tiny, remote fishing village in Newfoundland. The two slower *S*-class submarines had to be patient, though, plodding along, well astern of the sleek greyhounds.

The anchor lights from a dozen ships, waiting to form up for the next eastbound convoy, dotted the bay's wide expanse. Hardy local fishermen, oblivious to the cold or the holiday, were manning little fishing boats while out tending their cod traps. Lights from the windows of a few houses dotting the nearby hilly coastline to the east confirmed that a few more hardworking Newfoundlanders were also up early, waiting for their men to return with the day's catch in time for Christmas dinner.

On the bridge of *S-52*, Fred Wurster shivered, slapped his gloved hands together, and hugged himself to try to get the blood circulating. The little bit of heat rising out of the open bridge hatch was a mere tease, doing nothing to keep him warm. They were not due in port for another four hours. That transit would be on the surface all the way. Wurster was sure that his fingers would freeze solid and fall off before then.

"Bridge, Control," the 7MC speaker blasted. "Captain to the bridge."

Fred was still reaching for the microphone to acknowledge when Don Gorman emerged up the bridge hatch. "Morning, Mr. Wurster, and Merry

Christmas," the Skipper happily greeted him, his breath a fog as he looked up at a star-studded sky. Then, eyes wide, he added, "Bit brisk out, ain't it?"

"Merry Christmas to you, too, Skipper. Where I'm from, they call this 'damn cold!'" Wurster responded. He picked up his coffee cup where it had been sitting on the bridge fairing and turned it upside down. Nothing came out. "Even my coffee's frozen solid. You're up and about a bit early, aren't you? We're four hours out."

"Just thought I'd enjoy some morning air before breakfast," Gorman answered. "I hear that Cookie has been hoarding the cinnamon and pecans and he's going to use the last of it for breakfast rolls this morning."

"Great," Wurster grumbled with no enthusiasm. "Those chow hounds in the wardroom will scarf them all down before I ever get relieved."

Gorman laughed. "Well, maybe I can have a plate sent up with a pot of hot coffee. How does that sound?"

"Like the best idea ever," Wurster answered with a bit more zeal. At the same time, he responded to a friendly wave from a fisherman in a dory just passing down their port side. "Could be worse. At least I'm not out trying to pull a living out of these waters," he said as the fishing boat disappeared astern. "Those guys gotta be tough."

"Well, we're going to get a chance to observe these tough guys a hell of a lot more," Gorman replied.

"What you mean?"

"Message on this morning's boards," the Skipper answered. "The entire squadron is in the process of moving up here. The *Beaver* dropped anchor in Argentia harbor yesterday. Our orders are to tie up to her. We're being deployed to Argentia. And for a while, I suspect."

The *Beaver* was a submarine tender. Her presence at this out-of-the-way port confirmed this was no week-or-two arrangement.

"You mean we're not refueling and going on back to New London?" Wurster was confused. He had been looking forward to seeing Ellie Morton, his nurse-in-training girlfriend that he had been missing mightily. He had hoped to be able to call her from Newfoundland so she could meet them at the pier when they finally got back home. He had even had thoughts of a New Year's Eve marriage proposal. Now the Skipper was telling him they were not going home after all.

"Yep," Gorman grunted. He gazed out at the calm waters and the mostly dark shoreline before finally saying, "And just to make it interesting, this deployment is secret. We can't tell anyone where we are or what we're doing. Not even that girlfriend of yours. Or my wife, for that matter." The CO could see the disappointed expression on the young officer's face. "You're right, Fred. Too damn cold up here. I'm going down to breakfast. And I will send up some cinnamon rolls and hot coffee."

Wurster managed a weak smile. "Thanks, Skipper." He paused a moment. "And Happy New Year, too."

∞

Stan and Karen Ward had settled into the routine of an old married couple. Stan was spending long hours at "the office," piecing together mysteries—some quite disturbing—at the intel center. At the same time, the sudden uptick in activity at the submarine base meant that Karen was kept busy at the hospital. Several weeks before Christmas, they had moved out of the rooming house and into a little cottage up on Long Cove Road. Several of the single nurses with whom she worked were renting a house just around the corner from them. That meant Karen could share a ride, saving a lot of mileage on the old Chevy. And the price of gasoline had soared to almost twenty cents a gallon.

But this was a special morning for the Wards. The couple were about to enjoy their first Christmas breakfast together as a married couple. Then they would splurge and make long-distance holiday calls to his family back in Colorado and hers in Kansas. It was not lost on either of them that had Stan been physically able to become a submariner, he would not have been here for this holiday. Two of his "*Sugar*-boat" buddies—Brad and Fred—were off to somewhere in the Atlantic and Trip MacLean had been abruptly ushered off to the Philippines by the Navy.

Karen poured the coffee and dished out the eggs. Stan was buttering his toast and did not even notice the odd smile on her face. Then Karen suddenly announced, "I'm late."

"Late for what?" He looked up, confused. "It's Christmas Day. You got the day off, right?"

"No, dear," she said very slowly, as if she were waiting for a light to come on in that usual bright-bulb brain of his. "I'm late."

"Huh?" He held the knife poised midair, a pat of butter balanced on its end.

She repeated herself one more time, with emphasis. "I'm *late*."

It then dawned on Ward what his wife was saying. "What? How? When?"

She smiled and kissed him on the forehead before she sat down at the little table across from him. "As to 'what' and 'how,' I expect it was the normal way," she said with a laugh. "I'm about three weeks late, so Lieutenant, Labor Day might really be labor day for us this year."

Ward set the butter knife down, eyes wide. "Wow!" was the only response he could muster. Then he jumped up, grabbed his wife, pulled her up, and enveloped her in his arms, then gave her a long, passionate kiss. "Wow! I'm going to be a daddy!"

15

It was an especially rough roller coaster ride. A bitter-cold winter wind howled down the ice-covered Davis Strait and gained strength as it whipped across the Labrador Sea. The winter of 1940–1941 was already proving to be the coldest in the history of Atlantic weather records, and 1941 was only a month old. There was still plenty of time to test the integrity of the bottom of the thermometer.

Even submerged at a hundred feet, the *S-54* submarine pitched and bucked in the heavy seas a hundred nautical miles south of Cape Farewell, Greenland. Stephen Brewster, the Skipper, and Clark Manson, the XO, huddled around the navigation plot in control, grabbing coffee cups, butt kits, and anything else not tied down as it all slid back and forth across the chart that was taped down on the table. The chart itself was already well stained with coffee splashes.

To add to their misery, the ancient submarine was cold and dank. The one heater, up in the forward torpedo room, labored endlessly but could barely keep the temperature inside the boat above freezing. Condensation constantly dripped from the hull, soaking everything. The men had rigged canvas tents to direct the dribbles away to the bilges. The crew were bundled up like so many Eskimos, wearing every stitch of clothes they owned in an effort to stay warm.

Manson took a drag on his Lucky Strike, blew out a cloud of smoke, and proclaimed, "Damn, Skipper! We've been making racetracks all over this bit of ocean for a couple of weeks now. And what we got to show for it?" He stubbed out the butt as he answered his own question, "Nada! Not a damn thing except bruises from riding this bucking bronco."

Brewster nodded solemnly, continued studying the chart, then finally responded, "XO, let me bum a smoke. I ran out yesterday."

Manson tapped out another Lucky Strike from his pack. Brewster pulled out his Zippo and lit the cigarette, drawing deeply before he went on. "You're right, XO. No use complaining, though. Long as the weather topside is like this, ain't a whole lot we can do but avoid sharp objects when we take a tumble."

As if to illustrate, a particularly strong roll caused them to both grab for their freshly filled coffee cups as they slid away from them. Brewster hooked his just before it got to the edge. Manson missed his. On its way to the deck, the mug doused him from the waist down in a hot brown bath. The XO danced for a second, grabbed a rag to wipe off, then said, "Damn! That's the first time I've been warm this week."

Brewster smiled. "Probably the first shower you've had this week, too. But, as I was saying, we can't run on the surface any longer than it takes to get a charge. Too much chance of losing someone or getting folks hurt. Look what happened to the 52 boat on the run down. Lost a guy overboard and another's in the hospital. Not going to risk that. Not yet anyway. Maybe once we're actually in a shootin' war."

"If we just had a better idea when we could expect the Germans to get into range," Manson said in frustration. He was still busy mopping up spilled coffee from the deck. "It would make catching them a whole lot easier if we just knew when and where to look. Squadron isn't giving us any intel. With all those super-secret huff-duff stations the Brits have strewn around, you'd think they could tell us something."

"XO, that's a good idea," Brewster replied. "But we both know that squadron doesn't have any intel guys with them. All that stuff comes out of COMSUBPATFOR headquarters, and I doubt if they even know we're out here, much less care."

"We know the Brits are sending that dope out to their convoys," Manson shot back. "Why can't we just copy their broadcast."

Brewster shook his head and took another draw on his Lucky Strike. "For some reason, our British cousins are keeping all this very close to the vest," he answered. "I don't think they quite trust us to not tip the Nazis to their little game. But I figure a dedicated intel shop on the *Beaver* might be the ticket. Especially now that we're all going to be spending some time in Newfoundland, it looks like. Somebody who could at least sift through all the crap and send us the nuggets that affect whatever we're doing out here." The Skipper had a thought. "By the way, go ahead and put that in the patrol report. Maybe somebody that counts will read it. And I'll brief the Commodore as soon as we get back."

Manson got back to his feet just in time to brace himself against a hard shove from the roiling Atlantic waters. He tossed the sopping rag into a corner of the compartment. "Speaking of nuggets, where the hell is that wayward junior officer of ours? Brad should have finished his little Iceland boondoggle by now and be back out here enjoying all this sun and sand."

Brewster laughed. "Last message traffic said he was due in port New London this week. We know he hitched a ride home on a tin can bound for New York. COMSUBPATFOR says they'll be routing him our way on the next supply ship to Argentia. Probably be waiting for us when we get back."

An especially vicious roll sent *S-54* slewing sideways once again.

"If Davy Jones don't dispatch us to his locker first," Brewster responded. But there was little humor in the Skipper's words. He rubbed his hands together and shivered. "I'm going back to the motor room to see if I can get warm. Those motors are the only warm place left on this old tub."

∞

FBI Special Agent Ralph Flannigan took one step farther back into the shadows. The noon train from New York City was just pulling into New London Station. A small but happy crowd was forming inside the Romanesque brick station, there to greet travelers coming from the big city, many of them US Navy personnel or civilian employees coming back to home base from wherever Uncle Sam had sent them in the course of their jobs. Flannigan's intent was to be in a position where he could observe both the small, happy crowd and the passengers as they disembarked from the train. At the same time, though, he needed to remain hidden so his quarry would not be spooked. Neither one of them. The young naval officer or his sexy girlfriend. He needed the eventual confrontation to be on the agent's terms and in a better setting than this very public one.

Flannigan's problem was that the only good observation point was outside the terminal, and that put him directly in the cold north wind and a snow flurry. He was freezing and just about to give up when he spied the Schultz girl wheel into the parking lot, spraying gravel as she screeched to a stop in one of the few open parking spots. And there was that Johnson kid—haughty, privileged son of what was certainly a full-of-himself Admiral—just emerging from the station's main access doorway.

Flannigan pulled his Leica 250 Reporter camera from his overcoat pocket and began snapping photos. He was glad he had requisitioned it with a 73mm Hektar lens. That made it ideal for grabbing a quick, clear image, even at a distance, that could later be blown up into detailed, large-format prints. These images of the cute barkeep clutching tightly to the Navy officer—the powerful Admiral's kid—could soon prove to be a useful leverage tool.

The FBI man stepped farther back, against the redbrick wall, as the couple rushed out of the rail station and Johnson threw his bag in the car's trunk. He continued shooting pictures as they left the parking lot, pulled out onto Water Street, and then merged onto Route 1 to cross the Thames River. Flannigan had no reason to trail them closely. He knew exactly where they were headed. He cranked up his '39 Dodge and followed from a leisurely distance.

As expected, Debbie Schultz's Ford coupe was sitting in the Schultz family driveway on Cottage Street when Flannigan slowly drove past, took more photos, and went on. He eased around the corner onto Morgan Court and found a spot where he could pull over to sit and watch the car from between two other houses. There was not a whole lot he could do until the couple emerged again. He could only hope that the wet-behind-the-ears Johnson kid would be intimidated enough by the FBI bluster and the threat to his father's prominence to come through for him. Otherwise, Flannigan would have to tighten the screws some more. That was always ticklish with someone with the clout of the senior Johnson. He would just have to see how it played out, how the kid responded to the next not-so-subtle round of pressure.

Flannigan's patience paid off. It was almost time for the Schultz girl's shift at the bar when the couple emerged from the family cottage. Johnson drove. Debbie sat in the passenger seat but immediately moved over close to the officer. She had to be straddling the floor gear shifter. That thought warmed up the FBI man just a bit.

Flannigan dropped in behind the coupe and trailed it right up to the front door of Solomon's Tavern. The Schultz girl showed Flannigan a lot of leg when she hopped out of the coupe—those photos he might have to save for his own personal collection—and then, with a wave to her boyfriend, disappeared into the bar.

The FBI sleuth was not interested in the girl. Yet. Johnson was his target. The Navy officer spun the Ford around and drove the short distance to the SUBBASE main gate. Flannigan followed as Johnson headed for the BOQ parking lot. The young officer had just stepped out of the car and was retrieving his seabag when Flannigan stepped up beside him.

"Well, I'll be damned if it isn't Brad Johnson." Flannigan's tone was light, friendly. "Just back from the wars and already cozying up to the enemy."

Brad Johnson dropped his bag, clenched his fists, and took a step closer to the FBI agent. Within striking distance. "Agent Flannigan, if you don't quit..."

"Careful there, Lieutenant," Flannigan growled. "You just might be overmatched. Director Hoover trains us well, you know. And I suspect you don't want to get that pretty face all bruised up. Might be hard to explain to your sweetie."

He could see the young man deflate right in front of him, dropping his fists, taking a couple of steps back. "Now would be a good opportunity for you to tell me what you may have learned about our spy over there at Electric Boat. And if his baby girl is involved in any way. Anything helps. Even the smallest thing. And be quick. I ain't got all night. That traitor may be sabotaging submarines as we stand here in the snow and waste time."

"Listen, you son of a bitch," Brad Johnson responded. "I've already told you. Mr. Schultz is not a spy. Or saboteur. I think he'd turn himself in and plead for mercy from the court if he got caught jaywalking. He raises the Stars and Stripes on the flagpole in his backyard every morning before he goes to work. His only crime is being born German. Debbie is certainly not a spy, and you're crazy to even hint at such a thing. Look, I can't tell you what isn't there."

A cruel grin crossed Flannigan's face. He stuck his face close to Johnson's and, in a low, menacing voice, said, "Get this straight, son. The FBI does not make mistakes. But I need absolute proof that Heinrich Schultz is working for the Nazis so we can turn him and find out who his boss is. And who his boss's boss is. I don't really care how you get that proof. You ship out in two days."

Flannigan paused to let that bit of information sink in. Johnson's wide eyes confirmed it had. "If I don't have what I want by then, your daddy is going to get some very interesting information that he is going to have a hard time explaining to the US Navy, *The New York Times*, and President Roosevelt himself. Understand?"

Flannigan abruptly turned and briskly walked away into the veil of a snow shower. Brad Johnson stood there, watching him go, a sizeable knot in the pit of his stomach.

∞

Stan Ward dusted the snow from his wool coat and hung it up on a hook just inside the door to dry. Groton was once again on the receiving end of a powerful winter storm. The radio was warning everyone along the coast from New York City northward to expect another ten inches of snow by evening.

When Ollie Oglethorpe saw Ward come in, he immediately hollered to him from across the room. "Hey, Stan, I need to speak with you. Grab a cup and meet me in my office."

Ward waved to acknowledge his boss and reached for his coffee cup. He took a welcome, warming sip of the steaming brown brew as he walked into Oglethorpe's little cubicle. The place was a sight. Stacks of papers, books, and notes covered every horizontal surface. Stan had to carefully clear away some of the mess so that he could take a seat in the only available chair.

"So, what you need, boss?" the newly minted LT(jg) asked. "I'm still working to flesh out that intercept from Bermuda. So far, it's reading like a bunch of admin drivel. But I am learning the German process for requisitioning toilet paper and red cabbage for their U-boats," he reported.

The Commander chuckled. "I hate to pull you away from something so vital, but I have a job for you that just might be a tad more interesting." Then he busied himself reloading his pipe, tediously tamping the tobacco firmly into the bowl, and then applying the match as if it was some kind of ritual.

Ward was by now quite familiar with his boss's delaying tactics. It typically meant he had something important to say but wanted to be precise in how he said it. Stan knew to sit back, drink his coffee, and wait. When Ollie was ready, he would speak. There was nothing to be gained by trying to rush him.

Oglethorpe blew out a cloud of aromatic smoke and then, from somewhere behind the thick cloud, said, "You know that we have a squadron of boats deployed up to Argentia, right?"

"Yeah," Ward replied. "I've got some Academy classmates on a couple of those boats. Gotta suck, being up there this time of year."

Ollie Oglethorpe chuckled again. "Well, Stan, my boy, you're about to find out for yourself. Seems someone up there is bemoaning the lack of useful tactical intelligence for the people who are caught in a very dangerous non-war. They seem to think they need an expert immediately underfoot to advise. COMSUBPATFOR has tasked us to provide an intel team with an intel officer to lead them. I took a quick look around the room and you are it. Thank you for volunteering. Pack your seabag. Your ship leaves Thursday at 0600 for Argentia, Newfoundland, Canada."

"Hey, wait a minute," Ward spluttered. "Volunteering? I don't recall volunteering for anything."

Oglethorpe laughed again. "Well, Stan, what it came down to was either you or me was going, so you volunteered. Remember, that's the Navy way. Best tell that young wife of yours that you won't be home for supper for a while. And welcome to the joys of being a Navy wife."

A sour expression claimed Ward's face. "Speaking of Karen, how long are we talking about for this deployment? We just found out we're expecting our first child in August. I don't like the idea of abandoning her now and I sure want to be home when the little critter's hatched."

It was CDR Oglethorpe's turn to display a concerned expression. He chewed on the pipe stem for a few seconds, lost in thought, before he responded. Finally, he said, "Stan, we both know that there is a war coming, no matter what they're saying in the papers. Lots of guys are going to be leaving their wives to go off and fight. They may or may not ever come back home. We'll need to live with that. You're not exactly going into battle, but we need you to go out there to do something really important. Something that might mean more of those guys do come back to their mothers and wives and children." He paused, puffed a moment, then added, "I'll try my level best to get you home for Karen and the little scoundrel, but I can't promise anything, Stan. It's serious business up there. I hope you understand."

"Yep, boss," Ward replied reluctantly. He took a swallow of his coffee. It had already gotten cold and bitter. "Got it. The term we learned at the Academy when there was a tough assignment was to 'suck it up.' Just promise me you'll keep an eye on Karen for me. Now, I'd better go give her the news. Unless you want to deliver it for me."

"No, thanks." Oglethorpe held up both hands, palms out in surrender. "Best it comes from somebody she knows and loves."

Stan smiled grimly, grabbed his coat, and headed for the steps that led up and out of the basement.

∞

Brad Johnson was sitting on the bed in his BOQ room, staring at the wall, wondering what he should do about his latest situation, when the phone buzzed. It startled him. He grabbed it before it could deliver another raspberry. The operator at the front desk told him that he had a long-distance call at the desk, but that he could patch it through to the room phone. Johnson had a good idea who it was.

The line buzzed and popped and then he heard his father's voice. "Brad, welcome home! From what I'm reading, it sounds like you did real good out there. I'm proud of you, son. That's one reason for the call. The other is that your mother asked me to check with you to see if you could make it down here to DC this weekend. It's her birthday, remember?"

Brad Johnson laughed. "Dad, I'm your son, you know. Of course I forgot. Mom always forgives you when you forget. Maybe she will me, too. Please do your best to seek absolution for your boy, okay?"

It was the elder Johnson's turn to laugh. It was true that he had probably forgotten more family holidays than he had remembered. The Admiral was a very busy man. And even more so of late, considering the world situation. "I'll do my best, but can you make it down for dinner Sunday?"

"Wish I could, Dad, but I'm leaving tomorrow to go meet my boat. I can't tell you where that is over the phone, but you can certainly find out easily enough. With the ops we're doing and with some new switching around that's going on, I'm really not sure when we'll be back to Groton."

Devin Johnson answered, "That's sure a quick turnaround, even for the Navy. You just landed back here, and they've got you shipping out already. No leave at all. Is there anything you need for me to take care of while you're gone?"

Brad had a sudden bit of inspiration. There would never be a better time than right now to tell his father about the FBI, Special Agent Flannigan, and all the problems the seedy guy was causing or threatening to cause. He spent the next ten minutes baring his soul, explaining everything, with only an occasional "Uh-huh" and "Go on" from his dad. He ended the litany with, "Dad, Heinrich Schultz is as straight an arrow as anybody I know. Just because he was born German does not make him a spy for Hitler. The man's as loyal to the Stars and Stripes as you or me. Flannigan's just trying to railroad him for some reason that I can't fathom just yet. And he's threatening us to make me cooperate with his scheme. Dad, I really care about Debbie. And her father, too. We can't let him get away with this."

Except for a distant hum, the phone line was quiet. Brad Johnson was just about to conclude that their connection had been broken when his dad cleared his throat and said, "Son, I'm glad that you're telling me about this. I can't imagine it's easy for you. But none of this is your fault. Let me take a look and see what I can do. Your Special Agent Flannigan is almost certainly being pressured to show some positive results, to net some fish, big or little, for the press and for the government. This is the way the FBI works nowadays. Nobody cares if the charges are valid or not. They just want results, something they can crow about in the newspapers and on the radio. This guy's putting the hard press on you because somebody higher up the food chain is squeezing his balls. Flannigan sees you and Mr. Schultz as easy targets he needs to hit just to lessen the pressure on him. Flannigan, I suspect, would be an easy bug to squash, but J. Edgar Hoover plays major league hardball. It's complicated, but he wants his agency to be the primary law enforcement body in the government, and that includes foreign as well as domestic responsibility. And he has a lot of friends in intelligence, the military, and government who owe him favors. Let me see if I can find out for sure what's going on and then we'll figure out a way for me to take care of this crap. I don't want this to sound demeaning, but this is way out of your league, Bradley. You go back out there to that sewer pipe of yours and make us proud again."

Brad released a long sigh. It felt like a very heavy weight had just been lifted off his chest. "Thanks, Dad. I can't even begin to tell you how much better this makes me feel."

"Brad, that's what daddies are for," Devin Johnson's deep voice boomed strongly, reassuringly, over the phone. "And by the way, your mother will expect you to bring Debbie down to DC when you get back and have a few days."

"Absolutely, Dad. And I promise I won't bring every little personal problem to you to fix. I know you're busy."

"This one's not just a personal problem, son. This one involves a lot of moving parts and some real tough-minded higher-ups who can and do affect the lives and careers of a lot of people, never mind who gets hurt. Or worse." He paused, then said, "I love you, Brad. Be careful. Be damned careful."

"Love you, too, Dad." The younger Johnson paused for his own long moment. "I will."

∞

Oberleutnant Helmut Schmiel once again felt the dribble of cold water down the back of his neck. The *verdammt* periscope packing gland was leaking even worse. There was nothing they could do out here in the middle of the ocean to repair it. But maybe they could tighten down on the gland and hope it stopped leaking. But not tighten so much that he would have even more trouble turning the scope. It was already tough to push the thing around to where he needed it to point. The only alternative was that he would just have to carry a towel and live with icy seawater trickling down his spine.

"*Obermaschinist*," *Warrant Machinist*, Schmiel growled to a young submariner standing nearby. "Grab a wrench. Tighten down on the packing some more." The man scurried off to look for the tool. Schmiel had not taken his eye away from the periscope. The night outside was illuminated with dancing green, mauve, and pink colors all along the northern horizon. It was an especially impressive display of the aurora borealis. And, he suddenly noticed, the eerie, colorful light show was backlighting something running along on the surface of the sea.

A small freighter that appeared to be trying to sneak past him and his submarine.

U-boat Command had issued new orders to the *U-23* to patrol the waters at the mouth of the Cabot Strait, between Nova Scotia and Newfoundland. Schmiel's job was to watch for outbound convoys departing the Gulf of St. Lawerence, bound for Great Britain. When he encountered a collection of worthy targets, he was to radio home with details. Should he deem them big enough to justify attention, that warning would give the waiting wolfpacks plenty of time to gather for an ambush.

The Type VII-C U-boat had cruised to the southwest end of its search area and turned around to the northeast when Schmiel caught sight of the solitary target heading across the straits on almost a parallel course to the submarine. The ship would not be of interest to the wolfpacks. It was so small that it was not even worth one of *U-23*'s two remaining torpedoes. Schmiel watched as the ship raced across the horizon. He could see its high bow plowing into the oncoming seas. It looked like it had a single kingpost on the low main deck and then a high pilot house midships. Couldn't be more than five hundred tons maximum. Probably delivering supplies to some remote village or out-of-the-way Canadian outpost.

"*Steuermann*, left standard rudder, steady course north," Schmiel ordered the Helmsman. The freighter was going much too fast for the *U-23* to try to intercept it while submerged. He would need to surface and race out ahead. That was not a problem. He was planning on using his 88mm deck gun anyway. It would make quick work of erasing the little steamer.

The *U-23* emerged from the depths and raced ahead. *Oberleutnant* Schmiel climbed up to the low bridge while the gun crew raced out to man the 88mm deck gun. He did not want to miss even a second of the action.

Within a minute, the first shot was arcing from the German submarine's deck gun toward the freighter, which now moved along three thousand meters away, its crew and passengers still unaware they were under attack.

16

Brad Johnson and Stan Ward had just finished their supper, reminiscing the whole time about their escapades back at the Naval Academy. It had been a bit of serendipity that the two friends found themselves catching the same ride up from Groton to Argentia. But this was to be their last night at sea together. They were just about to cross the Cabot Strait, the stretch of open water that separated Nova Scotia from Newfoundland. After dinner, they decided to step outside onto the bridge of the *Emily Rose* and enjoy the night's brilliant display of northern lights.

The little coastal freighter was not just a water taxi for the two young officers. It was making its regular three-day run, laden with supplies for the submarine tender *Beaver* and for that ship's clutch of submarines. Operating those ageing "*Sugar*" boats in the demanding wintertime in the North Atlantic—and especially with the long runs some of them were being called upon to make lately—was proving to be much more challenging than anyone anticipated. The little *Emily Rose* had become a valuable resource shuttling spare parts, supplies, and diesel fuel up north every week. And ferrying naval personnel, mechanics, and other personnel required to maintain those subs and keep them at the ready there in the little fishing village, too. Johnson and Ward had managed to catch a lift on one of the *Emily Rose*'s weekly round trips.

The two classmates were standing at the rail, marveling at nature's light show when the peaceful night was suddenly shattered by a loud blast from somewhere behind them. Then a short moment later, a plume of water a hundred feet tall shot up a couple of hundred yards away from the steamer's port side.

"God, Brad, what was that?" Ward exclaimed.

Johnson was already running to the other side of the bridge, yelling over his shoulder, "Somebody's shooting at us!" He could not see the source of the ordnance until the second muzzle flash erupted in the distance.

"There!" he yelled and pointed at something eerily lit by the northern lights. Something sizeable, riding up and down on the swells. "U-boat, on the surface!"

The *Emily Rose*'s captain, Hans Schneider, a grizzled old salt, had spent a great deal of his life on the bridge of this very steamer, but, in all those years, no one had ever shot at him before. He looked in the direction the young officer pointed. The low, gray form of a submarine was barely visible. Schneider instinctively whipped the wheel over to try to run away from the attacker.

Johnson looked forward. No one was rushing to man the vessel's only gun. He turned to Schneider and shouted, "Captain, where's your gun crew?"

The old seaman shrugged and answered, "None o' me crew been trained how to use it. Navy just welded it to the deck one day and left 'er there. I figgered any of me boys what tried to shoot it would either get hurt or blow the bridge out from under me."

The weapon looked a lot like the four-inch gun that Johnson used and drilled on aboard the *S-54*. "Captain, give me a couple of men to pass us shells. I can shoot that gun and at least try to scare that bastard away. You just keep weaving around to make it hard for him to aim." Then, grabbing Ward by the shoulder, he said, "Come on, Stan, let's sink us a U-boat!"

Johnson raced down the ladder and across the main deck, then climbed up onto the gun platform. Stan Ward was a lot slower as he limped down the ladder and hobbled across the deck. By the time he made it up to the gun, Johnson had already grabbed a brass round from the ready service locker, shoved it into the chamber, and slammed the breech shut.

As he jumped into the pointer's seat on the left side of the gun, he yelled over at Ward, "Stan, you ever shot one of these things?"

"Second Class summer cruise, on a destroyer, but I mostly just passed ammo."

"Jump into the aimer's seat, here on the right side. Just spin the wheels until you're looking right at that U-boat through the sights. That's that telescope in front of you. When you see it, yell 'ready.' I'll shoot from over here."

Johnson guessed at the range and elevated the gun for three thousand yards. He felt the gun rotate around and heard Ward yell. He waited for the ship to roll up and then kicked down on the firing pedal.

The blast was unexpectedly vigorous and loud. Johnson was sure he would never hear again. The recoil jerked him backward in his seat. A lance of bright yellow flames shot out of the gun's barrel. Then they saw a tall column of water flare up just beyond the U-boat.

Close but no kill.

Brad climbed down from his seat and checked the breechblock open just as three sailors climbed up to join them on the gun platform. One kicked the hot, spent shell casing aside while another grabbed a fresh round from the ready service locker.

The U-boat's gun blasted again. This time the shot was close enough that the water column rained down and doused Johnson's makeshift gun crew. But they carried on, bracing themselves against the ship's erratic zigzagging course, fighting as if nothing else was happening around them.

Johnson climbed back up into the pointer's seat just as the sailors slammed a fresh round in the chamber and swung the breech closed. They stepped back as Ward rotated the gun and once again yelled, "Ready!"

Johnson dropped the range by five hundred yards and fired. This time he was prepared for the blast and noise.

This time, the shot fell just a little short of the targeted U-boat. The crew immediately began to reload. They may have been slowed by inexperience, and so far had not really been very accurate, but they were doing what they could to fight back against their ambusher. That U-boat Skipper would have to think twice about coming any closer for a less challenging shot. From out there where he was lurking, the sub Skipper had the same problem the steamer gun crew did. They were trying to hit a bobbing, weaving target. The difference was, one hit might hurt the *Emily Rose*, but the steamer was unlikely to sink from that blow. One hit on the German sub would almost certainly be fatal.

Before he let Brad know he was once again ready with the aim, Ward yelled, "Stand by! He's gone! We ain't got nothing to shoot at."

Johnson looked out in the shimmering darkness for any sign of their target. The ocean was empty of all but whitecapped wavetops.

The admiral's son whooped and laughed. "Well, buddy, we did it! We chased that Nazi and he's probably skedaddling down there."

"Maybe. Maybe not," Stan countered. "He may be trying to line up a torpedo shot right about now."

Brad snorted. "No way he could hit us the way Captain Schneider's poured on the coal and got us doing the boogie-woogie all the way to port. And besides, we're just too small to waste a torpedo on."

"You're probably right, but still..." Both men were climbing down from the gun platform.

"Besides, if he was going to torpedo us, he'd a done that instead of shooting at us with his deck gun, right?"

"Guess so."

"C'mon, let's go see if Captain Schneider has something a little stronger than coffee so we can properly celebrate our glorious victory over the dreaded *Kriegsmarine*."

∞

The bright afternoon sunshine glinted off the bare aluminum of the four-engine flying boat as it kissed the calm waters of Bowery Bay. A British flag and the aircraft's name, *Bristol*, were painted on the fuselage just below the cockpit, marking it as one of British Oversea Air's three Boeing-built flying boats. Kicking up a foaming white wake, the Boeing 314 Clipper slowed and then turned toward the new LaGuardia Airport Marine Terminal. The pilot shut down two of the engines as he taxied up to the pier, and then the other two while the Navigator and Engineer stood on the port sponson and tied the boat up.

Sir Roger Whittaker stood just inside the hatch, stretching his aching back as he waited for the signal that he could deplane. The flight from Foynes, Ireland, with a refueling stopover at Shediac, in Nova Scotia, had taken just over thirty hours. Despite the Clipper's much ballyhooed luxury, Sir Roger was exhausted. Yet he knew the roughest part of the trip still awaited him.

As he stepped onto the pier, a tall man wearing a heavy khaki trench coat approached, held out his hand, and said, "Welcome to the United States, Sir Roger. I'm Bill Stephenson from the BSC."

Winston Churchill had informed Whittaker that the British Security Co-ordination office would have someone meet him in New York and arrange for him to meet quietly with the right people to attempt to accomplish his goal. The Prime Minister had also told him that the BSC was actually a covert MI6 operation recently set up in New York to further the British war effort and to coordinate with its counterpart, the American OSS, the equally vaguely named Office of Strategic Services. William Stephenson, a Canadian, led the BSC effort from his headquarters in Rockefeller Center.

Stephenson ushered the First Sea Lord off the pier and toward a waiting car, a shiny new maroon Bentley Mark V. Stephenson watched with amusement the way Whittaker was admiring the luxury car's sleek lines. He laughed and said, "Sir Roger, in America, the rule is 'if you have it, flaunt it.' Quite useful, really. This car says money and power."

Whittaker nodded. "It certainly does. Not what I would expect an MI6 spy to be driving, even in America."

"Precisely. Deception by deflection. No one expects a spy to be so ostentatious and noticeable."

Stephenson held the door open for Whittaker and then walked around to the other side and climbed into the back passenger door. As the driver briskly pulled the car away from the pier, the BSC man reached forward to open a small cabinet from which he removed a crystal decanter and two glasses. "We'll have time between here and Manhattan to enjoy a whiskey while James negotiates the traffic. A little relaxation after your stressful flight. This is a forty-year Bowmore. I think you'll enjoy the mellow earthiness."

Sir Roger sat back, smiling, allowing the soft Moroccan leather to envelop him as he sipped the whiskey. He sighed. "Bill, I could imagine that I'm in the wrong business, this navy thing. Perhaps I should consider becoming a spy for His Majesty's Secret Service."

The saloon-on-wheels smoothly sailed across the Queensborough Bridge but then quickly got snarled in Manhattan traffic. It took almost forty minutes to negotiate the six blocks over to Central Park South and the Plaza Hotel. When the maroon vehicle swung into the main entrance to the swanky old hotel, the bellmen, anticipating generous tips, stumbled over themselves in a race to be the first to open the Bentley's doors and welcome the obviously very important and well-heeled guests to their fine establishment.

Bill Stephenson stood aside while the bellman retrieved Sir Roger's single bag. He again shook the Admiral's hand and said, "I must get back to the office and see to a few things. There's a war on, you know. I've taken the liberty of reserving a private table in the Oak Room for you tonight at 2000. Your guests will meet you there. I'll join you in the morning for breakfast at 0730. Should we need to journey down to Washington, we can make arrangements then." With that, he climbed back into the car and was whisked away around Grand Army Plaza and down Fifth Avenue.

Whittaker looked at his watch and decided he had a few minutes for a brisk walk before straightening up for dinner. Maybe a little window shopping on Fifth Avenue for the wife. She had mentioned something about a shop near the hotel called Tiffany's.

By the time he found his way back to the Plaza, his wallet was several hundred pounds lighter, but Mrs. Whittaker now had a sparkling new bangle to display at cocktail parties and formal affairs. And there was just enough time to dress for dinner.

He arrived in the Oak Room and was immediately led off to a private table hidden from the view of other diners. The two men he was meeting had already arrived. Both stood to greet him.

Admiral Devin Johnson said, "Sir Roger, so good to see you again. I trust that you had a comfortable flight. Please allow me to introduce you to Harry Hopkins. I assume you are familiar with Harry and his role within President Roosevelt's administration."

Whittaker shook hands with the tall but somewhat emaciated man, saying, "Yes. Yes, I am. And I'm most appreciative that you could break yourself away from the Washington bustle to come up here to meet with me."

Hopkins smiled as they took their seats, and said, "Happy to oblige. Besides, New York is practically my second hometown. Devin said that you wanted to meet discreetly. There is no such thing in Washington, I'm afraid. Especially nowadays with all the speculation about our position in the war. Our nice dinner tonight would be fodder for the front page of tomorrow morning's *Washington Post*." He waved his hand around, indicating the Oak Room. "This, I assure you, is much better."

The waiter arrived with fresh drinks and the menus. The men perused the leather-bound descriptions of the chef's finest efforts. Whittaker and Johnson both chose a filet mignon with asparagus spears, but Hopkins limited himself to a salad and some mixed vegetables.

"I'm afraid that my food choices are limited of late," he explained. "Stomach cancer. Doctor says no proteins and no fats." Tapping his glass for the wine steward, he continued, "But he didn't put any restrictions on the wine. This is an excellent Bordeaux."

There was idle talk until the food was served and then the waiters discreetly took positions out of earshot when Harry Hopkins, after taking a sip of wine, not so subtly changed the subject.

"So, Sir Roger, what is important enough for you to fly all the way across the Atlantic to have dinner with the Admiral and me this evening? Certainly not just for the filet mignon."

"I am here at the specific request of the Prime Minister," the First Sea Lord answered. "And I assure you it is not to once again lobby for even more vigorous participation by the USA in our little conflagration with Herr Hitler and his Nazis. However, Mr. Churchill is of the opinion that it is vital that he and President Roosevelt meet face-to-face at the earliest opportunity to work out cooperation agreements. Our nation is already at war, and we believe you will soon be, despite the opposition within your Congress and press. Winston has expressed that this proposed meeting should be discreet, certainly away from the press and any prying eyes. And, most importantly, hidden from any Nazi effort to intervene, violently or otherwise. Clearly, they would like the USA to remain neutral and might take drastic measures to keep it that way. Hence, this back-channel approach."

Hopkins put down his wineglass and dabbed his lips with his napkin as he formulated his response. "Sir Roger, please inform the Prime Minister that I will discuss this meeting idea with the President at my first opportunity. It is something that we have discussed already, although in very broad terms, but we do see the value in close communication with the Prime Minister. Defining precisely what form such cooperation between our countries would take in such turbulent times would make such a meeting productive. We are aware of the strategic implications, the levels of commitment, the logistics, those kinds of things."

Hopkins took another sip of wine. Admiral Johnson had remained quiet, but he finally asked, "Where and when is Winston considering holding this meeting?"

"We were thinking that, since both Winston and FDR enjoy going to sea in Navy ships, maybe they could have a chance meeting at sea, far from newspapermen and spies. Maybe some out-of-the-way location reasonably convenient to both sides of the Atlantic, like Newfoundland. And probably early summer, when the seas are a lot calmer, but certainly no later than August. We are aware of Mr. Roosevelt's legislative workload right now and the upcoming election. Winston is quite involved already with Greece, Crete, and Dakar, as well as the German action against our shipping and the British Isles themselves. But we also know that Nazi madman could be lobbing bombs into your East Coast by the end of the year."

Hopkins smiled, shaking his head. "Sir Roger, we well understand the threat to your country, and that only intensifies our concern for our own nation. And it is essential that we have communication all the way to the top of each of our governments. I see value in such a meeting, and I like this plan. I'll relay it to the President with my total endorsement." He folded his napkin and stood. "Now, if you gentlemen will excuse me, I can still make the last train home if I hurry."

"But no time for dessert, Mr. Hopkins?" Whittaker asked.

"No, no. Remember, no proteins or fats. But please. Enjoy something,

Sir Roger, compliments of the people of the United States of America. It's the least we can do. Good night and safe travels."

17

Oberleutnant Helmut Schmiel was not one to give up easily. Any kill, even the little coastal steamer that had boldly chased him under, would make his patrol report more impressive once he returned home. All was quiet aboard the *U-23* as it headed out toward the open Atlantic. Schmiel was both chagrined and mystified. The gun attack on the little vessel should have been quick and easy. Instead, the ship had put up a surprisingly effective fight that nearly sank his submarine. Lucky shots or not, Schmiel knew that even minor damage could have proven fatal for his boat this far from home. He could not afford to engage in any slugging matches. The submarine had been forced to seek the safety of the depths and quietly skulk away. He was not at all sure, though, that his superiors would accept his reasoning for not pressing the attack.

Schmiel huddled with his watch officers in the cramped control room to discuss what had happened and what they should do now. The First Watch Officer, with half a dozen war patrols under his belt, came up with the solution.

"*Herr Kapitan*, it was obviously a submarine trap, cleverly deployed. The British call them Q-ships, warships designed to appear to be innocent cargo vessels, meant to lure us to our death. We should simply torpedo it."

"*Verdammt*," Schmiel exclaimed as he slapped his fist down hard onto the chart table. "Claus, I suspect you are correct. The *scheißkerl* Q-ship was very nearly successful. But do we risk another attack?"

There were other considerations. The Chief Engineer's daily fuel report showed that they were already ominously low on diesel, with only enough to get home if they were very careful. Common sense told him that he should turn east immediately. But he still had two torpedoes in the forward torpedo room. Returning with unexpended ordnance was a cardinal sin to Admiral Dönitz.

"We will attack the Q-ship," Schmiel said decisively. "And we will sink it. First Watch Officer, steer us out ahead of its track. I want to be four hundred meters off of his track when we shoot. He is small and will have a shallow draft. We will risk shooting with a minimum run depth and trust that the *Kriegsmarine* for once built at least two torpedoes we can trust to run straight and true."

The *U-23* emerged from the depths into a cloud-covered night. Yet another late winter storm was likely blowing down out of Canada and had already obscured the night sky. That was a positive for the U-boat. After trying to conduct the previous fight under the brilliant northern lights, the clouds were a godsend.

Helmut Schmiel could not see the enemy steamer from his perch on the U-boat's bridge, but if the vessel had continued across the Davis Strait on the same course it had been heading, he calculated his submarine would be out ahead of it and in position in an hour. Then they would simply dive and wait.

It was just after midnight—within minutes of an hour later—when the steamer came over the horizon, directly at them. Schmiel watched through the periscope as the doomed little ship proceeded on. He waited until its angle-on-the-bow was a starboard ninety degrees. Then he ordered, "Set run depth to minimum. *Torpedo eins und zwei abfeuern!*"

The two G7a steam-driven torpedoes raced out of their torpedo tubes and turned directly toward their target. Helmut Schmiel watched as the two arrow-straight white lines, the frothy torpedo wakes, pointed directly toward the target. Anyone on the steamer who might have been looking would have seen them, too. But there was not a thing they could do but pray.

Schmiel sucked in a deep breath, ready for the flash then rumble of a successful hit.

There was nothing. They had missed.

The German Skipper stepped back from the periscope as it lowered. He growled, "They ran right under that U-boat trap. Those Brits will never know how close they came to death tonight." He slumped down tiredly onto a stool. "Let us head home, then. First Officer, come to course zero-nine-zero."

∞

LT(jg) Stan Ward made his official call on the Commodore, Captain Roderick Flynn, the day after the *Emily Rose* tied up alongside the *Beaver*. Ward had never met the former Submarine School Skipper, but Brad Johnson had been quick to fill him in on all the sea stories about "the Old Man." Given that Johnson's interactions with the SUBSCOL Commanding Officer—now the Squadron Commodore—were not always positive, his description may have been a little colored.

Ward labored up to the O-3 level and all the way forward to the Commodore's stateroom. Captain Flynn met him at the door and pointed him to a seat at the big conference table that took up most of the space in the forward part of the stateroom.

"Coffee?" Flynn offered, waving toward the pot sitting on a little side table with a clutch of heavy porcelain Navy mugs. Flynn grabbed his cup from his desk and plopped down at the head of the conference table. Ward quickly poured himself a cup and sat.

"Sounds like you had an interesting trip up here," Flynn said as he perused the after-action report on the table in front of him. "So, you and Mr. Johnson managed to scare away a U-Boat with the *Emily Rose*'s little popgun?" He chuckled. "Good work. Too bad you didn't hit it though. Even if that might have given some folks heartburn. Damn war that ain't a war. That makes it a mess."

"We tried," Ward answered, "but he dove before we could get a handle on that gun."

"Glad COMSUBPATFOR took our request to heart," Flynn said,

changing subjects. "We need real-time intel up here so we can vector our boats to where they can do the most good. Frankly, I'm convinced SUBPATFOR has too many fish to fry to give us the priority we need to be effective."

Stan took a sip of coffee. "That's why I brought a team along with everything we need for a real-time operational intel center right here on the *Beaver*. We just need a place to set up."

Flynn grunted. "We'll do the best we can, but as you've probably noticed, we're already a little cramped."

At six thousand tons, the *Beaver* was not a big ship, and it had been tasked with servicing an entire squadron made up of some truly ancient *S*-class submarines. Every available square inch was being used for something important. Ward would have to use his imagination, a bit of skullduggery, and some not-so-subtle bribes and threats to find space for his team to do their work. The simple fact that no one on the tender—including the Squadron Commodore himself—had the "need to know" nor did anyone have high enough clearances to even be allowed to enter the spaces where Ward's team would operate made the working relationships on the tender interesting. "Ward's Boys" became the name for the spooks that no one could talk to.

It took a couple of weeks, but Stan finally identified a small storeroom deep in the bowels of the ship that they could convert into a lockable workspace. They laughingly dubbed it "The Crypt." The space was kept locked at all times. An armed Marine guard was always posted outside. They also managed to commandeer a closet-like corner in the tender's radio room where they installed their own dedicated radio equipment. The *Beaver*'s crew stared curiously whenever they saw Ward's radio operator, armed with a .45, carrying a locked satchel handcuffed to his wrist and escorted by an armed Marine, make his way every few hours from the radio room, high up in the ship's superstructure, all the way down to The Crypt. There he disappeared behind the locked and guarded door.

When the intel boys had The Crypt up and running, and Stan was satisfied with all the extra security, he finally unboxed his pride and joy, the crown jewel of the intel center. Ollie Oglethorpe had given him one of America's few crude Enigma machines. Ward's Boys had hopes of working with Oglethorpe's team back in Groton to try to read the U-boat mail. But the damned *Kriegsmarine* had not cooperated, recently changing their code again. Despite their best efforts, neither team was able to read anything useful from their intercepts. Meanwhile, the British were still keeping whatever intelligence or code-reading ability they possessed to themselves for fear the Germans would somehow find out how much they had. So all Ward had to work with was whatever he could glean from the huff-duff information and his own quickly developing instincts.

He was not at all sure that would be enough to do the job he had been tasked to do.

∞

Debbie Schultz had an almost overpowering feeling that something was not right. She could not overcome the strong sense that she was being watched. But the parking lot in front of the tavern was empty except for her old Ford, which sat directly under the light pole. It was the only car in the lot at just after three a.m. So, if someone was watching, waiting for her to close up and leave work, they were well hidden back in the shadows. She locked the tavern's front door and clutched her purse tightly as she scurried across the gravel lot. She had been mugged a couple of times before, a hazard of working the hours she did, but she had taken some training and felt she could protect herself. Assuming the robber was not armed. Debbie was just unlocking the car door when she heard a voice from the darkness.

"Fraulein Schultz, we need to talk." A man emerged from the shadows and into the light, then stopped.

Debbie recognized the accent. It sounded exactly like her Uncle Ludwig. Bavarian. But this stranger's English was quite good. Uncle Ludwig's English was barely decipherable.

"Who are you?" she challenged. "And what do we have to talk about?"

"Who I am is not important," the man said. "What is important is that you be aware that the FBI has you under observation. You and your father. Were you aware of that?"

Debbie Schultz was mystified. Why would the FBI be interested in watching her or her father? They went after bootleggers and gangsters, right? Did they think the Schultzes were "rum runners" or something? And who was this mystery man standing in a gravel parking lot in the middle of the night, his face hidden in the shadows of the brim of his hat?

"I'm here to deliver a warning." The man's tone was calm, but his words were anything but soothing. "The FBI is now actively persecuting German Americans. We have done nothing to deserve their scrutiny or harassment, but they persist. We Germans must band together for protection."

He removed his fedora then and held it in his hands, fidgeting with the rim as he spoke. He was younger than she had at first thought. And he carried a sincere expression as he implored the young lady to believe what he was telling her. "They are already arresting Germans in New York. They claim they are rounding up a major spy ring working for the *Abwehr*, but all they are doing is locking up and trampling on the rights of hardworking, honest citizens."

The stranger looked around nervously, as if aware for the first time that he was standing in the light in the middle of an empty parking lot. "Look, you need to go before someone sees us together, sees us talking." He hesitated, his face grim. "But before you go, we need to set up a very private meeting with you and your father. Somewhere the FBI won't be able to listen in on our conversation." Reaching into his coat pocket, he pulled out a slip of paper. "Call this number from a payphone. Someone will answer and work with you to set up a meeting. Understand?"

Debbie Schultz took the paper, opened it, and saw it was indeed a phone number. When she looked up to ask another question, the man was gone. A cold wind blew trash and dust across the lot, but that was not what caused her to shiver.

She drove home in a daze. She had to think before doing anything else. She was pretty sure that she had just been approached by a Nazi spy. And right there in Groton, Connecticut! But what should she do? If Brad had been there, he would have known exactly what to do. Then she remembered something. Brad had given her his father's phone number, and he emphatically told her to call him if she ever needed help. Right now, Admiral Johnson was the only person within reach that she knew she could trust, but did she dare call him at this hour? She pulled up to the house, parked the car, and rushed inside.

Everyone was asleep, including her father, but she still was not sure if she should mention the stranger in the parking lot or the proposed meeting with him. Grabbing the phone, she dialed the operator.

"Long-distance please. I need to call Washington, DC. The number is Dupont 4316."

∞

The jangling phone woke Admiral Devin Johnson from a sound sleep. He grabbed the handset and answered quickly, hopefully before it woke Faye, his wife.

"Admiral Johnson," the breathless voice on the other end said. "Forgive me for calling so late. This is Deborah Schultz, up here in Groton, Connecticut. Brad said I could call you if I ever needed anything."

Johnson was already fully awake, a skill learned from his many years in command positions in the Navy and now in the higher reaches of the military in DC. He turned on his most reassuring tone. "Of course, Debbie. Brad told us that you might be calling. What's going on?"

Deborah Schultz spent the next five minutes describing the parking lot encounter in detail. And what she felt might be an attempt to recruit her and her father—who worked in a restricted area at Electric Boat where some new kind of submarines were being constructed—as spies.

Johnson thought for a few seconds, then he responded, "Debbie, I'm going to have someone from Naval Intelligence talk with you. This may be nothing, or it could be a very serious thing. My flag aide, Phil Sherman, will head up to Groton in the morning with one of their case officers to talk with you."

"Should I go ahead and set up the meeting like this guy told me to?" she asked.

"Let's discuss it with the case officer. We'll need to set some things in motion first."

Johnson could hear the stress in the young woman's voice when she asked, "So what should I tell my dad, Admiral?"

There was another pause, then he said, "Debbie, is it possible your dad might already know about these people? That they may have been talking with him already? Maybe tried to get to him?"

She was quick to answer. "No! No, of course not! My dad's the most patriotic man you'd ever meet. He loves this country. He was talking just the other day about how crazy those Nazi guys looked in New York City, marching through Central Park with their swastikas and that silly salute..."

"Okay, I believe you. But for now, please don't tell him about the man in the parking lot, the proposed meeting, our call, or your meeting with Phil Sherman. Same with Brad in the unlikely event he should contact you. Phil will take care of everything and advise about what should happen next. And you were right to call me. As you know, Brad cares a great deal about you, so that means Faye and I do as well."

Johnson heard the sigh of relief on the other end of the line. "Thank you, Admiral. I feel better already."

Johnson chuckled. "You really must call me Devin. And don't worry, okay? LT. Sherman will take care of everything."

When they had completed the call, Admiral Johnson sat on the edge of his bed and thought for a few minutes.

"Trouble at the office?" his wife groggily asked.

"Classified, honey. Classified."

"Same old excuse as always," she told him. "But this one sounded..."

"Go on back to sleep now."

"Aye, aye, Admiral. I have my orders." She turned back over as Johnson grabbed his robe and slippers and headed off for his study. He first called Phil Sherman and got him headed toward Groton. Then he riffled through his address book. It took him a few minutes to find the number he was looking for. Here was a chance to protect national security, help out his son's girlfriend, and maybe put FBI Director J. Edgar Hoover in a box, all in one fell swoop.

He dialed the number. There was only one ring before the phone was attentively answered.

"Office of Naval Intelligence, Watch Officer."

"Hello, this is Admiral Devin Johnson. I need you to call the Director and have him call me back at Dupont 4316 immediately. Tell him that it's urgent."

∞

Before he boarded the Pan American Airways Yankee Clipper aircraft, Archibald Coombs, official courier for His Majesty's Diplomatic Service, watched with great interest as the locked and sealed diplomatic pouch he had brought along with him was loaded into the plane's cargo compartment. The pouch was filled with classified and sensitive documents being sent from the Foreign Office bound for the British Embassy in Washington, DC. It was his job to guard it and see that no one tampered with it on the journey across the Atlantic.

With the pouch safely stowed, he stepped into the main passengers' cabin. The steward greeted him warmly and promptly showed him to his seat. There, without even asking his preference, the steward served him a chilled gin and tonic. This was Coombs's regular courier route. The steward made it his business to care for regular passengers.

Coombs felt a slight rocking as the big seaplane moved away from the pier at Lisbon's Cabo Ruivo Seaplane Base and out into the Tagus River. The fast-flowing river was a little choppy, but once the flying boat was airborne, Coombs knew he would be able to settle back for a calm flight, a nice meal, and a restful night. It was ten hours to their first layover at Horta in the Azores. A couple of these good gin and tonics, a nice supper, maybe a couple of night caps, and he could retire for the evening.

Meanwhile, down in the airplane's cargo compartment, Juan Sierra, chief steward for the Yankee Clipper, was hard at work. But he was not performing any Pan Am duties. He was busy working for the *Abwehr*, the Nazi spy service, who paid him much better than the airline did. He painstakingly removed the diplomatic seal on the courier pouch before picking the lock. By the time the Clipper had cleared the Portuguese coastline, he had the pouch's contents spread out on the deck and was painstakingly photographing every page. He finished and resealed the pouch in time to rejoin his staff up in the main cabin to help serve the evening meal.

Archibald Coombs enjoyed the slow-cooked *boeuf braise bourgeoise* with a 1932 Chateau L'Arrosee. He found the *framboises rafraichies* delightful and the Tesseron XO Cognac—recommended highly by Juan Sierra, the chief steward, who always showed the Brit special attention—topped the meal off with near perfection. After a whiskey in the lounge and a glance at the previous day's *The Mail* newspaper, the diplomat was ready to retire for the evening. He barely stirred when the Yankee Clipper touched down in Horta on the Ilha do Faial, in the Azores. He certainly did not see Juan Sierra pass a roll of film to one of the crewmen who was refueling the Clipper. He rolled over and remained soundly asleep when the Clipper was again airborne, heading for its next stop in New York City.

Admiral Wilhelm Canaris in Berlin, the chief of the German *Abwehr*, and US President Franklin Roosevelt in Washington, DC, would both receive British Prime Minister Winston Churchill's travel plans for a supposedly secret rendezvous in August 1941.

And they opened them at almost exactly the same moment.

18

Iceberg calving season came early to the Labrador Sea. The tidewater glaciers lining Greenland's western shores inexorably slid down to the sea and then formed huge ice shelves extending miles out over the Baffin Bay and the Labrador Sea. With a great roar, massive chunks of ice broke off the towering high shelves and floated out into a sea already clogged with icebergs. The frozen islands crashed against each other as the polar wind and Labrador Current pushed them south, and that, unfortunately, took them toward primary shipping lanes. Wind and water eroded the ice into bizarre but beautiful sculptures, looking for all the world like a parade floating by. The stark white ice, sometimes streaked with pale blues, greens, and browns, contrasted sharply with the blue-gray water and deep-blue sky. Sea birds, seals, and whales feasted on the abundant marine life that clustered around the icebergs, adding to the wild splendor.

Freddy Wurster stood on the *S-52*'s open bridge and marveled at the awesome beauty he was witnessing. Carefully keeping the surfaced submarine well clear of the icebergs, he weaved his way through the relatively clear channels between them. They had another day traveling these ice-clogged waters before they would be clear of the Labrador Sea and in their assigned patrol area south and east of Greenland. It was unbelievable that he had all of this striking scenery to himself. Beyond the submarine beneath his feet, there was not a sign of any other humans.

Nature's beauty contained a hidden danger, he well knew. Under each of the islands of ice was a massive hunk of hard, unforgiving berg that was over eight times as large as what was visible on the surface. These underwater mountains extended down to depths of three hundred feet or more. Undetectable by a submerged submarine and reaching over a hundred feet below the *S-52*'s test depth, the icebergs formed a barrier that made it too dangerous for them to transit while submerged. Just the previous week, their sister boat, the *S-53*, found this out the hard way after an underwater encounter with an iceberg. That submarine was now moored alongside the *Beaver* back at Argentia, repairing bent metal while waiting for a new periscope to be shipped up from the factory in Massachusetts.

Wurster turned around and yelled to his lookouts standing up in the periscope shears. "Keep your eyes open and your head on a swivel. We got two possible threats up here, ya know. Watch for periscopes from any U-boat dumb enough to be running submerged up here. But the worse threat is any patrol plane who didn't read that we're operating up here."

The lookouts each nodded and yelled back down, "Yes, sir!" Wurster was not sure if his warning was effective, but the young sailors did seem to be diligently scanning the horizon. Younger men were chosen for such duty because they typically had sharper eyesight.

"XO to the bridge," the 7MC blasted, but Lieutenant Simon McNeely's head had already popped up through the hatch.

"Afternoon, Fred," the XO said as he stood, sucked in some chilly, clean air, then looked around, taking in the impressive scenery. He reached into his shirt pocket and pulled out the ever-present pack of Lucky Strikes. Shaking one out of the pack, he offered it to Fred Wurster, then stuck it between his own lips when Wurster shook his head. After he lit up and took a deep drag, he said, "I thought I'd come up and grab a smoke. You need a relief for a few minutes?"

Wurster nodded, "Thanks, XO. I sure could use a head break. My bladder's hydroed from all the coffee. We're on base course one-zero-zero but doing some zigzags to dodge the icebergs. No contacts except them." He waved toward the ice-littered sea. "I'll be back as soon as I drain the lizard."

McNeely told him, "I relieve you," and gazed out toward the horizon. Wurster dropped through the hatch into the warmer atmosphere of the conning tower below.

The XO was just finishing his smoke when the port lookout yelled, "Aircraft!" and pointed toward the sun. "He's inbound! Coming fast!"

McNeely barely had time to turn and look that way. Sure enough, he could see—and already hear—a twin-engine plane diving toward them. Obviously, this guy had not seen the memo about friendly submarines in the area.

"Clear the bridge!" McNeely yelled. Reaching for the diving alarm, he yanked the lever twice.

Aoogha! Aoogha! The diving alarm sounded.

Over the 1MC the XO hollered, "Dive!" Dive!"

The lookouts had already gone down the hatch and McNeely was headed that way when the plane roared overhead, scant feet above the deck. The blue, white, and red roundels on the wings were plainly visible. That signified that he was supposed to be friendly. But the XO could also see the bomb dropping away from the aircraft's open bomb bay.

The bomb seemed to be falling in slow motion, headed directly for the spot on the bridge where he stood. McNeely realized he did not have time to get to the hatch. Instinctively, as he sprawled for cover, he reached over and slammed the hatch cover shut. The bomb arced just over the submarine's bridge so close that McNeely was sure he could see the writing on the gray shape as it flashed by.

The weapon exploded in the water a bare fifty feet from the submerging submarine. The ordered dive was well underway. Seawater already swirled up around McNeely. Then the concussion and wave from the bomb swept him right off the bridge, out into the sea. The cold hit him like a hammer. His head pounded. It felt as if his body was already frozen numb. Numb except for a searing pain in his left side.

With all the strength he could muster, he kicked toward the surface, though his legs balked. Once there, he tried to breathe but gagged on the seawater. Then he realized that he was alone. *S-52* was submerged, as ordered. The sea was empty except for the ever-present icebergs. And the sky was empty, too. The "friendly" had apparently gone on in search of other targets.

A feeling of calm acceptance came over Simon McNeely. If he was destined to go, there were far worse and more painful ways. He lay back, floating, and waited for the sea to lull him to sleep and then swallow him up.

The *S-52* popped to the surface a hundred yards from the XO. Don Gorman, the Skipper, was still maneuvering the boat closer to the overboard man when Fred Wurster dived over the side. With a few powerful strokes, he swam over to where McNeely floated. It only took a couple of minutes for crewmen to pull McNeely and then Wurster up out of the water. Doc Jones immediately started first aid on the wounded XO, applying a pressure bandage to a deep, bleeding gash on his left side.

Gorman looked down from the bridge at the dripping-wet and shivering Wurster and shook his head. "Damn it, Fred. We've got to stop these cold-water swim calls of yours."

Wurster only half laughed. "I'm all for that. It'll be a week before I quit pissing ice cubes."

∞

It was a moonless, pitch-black night. Like a ghost, the German submarine *U-23* emerged from the depths and headed on the surface toward the French coast to the east. The *schnellboot* was on station, waiting precisely where U-Boat Command had designated for the rendezvous between the U-boat and its patrol boat escort. *U-23*'s commanding officer, Helmut Schmiel, answered the flashing light challenge and then steered his submarine to closely follow the escort boat home.

Dawn was breaking when the *U-23* passed the island of Ushant and then headed toward Camaret-sur-Mer. The *schnellboot* led the submarine on a twisting, erratic course through the protective coastal minefields and past the submarine boom that crossed the channel at Fort de Cornouaille. The massive underground U-boat bunkers were still under construction at the former French naval base at Brest, so Schmiel was directed to moor the

U-23 with his squadron mates at a well-protected pier inside the breakwater.

Finally, the last line was secured, the precise time noted, and the U-boat's mission was officially completed. Schmiel could already taste the champagne at the Bar Royal, but only after a long, hot bath at the Hotel Majestic. Then he would get gloriously drunk as he compared sea stories with his fellow U-boat *Kommandants.* They would see who of the group was still alive and toast the warriors who would not be coming home. From reading the radio traffic, he was pretty sure that neither Müller nor Meier would be at the Bar Royal. All communication with their boats had stopped a couple of weeks before. But Koch and Smit would be there to buy a round. And maybe Gunter Hessler, too. He was a good man, even if his father-in-law was Karl Dönitz.

Schmiel had just stepped ashore when a big Mercedes screeched to a halt right next to him. *Kapitänleutnant* Albert Hoffman climbed from the back seat. He sharply answered Schmiel's salute—the old, traditional Prussian salute, not the Nazi outstretched arm—and offered a welcoming smile. The two were old shipmates. Neither was a Nazi.

"Helmut, welcome home," Hoffman said as he proceeded to envelop the smaller man in a bear hug. "It appears you have enjoyed good hunting. Another patrol like this one and I believe I can see a Knight's Cross in your future."

Schmiel shook his head. "Albert, you well know I do not care for such baubles. Just let me do my duty and then bring my crew home."

Hoffman laughed and slapped his former shipmate on the back. "At any rate, I have authorized a week of relaxation for you and your crew in Brest's best bars and whorehouses. Then I have a very special mission for you that will keep you quite busy for a bit. Enjoy your leave, my friend, then come and see me in one week. If you succeed on this mission, you will be awarded a Knight's Cross, and probably from Herr Hitler's own hand. Whether you like it or not." Then Hoffman sniffed and frowned. "And for God's sake, get a bath first. You smell like you have spent the last six weeks inside a pig boat."

∞

Admiral Devin Johnson stole a glance out of the floor-to-ceiling second-story window. Constitution Avenue was clogged with evening traffic as the politicians and bureaucrats fought for a few car lengths' advantage on their nightly battle to get home to Arlington or Chevy Chase in time for dinner and to listen to *Texaco Star Theater* with Fred Allen or hear the news from Lowell Thomas on NBC. Secretaries and janitors stood on the sidewalks and waited patiently for their bus to Anacostia or Northeast.

It would be a while before Johnson could even think about his own journey home. By then, the streets would be empty, traffic no issue. And the radio would have switched to big band music or silly comedies. He sighed and turned his attention back to the ongoing meeting. Secretary of the Navy Charles Edison was deep into a discussion with the Chief of Naval Operations, Admiral Harold "Betty" Stark. The CNO was not happy about doing anything to disrupt his long-planned fleet training for what he had already described several times as "a damn political stunt."

Edison used his smoothest, calmest tone to try to placate the irate Admiral. "Now, Betty, let's look at this calmly, rationally."

"So now I'm not rational!" Stark roared. "Damned politicians! Let's talk about 'rational.' This administration has had me fighting a war that's not a war for two years now. I'm supposed to be getting ready to engage in a major naval war—likely on two oceans in two different hemispheres and against some of the world's most powerful navies—and he still goes and gives away fifty of my destroyers despite my objections to such larceny. Now, FDR wants a frontline cruiser and a half dozen destroyers so he can take a summer cruise right smack-dab in the middle of our annual major fleet exercise as we try our damnedest to prepare for the inevitable conflict coming our way. And to top it off, this cruise of his is so secret that I can't even give the commanding officers of any of the vessels involved a speck of any warning or critical details of what's going on."

"Betty," Edison admonished, "he is the Commander in Chief. And we sure can't let the Germans even sniff a hint that the president is going anywhere outside the country or meeting with Churchill. They know that ratchets up the chance of our joining a war as an ally of Great Britain, and even somebody as crazy as the Führer doesn't want that to happen. At least, not yet." Pulling a sheet of paper from a buff-colored file on his desk,

Edison read, "Churchill says that he is coming over on the *Prince of Wales*. Says he needs something with firepower in case the Germans do get wind of this powwow and send out one of their battleships."

Stark pounded the table with a closed fist. "Damn it, Charles! Do you really think Hitler would attack a ship with Churchill on board? Or the President of the US? Or both?"

Edison looked over the top of his spectacles at the CNO. "Yes. Yes, we do. Oh, they would more likely threaten with their mere presence, assuming the meeting would be cancelled if there were battleship guns aimed their way. But if the only way they could prevent this meeting was... well...we've seen what they've done in Europe already."

Stark considered Edison's reasoning and appeared to calm down. "Then what do we know about what Hitler and his *Kriegsmarine* might have available?"

"The pocket-battleships *Scharnhorst* and *Gneisenau* are up somewhere in the Norwegian fiords along with the battleship *Tirpitz*. It would take some serious firepower to counter them if those three sortie. And intelligence is telling us that the *Bismarck* is about ready to leave Kiel for sea trials with the heavy cruiser *Prinz Eugen*. Now, you see why Churchill wants the newest and best firepower he has for protection?"

Stark shook his head. "All the more reason not to do this face-to-face stunt. And I don't have a battleship to give the President. Those that aren't already in the shipyards being modernized are all way out there in Pearl Harbor, trying to make the Emperor of Japan think twice about what he's doing in the Pacific."

Johnson interrupted. "Betty, the President doesn't need a battleship. We're meeting on our side of the pond. I don't see any German battleships being a threat. We'll have plenty of warning if one breaks out. U-boats are a much more realistic problem. We need a ship that's fast enough to make a U-boat attack a problem for the Germans and yet big enough to house the President and his staff. That's why we're asking for a heavy cruiser. What do you have available?"

The CNO rubbed his chin, thinking. "In the past, the President has shown a strong preference for riding the *Houston*, but we just moved her to the Asiatic Fleet. The *Augusta* is available. She's a sister-ship. I suppose we could redeploy her even if she was going to be part of the exercises. She's just coming out of a shipyard maintenance in Mare Island and is heading through the canal and up to Newport as we speak. I'll order her to a shipyard here on the East Coast to be fitted out to haul the President. But be aware, BUSHIPS is going to need to really hump it to make this schedule work."

Charles Edison looked over his spectacles again, but this time he smiled. "I know that you can make it happen, Harold."

With that final exchange, the meeting broke up. Johnson did not hang around for the inevitable small talk that followed these type of get-togethers. There was much that demanded his attention back in his office.

Sure enough, as he walked through the door, his secretary informed him that Phil Sherman was on the phone, calling from Groton, Connecticut. Johnson hurried to his desk, grabbed the phone, and answered with, "Phil, what you got?"

"Good evening to you, too, Admiral," the flag aide responded, then immediately shifted to seriousness. "There have been some significant developments. At my direction, Miss Schultz has called the Germans and arranged a meeting for tomorrow night in New London. We'll have the meeting under observation. I have a team of Naval Intelligence agents up here. We have provided a store of phony stuff for her to feed them. She's tough, Admiral. And mad as hell."

"Just make sure you keep her safe," Johnson directed. "What else?"

"Your good friend FBI Special Agent Ralph Flannigan has raised his head again," Sherman growled. His tone of voice confirmed that Flannigan was not his favorite person. "He has been keeping Miss Schultz under observation. I gotta say, the guy is not very professional. We've been trailing him the entire time and he's none the wiser. We watched him as he installed a wiretap on the phone line at the Schultz house."

"What?" Johnson exclaimed. "Doesn't that SOB know that wiretaps are illegal? I'm pretty sure that the FBI knows about the Communications Act of 1934. Even if he tries to build a case with phony evidence, it'll get tossed as inadmissible. But just having the FBI suspecting you're a den of spies would ruin the Schultz family's name."

"Boss," Sherman answered, "I really don't think he cares. He's going to nail those folks any way he can. We're planning on feeding him a ton of crap on the wiretap, too, just to see how gullible he really is."

Johnson laughed. "Phil, make it good. I want to see this guy way, way, way up the river, making little rocks out of big rocks at the behest of the federal judiciary. And if it slows Hoover down, it would be a good thing, too, I think." There was a pause, then, "And from the other side, you seeing anything suspicious with Debby or her daddy? I'd be surprised, but..."

"Believe me, sir, we're working that angle as hard as we can without raising any suspicion. So far, they're as pure as the driven snow. Except for that juvenile charge on Mr. Schultz for egging the principal's house on Halloween, 1906, two years after he got off the boat from Deutschland. Nothing since. Not even a parking ticket. But they do consume an inordinate amount of sauerbraten and red cabbage. That don't make 'em spies. Just dyspeptic."

"Good. Good work. Keep me posted."

∞

Stan Ward rested his elbows on the desk and lowered his forehead into his cupped hands. That allowed him to take pressure off his aching neck muscles while he stared downward at the legal pad. The letters and numbers penciled onto the lines on the page were just so much gibberish. The page header informed him that the HF transmission on which these notes were based had been overheard on the U-boat circuit "*Amerika* 2," a frequency typically used by the *Kriegsmarine* to communicate with their U-boats operating in the Western Atlantic. There was also a note confirming that HF/DF—direction-finding stations dedicated to monitoring high-frequency radio transmissions—had a good idea where these transmissions came from. They had triangulated it to the Lorient broadcast station in northwest France.

That was all well and good, but it did not tell Ward what he really needed to know. What did the message say and who was on the receiving end of the transmission?

He had a tall stack of handwritten pages to work through, and that was only from the previous day's intercepts. But they were all the same gobbledygook, only from different shore stations and U-boats.

Ward stepped over to the small-scale chart of the North Atlantic that he had taped to a bulkhead in his new office deep in the bowels of the *Beaver*. The chart was peppered with pushpins. Each pin was color-coded for a date and had a little paper tag that referenced a particular intercepted piece of radio traffic. The color coding indicated the best guess for individual U-boats known to be out of port and on patrol. Ward's crew had stumbled upon a clever way to discern which boat was which. Every radio operator had a distinctive "fist," identifiable idiosyncrasies in the way they tapped out the dots and dashes of Morse code. Some made the "dahs" much longer than other operators, others had telltale spacing between letters and words, and some had an almost musical swing to their transmissions. Ward's team had been working hard to identify particular "fists" and assign them to known boats. With that bit of knowledge, they could now track U-boats across the Atlantic, and in many cases, helped by other more detailed intelligence, know exactly which boat it was and even who skippered the submarine. But it was not real time. They could not send someone to attack the U-boat. Not yet, anyway.

Ward stared at the colorful array of pins on the chart. Maybe he could deduce what was happening if he looked more closely somehow at the geography of the problem. Then he remembered a church project he had once done back at First Presbyterian in Lamar. He had used strands of his mother's knitting yarn to track the movements of Jesus across a map of the Holy Land. Now, he tied pieces of string between like-colored pins on the chart on the bulkhead and watched as patterns began to develop. Next he took a compass and spun circles around each pin with a diameter of how far the submarine could reasonably travel in a day. Some of the pins, strings, and circles made no sense at all, like the boat that would have had to travel five hundred miles in a day to get from one point to the next. There had to be a mistake in the data or the interpretation of the data there.

But many more of them made perfect sense. A light switched on inside Ward's mind. He not only could get a pretty good idea of where the U-boats were, but he could also see where they would be able to go to in a given period of time. And, if he could do that, then he should also be able to move the squadron's patrolling submarines into positions where they were most likely to find German submarines.

Staring at the pins, strings, and circles, Ward saw an exciting opportunity. He grabbed his hat and dashed out the door, startling the Marine guard standing watch there. Then he hobbled up ten decks to the Commodore's office as quickly as he could manage. He was breathless when he knocked on Captain Flynn's door and burst in at the squadron CO's grunt.

"Commodore, we need to get a message to the *54* boat right away!" Ward exclaimed, even as he struggled to restore oxygen back into his lungs. "They need to be...at the southern edge...of their patrol area within...the next twelve hours." With that, he braced himself against the bulkhead for support and sucked air.

Flynn, unsettled by the sudden interruption and the young officer's excitement, looked up from the file he was working on, mouth open and eyes wide. "Okay, exactly why is that, Mr. Ward?" Flynn asked, head cocked sideways.

"There is a very high probability that they will find a couple of U-boats operating down there, right on the edge of their patrol area, sometime in the next twenty-four hours."

"How do you know that? Little bird tell you?"

The intel officer stood erect and answered assuredly. "Commodore, you know that I'm not allowed to tell you that. Let's just say we can benefit from 'operational analysis.' That's the best I can do."

"What I'm hearing is that you want me to move *S-54* around based on one of your wild-ass guesses," Flynn shot back, challenging Ward's declaration. "Do I have that correct?"

Ward responded, "Except I would call it a 'SWAG,' a *scientific* wild-ass guess, but yes, that's pretty much it."

Flynn laughed and stood, hands out in surrender. "Okay then, let's go down to the Ops Center and get 'em moving that way before I change my mind."

19

Debbie Schultz turned left onto Neptune Avenue. Lights had just begun blinking on in the small but comfortable-looking houses that lined the streets. Children played on well-kept front lawns while a few of the residents were out for strolls, taking advantage of the springtime evening.

She had not been down to this end of New London since the devastating hurricane of 1938 pretty much leveled the town. She still had flashback memories of hunkering down in their basement as the wind screamed for hours. Although the storm made landfall in the afternoon, it was well past midnight before her father deemed it safe enough to leave the cellar. She especially remembered emerging into utter darkness. The only damage she could see in the gloom was the big elm tree in the front yard, knocked over and blocking the street. But the next morning, in the bright sunshine, she saw plenty of destruction. Across the river, New London appeared to have been steamrolled. Ocean Beach and the cottages that lined the shore were nothing but heaps of rubble. The sandy beach where she learned to swim was gone, swept out into Long Island Sound.

Driving through the area, she marveled at how much the restoration efforts by shoreside communities had accomplished. Only the lines indicating the height of the flood surge on buildings hinted of the depth of the disaster. Most of the cottages along the Thames were still in some stage of rebuilding. Soon the entire city would look as if nothing had ever happened.

Down at the Point, New London had taken a different tack, claiming about fifty acres of beachfront property and turning it into a park, scheduled to open in a couple of months. But tonight, it remained a construction site. And that was where Debbie was headed for her clandestine meeting with the mysterious German.

Parking the old Ford, she had to clamber over piles of construction debris and make her way to the nearly complete bandshell. In the darkness, she stumbled several times on materials workers had left lying around. A flashlight would have been helpful, but the German was specific on that point. A flickering light might draw unwanted attention from the law-abiding neighbors or local police.

Debbie shivered at the thought of being out here all alone. She was confident she could handle rowdy sailors at the bar and, indeed, had done so a few times. But now, she could only hope that Phil Sherman and his Naval Intelligence agents were close enough to help her if she needed them.

It was even darker inside the bandshell. It reminded Debbie of one of those spy movies where the bad guy pulled a hood over the heroine's head so she could not see her attacker.

But there did not seem to be anyone else around. The quiet, the stillness was ominous. She was just about to leave the dark bandshell and hurry back to her car when a deep, guttural voice broke the silence. "Fraulein Schultz, it is good that you have agreed to join us."

The voice startled Schultz. She yelped impulsively and took a step backward, almost falling.

But it was not the same man as the one in the parking lot. This voice was much deeper. Deeper and with an even more pronounced Bavarian accent. It came from somewhere far back in the shadows. Shadows so murky she could not even discern a shape in that direction.

"I can't see you," Schultz complained, struggling to control her voice. "Please, come to where I can see you so we can talk."

"No. Believe me, it is much better if you do not see me," the voice responded. "Then you cannot identify me, so we are both much safer if the

FBI should ever have reason to question you. Now, have you spoken with your *vater*? What does Herr Schultz say about helping the Reich?"

Debbie gulped. It was time to put the scheme to the test. And do it without even a hint that she had been briefed by anyone on what to say. Would this seasoned spy buy her story?

"Father is very angry with the way our *Deutschstämmige*...our immigrant people...are being treated by the American government anymore. The way we are being singled out for abuse by the FBI."

"*Das ist gut*," the voice confirmed, clearly pleased with her answer. "As proof of his and your loyalty, you must ask Herr Schultz to obtain a copy of the specifications for the new storage batteries for the submarines on which he works. The more detailed, the better, but he must be cautious and not get found out. When he has the information, park your car under the last light pole at the northeast corner of the lot at that tavern where you work, leave the specifications on the rear floorboard behind the driver's seat and the car door unlocked. That will be our signal that you have done as requested. Someone will contact you then. You will be well compensated for your risk and efforts as well as knowing that you have helped the cause of restoring the Fatherland to its rightful place in the world order after the indignity and suffering from the Treaty of Versailles. And there will be more opportunities, I assure you. *Guten abend, fräulein*."

There were rustling noises in the darkness, like a rodent scurrying away, and then only silence. She stood there for a few minutes, waiting, but said nothing more. The man did not speak again.

Slowly, she made her way back to her car, careful not to trip over the construction materials. Phil Sherman sat in the passenger seat of her car, waiting for her. She noticed the dome light did not come on when she opened the driver's side door and slid into the seat.

"Did you hear all that?" she asked, trying to regain the ability to breathe normally again.

"Yeah, we got everything. Bill was just outside the bandshell and heard every word," Sherman answered. "We got a tail on the guy now. I'll be honest with you, Debbie." She sucked in a deep breath as Sherman went on. "We're dealing with more here than we first thought. We figured these were a couple of local guys, doing what they could for Hitler just for the money and not necessarily Nazi pride. But you may have uncovered something bigger, a sophisticated spy ring. You did good. Real good."

Debbie exhaled. All the tension from the evening flowed from her body. She could not remember when she had ever felt so damned tired.

"Thank you, Lieutenant, but right now, I just want to go home and go to sleep."

∞

Stephen Brewster sat in *S-54*'s wardroom with Clark Manson. The message that directed them to take their submarine south rested on the table between them. Manson lit a cigarette, tossing the match into the ashtray.

"I gotta wonder who's suddenly getting all this great insight into U-boat plans," he said. "Any idea, Skipper?"

Brewster took a swig of coffee, then answered, "Nope. I can't imagine the Brits are suddenly sharing. Maybe we broke the German's code or something. But doesn't really matter, XO. They tell us where and when to go. We go." He stood and headed toward the control room. "Let's take a look at the charts and get our asses moving."

Brad Johnson met the command team when they gathered around the navigation plot. Manson grabbed a parallel rule and laid it down between the spot where they currently floated and the one where they wanted to go. Then he carefully slid it across the chart to the compass rose. Looking up, he said, "Skipper, recommend course one-six-five."

Brewster nodded. "Thanks, XO." Turning to Johnson, he ordered, "Officer-of-the-Deck, steer course one-six-five." As the boat was swinging to the new course, the CO said, "Brad, make sure the sonar operator's alert. And keep a sharp periscope watch. Squadron's repositioning us and telling us to expect some U-boat company in the next day or so." He started to leave, then turned back. "And, Brad, plan on surfacing as soon as it's fully dark. I want to keep the battery topped off, but I don't want to be running on the surface in daylight. Not with U-boats in the same waters with us. Best make sure your foul-weather gear is laid out on the main motors so it's nice and warm when you head up to the bridge. It ain't gonna be warm or dry up there."

"What exactly am I supposed to do if we see a U-boat?" Johnson asked. It was still confusing on exactly where the US Navy fit in this cockeyed war/non-war.

"Our orders are to get on the horn and report it," Brewster told him. "No matter how bad we may want to shoot 'em for all the mess they're making out here, right now, we shoot only in self-defense. Make sure that Sparks has the radio frequencies for both the Escort Common Circuit and Western Approaches Command Circuit. Those are the folks who need to know that the sharks up here have some really big teeth."

∞

Sublieutenant Geoff Chandler stared out at a dark sea. He was standing alone on the bridgewing of HMS *Chestnut*. The Royal Navy, in its wisdom, had decided that he would now be a permanent member of the trawler's crew. At least until they found some better assignment for a junior officer who had already had two ships shot out from under him.

A stiff breeze blew out of the west, pushing clouds in, obscuring the sky and a full moon. Somewhere out there to the southwest, Convoy HX-34—forty merchant ships laden with aviation fuel, bombs, and bullets to feed the voracious air war over Europe—was heading toward their rendezvous three hundred miles south of Greenland. The *Chestnut* was one of four trawlers coming down out of Iceland to reinforce the convoy escort as they crossed the dangerous stretch of ocean over to the Western Approaches. The trawlers would add some firepower and rescue assistance to the two destroyers and a frigate, vessels already run ragged from being on continuous escort duty.

Chandler could just make out the shapes of the other three trawlers in their own little group. The *Olive* and the *Pine* lay to port, while the *Hazel* was three hundred yards to starboard. All of them were riding easily in the state-three sea.

Lieutenant Jamison Cochrane, the CO of the *Chestnut*, stepped out onto the open bridge. He held two steaming coffee cups.

"Evening, Geoff," he said, handing a cup to Chandler. "Nice night, quiet."

"Thank you, sir," Chandler said as he took a sip. "Let's hope it stays that way. Anything new on the wireless?"

"Nothing much," Cochrane said. "Just a reminder that those American submarines are operating to the north. They should be better than a hundred miles off, so they should not be any problem for us having them underfoot."

Cochrane stood looking out toward the horizon for a few minutes. Then he took a sip of his coffee. He grimaced and threw what remained over the side. "Cold! I hate cold coffee! By the way, I asked the First Officer to change the watch bill. The Second Officer will be up to relieve you in a bit. You'll have the midwatch. We're scheduled to rendezvous at 0300. I want you on watch for that."

Chandler answered, "Aye, sir," but he was speaking to the Skipper's back. Cochrane had already disappeared into the bridge house, off to procure a cup of hot coffee.

∞

Brad Johnson had grown to love midwatches while running on the surface. He had the darkened sea and the star strewn sky all to himself. The full moon made a silver path across the sea like a strand of decorative lights. The air was brisk and clean, certainly less fragrant than below. The twin diesels burbled comfortingly in the background. The old *S-54* seemed to be alive, vibrating in anticipation as it pushed through the water.

"Bridge, Conn, battery charge is complete," the 7MC blared, disturbing his revery. "Answering bells on both main engines."

"Very well," Johnson spoke into the mike. "Inform the Captain and tell him that with his permission, I'll dive the boat."

But a voice from above him instantly changed things. "Mr. Johnson, I see a shape, two points off the starboard bow," the starboard lookout called down from his position up in the shears. "Can't see it clearly, even in all this moonlight, but it ain't very big."

Brad Johnson swung his binoculars around to look. Then, immediately he hollered, "Clear the bridge!" Reaching down, he yanked the diving alarm twice. Over the 1MC, he ordered, "Dive! Dive!"

Johnson was still sliding down the ladder into the conning tower when the Skipper, yawning and wearing only his skivvies, appeared. He did not even have to ask the question.

"U-boat! Two points off the starboard bow!" Johnson breathlessly reported. "Best guess on range, two thousand yards."

Brewster raised the attack periscope, turned it in that direction, and looked out.

"Yep, there he is!" He looked up and said, "Mr. Johnson, man battle stations. Make tubes one and two ready. Set their run depth at ten feet."

Johnson passed the orders down to the torpedo room just as the sonar operator reported, "Sonar contact, bearing zero-nine-six. Sounds like a submarine diesel engine."

Clark Manson climbed up to the conning tower and reported, "Ship manned for battle stations, Skipper."

Brewster nodded and replied, "Very well, XO. Now, get down to radio and get a report out on this contact. Have Sparks send it on the Escort Common Circuit first, then Western Approaches, before he sends it to squadron."

Brewster put his eye back to the periscope. "Now, let's track this sucker. Observation on the U-boat, bearing mark." The Quartermaster pushed the button on the "pickle" to send the periscope bearing to the torpedo data computer and read the bearing off the circle in the overhead above the periscope. "Bearing zero-nine-two," he called out.

Brewster adjusted the periscope stadimeter and yelled, "Range, mark!"

The Quartermaster read the stadimeter dial and reported, "Range, two-one-hundred yards."

The COB stuck his head up through the control room hatch.

"Excuse me, Skipper. I brought you your robe and slippers. You'll be a lot more comfortable and a bit warmer."

∞

Geoff Chandler glanced over at the ship's clock on the after bulkhead of the *Chestnut*'s bridge. The illuminated dial read 0245. The convoy should be steaming over the horizon any time now. He used his binoculars to scan the horizon, but nothing was visible save for the other three escorts waiting for the rendezvous.

The speaker on the HF voice radio on the back bulkhead abruptly buzzed and crackled. Chandler carefully adjusted the fine tuner for the Escort Common frequency. Most likely the Escort commander was trying to contact them to coordinate the meetup.

But the speaker blared an unexpected message. "All ships copying this circuit. All ships copying this circuit. This is US Submarine *S-54* reporting U-boat contact. Posit five-six degrees four-nine minutes north, four-one degrees four-zero minutes west. I say again, visual contact on German submarine. Posit five-six degrees four-nine minutes north, four-one degrees four-zero minutes west. U-boat is on the surface. *S-54* is submerged."

Chandler looked at the navigation chart. Jesus! That German sub had to be in sight right now! He was reaching for the phone to call the Captain when Jamie Cochrane stepped through the hatch.

"I heard the Escort Common circuit report," Cochrane said. "*S-54*? Isn't that your friend Johnson's boat?"

Chandler answered, "Yes, sir. And that U-boat is close by. I suggest that we man the deck gun and go hunting before we collide with the bloke."

Cochrane agreed. "Mr. Chandler, bring the ship around to point the U-boat and increase speed to flank. I'll get our sisters in a line abreast. Let's catch that bastard before he dives."

The four little trawlers spread out a thousand yards apart and charged off to the north. The full moon illuminated the sea, making visibility easy.

"U-boat! One point on the starboard bow!" the starboard bridge lookout yelled.

Chandler took his binoculars and had a look. "Captain, I make the range at three thousand yards. Recommend we take him under fire."

Cochrane quietly answered, "Very well, Mr. Chandler. Engage the U-boat." Then he passed the information to the other three sisters.

Geoff watched the German vessel as *Chestnut*'s quick-firing 12-pounder forward gun belched. The sub was obviously unaware of the imminent attack. The first shot fell a few hundred yards short. The second shot was a hundred yards long.

But the U-boat was not defenseless and its 88mm deck gun answered. The round screamed overhead and landed just beyond the *Chestnut*. Chandler involuntarily ducked although he well knew such a response was futile.

The three sisters joined in the fray as they charged forward. The water around the U-boat quickly resembled a forest of water columns, plumes created by near misses. Then someone's shot struck home. A pillar of flame and smoke burst from the German submarine. Steel pieces and human bodies were tossed high into the air. Chandler could easily see German sailors jumping from the sub's deck and into the water. The trawlers kept firing, though, with shots falling on and around the doomed U-boat.

In a whirlpool, the mortally stricken vessel disappeared beneath the surface just as the destroyers that had been escorting Convoy HX-34 raced in from over the horizon. They were obviously itching to join the fray. As they approached where the U-boat had gone down, the pair of warships tossed depth charges into the sea from their K-guns and rolled ash cans off their sterns. The water all around was quickly boiling up from the thunderous underwater explosions.

Geoff Chandler grabbed the radio microphone and screamed, "Cease fire, you stupid sods! There's an American submarine out there for God's sakes!"

There was a short pause and then a voice on the speaker hissed, "This is Commodore MacGyver. I want to know who is calling me a stupid sod!"

Chandler ignored the message and hung the microphone back on its hook.

But the random, wild depth charging had stopped.

20

LT. Phil Sherman knew that he was in well over his head. After all, he was the flag aide to a Washington-based Admiral, not a counter-espionage spymaster. Admiral Johnson had tasked him with unraveling a rogue FBI agent's attempt to strong-arm a young lady who happened to be the boss's son's girlfriend. The task had become very complicated from there. It now appeared they had accidently kicked over a major Nazi spy ring. And FBI Special Agent Ralph Flannigan, assigned to investigate the area for the presence of Nazi spies, had been spending all his time and effort trying to implicate Debbie Schultz's father as an enemy agent. The clueless FBI man had no idea Naval Intelligence was trying to help catch real enemy agents.

Sherman reported all of this to Admiral Johnson on the night Debbie first made contact with the Nazis. The Admiral told him to sit tight until he got back with more instructions. Just keep an eye on Miss Schultz and have her play along with the Germans. And, whatever else he did, keep her safe.

Meanwhile, Naval Intelligence had gotten busy and put together a set of documents that ostensibly were the plans for the new *Gato*-class submarine battery. Sherman was no submarine battery expert, but the documents sure looked real to him. But the experts assured him that if the Nazis tried to exploit these plans, it would send them down a deep rabbit hole. The documents showed that the Americans had an amazing new secret battery technology that hopefully the *Kreigsmarine* would expend a lot of time, manpower, and reichsmarks trying to duplicate.

Sherman sat at the Schultzes' kitchen table and watched as Heinrich Schultz laboriously copied the documents onto sheets of lined notebook paper with a stubby, dull pencil. Then he folded each sheet before crumpling it and stuffing it into his lunch pail. The result was a pile of pages that looked like Mr. Schultz had copied them down while at work at Electric Boat's shipyard and then smuggled them out in his lunch pail, right along with the remnants of his daily schnitzel sandwich.

Sherman was pleased that Mr. Schultz had agreed to go along with the plan once the Navy man had told him what was going on. Agreed only after threatening to take his shotgun and blow holes in "them damned spies!" Sherman slipped the pile of papers inside a copy of New London's daily newspaper, *The Day*. Handing the bundle to Debbie, he said, "It's your turn now. Just follow the instructions they gave you to the letter. Put this on the floor behind the driver's seat. Park under the light at the northeast corner of the tavern lot, and leave the car unlocked."

"Okay." Debbie Schultz nodded nervously as she grasped the folded newspaper.

He noticed her hand was trembling. Sherman placed his hand over hers and said, reassuringly, "Don't worry. Someone will be watching over you every second. Nothing's going to go wrong."

"Best it don't, Lieutenant," Mr. Schultz said. "I got plenty of shells for that old .410 and lots of practice on rats."

Debbie calmed her father down with a hug, pulled on her coat and quietly walked out the door. Sherman waited a few minutes—all the while assuring Heinrich that Naval Intelligence men would keep their eyes on his daughter until she was inside, at work—and then he followed her. As he pulled out onto Cottage Street, he watched Debbie's Ford turn left onto Broad Street. But then, another car pulled away from the curb two houses up and turned left onto Broad behind her. It was Special Agent Flannigan's '39 Dodge.

Sherman cursed under his breath. Flannigan! And he was going to screw everything up! Maybe keeping the FBI in the dark so far had not been the best plan. But Sherman was not quite ready to concede that point.

He gunned his engine and shot down the street, wheeled right onto Broad, and then slewed left onto North Street before swinging left and then hurrying down Bridge Street. Debbie was just pulling up to the intersection of Church and Bridge when Sherman sped right on past her. And past Flannigan, two cars behind Debbie. They were behind him now. He turned right onto Fairview and slowed. He still was not sure how he would get rid of the bothersome FBI agent, but at least he was now in a position where he could do something if the agent tried to make a move.

The rest of the drive up Military Highway to the Solomon's Tavern parking lot was calm and quiet. The place was already bustling with off-duty sailors and shipyard workers grabbing a beer before heading home from a day's work. Sherman chose an inconspicuous parking place at a curb outside the parking lot. From there, he could sit and watch without drawing attention. Debbie Schultz pulled into the lot and dutifully parked under the light pole at the northeast end. Sherman could see her glancing around nervously. And somehow, she was ten minutes early for work. Sherman's men may or may not be in place yet to watch her and then keep an eye on her car.

Special Agent Flannigan was only seconds behind her. He was not subtle at all. He pulled up alongside her car and stopped. Then got out and went around to confront Debbie.

Still no sign of the detail assigned to watch her. Protect her.

Sherman cursed, then reached into the glovebox and pulled out his M1911A1 service automatic. He had never fired the gun in anger, and it had been over a year since he had even done any practice shooting on the range. He checked that the pistol was "cocked and locked" before slipping it into his jacket pocket and stepping out. He calmly walked over to where Flannigan was now trying to manhandle Debbie out of her car and into his. She was resisting, yelling for help.

Sherman started to run toward them when a car full of sailors slewed into the gravel lot in a fog of dust and spray of stones. The vehicle would have hit him for sure if the Lieutenant had not jumped back and rolled out of its way. By the time he could get back to his feet, Flannigan's car was pulling out onto Crystal Lake Road with Debbie a prisoner in the car.

Sherman ran back to his car, started it, and gave chase. Flannigan had a significant head start but Sherman was pretty sure he knew where the agent was headed. The FBI satellite office over in New London, across the river. But that was only a guess. If the agent took her someplace else and he lost them, he would have to deliver some bad news to her father, and to the Admiral.

He turned down Military Highway, heading toward the Thames River Bridge, trying to keep the car in sight. Traffic abruptly came to a halt just as Sherman was passing beneath the railway underpass.

The drawbridge was coming up.

Sherman jumped from his car and sprinted down the highway, past a line of stopped cars, then out onto the auto bridge. Out of the corner of his eye, he caught a glimpse of a couple of sailboats and a small freighter, all heading upriver. The reason the drawbridge was up. He had at least until they passed by before it would be lowered again.

He could only hope Flannigan was stuck on this side of the river. If not, they were gone. Then he caught sight of the FBI agent's car, out on the bridge, third car back.

Sherman pulled his .45 out of his pocket and eased up along the driver's side. He could only hope his uniform would dissuade some motorist from trying to play hero, try to stop what might appear to be a mid-bridge mugging.

He tapped on the window and motioned for Flannigan to lower it. Before the agent could say anything, Sherman ordered, "Put your hands on the wheel where I can see them. You are currently interfering with a federal investigation involving national security. You could also be charged with kidnapping."

Flannigan sputtered, "I'm an FBI Special Agent! Back off! You can't meddle in a Bureau investigation!" The agent started to reach for something in his coat, maybe his ID, but Sherman touched his cold gun barrel to the man's cheek.

"Yes, I can. I'm the one with the gun." Glancing over at Debbie Schultz, in the far corner of the front passenger seat, he said, "Now, Miss Schultz, if you will come with me. Very Special Agent Flannigan won't be bothering you anymore." Looking back at Flannigan, he added pointedly, "Will he?"

The agent shook his head and looked down at the dashboard, defeated. This time. He would not meet Phil Sherman's eyes.

The pair walked back across the bridge, leaving the FBI man sitting there, perplexed, wondering what had just happened. They did a U-turn in Sherman's car just as traffic started moving again and quickly drove back to Solomon's Tavern.

One of the two Naval Intelligence agents who had been assigned to watch the Schultz car met them at the door.

"And where were you ten minutes ago when we needed you?" Sherman asked with no other greeting. Debbie was already behind the bar, putting on her apron, fending off the first lecherous customer of the evening.

"They said 1750. I was here at 1750. I saw the lady's car over there already where it was supposed to be, but I never saw her."

"We almost lost our operative. If you're ten minutes early, you're twenty minutes late, understand?"

"Sure, boss."

"So, what you got?"

"Somebody came out of the bushes. Five minutes ago. Walked right over to the car and grabbed the file like he didn't have a care in the world. Then he disappeared back into the bushes."

Sherman listened and then asked, "Where is he now?"

"Bill's trailing him. I got no idea where they went."

Sherman replied, "Okay, so they took the bait. Now, all we can do is wait and see how badly Flannigan screwed this all up. And do our best to keep an eye on Miss Schultz and her dad. Got that?"

∞

LT(jg) Stan Ward stood on the bridge of the *Emily Rose* as it passed beneath the upraised Thames River drawbridge, just behind a couple of sailboats. Hans Schneider, there next to him, blew the ship's horn as the little freighter cleared the highway bridge and then the railroad one. That signaled to all the cars stuck up there that they would soon be back on their way home to supper. But it also signified that the ship's journey down from

Argentia, Newfoundland, was almost complete. Another two miles upriver and then they would be tying up at the submarine base piers.

"Anxious to get home?" Captain Schneider asked Ward.

"You bet, Hans!" he enthused. "Even if it's only for a week and it's for work."

He had not expected to be back in New London so soon, but his work on helping intercept the lurking U-boat had caused a great deal of curiosity among members of Naval Intelligence. They apparently wanted an in-person briefing. And Ward was not about to argue.

"Well, that pregnant wife of yours will be happy," Schnieder replied. "How long till the baby's due?"

"Best we can figure, in August," Ward answered. He was intently searching the shoreline, hoping to catch a glimpse of their beat-up Chevy roadster parked at one of the observation points along the river. But it was not surprising it was not there. He had not been able to send a message to Karen that he was coming home for a few days. Security had tightened dramatically of late and would not permit such sharing, no matter how innocent. His best hope would be to call the hospital once they had tied up. Her shift did not end until 2000. But surely Karen could break free from her nursing duties a few minutes early to meet her husband, home from the wars. Well, to be diplomatically correct, the "non-wars."

The little freighter chugged on up the river, battling the Thames current every inch of the way. They were traveling so slowly that Ward was sure that the *Emily Rose* was losing the battle with the river and might be flushed right back out into the Sound. But finally, they pulled abreast of the North Pier, in the shadow of the submarine escape tower.

Stan stood up on the bridge wing and watched as the crew secured the *Emily Rose* to the pier. Then he spied Ollie Oglethorpe standing at the head of the pier, pipe firmly clenched in his teeth, sending up smoke signals. It was still a mystery to Ward how a Navy Commander got away with wearing an old, beat-up, tattered cardigan sweater. It certainly was not Navy issue.

Then he could see someone else, someone getting out of the passenger side of Ollie's car. But it couldn't be!

Karen! Stan bounded down the ladder as fast as his bad leg would allow, and across the brow seconds after it landed. Then it was real. She was in his arms, where she belonged. All was right with the world.

Oglethorpe gave the newlyweds a few minutes before he pointedly cleared his throat. The couple slowly broke away from a particularly long kiss. Stan looked up, a broad grin and smeared lipstick across his face.

The Commander reached into his pocket, took out his car keys, and tossed them to Ward. "Take your wife home and then meet me in the Ops Center. We have work to do," Oglethorpe told him. With a dismissive wave, he headed off, walking up toward the COMSUBPATFOR headquarters building as the Wards headed out toward home.

It was a couple of hours before Stan made an appearance back in his old haunt, in the basement Operations Center. Oglethorpe looked up from the report he was studying when Stan came in.

"Didn't figure I would see you until morning," he said with a laugh.

Ward tossed him his car keys and replied, "Figured it was bad form to make the boss walk home. Besides, you said we had work to do. So, to what do I owe the good fortune of being called back here?"

Oglethorpe waved him to a chair and spun around the report he had been perusing so that Stan could see it.

"We're starting to make some headway on cracking this new version of the Enigma code," Ollie explained. "The Brits are still no help. They figure if they cut us in on what they know, it'll instantly get leaked and go right back to Hitler's *Abwehr* guys and they'll immediately change the code. But we're doing what we can, using brute force to reliably decode maybe twenty-five percent of some of the messages. They're still late for any kind of action, but at least we're starting to piece it together."

Ward nodded, still studying the report. "Twenty-five percent is twenty-five percent better than nothing, I guess. Looks like you guys have been doing fine without me, so what can I do to help out?"

"I was really interested in that report you sent down, the one about operational analysis and tracking signals," Oglethorpe answered. "It occurred to me that maybe we could combine the two approaches and make some real gains. You know, putting two and two together. Putting the easy outside jigsaw pieces together first, then filling in the middle. I want us to put our heads together and bounce ideas for a bit. Come up with a plan for cracking this nut. And that's hard to do if you're up there in Canada in the bilge of a submarine tender."

"Okay," Ward responded. "But it would be a lot easier if we had a clue of what the message traffic might be about. They could be trying to order toilet paper, or they could be vectoring a wolfpack onto a convoy?"

Oglethorpe got really quiet for a minute. Then, a serious expression on his face, he leaned forward in his chair, stopped puffing on his pipe, and explained.

"This is even higher classified than what we normally deal with. No one in this room knows about it but me. And now so do you. Churchill and Roosevelt are planning a powwow up in your neck of the woods in early August. At Argentia. They will be discussing the possibility of the US entering the war, among other things. Such a get-together might well invite German attention. And possibly action. We need to sift through all the U-Boat command message traffic to see if they have gotten a hint about this meeting, and, if so, what they're planning to do about it."

"Man, you really think they might try to assassinate two of the most powerful men in the world?" Stan asked.

"Doesn't matter what I think. We just have to see what the Germans know and what they plan to do with that information." The Commander sat back and resumed puffing away.

"Okay, boss. Then, I suppose we ought to get to work."

"Indeed. That is, if you still have the strength after"—a broad wink—"dropping your wife off at home."

21

A cold fog fell over the Brittany coast. *Oberleutnant* Helmut Schmiel could barely see the deck gun, only five meters in front of where he stood on the bridge of the *U-23*. The barest hint of a smile crossed Schmiel's normally dour face. The thick fog was perfect to mask his underway. If luck held, and the meteorologists were correct for once, the *U-23* would be well out to sea and submerged before the British air searches had any chance to find them.

Schmiel waved to *Oberleutnant* Karl Smit, standing on the bridge of the *U-144*, tied up inboard of the *U-23*. Smit and the *U-144* would follow him out to sea and accompany them on their special—and very secret—mission.

"Good hunting, Karl," Schmiel hollered across to the other U-boat commander. "Schnapps at the Bar Royal when we return."

"*Ja*," Smit responded with a laugh. "You buy."

Schmiel ordered lines cast off and sounded the ship's horn. Horns from ships all around the harbor answered, wishing the warrior a successful hunt. Diesel smoke contributed to the cloying fog as the *U-23* moved out into Brest's inner harbor. The *schnellboot* was waiting at the sea wall to escort the U-boats out to sea, away from the coast of France. Schmiel looked back to see the *U-144* following them a few meters astern.

The little convoy carefully picked its way through the narrow channel, avoiding the rocks, small islands, and defensive minefields that dotted the way. The fog was dissipating, blown away by the prevailing southerly winds out in the Iroise Sea.

Schmiel signaled the *schnellboot* with his flashing light, thanking the escort boat and releasing it to return to Brest. The *U-23*, closely followed by the *U-144*, disappeared beneath the waves.

∞

Stan Ward reviewed the latest intercept traffic. It was well past midnight. He was alone, in his ops center deep in the bowels of the *Beaver*. With Karen nearing her due date and him once again a thousand miles away, there was nothing for Ward to do but try to tamp down the worry with work. Ollie Oglethorpe had promised him that, once this crucial Presidential meeting was done, he would do everything in his power to get Ward back to New London, but, for right now, "the needs of the Navy" meant that he was stuck on a submarine tender in this tiny, isolated bit of Canada. And when he was off duty, there was little to occupy his time—and mind—but to find a sunny spot and watch the fishermen coming and going. At least the summer weather made it more pleasant to do so. Still, he was not off duty that much.

Ward took the clipboard with the radio-intercept traffic and laid out the new information on his wall chart. More push pins and bits of string showed that two new U-boats had come out from Brest and were now in the North Atlantic. Both boats were sending a lot of traffic. And probably getting a lot, too, but Ward could not tell that until they had some more profound breakthrough on the Enigma machines.

The much more rudimentary pushpins and string showed that the two boats were heading pretty much directly across the Atlantic. Why weren't they swinging north? Two large convoys, a fast one and a slow one, were both progressing toward Ireland just a few hundred miles north of those two U-boats. A couple of fat, juicy targets like those should be attracting every wolf at sea, but these two were ignoring them. Ward could only assume that they had another, more important mission. But what could it be?

He stared at the chart, imprinting every detail in his mind. He had a thought. Taking a pair of dividers, he walked off the distance from the two German subs' current position to Argentia. Then he calculated the time it would take the U-boats to traverse that distance if they maintained their steady pace. Finally, he took a close look at his notes on the calendar hung on the bulkhead across the desk from him.

Jesus! It worked out. His calculations had them arriving—if they continued their current course and speed—in the vicinity of Argentia a day before either the *Prince of Wales* or the *Augusta* arrived with their VIP passengers. Ward hastily folded up the chart, grabbed his hat, and rushed out of the ops center, once again almost bowling over the sleepy Marine guarding the door.

The squadron duty officer, sitting at his desk in the *Beaver*'s communications shack, was also struggling to stay awake when Ward came barreling in. The duty officer jerked awake and then listened as the wild-eyed LT(jg) tried to explain why he needed to speak with the Commodore "right damn now!" And he would not listen to the fact that it was well past midnight and the Commodore was certainly sound asleep. It took some loud discussion and dire threats before the duty officer relented and called the Commodore's stateroom.

He handed the phone to Ward while it was still ringing and said, "Here, you wanted to wake him. You take the blast of crap that's gonna generate."

"Flynn." The hoarse voice confirmed he was barely awake.

"Commodore, this is Stan Ward," he blurted out. "I need to talk to you right away. It's important and it can't wait."

"All right," Flynn growled and yawned. "Give me five minutes and meet me in my stateroom. And, Ward, this damn well better be important."

Stan took a couple of deep breaths, paced around the comms shack nervously for precisely four minutes, and then rushed back down the passageway to the Commodore's cabin. He knocked and then entered when he heard an irritated growl through the door.

Ward quickly unfolded his chart and started to explain what he had deduced, that two U-boats were apparently coming their way, and their arrival would put them in the vicinity at a time when they could intercept warships on their way to a high-level summit meeting at Argentia Station.

But there was one problem in explaining the urgency to Commodore Flynn. He still knew nothing about any meeting between Roosevelt and Churchill, much less that it was occurring in his backyard in less than a week. The meeting was that secret.

Ward carefully explained as best he could about the intercept intelligence and what he inferred from it. But he could not tell the Commander exactly why it was such a big deal.

Flynn listened quietly. Then he said, "Mr. Ward, I don't know a damn thing about what you are telling me. You expect me to believe that some high-ranking muckety-mucks are coming here for some kind of super-secret confab and that the Nazis are sending a couple of U-boats all the way to our little harbor to attack them. And this is all based on some pins that you stuck in a chart of the Atlantic?"

"Yes, sir." Ward nodded vigorously. "That is exactly what I'm telling you. The *52* boat and the *54* boat are both in port. We need to get them underway and send them out to try to find those U-boats and stop them before they even get close. The only other option would be to postpone or move that meeting, and I doubt either...well, either of the main attendees... would be keen on that."

Commodore Flynn stared at the excited officer for a few seconds, eyes still sleepy, face incredulous. Then he said, "I know that you have access to intel that I don't have clearance for. Nothing I can do about that. But I'm not getting boats underway based on some JO's half-baked ideas and guesses. You get hold of COMSUBPATFOR and have them order me to deploy those boats. Then I will do so. Now get out of here and let me sleep."

Dismayed and disheartened, Stan Ward slunk out of the Commodore's cabin and walked back to the comm shack. It took him nearly an hour to draft a message to Ollie Oglethorpe. Ollie should be able to walk upstairs and talk to the Admiral. That might be what Commodore Flynn needed to get things moving.

If not, if either Oglethorpe or the Admiral had the same opinion of Ward's interpretation of the data as Commodore Flynn, then things would just have to play out. And Ward could only pray he had arrived at a wrong conclusion.

∞

Admiral Devin Johnson read the message one more time. Its content really wasn't a surprise, but he was caught off guard that it was finally all happening. The mechanics for the historic meeting between Churchill and Roosevelt were now lurching into motion, and the results of that get-together would have an enormous impact on world history. The message was from the US Embassy in London. Churchill, accompanied by Roosevelt's top advisor, Harry Hopkins, had just departed London by train, bound for northern Scotland. From there a Royal Navy destroyer would ferry them on the short ride to Scapa Flow. Once in that vast Royal Navy anchorage, the party would board the battleship HMS *Prince of Wales* to begin the voyage across the Atlantic.

Johnson read the detailed schedule in full once more before yelling through his office door to the secretary, "Get me SECNAV on the phone. Pronto!"

It took a few minutes for Secretary Edison's office to locate him. He was up on Capitol Hill, meeting with Senator Vinson. When Johnson was finally patched through, he reported, "Mr. Secretary, the Prime Minister is on the move. It's time to get the boss headed north."

"Is everything ready?" Edison queried. "I don't want to get the President moving only to have him sitting around cooling his heels at some train station."

"Yes, sir," Johnson quickly responded. "Everything is as ready as we can make it. The press already has the story that he's taking some foreign dignitaries on a ten-day fishing junket. They're running with it. Some are already giving him flack for going fishing while Japan and Germany are causing such a ruckus."

It took a couple of hours for the final coordination, so it was early afternoon before the presidential train pulled out of Union Station in Washington, DC, for its eight-hour journey to New London, Connecticut. Cheering crowds lined New London's streets as the President, sporting his jaunty cigarette holder, waved happily from the backseat of the limo as it made its way across the Thames River to the submarine base.

The presidential yacht, *Potomac*, was waiting, tied up at Alpha Pier at the submarine base, as invited dignitaries from several countries boarded. Roosevelt was whisked aboard as soon as he arrived at the pier. The impressive yacht steamed through the night and anchored off Martha's Vineyard, where the foreign dignitaries were stealthily put ashore. Then the yacht raised anchor and headed out to sea. Once over the horizon, it rendezvoused as planned with the cruiser USS *Augusta* and—when no aircraft, ships, or submarine periscopes were to be seen—President Roosevelt was swung over to the Navy vessel.

With the President aboard, the *Augusta* pointed north toward Newfoundland. The *Potomac* turned around and made its way back toward Cape Cod. One of the Secret Service agents aboard, wearing a white fedora, a blanket across his lap, and sporting a distinctive cigarette holder, sat on the yacht's fantail and waved at more cheering summer crowds along the shore as the *Potomac* motored through the Cape Cod Canal on its way to the fishing grounds off Provincetown.

∞

Ollie Oglethorpe quickly read, and then reread, Stan Ward's message from the overnight message boards. Thinly disguised amid all the "navalese" of a standard US Navy communication, Ollie could easily determine that Ward was frantic. Frantic but confident in his analysis. He could see that the bright young officer had used his analytical skills to deduce a potentially significant threat to the Argentia meeting and to the two world leaders who were already enroute there.

It was time to take action. Maybe past time.

The moment he knew Admiral Edwards would be in his office—thankfully, the Admiral was an early riser, on duty by 0700 most days—Oglethorpe grabbed the message and bounded upstairs, taking two steps at a time. It was sometimes convenient having the boss, Commander Patrol Force Submarines, one floor above his own ops center. He was standing in Rear Admiral Richard Edwards's outer office, enduring the baleful stare from the Admiral's Yeoman, when he realized he had forgotten to remove his old cardigan sweater before rushing upstairs. Well, it was too late now.

The Yeoman Chief swung the heavy oak door open and waved Oglethorpe into the Admiral's office.

Admiral Edwards glanced up at Oglethorpe after he finished signing some document, carefully replaced the cap on his fountain pen, and laid it on the desk as the Chief closed the door behind the intel officer.

"Ollie, dammit!" Edwards growled. "I'd heard stories about how you run that little kingdom of yours down there in the cellar, but I never gave them any credence. Now, I'm not so sure. In the future, I would very much appreciate it if you would wear a proper uniform in my office. Understood?"

Oglethorpe blushed crimson. "Yes, sir! I'm very sorry, sir! I was in a hurry with some very important information that requires immediate action. I didn't think."

"Well, what is this emergency that demands my immediate attention?" the Admiral asked, holding out his hand for the message that Oglethorpe was thrusting his way.

"Admiral, we have reason to believe that the Nazis have learned of the upcoming meeting in Argentia and are positioning U-boats to intercept the *Prince of Wales* and the *Augusta*!" Oglethorpe exclaimed. "It's all based on communications traffic analysis, but I'm afraid that it is pretty convincing."

Edwards read Ward's message carefully and looked up. "I see the logic in Mr. Ward's argument, but there are no hard facts to nail his conclusions to. Those subs could just be hunting and killing farther west than typical. Or setting up a picket to spot convoys sooner. God knows, they've been ranging far and wide of late."

Oglethorpe's face fell. Admiral Edwards was about to tell him that he was chasing ghosts and then unceremoniously toss him out of his office. "But, sir," he pressed. "This meeting is too important to..."

Edwards cut him off in mid-sentence with a raised hand. "This meeting is far too important to take any chances. If the President or Mr. Churchill should be hurt...or worse...it would create chaos unlike anything we've ever seen. Just the kind of thing Adolf Hitler would be aiming for. Let's get those submarines that we have stationed up there out of the barn and looking for these U-boats." He hollered in the general direction of his office door, "Chief! Come in here!"

The Yeoman Chief stuck his head in.

"Chief," Admiral Edwards ordered, "get a priority message to that squadron commodore up in Argentia. What's his name, Ollie?"

"Flynn, Captain Flynn."

"Yeah, Captain Flynn. I keep forgetting we exiled him up there in the wilds of Canada. Chief, tell him I want all his subs deployed and out looking for suspect U-boats that might approach Argentia Station. They should be accompanied by appropriate surface vessels, as well, depending on what he has available. And I want every asset at sea yesterday. Understand?"

The Yeoman was backing out the door when Edwards added, "And get me Admiral Johnson on the phone. Try his residence first. Washington needs to know about this."

When the door was shut again, Edwards turned to Oglethorpe and said, "Ollie, give that young Ward fellow a Bravo Zulu from me. It takes a lot of balls as well as smarts to go over your boss's head when you are sure that you are right."

Oglethorpe nodded in agreement and started to back toward the door. Edwards smiled and added, "Next time you are up here, please wear your shoes."

Ollie looked down. At his bedroom slippers.

∞

Brad Johnson and Fred Wurster were enjoying one of those rare moments when they were both in port at the same time. It was lunchtime and the *Beaver* wardroom was serving cheeseburgers and French fries. That was too much for the ravenous young submariners to resist.

"How are things on the 52 boat?" Johnson asked as they waited to be served. The two junior officers were well down on the seniority list and would wait for several minutes before their plates arrived.

"Interesting is the best way to put it. With the XO still out of commission, Jim Shelton is going to be acting XO," Wurster replied. "Saw the XO down in the tender sick bay this morning, living the life of Riley. No duties, no junior officers to harass, just kicked back. Says he will be back in a week or so. I can't wait." Sarcasm dripped from the last comment.

Plates of hot food appeared in front of the two. The initial feeding frenzy was conducted mostly in silence. Then Brad Johnson picked up his napkin and wiped grease from his chin. "Got a letter from Trip this morning," he offered up.

"And what does our wayward world traveler have to say?" Wurster asked as he dribbled more ketchup onto his fries.

"Well, he finally landed in the Philippines," Johnson answered. "He spends a lot of words bemoaning how hot his "*Sugar*" boat is with no air conditioning way down there in the tropics."

"Poor baby," Wurster's voice oozed false sympathy. "He could be up here with us, cuddling up to the diesel engines just to get our hands warm."

Brad Johnson ignored Wurster and went on. "Seems that the Manila Army and Navy Club is quite the social scene, though, and that fits Trip to a T. Our Senator's son is blending right in. Golf in the morning, bridge in the afternoon, and then a cocktail party at the Officer's Club 'til they run him out."

Wurster shook his head. "Sounds a lot like our social life. Diesel repairs in the morning, an afternoon stores load, then an evening battery charge."

They were both laughing and reaching for the ice cream when Jim Shelton and Clark Manson walked into the wardroom together. The pair walked directly over to Johnson and Wurster's table. They were not smiling.

Shelton glanced at the unfinished meal in front of them and said, "Fred, we got emergency sortie orders. Grab your stuff and hurry back to the boat. We shove off in an hour."

Manson nodded. "You too, Brad. We're pulling out right behind the 52."

Wurster ran to his stateroom on the tender, grabbed his toilet kit and clean clothes, stuffed it all into his seabag with no regard to packing or folding, and hurried down toward the *S-52*. The clothes that he had sent to the ship's laundry that morning would just have to wait until he came back.

He climbed down the accommodation ladder from the tender to his submarine to find it a madhouse of activity. Pallets of groceries were being lowered by the tender crane to the submarine's deck. Boxes of last-minute stores were being shoved down the hatches to waiting hands below. Fueling hoses snaked across the weather deck and were already topping off the submarine's diesel oil tanks.

LT(jg) Wurster managed to worm his way belowdecks through all the activity and toss his seabag onto his bunk before fighting his way to the control room. Jim Shelton, the Weapons Officer/XO, and Brent Halloran, the Engineer, were huddled there with Don Gorman, the Skipper, fervently discussing something.

Gorman looked up and saw Wurster. "Fred, you're Officer-of-the-Deck for the underway. Get to the bridge and get topside cleared." Gorman glanced at his watch. "We are underway in forty-five minutes, come hell or high water."

Wurster nodded and rushed up the ladder to the bridge. He looked down at the main deck. It reminded him of some wildly out-of-control Saturday farmers market being piled onto the decks and stuffed down the hatches of a submarine. There would be no way to get this all cleared and do an underway in three-quarters of an hour.

Then he caught sight of Chief Wankel supervising the fueling operation. He cupped his hands around his mouth and yelled, "Chief Wankel!" When the Chief looked up, he waved for him to come over to the base of the bridge.

The Chief Engineman hurried over and looked up at Fred from the deck. "What you need, Mr. Wurster?"

"We're underway in forty minutes," Wurster said. "I need for you to wrap up fueling right away. And can you help me clear topside?"

"Sure thing, sir. We're about done anyway." He trotted back to his fueling party and issued a couple of orders. Then he turned to the stores loading party and had a few words with them. As if by magic, the confusion topside began to dissipate. The fuel hoses were drained and snaked back up to the tender. Pallets and empty boxes disappeared, lifted up and piled on the tender deck.

Wurster glanced at his watch. Fifteen minutes to go. He gave the order to start the diesels and to shift electrical power to them. Line handlers were mustering at the mooring lines fore and aft. The shore power cables and the potable water hoses were being pulled up onto the tender when Don Gorman climbed up onto the bridge.

Wurster reported, "Ship's ready to get underway with the exception of the brow, Skipper. Request permission to remove the brow."

Gorman nodded. "Remove the brow, then cast off all lines."

Just as the lines dropped into the water, Wurster blew one prolonged blast on the ship's whistle. He heard the answering whistle of their sister boat on the other side of the *Beaver*, indicating she was ready to depart as well. He looked up to see QM-1 Obrien unfurl "Old Glory" and run it up the mast.

S-52 was officially detached from shore and underway.

As the sub slipped out of the anchorage and into Placentia Bay, Wurster glanced over at Don Gorman. "Skipper," he asked, "what's the mission this time? Why all the secrecy and sudden rush to get out to sea?"

"Well, Fred," Gorman said, "I'm about to go below and tell everyone what's up, but you're stuck up here for a bit. Seems that Winston Churchill and FDR are both headed up here for some sort of super-secret conference. The Intel weenies are afraid that the Nazis may have caught wind of this little meeting and may be sending some U-boats to break it up. We're being sent out to find these U-boats first and send them to Davy Jones's locker." Gorman watched as the shoreline grew farther away. "Freddy, we may just be on the next Great War's very first war patrol."

22

Debbie Schultz turned on the "Closed" sign, locked the door to Solomon's Tavern behind her, and headed out across the gravel parking lot. She waved goodnight to Kelsey, the last of the bartenders to go home, as he drove past, hurrying home. It was a dark, moonless night, though she thought she might just be able to see the first tinge on the horizon of the next day's sun. Few nights went by when, as she left work, she did not think about past harrowing events that had taken place in this very parking lot. Even though it had been a couple of months now since her encounter with the Nazi spy and since Special Agent Flannigan had tried to kidnap her. No one from either side had tried to contact her, so she had almost forgotten about all that. It had been so uneventful that Phil Sherman returned to Washington, claiming things were getting very hectic back at the "plant," his pet name for his office in DC. He faithfully promised her that Naval Intelligence agents were still there, still keeping an eye on her, and they would make certain nothing happened to her or her father.

As she walked briskly to her car, Debbie looked all around the empty parking lot. If someone—friend or foe—was keeping an eye on her, they were certainly doing a good job of remaining out of sight, way back in the shadows. As far as she could tell, she had the dark parking lot and the star-studded night sky all to herself. Even so, she was relieved when she got to the car, grabbed her car key from her purse, and inserted it into the lock.

"Fraulein Schultz."

She jumped when the voice startled her. The same deep Bavarian-accented voice from before. The man emerged just enough from the shadows so she could see him, but he was still ten feet away. His broad hat brim was pulled down so far that she could not see any of his face. Only that he wore a full-length trench coat. All she could tell for sure was that he was tall. Maybe slim, too, but the coat hid that.

"Must you always startle me that way?" she asked, trying to control her breathing. And the situation.

"I apologize. But I bring you good news. The *Vaterland* is most appreciative of your last work. The information you and your father provided us is proving very valuable."

"Just how valuable? I hope you and the others are not wasting what we worked so hard and risked so much to deliver," Schultz shot back. Despite her pounding heart, she stayed right on script. Phil Sherman's NIS agents had drilled into her that she needed to establish her bona fides, her motivations, her ownership of her part of the operation with the Germans. Give them no reason to question her loyalty to her ancestral homeland or her desire to make money in the process.

"Ah, the American mercenary instinct," the Voice said with a chuckle. "I believe you will be pleased with the generous recompense you will find waiting for you under the doormat at your front door. And *danke* to Herr Schultz as well, though we believe it still prudent to keep all contact through you, fraulein. To show the appreciation of the much-abused German people for your work on their behalf, you have both been raised to the rank of *Oberstleutnant* in the *Abwehr*. Herr Schultz has been awarded the Iron Cross, Second Class, for his stellar service to the Reich. All this to remain secret for the time being, of course. And be assured your efforts have been personally acknowledged by *der Führer und Reichskanzler* himself, *heil* Hitler!"

Debbie fully expected the Voice to click his heels and snap off a Nazi salute. Instead, he changed topics. "We have a new assignment for you. The *Kreigsmarine* desires the plans and specifications for the advanced torpedo data computer that is being installed on your new submarines under construction at Electric Boat. Expect to also find a Minox camera and film beneath your doormat. Tell your *vater* that the camera is much faster and safer than hand-copying the files. Signal us in the normal manner when you have the information."

The Voice abruptly turned and disappeared into the darkness. Debbie stood there a full minute, half expecting someone from Naval Intelligence to emerge and let her know he had witnessed the chat. No one did.

She was lost in thought for the entire drive back to the house on Cottage Street. She parked the old Ford and rushed up onto the porch. Sure enough, there was a telltale bulge under the doormat. She looked around. The neighborhood appeared to be asleep. And no Naval Intelligence people that she could see, either.

Lifting the mat, she found two packages wrapped in thick packing tape and cardboard. She carried them inside, to the kitchen table, and used one of her late mother's carving knives to open them.

One envelope contained a thousand dollars in twenty-dollar bills. That was more money than she made in an entire year at the bar, even when tips were good. But she assumed she would have to turn that over to the government. For evidence or something.

In the other package was a tiny camera and a dozen very small cannisters of film plus a small booklet with instructions. In German.

She used the phone on the kitchen wall to call the emergency number that Phil Sherman had given her. This certainly qualified as an emergency, or at least something the Navy spy-catchers would want to know immediately. The call was answered on the second ring.

"Yes, Miss Schultz. Are you in danger? Our agent is five minutes away."

"Five minutes" gave Debbie a moment's pause. A lot of bad stuff could happen in five minutes. "No, I'm okay. But they have made contact again and assigned us a new mission. I need to speak with Phil Sherman."

"He will call you in the morning. Since the *Abwehr* agents contacted you again, our instructions are to open a counter-espionage operation. Lieutenant Sherman will explain what that means when you talk."

She was not able to find much sleep. She even heard Father getting ready for work, fixing his breakfast, but she decided to wait to share this latest development with him until she spoke with Sherman. It was late morning when she gave up on sleep. She got up, got dressed, and was pouring herself her first cup of coffee when she heard a knock at her door. She considered not responding, just in case it was someone from the *Abwehr*. Or worse, the FBI. But either one of them would know she was home and alone. And they could come in violently if they really wanted to talk with her.

She grabbed her cup and went to answer the front door. If it was Flannigan, the FBI man, she would, without hesitation, give him a face full of hot joe.

Phil Sherman and a man she had not seen before stood there, patiently waiting.

"Good morning, Debbie," Sherman said with a broad smile when she opened the door. How in the world had he gotten to Groton so fast? It had been only a little over six hours since she spoke to the agent. And it was at best an eight-hour train ride from Washington.

"The Admiral is in New York for some meetings, so I decided to drive over after I heard about your little meeting last night." Well, that explained the quick personal visit. "May we come in?"

Debbie opened the door for them. Then looked up and down Cottage Street for any signs the Germans might have seen her guests arrive. "Of course. There's fresh coffee in the kitchen."

The two men took the offered coffee and sat at the kitchen table. To Debbie, it looked as if they were ready to discuss the weather or the Red Sox season. "Miss Schultz," Sherman began, "since the Germans have chosen to contact you again and ask for more information, Naval Intelligence has decided that this is a good counter-espionage opportunity. We want you and your father to be double agents and continue to feed the Nazis the bogus stuff that we give you." He smiled. "There is a side benefit. Whatever the Germans pay you is yours to keep. And it's tax-free, since reporting it would be a violation of national security."

Debbie drew back. The money was a nice touch, but the risks were unknown. One other thing bothered her, too.

"But we are not at war with Germany or anybody else I know of," she said. "I don't understand all this spy nonsense. It's like those Hitchcock spy movies. We'd be double agents or something. I've seen more than enough already to worry that it could be dangerous. For me and for Father. Maybe even for Brad since his dad is an Admiral."

"Debbie, don't worry," Sherman reassuringly told her as he sipped his coffee. "We'll always have someone watching over you. We will keep you safe. None of us knows if war is inevitable or not, but right now, I would not bet against it. And Hitler and his spies being so active and aggressive is a sure sign." He pointed his cup toward the other man who had so far only offered a mumbled "Good morning" and a nod. "But I do need to tell you that George Klemp here will be taking the lead on this operation from this point forward. Things have moved well out of my bailiwick, and I need to go back to working for the Admiral. We got plenty going on down at the plant. However, if you need me or just want to talk, you have my number. Please call."

"One question, Phil," Debbie asked. "How long will we be doing this?"

But it was George Klemp who answered. "Until the coming war is over. Until the Germans have some reason to question your information, value, or loyalty. Or until the *Abwehr* shuts down this spy operation."

"In other words, you don't have a clue," she responded, but not in a negative way. "I'm doing this because I love my country. That might sound corny but it's the way I feel. I can't speak for my father, but I know how much he loves America, and he will do all he can. I know you can't totally guarantee our safety or his, but for right now, I suppose that's a risk we're willing to take."

Klemp nodded. "That's great to hear. With Nazi parades marching down Fifth Avenue in Manhattan and holding rallies in Central Park and Japan jerking our diplomats around while they gobble up the Pacific Rim, it's a scary time." Klemp drained the last of his coffee. "Look, there's one more thing. This is a very highly classified operation. Top secret. No one can ever know about it or what your role and your father's role is in it all. That includes your boyfriend, LT. Johnson. Admiral's son or no, he cannot know anything. Period."

Debbie nodded. "The way the Navy's keeping us apart these days..." She looked out the kitchen window. A large cardinal sat on the outside window ledge, head cocked, looking for all the world like he was eavesdropping. She nodded toward the bird. "Maybe you should tell that guy out there to not tell anybody what he knows, too."

All three laughed but with minimal spirit.

∞

Oberleutnant Helmut Schmiel stood behind the Enigma operator, looking over the man's shoulder, reading the message as it slowly emerged from the typewriter-like machine. Schmiel had not experienced anything like this mission before. *Befehlshaber der Unterseeboote* Karl Dönitz, well known for "playing chess" with his boats, was personally directing both Schmiel's *U-23* and Karl Smit's *U-144* in minute detail. Schmiel was beginning to feel that Admiral Dönitz was telling them "how to stuff a *wurtz*." The Supreme Commander of German U-boats was sending frequent long messages telling the two Captains every detail of what he wanted done and then requiring that they promptly acknowledge his orders, as if they were a couple of trainees in submarine school.

Schmiel glanced over at the navigation chart and mentally measured the kilometers that he still needed to transit. He was not at all sure that he could race fast enough to get a shot at the *Augusta* and satisfy the demands of the Admiral. There was little consolation in the fact that Smit and *U-144* had it even worse. His assignment was to attack the British Battleship *Prince of Wales* with the Prime Minister on board.

Schmiel solved the time-distance problem in his head. He came to the only conclusion available to him. They would need to surface and run at a flank bell nearly all the way to the attack position. That meant throwing caution to the wind, ignoring the Allied air threat while they raced ahead, burning more diesel in the process.

At his command, the *U-23* leaped up to the surface and charged ahead. The pit log showed that they were making better than thirty-eight kilometers per hour when Schmiel climbed up to the U-boat's bridge. A wave crashed over the low bridge just as he emerged from the hatch, drenching him and everybody else standing there. Rain squalls and low storm clouds prevented him from seeing much of the ocean, but it also hid the *U-23* from the Allied hunters.

"*Kapitän*," the bridge speaker blasted. "New message from U-Boat command. *Prince of Wales* and three British destroyers sighted five hundred kilometers due south of Iceland by Condor aircraft. Estimate speed forty-five kilometers per hour and on course two-four-zero. The Americans are reporting that the *Augusta* will arrive in Argentia at the same time."

"*Suhr gut*," Schmiel grunted in reply. "Acknowledge receipt and inform U-boat command that we are now on the surface running at flank. Tell them as well that we will need to rendezvous with a *milchkuh* after the attack to take on fuel." A *milchkuh*—literally a "milk cow"—was a Type XIV German submarine specially designed to replenish other subs.

"*Ja, Kapitän.*"

Schmiel could picture his counterpart, Karl Smit, running on the surface a few kilometers to the south, standing on the bridge of the *U-144*, doing and saying much the same thing.

Including giving the bridge railing a sound kick in frustration.

∞

Stan Ward spread his chart of the Atlantic Ocean out on Commodore Flynn's conference table. The *Prince of Wales* was plotted heading west-southwest from Scotland at a reported twenty-eight knots. The *Augusta* was north-northeast-bound from New London, making twenty-five knots. And the squadron's submarines—four of the boats already out on patrol and two, the *S-52* and *S-54*, racing out to take their positions—showed up on the chart as well. Stan had added his best guess based on his simplistic pins and string of where the two German U-boats likely were. They were providing plenty of intercepts, so he was getting more and more comfortable with the accuracy of his analysis. The submarines had not varied course or speed at all since departing France.

"Commodore, this is the current layout of everyone's position," Ward explained. "Both U-boats are still well to the north of the convoy routes where they usually are at play. These two guys are not showing any interest in the eastbound convoys. Or anything else. They're coming this way straight as an arrow and as quickly as those boats will go."

"Okay, Stan," Roderick Flynn said as he stood there intently studying the chart. He had been briefed on the details and importance of the upcoming meeting at Argentia, and who would be among the star attendees. The gravity of the situation, complicated by the behavior of the U-boats, now rested heavily on the Commodore's shoulders. He rubbed his chin for a few seconds as he thought. Then he said, "It looks like those two bastards are going to blast right through the patrol areas for two of our boats tonight. Chances of them making contact in that big old ocean are slim to none. What's your best guess on where they plan to ambush the heavies?"

Ward stood back and carefully phrased his answer. He would have preferred far more data to base his response to the boss, who now stood there, hands on hips, awaiting his reply. A reply that could affect the course of history.

"If they keep charging like they are, the dynamics work for an attack right here, just outside Placentia Bay. And if I were the Germans, that's where I would attack. No chance of missing the heavies in the night in a stormy sea. Both ships will be right here and, so far as the Germans know, unaware, and with their guard down. Ducks on a pond. I doubt they'd attack either one separately. Their chances are much better to bag them both right out there..." He pointed out Flynn's window, overlooking the bay and the ocean beyond. "And they wouldn't want to prematurely alert anyone to the possible full objective of their mission."

Flynn nodded, lips pursed, brow deeply furrowed. "That's just exactly what I was thinking. And we don't have anything here to take them out. With all our subs at sea now and most of our tin cans escorting convoys to Britain." He picked up a pair of dividers and walked off some distances on the chart. "Way I figure it, we've got a little less than two days. Just enough time to turn *S-52* and *S-54* around and get 'em back here, on station, guarding the gates to Placentia Bay. If those German boats slow or take a different course, we can always vector our boys to intercept."

Ward nodded his agreement. "I think it will be. Historic, that is. But those guys on our subs are going to think we've lost our minds, jerking them around like that." Two of his friends, Fred Wurster and Brad Johnson, were riding those boats. He knew full well what their thoughts would be when they got ordered to do a U-turn, away from where everyone knew the potential targets were located.

Flynn grabbed the phone and dialed the comms center. "Duty Officer, get a message out to the *S-52* and *S-54*. Tell them to return to Argentia and to pour on the coal getting here."

∞

LT(jg) Brad Johnson stared out at the limitless blue horizon from his familiar vantage point on the bridge of his *S*-boat. The storms of the last few days had blown off to the east. As far as he could see, he and his submarine had the ocean to themselves. Only a couple of icebergs slowly made their way south, drifting down toward the shipping lanes, glittering in the sun. The calm sea was disturbed only by the *S-54* plunging forward at a full bell. And by a pod of white-beaked dolphins that played on the sub's bow wave, jumping into the swell, surfing along for a few seconds, then diving deep before coming back up and doing the whole thing again. Johnson enjoyed watching their playful antics. He could only hope that thing about dolphins promising good luck held true this time.

The *S-54* was well to the north of the convoy routes, heading out to intercept the *Prince of Wales* as it raced down from Scapa Flow. And, in the process, to intercept two U-boats supposedly stalking the British ship. He was not sure where his Academy classmate Fred Wurster and the 52 boat were, but they were most likely only a few miles to the south. Those U-boats that everyone seemed to be so worried about should still be several hundred miles to the east unless they had diverted by now to their usual hunting grounds.

Johnson was most confused about how this was all supposed to play out. Even if all the boats in the squadron somehow got into a perfect north–south line from Greenland down to the convoy routes, there was little chance that they would even see the U-boats. The North Atlantic was an awfully big ocean, and the German submarines were an awfully small and very elusive pair of targets. The latest message traffic said that, based on some unspecified kind of intel the guys back home were seeing, the Germans were thought to be running on the surface at top speed. That was curious, and it would make it easier to spot them, but it also meant that the quick moment of potential encounter would pass in one hell of a hurry. Maybe in the dark of night. Or the middle of rain squalls that were so common and sudden up here.

And if they did see the U-boats, their orders were to shoot. Shoot, even if, so far as Johnson knew, there had been no declaration of war. Surely, they knew how difficult it was for one submarine to sink another.

"Bridge, this is the captain," the 7MC blasted, shaking him from his reverie. "Our orders have been changed. Reverse course to two-one-zero. Come to ahead flank. We're heading back to the farm to guard the barn door."

Johnson gave the bridge rail a hard kick. And vowed he would find out what flunky had decided to reverse their course and bring them all the way back to Argentia Station instead of operating out here where they might be able to do some good.

He'd give that son of a bitch a piece of his mind and maybe even a punch in the nose.

23

Fred Wurster climbed up to the *S-52*'s tiny bridge. It was midnight, time for him to relieve Brent Halloran as Officer-of-the-Deck. When he got to the bridge, he found the submarine's Engineer Officer busy, talking over a sound-powered phone. Halloran glanced over at his relief, smiled, and held up a hand. Watch relief would have to be delayed until the current conversation was completed. Wurster waited patiently, looking out at the moonlit sea. Finally, Halloran finished his conversation and returned the phone to its holder, shaking his head.

"That was Chief Wankel," he told Wurster. "Seems we have zero ground on the port main motor. Chief thinks oil has soaked into the insulation again. Said if we didn't fix it now, we'd have a fire soon. Anyway, the port main motor is out of commission while the electricians try to clean it. They already broke out the torpedo fuel alcohol to try and dissolve the oil. That means if you have to dive, you'll only have one main motor." The submarine's two battery-powered electric main motors turned the sub's twin screws when the boat was submerged.

Wurster nodded. "Got it." Being without one of the main motors would not affect them while they ran on the surface. Then they would be powered by the two big MAN diesels. Since they were hustling back to Argentia, making top speed on the surface, they likely would not need to submerge.

But if they did dive with only one main motor, they could only use one of the *S-52*'s shafts. That meant they could only make about four knots.

Halloran shook his head. "Anyway, I'm cold, tired, and hungry. I expect I'm gonna spend the next several hours nursemaiding the electricians, and not in my nice, warm bunk." He pointed at the bridge compass repeater. "Steering course two-one-zero, ahead flank. No contacts."

Wurster confirmed with, "Port main motor out of commission, steering two-one-zero, ahead flank, no contacts. I relieve you."

Halloran replied, "I stand relieved, laying below." And he was gone.

Wurster rested his arms on the bridge rail and stared out into the night sky. There was a full moon, high overhead. It lent everything a silvery glow while a bowlful of stars twinkled above. But Wurster's mind was not on nature's lonely beauty. He was trying to work out in his own head just what the hell was going on.

First, they had charged east as fast as they could go to find some Nazi U-boats hell-bent on sinking a British battleship. Then, abruptly, here they were charging back westward as fast as they could go to protect Argentia from those same Nazi subs. And as a result of all the charging around, they had a main motor out of commission. Someone back home and high up the chain of command needed to understand that these old "*Sugar*" boats—all built before the mid-1920s—could not handle a whole lot of jerking around before something went seriously wrong. Like losing a main motor.

"Bridge, Navigator," the 7MC blasted, interrupting his deep thoughts. "Recommend coming left, steer course one-nine-zero."

Wurster grabbed the 7MC microphone and responded, "Bridge, aye." Then he ordered, "Helm, right ten degrees rudder, steer course one-nine-zero." Looking over his shoulder, he saw the wake behind him was smoothly arcing around to the south. He eased back and took a sip from his coffee cup. Glancing up, he noted that the lookouts were diligently scanning the horizon. He sighed. Hopefully, it would be a quiet and uneventful midwatch. Then breakfast and some sleep.

By 0300, Wurster was struggling mightily to stay awake. Coffee was just not doing the trick anymore. His head dropped down and then he jerked himself awake. He checked his wristwatch, a gift from his folks when he graduated from the Academy. Another hour to go before his relief came up.

"Officer-of-the-Deck," the after lookout suddenly hollered. "Sir, I have a contact low down on the horizon. Two points abaft the starboard beam. Can't make it out yet."

That brought Wurster fully awake. He swung around to peer in the direction the young lookout pointed, but he could not see anything. Not even with the help of the full moon. The lookout, though, was on a platform a good six feet higher. That meant he could theoretically see half a mile further than anyone on the bridge could. But the forty-foot periscope had a height-of-eye a good twenty feet above the lookout.

"Control, Bridge." Wurster sighted down the bridge compass for the true bearing as he keyed the 7MC. "Possible contact, bearing zero-eight-zero, hull down on the horizon. What do you have on the scope from that bearing?"

QM-1 Clancy Obrien promptly answered, "Officer-of-the-Deck, I'm seeing three contacts around that bearing. Best estimate of range, twenty thousand yards, too distant to classify."

Pretty much right on the far horizon, ten miles away. "Very well, report the contacts to the Captain, and start a plot on them," Wurster directed.

A ship off to the east-northeast of where *S-52* was running would be rare, but not impossible. They were well north of the Grand Banks and hundreds of miles away from usual convoy routes. Three ships, steaming together, coming from that direction at that speed could only mean one thing. The *Prince of Wales* battle group was out there and quickly overtaking them. But they were not expected, at least according to the intel message that Wurster had read before he came on watch, until tomorrow sometime.

"Mr. Wurster, dive the ship!" Don Gorman's voice blasted from the 7MC.

Wurster yelled up at the three sailors above him, "Lookouts below! Clear the bridge!" When he saw the last man drop through the hatch, he hit the diving alarm twice, yelled, "Dive! Dive!" over the 1MC and followed them through the hatch.

Gorman was standing by the navigation plot when Wurster dropped to the deck. He looked up and said, "Officer-of-the-Deck, come to course south. Make your depth four-five feet."

Gorman turned and rotated the handwheel to raise the periscope.

"Number one scope coming up for a look-around." He squatted down and met the periscope as it emerged from the well. Flipping down the training handles, he rose with the scope and slowly walked it around in a complete circle. Stepping back, he said, "I see four ships. Looks like three destroyers out ahead of the heavy. The big guy is still hull down, but I'm pretty sure it's the *Prince of Wales*."

The sub's Skipper put his eye to the periscope again. "Yep, that's the *Prince of Wales*, all right. Can't mistake that silhouette." He lowered the periscope and stepped back once more. "Mr. Wurster, come to course zero-nine-zero. I want to get well off these guys' track so we don't inadvertently get run over. They ain't likely to be friendly to any submarines out here."

As the *S-52* slowly moved away from the course of the charging British warships, the sonar operator suddenly clamped his headphones tightly to his ears and let out a, "Whoa!" He listened for a few seconds, then he reported, "Captain, I'm hearing something on bearing one-four-six. It's really weak, but it sounds like something with a shaft rub going on."

Gorman stepped back to the little sonar cubicle and picked up the spare headset. The sonar operator carefully trained the hydrophones so that they were listening to this new and curious noise source.

"There, Skipper," he said as the sonar hydrophones were aimed right toward the sound, "Hear it? Sort of a whoop, whoop, whoop sound?"

Gorman held up a finger. "Got it. Damn ocean's getting mighty full all of a sudden. I think we've just found one of the U-boats we came out here to look for. He's coming up well behind the Brits. They're making better than twenty-eight knots. No way he can catch up now. Especially not if he stays submerged. Hell, not even if he surfaced and ran all out."

"He doesn't have to," Jim Shelton, the acting XO, offered. He pointed at the chart. "All he needs to do is follow along until they all round Cape Freels. Those Brits will be slipping into their anchorage in Placentia Bay. That U-boat captain will be shooting fish in a barrel."

Gorman stared down at the chart. Shelton was right and they needed to act fast. If the U-boat got past them and they lost it, they might not find it again. There was no one left to stop it and protect the British Prime Minister and most of his War Cabinet.

"Let's get in position and shoot this guy," Gorman said.

"Even if we're not at war with Germany?" Shelton asked. Then he grinned and added, "Just playing devil's advocate, Skipper."

"We got our orders. If we see 'em, we shoot 'em. XO, set up to plot the U-boat using sonar. We'll try to keep up and then shoot him once he slows enough and sets up for his own attack. When we get a good solution, I intend to shoot a four-shot spread from the bow tubes. Make the weapons in tubes one, two, three, and four ready."

Shelton set his team to work plotting sonar bearings to find the German sub's course, speed, and range. It was a tedious, intuitive process that took time and usually resulted in an imprecise answer at best. Had it not been for the distinctive noise the U-boat was making, they likely would have lost contact altogether.

"Skipper," Shelton reported, "we need to come to two-zero-zero to cut this guy off or he's going to get way, way out in front of us. He has a three-degree-a-minute right bearing rate, so he is hauling butt."

The sonar operator chimed in, "Turn count for a seven-knot target."

"Skipper, we got a problem," Fred Wurster piped up. "He's making seven knots. The best we can do on a single main motor is four. No way we catch him before he gets there and does his nasty business."

McNeely agreed. "My solution has him three thousand yards ahead and pulling away. Even with all that racket he's making, we'll lose sonar contact pretty soon."

"But if we surface for speed," Wurster added, "he'll know we're here and try to stop us. Or one of our friendlies might sink us, too."

"Tell Chief Wankel to button up the port main motor," Gorman directed. "I don't care if it has a zero ground, we got to have that motor online."

Brent Halloran, the Engineer, started to object. "But, Skipper, that has a good chance of causing a fire if..."

"Right now, Eng, I'll risk the fire. We need to get that U-boat."

It took Chief Wankel and his team fifteen minutes to get the port main motor back up and online. By then the U-boat had increased the range enough that the *S-52* had lost the sonar signal entirely.

The Skipper stared down at Jim Shelton's plot. He projected the U-boat's course and speed out into the future.

"Weps, let's assume that he's trying to get into a shooting position. He's going to round Cape Freels before he slows. Then he's going to try and slip into the bay real quiet like to get set up for a stable shot." Gorman traced out his idea on the chart with a finger. "I'm going to run at flank until we get a thousand yards behind him. We should regain sonar contact by then."

The *S-52* surged ahead. With a top submerged speed of eleven knots, they now had a four-knot speed advantage on the U-boat. At least, they did so long as the port main motor held out. Gorman spread out his fingers across the chart and estimated the distance between the two submarines. He guessed that they would need twenty minutes to catch back up again. That would place them at the entrance to Placentia Bay, south of Argentia Station. Until then, all they could do was charge ahead, listen, and wait.

"Skipper, regain sonar contact," the sonar operator happily reported. Gorman glanced up at the clock. They had run for precisely seventeen minutes. Gorman allowed himself a slight smile. Not bad for measuring with his fingers and doing the math in his head.

And, so far, the motor had held its own.

"Contact has the same shaft rub, still making turns for seven knots. It's the U-boat for sure."

Gorman looked at the plot solution, then he studied the position keeper on the torpedo data computer. They still were not quite close enough. If the *S-52* launched the attack too soon, the German would hear the torpedo launch and have a good chance to get out of the way.

"Weps, let's get down to five hundred yards from the murderous SOB. I'm going to point him for a zero gyro shot."

The *S-52* had just slowed when Chief Wankel loudly reported, "Smoke! Smoke from port main motor!" Then, "Fire! Fire in the motor room!"

Tendrils of smoke were already creeping into the control room. Gorman coughed and yelled, "Mr. Wurster, secure and isolate the port main engine. Make your depth four-zero feet. Raising number one periscope." The CO squatted by the scope as it slid up out of its well. Turning to Halloran, he ordered, "Eng, you fight the fire. The Weps and I will do the attack."

S-52's periscope broke the surface to find a bright, sunny day with blue skies to the horizon but no hint of the life-and-death drama playing out beneath the calm surface of the sea. The *Prince of Wales* was in perfect view a couple of thousand yards ahead, slowly maneuvering into its anchorage.

Then, as Gorman looked around for any other ship—to be sure nobody would be in the path if one or more of his torpedoes missed their target—he spied something else. Something unmistakable. A phone pole suddenly poked up from the water. And it was just a couple of hundred yards ahead.

The German U-boat! And he was in a perfect spot to attack the British battleship!

"Observation on the U-boat!" Gorman yelled. He spun the periscope so that the vertical reticule was precisely on the emerging periscope, giving him a perfect point of aim. And there was no sign of any other vessel beyond the telltale German periscope.

"Shoot tube one!" Gorman ordered without hesitation. "Shoot tube two!" The whoosh of high-pressure air signaled that the first two torpedoes were out of their tubes and on their way. "Shoot tube three! Shoot tube four!"

The spread of four fish were now racing toward the German. He and his treacherous crew had less than thirty seconds to live. And their attempt to assassinate Winston Churchill was about to come to an explosive end.

"Fire...fire has spread...to the maneuvering room!" Chief Wankel reported while coughing uncontrollably. "All personnel clear...clear of the room. Except McGee. I can't find McGee! The main motors are secured and electrically isolated. I gotta go back in and find McGee!"

Champ McGee, one of Chief Wankel's electricians, had been working on the port main motor, down in main motor room lower level. Now he was unaccounted for.

"Belay that, Chief! Get that fire out before we lose the boat! He'll turn up." Gorman turned to Shelton and ordered, "Weps, lay aft and take charge. We need to get fire hoses on that fire." Turning to Fred Wurster, he added, "Officer-of-the-Deck, we've lost all propulsion. Trim the boat to maintain a zero bubble."

Just then a pair of jarring explosions rocked *S-52*. Gorman looked through the periscope toward the German just in time to see its broken hull jump out of the water and then disappear back down into the sea.

"Mr. Wurster, blow all ballast! Get me on the surface as quick as you can," Gorman ordered. "And for God's sake, make sure you get the American flag up real quick. We don't want to get shot by the Brits after we just saved their Prime Minister. Signal them and anybody else who can see our light that we're US Navy and that we have a fire and need help."

The American submarine shot up out of the blue depths and then wallowed about in the calm seas. Until the fire was out, there was no way to start the diesels or to see if they could actually shift propulsion back to them. Until then, the sub was entirely at the mercy of the current, wind, and waves.

Fred Wurster and three lookouts clambered up out of the smoke-filled boat. A black fog billowed from the bridge hatch. Wurster leaned over the rail and took deep drafts of cold clean air, trying to expunge his lungs of the acrid smoke. He grabbed the Aldis light and began flashing signals for all he was worth in the direction of the *Prince of Wales*. Over and over, he identified his ship and requested assistance for a fire aboard.

He also prayed. Prayed those aboard the British battleship would believe his messaging and not start shooting and ask questions later.

"The fire is out!" the 1MC blasted. Then Gorman climbed up to the bridge, hacking and wheezing. Wurster barely recognized the smoke- and soot-painted visage of the Skipper. When he finally found enough breath, he said, "Mr. Wurster, start the diesels to clear the air in the boat. Get all personnel topside until the smoke's cleared. We're going to need help and maybe a tow. Tell the *Prince of Wales* that we have injured personnel and require medical assistance."

Then Gorman took a long look ahead, at the spreading oil slick a couple of hundred yards away from them. A small smile played on his lips before he began coughing again.

Maybe the old *S-52* was a rusty relic from the last war, beat up and obsolete. But the old girl had just done the job she was built to do.

24

The explosions off to the east brought an unusually broad smile to Helmut Schmiel's face. That could only mean that Karl Smit and his *U-144* had completed their mission, sending the *Prince of Wales* to the bottom of Placentia Bay. In all probability, Herr Churchill and his tag-along flock of officious bureaucrats and lackeys were feeding the Canadian fishes. Now it was up to Schmiel and the *U-23* to complete the success and add the American President to the war casualty list.

Schmiel had positioned the German submarine thirty kilometers north-northwest of Point Lance, Newfoundland, where Placentia Bay opened to the Atlantic. This put his submarine directly in line with the course the American cruiser *Augusta* should be on while approaching the rendezvous at Argentia Station. His plan was to be patient, attacking the Americans while they were busily preparing to anchor. That would be when they were most vulnerable, least suspecting, and certainly distracted. The Americans would be entering the port after a dangerous run up the East Coast, likely convinced they were safely inside a protected anchorage.

At that point, Schmiel's strike on behalf of the Führer and the Fatherland would have taken place. But Smit's earlier-than-planned attack on the *Prince of Wales* had instantly changed all of that. The Americans would be fully alert now. Indeed, the flotilla bringing the President and his entourage might very well turn around and hurry back toward home before *U-23* ever had a chance to launch their torpedoes. He, too, would have to attack earlier than he would have liked.

"*Kapitan*," the *Erste Wachoffizier* (First Watch Officer) called to Schmiel from his station at the periscope. "I see smoke on the horizon to the southwest."

Schmiel grabbed the periscope and looked to where it was pointed. A dark wisp of smoke marred the otherwise clear blue early morning sky. "Bring me up a meter," he ordered. Maybe, with slightly higher height-of-eye, he could see what was causing the smoke. Indeed, he saw the warships he had been waiting for, the smoke from their stacks, and they were steaming directly toward where he stood. An American heavy cruiser! Then he saw a light cruiser and five destroyers fanned out ahead as escorts.

Perfect! All he had to do was sit where he was and wait while the Americans came to him. Then he would sink the American heavy cruiser—and maybe a destroyer or two—before making his escape amid all the panic and confusion.

As the Americans nonchalantly steamed ahead, Helmut Schmiel maneuvered his submarine only slightly so that they were about five hundred meters to the southeast of the Americans' course. That gave him an ideal position to launch his ambush. And he slowly, incrementally lowered the submarine's depth so that he could just make out the enemy ships over the wavetops, assuring they would never see him before or after the deed was done.

"Make the torpedoes in all forward tubes ready to launch," Schmiel ordered.

It was almost time for him and his crew to dramatically alter history and likely assure the continued success of the Third Reich.

∞

LT(jg) Brad Johnson stood back in the corner of the *S-54*'s musty, cramped control room. The ancient S-boat had just raced eastward, a third of the way across the Atlantic Ocean, only to be ordered to zoom right on back, retracing their course to Newfoundland. Once they got back to the port from which they had so hurriedly departed, the boat was cryptically told to stand by, not to enter port, but to guard the entrance to Placentia Bay. To remain within their newly assigned patrol box and to stay at least two miles clear of the *S-52*'s assigned area. And to do it without being detected. Evidently, it was important to someone that the American submarine not be observed while it sailed back and forth across the harbor entrance. Johnson did not understand the whys behind all the decisions being made of late, but he had been in the Navy long enough to know that it was not necessary for him to know why. He only needed to know what his duty was and then, by God, do it. And right now, his duty was to guard "the barn door."

An odd thought caused Johnson to smile. Too bad his buddy, Stan Ward, was stuck with shore duty only a few miles away, inside the bay. The former Colorado farm boy would know what a real "barn door" looked like.

The only excitement so far had been the big explosion about an hour earlier, to the east, over toward the *S-52* patrol area. So far, they had no idea what that had been, but Johnson could only hope it was "us" sinking "one of them." But if one of the U-boats they had been looking for made it to Placentia Bay, it was likely the other one was lurking close by as well.

Suddenly, the sonar operator held his hands to his ears, jerked his head back and forth as if that aided his hearing, and then turned around. "Mr. Johnson, I'm hearing noises bearing two-three-three. Metallic transients. And they're pretty close."

"Any idea what it is?" Johnson asked.

"No, sir. But I'm pretty sure it's close all right." The sonar operator hesitated for a moment, as if he dreaded completing his assessment. "Sir, it sounds like torpedo tube doors opening."

"Go active on the WCA and get me a range," Johnson immediately ordered. Then he turned to Master Chief Lafour, his Diving Officer, and ordered, "COB, man battle stations!"

The "Bong! Bong! Bong!" of the general alarm had barely silenced throughout the submarine when the sonar operator reported, "Positive return on an active contact. Range eight hundred yards, bearing two-three-one. Positive submarine."

Gotta be one of those U-boats, Johnson thought. *Over here, near the route the President's vessel would be taking. Their sister boat, the S-52, would be in her patrol area miles to the east of here, right? Couldn't be him they were hearing.*

Stephen Brewster, the *S-54*'s Skipper, bolted into the control room and asked, "What you got, Brad?"

"Submerged submarine, bearing two-three-one, range eight hundred yards," Johnson hurriedly replied. "It sure sounds like he's getting ready to shoot at somebody, but no reason to think he knows we're here, so—"

"I got multiple screws, southwest!" the sonarman interrupted. "Gotta be five or six ships."

"The President's convoy," Johnson guessed.

Brewster climbed a few rungs of the ladder to stick his head up into the conning tower. People were still scurrying to their battle station positions. Clark Manson, the XO, had just donned his sound-powered phone headset and was receiving reports from the various stations around the sub, confirming they were where they were supposed to be.

"That's gotta be a U-boat and they're about to shoot our Commander in Chief." Brewster climbed another rung and shouted, without hesitation, "XO, make tubes one through four ready to launch. And we need to be quick."

Manson relayed the order over the phones, and then, a scowl on his face, looked down at Brewster, still halfway between the control room and the conning tower. "Skipper, forward torpedo room reports tubes one and three ready. Problem getting launch air to the port side tubes. They're troubleshooting."

"Damn it! XO, set run depth for twenty feet and launch tubes one and three at the target if that's all we got ready." He climbed on up the ladder to the conning tower.

They were now at war. And they were only halfway ready for it.

A muted "whoosh-bang" followed by a second similar sound confirmed the two starboard-side torpedoes had been launched.

Even so, Manson reported, "One and three away!"

"XO, get the starboard tubes reloaded and those damn portside tubes fixed," Brewster ordered. "I really don't like sitting here with no way to attack if those two fish miss."

∞

"*Kapitan!* Active sonar!" the *Gruppenhorchgerät* operator yelled. "*Amerikanisches U-Boot*." The operator clamped his hands to his headset for a moment. Then, wide-eyed, he shouted, "Torpedoes in the water! The *Amerikanisches U-Boot* is shooting at us!"

Helmut Schmiel ordered, "Make your depth fifty meters." He lowered the periscope and shouted, "Right full rudder, steady course north." The *Amerikanisch* had shot while he was at periscope depth. Their torpedoes would be running at five or six meters. All he had to do was get below the depth for those torpedoes. His quick maneuver would give him a chance to figure out what to do next. A wrong decision now would be lethal. And they might miss the opportunity to complete the mission.

Neither outcome was an option.

But the *verdammt Amerikanisch* had ruined his perfect shot setup. He would need to get into position again while being torpedoed. Then, he could attack his primary target and, if possible, he would shoot the American submarine as well.

But why had the US submarine only launched two torpedoes? Schmiel or any other good U-boat Captain would have shot a full complement from his forward tubes, increasing the chances of a fatal strike. American incompetence? Maybe so.

Schmiel allowed fifteen minutes to pass after evading the onrushing torpedoes before he was ready to attack again. The *gruppenhorchgerät* operator reported that he could still hear the surface ships, but he no longer heard the active sonar of the US submarine. Schmiel decided that he had to risk the Americans finding him again. He needed to be at periscope depth to attack the cruiser.

"Make your depth fifteen meters, all ahead dead slow," he ordered.

Schmiel eased the periscope up so that it just broke the water. He was pleased by what he saw. The American warships were once more about to be in the perfect position for him to shoot, as if on parade across his sights. If they were even aware of the American torpedoes—now long gone—or unduly concerned about the earlier sinking of their British counterparts, they only showed it by zigzagging predictably, not dramatically so. Nor were they speeding toward safety. He estimated the range to the cruiser, his most important target, to be about two thousand meters. The angle-on-the-bow was starboard forty-five. He would let the problem generate for a couple more minutes. He wanted to shoot just before the cruiser presented its broadest aspect. That way the torpedoes would arrive when the whole length of the ship was visible. This meant that he had the best chance of getting a hit. Nothing to do but to wait. And wait quietly so the American submarine would not find him again.

∞

"Skipper, U-boat dead ahead!" Brad Johnson yelled. He had relieved Brewster on the periscope for a few minutes while he concentrated on getting the torpedo room back ready to go. "I see the tip of his periscope and he can't be more than five hundred yards away!"

Brewster grabbed the scope and looked.

"Shit!" he muttered. The SOB had not been spooked at all by the near miss of the two American torpedoes. No, the crazy bastard was ready to shoot again, and this time *S-54* did not have anything ready to stop him. The four bow tubes—two still being reloaded and two out of commission—were not available right now and there was no time to turn around and shoot at him from the stern tube.

Well, Brewster thought, *I still have one weapon I can use.*

"All ahead flank," he ordered. "COB! Order the forward torpedo room evacuated, and the door dogged shut. Everybody hold on tight! We're going to ram that SOB! Sound the collision alarm!"

He looked through the periscope to make sure the reticule was aimed directly at the German periscope.

Then he spoke into the microphone, "All hands, brace for impact!"

∞

"Stand by to fire torpedoes!" Schmiel ordered.

The German commander allowed himself just the trace of a cruel smile. He finally had the Americans—including their President—just where he wanted them. The perfect firing position. Like one of the first problems presented to prospective commanders at the *Unterseebootsabwehrschule*. He would shoot the four forward torpedo tubes at the cruiser and then swing around and fire the stern tube at the nearest destroyer. With skill and a bit of luck, his crew could reload the forward tubes in time to turn back and shoot one or two more of the destroyers before he needed to evade. Maybe even sink the entire convoy!

He was opening his mouth to give the launch order when holy hell broke loose. The lurching, grinding crash came as a total surprise. No one aboard the German boat had time to ponder what might be happening. Schmiel was knocked off his feet, thrown hard into the torpedo launch panel. Many of the crew were injured when they were brutally tossed about. The *U-23* heeled over as the US Navy boat rammed it, riding up and over the U-boat after striking her directly amidships. The *S*-boat's heavy, blunt bow crushed through the smaller German submarine's 18mm-thick Krupp steel pressure hull, opening her up like a tin of fish.

Oberleutnant Schmiel, badly injured but still determined, struggled to pull himself up. He managed to reach and jam down on the firing buttons for the forward torpedo tubes only seconds before the cold waters of the Atlantic rushed in and immediately filled the *U-23*'s control room.

This last desperate act was Helmut Schmiel's final service to his Führer and the Fatherland.

Two German torpedoes shot out of their torpedo tubes, zooming toward the *Augusta*. The cruiser's deck gang, mustering on *Augusta*'s forecastle in preparation for dropping the anchor, had ring-side seats for the developing drama. They shouted warnings and pointed at the two white arrows streaking through the water right at them. The two German torpedoes, off aim from the collision, passed a scant fifty feet ahead of the cruiser. After the big ship had begun a sudden but late turn to try to avoid them—and after they had missed their intended target—the torpedoes exploded in shallow water at the end of their runs several thousand yards away, injuring only stones and mud and an unfortunate school of codfish.

The *S-54*, her bow badly crumpled and with a decided bend to port, lurched to the surface only five hundred yards from the *Augusta*. A pair of destroyers rushed over with guns trained and circled the sub until they could identify the sudden intruder. It took a few minutes for the submarine to man the bridge and to communicate with the American warships. When everyone could breathe again, the little convoy with the badly damaged submarine proceeded on to Argentia Station.

Meanwhile, the *U-23* slowly sank downward until coming to rest—all hands lost—on the rocky bottom of Placentia Bay.

25

The sun was disappearing over the Burin Peninsula to the west as Brad Johnson climbed up to the bridge. He was to conn the damaged *S-54* up Placentia Bay toward Argentia and into port. The smooth, calm blue waters and the sea breeze offered an almost shocking counterpoint to the brutal sea battle that had just been fought in these now placid waters. Only the submarine's badly crumpled bow and partially flooded forward torpedo room were visible signs of the fight. The other casualty, the U-boat, was not visible and no longer a threat to anyone.

The battle group left the USS *Sampson*, one of the destroyers, to shepherd the submarine safely home while the rest steamed on to their predetermined anchorage near the British contingent. The sleek destroyer made slow, lazy circles around the crippled submarine as it plodded toward its berth. At four knots, Johnson knew that it would take them until well past midnight before their journey ended. In the meantime, the crew was busy with damage control, trying to stop the flooding while they pumped the torpedo room dry. So long as nothing catastrophic happened, they should be able to make it to their berth, broken, battered, but still afloat.

Stephen Brewster climbed up out of the hatch, carrying a pot of coffee and two cups. "Thought I'd come up and enjoy the sunset for a few minutes," he said as he handed Brad a cup and proceeded to fill it. "It's been a busy afternoon and promises to be a busy night."

"Yes, sir," Brad Johnson agreed. "Thank you for the coffee, sir. How's it coming below?"

"The old girl took some damage when we rammed that bastard, of course. But it could have been worse. The drain pump's keeping up with the flooding so far," the Skipper said. He put his arms up on the bridge rail and leaned against it. His uniform was drenched in sweat, and it was clear the CO was exhausted. He slumped tiredly against the steel rail. "The guys are doing their best with damage control so we can at least get ourselves alongside the *Beaver*." He took a sip of his coffee. Then a gulp. "Hope you don't have any plans for any social soirees back home anytime soon. I'm guessing voyage repairs are going to take several weeks. Then we'll be off to the shipyard for a while."

"Any word from the 52 boat, Skipper?" Johnson asked. He was still worrying about Freddy Wurster.

"Last we heard, they got the fire out," Brewster said. "The Brits were taking her under tow. No reports of any serious casualties. One man unaccounted for."

Johnson's stomach turned over. But there were probably thirty-five or forty men on the *S-52*. Slim chance the missing one was Freddy. Brad had another thought.

"Sir, I just wanted to say, what you did out there is about the bravest thing I could ever imagine, and—"

"Doc to the bridge," the 7MC interrupted.

Brewster held up a hand. "If we do go to war someday, you'll likely skipper a boat, Johnson, 'cause you're a good sub officer. God knows we'll need plenty of those since none of us have ever taken a submarine to war. Even if we had, this next one's going to be completely different, and these pig boats will play a much greater role. Mark my words. And if we are at war, you'll have to do some crazy things, too, if we intend to win it. But it'll take a whole new kind of submarine and a whole new breed of Skippers..."

The sub's corpsman emerged from the hatch just then. He took in a deep breath of fresh air before he turned to the Skipper, unaware he was interrupting the conversation. "Reporting the status of the injured, sir," he said. "Nothing too serious. Cookie got a nasty bump on his noggin from getting bounced around the galley when we hit. Might be a concussion. Sparks has a broken arm, but not the one he uses for the Morse key. Rest are a bunch of cuts and bruises. I put some sulfa powder on a couple of the worst ones and passed out a lot of aspirin. They'll all live."

Brewster nodded. "Thanks, Doc. Go ahead and give them each a shot of the medicinal brandy, too."

Doc looked at the exhausted Brewster. "You could use a shot yourself, Skipper, and a good night's sleep."

Brewster gave a half laugh. "Once we're in port, Doc. Once we're in port."

∞

The *S-52* moved deliberately through the water. A heavy manila line extended out of the towing fairlead at the very bow of the boat. The line dipped underwater and then emerged again a dozen yards astern of His Majesty's Canadian Ship *Assiniboine*. The *River*-class Canadian destroyer was towing the badly damaged and powerless submarine into port.

Most of the submarine crew were resting on the deck, catching the last of the sunlight and breathing the clean, smoke-free air. The only personnel belowdecks were busy overhauling the fire and inspecting the extent of the damage. Fred Wurster, covered with soot and dirt, was assisting Chief Fritz Wankel back in the motor room. The pair were trying to see if they could restore propulsion, lining up the systems so that the diesels would turn the screws.

The *S-52* had a direct-drive system. That meant that the diesel engines were directly connected with a clutch to the shafts that turned the boat's screws when they were running on the surface. When they were submerged, the clutch was disengaged. The main motors, built right around the main shafts and powered from the battery, then propelled the sub. The problem was that both clutches were located in the main motor spaces. There was no way to know if they could be operated, or even if the shafts would rotate, until Wankel and Wurster fought their way down into the bowels of the motor room.

Even with one of the diesels running, offering no propulsion but sucking clean air into the boat, the place still reeked of smoke and burnt electrical insulation. Discarded fire-fighting gear was strewn all about for them to stumble over. Pressurized fire hoses still snaked around the tightly cramped area. The space was midnight dark, too. The battery disconnects had been opened during the fire to electrically isolate the main motors. With the disconnects open, there was no electrical power for lights, fans, or anything else. The two submariners were forced to work with only a couple of battery-powered battle lanterns for light.

Wurster was down in the bilge, wading through nasty, thigh-deep water, struggling to make his way aft to the starboard clutch. Just then, his light played across what appeared to be a bundle of clothes. Curious, he made his way closer to check on it what it might be.

Something protruded from the clothing. Something that looked like a man's hand. A shriveled hand contorted into a claw.

Wurster retched.

Then, when he got control of his gut, he called out, "Chief, I think I found McGee."

It appeared the electrician had decided he could best survive the fire down in the bilge. That had been a bad decision. The trapped smoke alone would have been enough to take him out.

Chief Engineman Wankel had tears making lines through the soot and grit on his cheeks as he lifted the body out of the bilge and started back up out of the motor room.

"I said I'd come back to get you, Champy. But I'm too late." He had at first insisted he would drag the man out of the bilge by himself. But when he struggled to lift McGee up to the deck, he realized he could not do it alone.

"Mr. Wurster, could you help me here, sir," he finally pleaded.

Together, the two men carried McGee's body up to crews' berthing and laid him out on one of the bunks. Wurster grabbed a blanket and quickly covered him. Then he turned to Wankel and put a hand on the big, tough man's shoulder.

"Come on, Chief. Let's go tell the Captain we found our shipmate."

∞

Sunrise found the two damaged *Sugar*-boats tied up alongside the *Beaver*. There was plenty of activity. A steady stream of sailors from the two submarines made their way up to the tender, more than ready for some well-earned rest in the far more spacious berthing available for them there. Another steady parade—this time of tender workers—climbed down to the two boats to survey the damage and begin formulating a plan to get them back into service.

Stephen Brewster and Don Gorman met in the passageway outside Roderick Flynn's stateroom. Their instructions had been to report to the Commodore's stateroom as soon as the boat was safely moored. Neither had an opportunity to clean up from their harrowing sea battles. They both still smelled of the boats. Brewster's uniform was streaked with soot. Gorman's was soaking wet and sweat stained.

They did not have time to compare notes but quickly promised each other they would do so at the first opportunity. But definitely over a gallon mug of beer each in some warm and dry bar somewhere.

Gorman knocked and they both marched into the Commodore's stateroom. The conference table was already set for what appeared to be a sumptuous breakfast. They were not the first to arrive. Two officers, both with a great deal of gold on their sleeves, were already helping themselves to coffee from an ornate and sizeable urn.

Commodore Flynn made the introductions. "Admiral Whittaker, Admiral Johnson, may I present Commanders Brewster of the *S-54* and Gorman of the *S-52*. Commanders, Admiral Sir Roger Whittaker, First Sea Lord of His Majesty's Navy, and Admiral Devin Johnson, Special Assistant to SECNAV."

They all shook hands and that was the end of the formalities. Don Gorman started to apologize for their disheveled appearance, but Sir Roger clapped both Skippers on their backs. "Jolly good show, both of you! Fine examples of fighting seamanship. I hope you know just how your bravery and decisions affected history. Someday, you will know the full story. And when this war is finally finished, maybe the entire world will know of your exploits."

Devin Johnson toasted with his coffee cup. "Never doubted for a second that you'd get the job done. Bravo Zulu to your crews. And I know I do not have to mention that any and all things to do with this operation must be kept completely secret. Please be sure your crew is aware of this as well."

Whittaker added one more morsel. "There will be a formal announcement of this conference later for the media, but the agreement our leaders will complete this week—the plan is to eventually call it the 'Atlantic Charter,' though diplomats and politicians can be quite indecisive in such things—will certainly become the working model for how we and our allies prepare for the struggle against Mr. Hitler and Emperor Hirohito. And you men have, through your bravery and skill, assured this meeting could actually take place."

As they were sitting down to breakfast, Sir Roger announced, "Oh, and by the by, the Prime Minister wants to host a cocktail party on the *Prince of Wales* with your wardrooms as guests of honor this evening. The Warrant Officer's Mess will host your crews."

Commodore Flynn cast a baleful eye in the direction of his two submarine commanders. "I know I do not even have to mention it, but you and your officers will be on your best behavior tonight," he sternly directed. "We will not tolerate a submarine-generated international incident, right?"

The two COs nodded. But they barely suppressed smiles as they likely had similar thoughts. They had just sent two of Mr. Hitler's prized U-boats and probably close to a hundred of his best submariners to the sea floor.

It would be damn near impossible for a cocktail party to create any bigger submarine-generated international incident than they already had!

EPILOGUE

To Fred Wurster, it felt as if he had spent an hour or two in pure heaven. In reality, it had been only fifteen minutes in a steaming-hot shower. No matter how much he lathered, rinsed, and repeated, though, he could not wash away the stink. The natural aroma of a diesel submarine and the sooty smell from the motor fire still seemed to exude from every pore of his body. He finally gave up on trying to eradicate the odor and allowed himself to luxuriate in the hot water.

"Wurster, you're not the only guy that needs to use this shower!" Brent Halloran yelled as he beat on the shower's stainless-steel door with a fist. "And you damn well better not use all the hot water!"

Wurster finally relented and reluctantly turned off the wonderful cascade. It had been the same when he played football for the Academy. One of the best parts of any game or practice was the shower afterwards. His teammates had been just as irked at him then, too. After a quick dry-off, he wrapped the towel around his waist and left watery footprints all the way down the passageway to his stateroom.

After a couple of weeks crammed into the claustrophobic spaces of the *S-52*, everything about the tender felt bigger, roomier. The stateroom that he was sharing with Brad Johnson was positively palatial. When he stepped into the compartment, he found Johnson almost dressed in a freshly cleaned and starched khaki uniform.

"Where'd you get the clean uniform?" Fred asked.

"Laundry delivered it a few minutes ago. All cleaned, pressed, and starched. You could shave your ugly mug on those pant-leg creases. Yours is hanging over there." Johnson pointed to the steel lockers that filled most of one entire bulkhead. "It still smells like the boat, though. Seems they worked overtime to get us gussied up to meet the bigwigs," Johnson said with a laugh. "Although, I'll admit, it's the first cocktail party I've ever attended in working khakis."

Wurster got busy putting collar devices and his gold dolphins on his shirt. "Well, our glorious leaders will just have to understand, there ain't no room on a *Sugar*-boat for a set of dinner dress whites. And never a chance to wear 'em if there was."

Johnson stood and checked himself in the full-length mirror hanging on the back of the door. He looked at his watch. "Hurry up, Freddy. Commodore's launch leaves in ten minutes. Wouldn't be good form to be late for this shindig."

The two friends hurried down to the *Beaver*'s quarterdeck, where they ran into Stan Ward standing there waiting, tapping his foot and making a show of checking his pocket watch. After much handshaking, the three classmates climbed down the accommodation ladder to the Commodore's launch and found seats. Commodore Flynn arrived just then with the two submarine Captains—Brewster and Gorman. When the three were seated in the stern-sheets, the boat cast off, heading across the harbor to where the massive *Prince of Wales* lay at anchor.

As the launch was tied up alongside, Wurster looked up at the steel wall towering over them and at the steep accommodation ladder heading up the near-vertical side of the vessel. He gulped. "Guys, I ain't never seen a ship this big. Closest thing might've been that right tackle, Brosey, from Notre Dame back in '38."

The officers had no choice. They carefully climbed up the accommodation ladder to the battleship's main deck. There they were greeted by the ringing of the ship's bell, bosun's pipes, and side boys, all in the finest tradition of the Royal Navy.

An officer, fully rigged out in the Royal Navy Lieutenant's mess dress uniform, met the American submarine officers and offered to guide them to the flag mess. Brad Johnson looked hard at the Lieutenant.

"Geoff?" he questioned. "That you?"

"'Tis indeed, Mr. Johnson!"

"Last I saw of you, you were waving bye-bye to me from the bridge of the *Chestnut* in Reykjavik after we had that nice cruise together up the fiord in Greenland."

Geoff Chandler laughed, shook Brad's offered hand, and explained. "The Admiral posted me to this assignment since I speak fluent American." Then he went on to answer the real question. "After that incident on the old *Chestnut*, she was paid off for a major overhaul in Glasgow. After a couple more encounters with Mr. Hitler's U-boats, I got assigned as Assistant Navigation Officer here on the *Prince of Wales*. It looks like I once again owe a debt of gratitude to you Yank submariners for saving my arse."

"Least we could do to make up for that unpleasantness back in the late 1700s." Johnson laughed as he responded.

The reminiscing continued as Chandler led the way up a score of ladders. Finally, he opened a door into a spacious room, richly appointed with leather and oak. A large bar filled one whole bulkhead. Several dozen officers stood around, nursing glasses filled with various hues of amber-colored liquids. None was below the rank of Captain.

"Ah, our guests of honor have arrived," a stentorian voice announced from somewhere back by the bar.

Chandler ushered the American submariners over to the bar where an older, rather rotund gentleman sporting a Royal Navy uniform with no rank stood. He had a whiskey in one hand and a cigar in the other. Winston Churchill had a smile on his face. So did President Roosevelt, nursing a martini, a cigarette in a holder in his lips as he sat next to the British Prime Minister.

"Gentlemen, the sun is well past the yardarm. Get yourself a drink," Churchill said. "Fortunately, the Royal Navy never had to contend with Josephus Daniels as the First Lord of the Admiralty. We never would have countenanced a General Order 99." Turning to FDR, he went on with a chuckle, "Franklin, weren't you the Assistant Secretary under the unlamented Mr. Daniels? Where did he get such bad advice?"

Josephus Daniels had been Woodrow Wilson's Secretary of the Navy during the Great War. A devout prohibitionist, he famously banned the presence of alcohol aboard any US Navy vessel with his General Order 99. The order remains in effect.

FDR took a telling sip of his martini and smiled. "I'm afraid Secretary Daniels did not always seek or listen to sound advice."

Once everyone had a glass of his favorite beverage, Churchill tapped on his own glass with a spoon, calling for silence. Then, looking at the assembled submariners, he earnestly said, "To these men we owe our lives. These warriors made our meeting here and the worthy tenets to which we have agreed a reality. They are therefore responsible, in part, for a set of common principles that will solidify our joint efforts through the difficult times that lie ahead." He held his glass high, laughed, and said, "Not to mention that in the course of their duty they saved the hides of two old politicians! A toast to these brave submariners."

He was answered by a loud acclamation of, "Hear! Hear!"

FDR held up his hand for silence. Then he said, "Of course, you and your crews must understand that you cannot speak a word of what happened out there. The world must not know how close to disaster we actually came. Such disclosure would give Mr. Hitler far more credit than we are willing to give him. Someday, maybe. Someday we can tell the world and see you are properly recognized." He paused for a moment, the room becoming very quiet. "Now, there is another warrior here with us tonight, not a submariner, who should be acknowledged as well. Lieutenant Stanley Ward of the US Navy figured this all out based on very limited information and convinced others of what was about to happen. Then he had the fortitude and initiative to get our plan of action in play. Otherwise, I fear these recent events would have had a far different outcome. To the good Lieutenant!"

After the toast and another enthusiastic round of huzzahs, FDR looked over at the young submariners and said, "Gentlemen, I echo the Prime Minister's words. In addition, I bring you a bit of news that I believe you and the rest of your crew members will be happy to hear. Your boats are going to be out of commission for quite a while for repairs." He chuckled and took a puff of his cigarette. Then, with his trademark chin-in-the-air smile, he went on. "You seemed to have put them through rather harsh treatment despite their being such antique vessels. It is my opinion, and that of the US Navy staff, that it would be a serious misuse for proven warriors like yourselves to be sitting in a shipyard for the next year or more. I have directed Admiral King to have you all reassigned to submarines now based in Pearl Harbor, Hawaii, where the weather is much better than here. No offense, Mr. Prime Minister, about the climate here in your Commonwealth."

Churchill nodded. "None taken."

Roosevelt looked around the room. "Please understand this is no vacation. We have much work to do to re-jigger how we fight our submarines, and how we shall employ the new vessels that will soon be brought into commission. But I'm pleased to inform you that your assignment to the Pacific will come only after you enjoy a thirty-day leave back home. The *Sampson* will sail tomorrow morning, transporting you back to New London tomorrow."

∞

The three friends stood along the rail of the *Sampson* as she steamed up the Thames. They watched as the sleek destroyer swung around in the current and gently kissed the upstream side of Alpha Pier.

"We're home, guys," Stan Ward said as he anxiously scanned the waiting crowd on the pier. He did not see the one face that he was looking for, but he did see Ollie Oglethorpe waving wildly and animatedly dancing from one foot to the other. But where was Karen? Their arrival time had been radioed ahead and immediate families and designated friends notified. Stan was certain she would be there. Unless there was some kind of dire emergency at the hospital, of course.

Brad Johnson could make out Debbie Schultz, looking for him amid all the men on the destroyer's deck. She was gorgeous, wearing a nice pink sundress. *Thank you, Lord, for late summer in New England*, Johnson thought.

Ellie Morton, in her nursing student uniform, was standing next to her, smiling and happily waving. Johnson nudged Freddie Wurster and pointed to the pair of ladies at the head of the pier.

"Somebody's glad to see us, buddy!" Johnson happily observed. "Even you!"

Lines were just being thrown across when Ollie Oglethorpe yelled across the short stretch of brown water between warship and pier. "Stan, hurry up! Karen's in labor! You're about to be a daddy!"

Wurster looked over at Stan and noted his suddenly pale, dumbstruck visage. "Hey, dummy, wake up!" he said as he poked Ward on the shoulder. "You need to get off this garbage scow and get on up to the hospital. We'll collect your stuff and meet you there."

The brow had just touched down on the ship's deck when Stan Ward hobbled across it at a speed that neither Wurster nor Johnson had seen him move before. At least since the bus accident. Oglethorpe grabbed the young Lieutenant and hustled him into his car. They disappeared up the hill in a spray of gravel, Ollie honking his horn to move slow traffic and pedestrians out of his way.

The two submariners grabbed their seabags as well as Stan's before wading into the crowd on the pier. After "welcome home" hugs and kisses all around and a brief update on what was going on with Stan, the foursome ventured up the hill to the base hospital on foot, the only way they could get there. Oglethorpe was in the waiting room matching steps with Ward, both men pacing nervously back and forth, doing their best to wear out the new hospital's brand-new carpet.

No news yet, they reported. But they expected to have a baby any time now. Everyone settled down for the wait as they caught up with each other's lives over the last few months.

The sun was setting behind the hills on the New London side of the river when the doctor finally emerged from behind the swinging doors. He smiled, inquired about which man was the "daddy," and then offered his hand to Stan.

"Congratulations! You got yourself a boy. Mother and son are doing fine, though like most sailors, the little tyke's complaining about any and everything at the top of his lungs."

"Can I see them?" the excited new father gasped.

A boy. He had a boy.

"Sure, in a few minutes when we get everybody presentable. The nurse will come and get you when everything's ready."

"What are you naming the varmint?" Ollie asked.

Stan had to think about that question. "Jeez, Karen was so sure it was a girl, that was mostly all we talked about. But we did think, if it somehow happened to be a boy, we might name him Jonathon. Jonathon, after my father. But we'll probably call him Jon."

"I like it," Brad Johnson said, smiling, nodding. "Sounds like a high-ranking officer's name to me. 'Admiral Jon Ward.'"

Everyone cheered and slapped Stan on the back until the nurse came out to shush them and to usher Stan back to meet his son for the first time.

Darkest Before Dawn
The Tides of War Book 2

In the aftermath of Pearl Harbor, four young submariners are thrown into the chaos of war.

December 7, 1941. Pearl Harbor lies in ruins, the U.S. Pacific Fleet is crippled, and Japan sweeps unopposed across the Pacific. America, no longer able to stand aside, rests its hope on rust-covered submarines manned by young, untested officers and crew.

Four friends, newly commissioned from the U.S. Naval Academy, are thrust into the heart of the conflict.

Alistair, a rich, entitled playboy, becomes a reluctant leader after his boat is sunk. Stranded on a remote tropical island, he and his crew wage a desperate guerrilla war against overwhelming odds. Stan, sidelined by a devastating injury, is pulled into the depths of naval intelligence. With cunning and perseverance, he struggles to unravel the Japanese naval code JP-25 and feed the vital knowledge to the sailors while staying one step ahead of the onrushing Japanese Army.

Meanwhile, Fred and Brad fight the war onboard America's latest submarines, pioneering deadly tactics beneath the waves to halt the enemy advance and rewrite the rules of warfare.

Amidst the brutal reality of naval combat, these young sailors must overcome impossible odds. Armed only with bravery, resilience, and brotherhood, they confront a ruthless enemy, determined to prove victory isn't dictated by firepower alone.

ACKNOWLEDGMENTS

As much as we would like to say that these stories "write themselves," that is just not the fact. We take a great deal of pride in making our tales as historically and technically accurate as possible. When dealing with the somewhat obscure immediate pre–World War II timeframe, we found research to be a little more complicated than a simple web search. We would like to thank Wendy Gulley and her staff at the Submarine Force Museum Library for their assistance in digging into the files for the prewar New London Submarine Base and FDR's 1941 visit there. If you are in the general New London area, a stop at the Submarine Museum is well worth your time. Say hello to Wendy when you visit.

Our thanks to naval historian Norman Polmar for turning us onto the Naval History and Heritage Command cache of naval ship's histories and to Norman Friedman for his excellent and detailed *US Submarines Through 1945, An Illustrated Design History*. Both were vital assets in getting the "*Sugar*" boats right.

Once we finished our initial scribbling, Cate Streissguth and her team at Severn River Publishing performed their usual miracles in turning our musings into a coherent story. It is good to work with professionals.

None of this would be possible without the love and support of our wives, Charlene (Don) and Penny (George).

ABOUT GEORGE WALLACE

Commander George Wallace retired to the civilian business world in 1995, after twenty-two years of service on nuclear submarines. He served on two of Admiral Rickover's famous "Forty One for Freedom", the USS John Adams SSBN 620 and the USS Woodrow Wilson SSBN 624, during which time he made nine one-hundred-day deterrent patrols through the height of the Cold War.

Commander Wallace served as Executive Officer on the Sturgeon class nuclear attack submarine USS Spadefish, SSN 668. Spadefish and all her sisters were decommissioned during the downsizings that occurred in the 1990's. The passing of that great ship served as the inspiration for "Final Bearing."

Commander Wallace commanded the Los Angeles class nuclear attack submarine USS Houston, SSN 713 from February 1990 to August 1992. During this tour of duty that he worked extensively with the SEAL community developing SEAL/submarine tactics. Under Commander Wallace, the Houston was awarded the CIA Meritorious Unit Citation.

Commander Wallace lives with his wife, Penny, in Alexandria, Virginia.

Sign up for Wallace and Keith's newsletter at
severnriverbooks.com

ABOUT DON KEITH

Don Keith is a native Alabamian and attended the University of Alabama where he received his degree in broadcast and film. He has received awards from the Associated Press and United Press International for newswriting and reporting. He is also the only person to be named Billboard Magazine "Radio Personality of the Year" in two formats, country and contemporary. Keith was a broadcast personality for over twenty years, owned his own consultancy, co-owned a Mobile, Alabama, radio station, and hosted and produced several nationally syndicated radio shows.

His first novel, "The Forever Season." received the Alabama Library Association's "Fiction of the Year" award. Keith has written extensively on historical subjects including World War II, submarine warfare, and fiction, biographies, and non-fiction works on a variety of subjects. He has published more than forty books, two of which—HUNTER KILLER and COLORS OF CHARACTER—have been adapted for the screen.

Mr. Keith lives with his wife, Charlene, in Indian Springs Village, Alabama.

Sign up for Wallace and Keith's newsletter at
severnriverbooks.com